"Are you in some kind of trouble?" Cade finally asked.

Leah turned away. "Why would you ask that?"

"I don't know. Something about the way you've acted since...well, since I pulled you from the snow. Like you're scared. Why are you in such a hurry to leave? I thought you were staying in the cabin tonight?"

She glanced at him. "I never said I was staying. I asked you to give me a ride back, that's all."

"I just want to help."

Leah sighed. "I know."

"I could take a look at it for you." Now, why would he offer that up—an attempt to snag her?

"No." Her reply was too emphatic.

He glanced her way, trying to watch her and the road. To his surprise, a timid smile broke through.

"Not tonight, that is," she added. She was trying to be friendly, warm up to him, but still, it seemed forced.

He risked another glance over and caught her eyes—there he saw the truth. She was terrified and hiding something.

Who are you, Leah Marks?

PERIL ON THE MOUNTAIN

ELIZABETH GODDARD

Previously published as *Buried* and *Untraceable*

LOVE INSPIRED
INSPIRATIONAL ROMANCE

LOVE INSPIRED®

INSPIRATIONAL ROMANCE

ISBN-13: 978-1-335-23089-8

Peril on the Mountain

Copyright © 2020 by Harlequin Books S.A.

Buried
First published in 2015. This edition published in 2020.
Copyright © 2015 by Elizabeth Goddard

Untraceable
First published in 2015. This edition published in 2020.
Copyright © 2015 by Elizabeth Goddard

This edition published by arrangement with Harlequin Books S.A.

For questions and comments about the quality of this book,
please contact us at CustomerService@Harlequin.com.

Love Inspired
22 Adelaide St. West, 40th Floor
Toronto, Ontario M5H 4E3, Canada
www.Harlequin.com

Printed in U.S.A.

CONTENTS

Elizabeth Goddard is the award-winning author of more than thirty novels and novellas. A 2011 Carol Award winner, she was a double finalist in the 2016 Daphne du Maurier Award for Excellence in Mystery/Suspense, and a 2016 Carol Award finalist. Elizabeth graduated with a computer science degree and worked in high-level software sales before retiring to write full-time.

Visit the Author Profile page
at Harlequin.com for more titles.

BURIED

This is how we know what love is: Jesus Christ laid down his life for us. And we ought to lay down our lives for our brothers and sisters.
—*1 John* 3:16

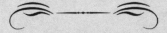

This story is dedicated to all the true heroes
in the world—men and women
who risk their lives for others.

Acknowledgments

It takes many people to write a novel and I thank my wonderful and amazing family first and foremost—my husband and children who let me spend hours far away from them in another world. Thanks to Shannon McNear—you are always there for me! I couldn't do it without you, friend. Writer friends Kathleen Y'Barbo Miller and Kellie Gilbert assisted me in figuring out my legal matters. I especially appreciate the technical expertise from my new friends in Juneau. I couldn't have come close to getting things right without the time and detail they offered. Bill Glude of the Alaska Avalanche Information Center, Doug Wessen, president of the Mountain Rescue Association, and my friend who works for the US Forest Service in Juneau. If I got anything wrong, that's all on me, but remember, I write fiction, and I created a whole new town.

ONE

Mountain Cove, Alaska, North of Juneau

Gasping for breath, Leah Marks ran for her life, working her way through the deep snow from last night's winter storm, the semiautomatic in her pocket pressing into her side. What she wouldn't give for a pair of snowshoes.

How had Detective Snyder found her here?

At least she'd seen him from a distance, giving her a few more precious seconds to make a run for it. She had to escape. She wouldn't use her weapon against him unless she had no other choice. Shooting a police detective, even if he was a dirty cop and a killer, wouldn't win her any points no matter which way you looked at it.

Approaching Dead Falls Canyon, she left the tree line and took the biggest steps she could, her hips aching with the effort. She couldn't outrun him this way, but she reassured herself with the fact that he struggled with the same obstacles.

The deep snow would hide the hazards, and Leah

counted on that. As she made her way, a snowcapped Mount McCann loomed in her peripheral vision. She'd spent enough time on the ski patrol in the Cascades during her college days to recognize the avalanche risk was high.

As she entered the danger zone, a glance over her shoulder told her Snyder was gaining on her. As strong as she was, she couldn't keep up this pace, and as if to confirm the thought, she stumbled headlong into the powder. Leah grappled and fought her way out, gulping panic with each breath.

With her fall, she'd have to turn and face him much sooner than she'd hoped. Leaving town and hiding in an off-grid cabin in Alaska hadn't bought her enough time. Hadn't bought her safety.

"Leah!" he called, his voice much too close.

Heart hammering, she turned to stand her ground. Stared into his stone-cold eyes. Breathing hard, he flashed a knife as he approached; smirking because he'd finally cornered her.

Dressed to kill, he was in black from head to toe—a dead giveaway against the white-carpeted mountains.

So that's what death looked like.

Funny that she'd worn white camouflage hoping to remain hidden, for all the good that had done.

Cold dread twisted up her spine. She thrust her hand into her pocket to reach for her weapon.

It was gone.

No! She must have lost it when she'd fallen. Snyder now stood between her and the snow she'd crushed with her tumble. Between her and her gun.

"Give me what I want, Leah." His dark eyes flashed from the opening in his ski mask.

"Why? So you can kill me like you killed Tim?" She had no idea what Snyder wanted from her, what he thought she had, but she'd witnessed him commit murder. No way would he let her live.

A thunderous snap resounded above them.

A crack appeared in the white stuff beneath Leah Marks's boots.

The ground shifted.

Before she could react, before she could think, the avalanche swept her away—swept Snyder away, too—along with everything she'd been taught about how to survive. Carried away by a daunting, crushing force, heavy and swift to kill, she was helpless to stop the power that gripped her with icy fingers.

Roared in her ears.

Terror seized her as the megaton of white powder ushered her along to a frozen grave, an untimely death, as though she was nothing more than a twig. One brutal way to die had been exchanged for another.

And then…

Her body slowed before easing to a stop. The snow settled and held her inside.

Frozen silence encased her, shrouded her in muted gray light.

Think. What did she do now? Something. There was something she must do and she must be quick. To act before the snow compressed around her.

Fear temporarily gave way to determination as survival tactics filled her thoughts. She took in a breath to expand her chest, give her breathing room. With her left hand near her face, she scooped snow away from her mouth and nose before it hardened completely. These things she did while thrusting her arm toward the surface in what she thought was the right direction. If only she could breach the packed snow and force her hand through. Before she could complete that one last task, increasing her chance of survival, it was all over. There was no more give to the snow—it had locked into place.

Buried alive. She couldn't move.

Icy grayness weighed on her.

She wouldn't dig her way out of this one. She hadn't planned for things to turn out this way. Panic the likes of which she'd never known choked her, compelling her to gasp for air.

That would kill her faster. She had to conserve her oxygen.

Inhale…exhale…

Minutes. She had minutes, if that, thanks to the small air pocket she'd created. She'd been given another chance to live, one small chance in a million. Or maybe she would die, but at least Snyder wouldn't be the one to kill her.

Calming her breaths, she prayed someone would find her in time.

But if that prayer was answered by the wrong some-one…

She was dead anyway.

From the helicopter, Cade Warren stared at the north-east face of Mount McCann, struggling to remember the innocence and joy of a carefree childhood spent in the mountain's shadow. But the images from two days ago still haunted him.

Snowboarders out seeking a thrill. Kids who believed they were invincible. By the time they'd called him to assess the avalanche danger for a search and rescue team, the victims were already dead.

Beside Cade, his friend and coworker Isaiah Callahan flew the helicopter deep into the hidden mountain crags.

Cade scraped a hand over his rough jaw. They did more searching than rescuing.

He pushed the thought away, reminding himself that that wasn't what they were there for this time. Today they were supposed to forecast the mountain, assess the avalanche threat in their roles as avalanche specialists.

"I don't get it," Cade said. "Why don't people read the forecasts?"

"They read them." Isaiah directed the helicopter to the right, angling a little too sharply for comfort. "They think it won't happen to them."

People didn't want to pay attention, which was why Cade's father had always struggled to get enough funding for the Mountain Cove Avalanche Center he'd founded. With his death, his father's frustration had now become Cade's.

The death tolls this week had been brutal, making Cade even more determined to do his job. He turned his attention back to the mountain. In the distance he could see the glaciers spilling from the Juneau Icefield.

Strange that in spite of all his expertise, his father

had died in an avalanche, trying to rescue someone. Cade was still trying to make sense of it all.

The one thing he knew was that his father had a reputation with the town of Mountain Cove as a real hero—a reputation that Cade strived to earn for himself. But he doubted he'd ever come close to being the hero his father had been.

"So far we have what—two hundred potential snow slides?" Isaiah asked.

Before he could answer, Cade's pager went off. He pulled it from its clip and looked at the screen.

This is a callout for SAR on an avalanche in Dead Falls Canyon…two victims. Meet at Crank Point. Respond on Code One frequency… Case No. 5547.

Cade stiffened. Not another one. He glanced at Isaiah. "Dead Falls Canyon. We can get there in time."

His pulse ratcheted up.

Maybe today he could make a difference.

Isaiah grinned his agreement and steered the helicopter east. First responders rarely made it in time to dig someone out of an avalanche. Cade and Isaiah were already in the air, near the avalanche.

They could serve as the immediate action team.

While Isaiah flew them over the harsh winter terrain of the backcountry, Cade communicated their plans, even as he wondered how and why someone would be in the remote area, especially after last night's storm.

The call had come in three minutes ago. Cade set his stopwatch to track the critical first fifteen minutes.

They only had twelve left, if the witness had made the call immediately. Cade went over a list in his head, glad they always carried equipment in the helicopter for such an occasion. Probe. Shovel. And they each wore a transceiver at all times, in case the unthinkable happened and the helicopter crashed. There was also bivouac gear in the event they were stranded on the mountain.

Maybe today would be the day he could save a life instead of recover a body.

Eight minutes.

Cade tensed, praying that the area would be stable, that he would know where to search. Even if they arrived in time, there were safety issues to consider. They'd need to examine the crown and path for debris, look for ski poles, gloves, goggles—anything that might tell them where to look.

Right around the ridge, Dead Falls Canyon came into view—a deep chasm, rugged and lethal, in the heart of avalanche country. Cade tensed at the ominous sight. Breath forced from his chest as though he were the victim crushed in the slide.

Isaiah sucked in air. "A big one."

"No kidding." Cade looked at the crown where the avalanche began, then down over the resulting debris field. "Six, seven hundred feet wide. Eight hundred long."

"Could be ten, twelve feet deep in some places, Cade. What do you want to do?"

"Get me down there."

"You sure it's safe?"

Is it ever? But whoever was buried, if they were

still alive, would die if he didn't do something now. He hadn't been there to save his father that day and he'd never forgiven himself.

"I'll take my chances." Five minutes left on the stop-watch.

He swallowed. It could take him longer than that to find the victim much less dig them out.

"Someone's waving at us down there," Isaiah said.

"The witness," Cade mumbled under his breath when he spotted someone layered in winter wear. He wasn't digging, but maybe he could give a few more details about where the victims were last seen on the slope.

"There's no place to land here," Isaiah pointed out, hovering the helicopter over the snow. "I'll need to toe in, touch one ski down while you grab your gear. I'll find somewhere to land, if possible, and hike over to help you."

Cade stared at his friend—a man he'd grown close to over the past three years. "Don't set her down. Don't even think about joining me until you assess the avalanche danger."

Isaiah didn't have a degree in glaciology like Cade. Didn't have the years of training under a mentor like Cade's father that Cade had.

Of the two of them, Cade was far better prepared—and it still might not be enough. At thirty-three, he didn't have near the experience or training he needed. He'd lost his father much too soon.

"Understood?" Cade stared him down.

"Aye, aye, captain." Isaiah saluted him.

Three minutes.

Isaiah touched the helicopter down long enough for Cade to grab the trauma kit, gear up with his equipment and step out. The landing zone was tight, and Cade kneeled next to the helicopter, the *whop-whop-whop* of the rotor blades drowning out all other sounds. He gave Isaiah the thumbs-up and watched the helicopter lift off and away.

The witness headed in Cade's direction and, in turn, he hurried toward the man, hoping to get the needed information. In the meantime he turned his beacon from transmit to receive and prayed for a signal.

Cade wanted to know what the witness was doing out here in the first place when the avalanche danger was considerable, but there was no time. Two lives were in the balance.

His ski mask hiding everything but his eyes, the man pointed to a place between the trees a few yards away. Not good. "Over there. I think I saw them—a man and a woman—go down, but it's hard to tell where they ended up."

Knowing the range of his beacon, Cade nodded and hurried to where the man pointed, moving down the center of the debris field, listening, looking for that life-saving signal. And then he locked on to that precious sound.

There was a chance…

He marked the spot.

Please, God, let me save this one.

He'd trained for this moment so many times—learned how to locate a beacon and dig quickly. He knew how to assemble his probe without wasting precious seconds. But rarely had he had the chance to use this particular set of skills with the real possibility of finding a survivor.

Two minutes…

Cade hoped to be a hero today, even though he'd never live up to his father's reputation. Pulse pounding, he reined in his chaotic thoughts, shut out the fear and panic. Stayed focused on the tried-and-true rescue strategies that worked.

Heart bursting, he assembled his probe—an eight-foot collapsible rod. He drove it into the packed snow, hoping to feel something—someone—beneath the surface. He kept searching and probing until finally the probe hit what felt like pay dirt only a few feet down.

A few feet and not ten or twelve or twenty.

God, please…

He tossed his probe to the man who'd witnessed the avalanche. "Start probing for the other victim."

Cade's breath hitched as he thrust the shovel into the snow, hoping he'd made the right decision to send the other man away. Then Isaiah appeared by Cade's side and helped with the digging.

Within a couple of feet they reached a hand.

Thirty seconds left on the clock and counting…

Sweat poured from Cade in spite of the cold, in spite of the fact that he was in top physical condition for his job. Together, he and Isaiah created a tunnel into the snow, searching for the face that connected to the hand. No time to stop to check for a pulse when seconds counted.

There!

"Establish an airway, stat!"

They dug the snow out and away from the pinched features of a young woman so that she could breathe. Vivid blue-green eyes blinked up in surprise and relief, sending his heart into his throat. She was still alive—though he wasn't done saving her yet. If they didn't free her completely and soon, she could still die in her icy grave from hypothermia or internal bleeding. Also, Cade couldn't forget she hadn't been alone.

"You search for the other victim. I've got this," Cade told Isaiah. "I could only get one beacon signal, though."

"You sure?"

"Yeah. I can dig her out." But he couldn't tolerate letting someone die when they could save both victims. Even though they'd passed the first fifteen minutes, victims had been known to survive up to two hours on rare occasions. For the first time in a long time, Cade was on the scene in time and every choice he made could save.

Or kill.

Isaiah left his side. From his peripheral vision, Cade saw him set his beacon and assemble his probe to search for the other victim. But where had their witness gone?

Great.

Failing to keep track of the witness would be a mark against him within the search and rescue team ranks.

No time to worry about him. Cade stared down into the air tunnel and concentrated on digging out this survivor—fortunate beyond reason—careful to avoid collapsing the tunnel, the only thing keeping her alive.

TWO

Leah sucked in a breath, trying to push down the rising panic. Except for her right arm, she couldn't move her body. But at least she could breathe. She blinked up at her rescuer—warmth and respite spilling from his determined eyes, the fierce green of a country spring in the mountains. Streaks of snow clung to his coffee-colored, wavy hair, and though he looked a little rough around the edges, he wasn't Snyder—the man who needed her dead.

Relief filled her and overflowed in an exhale accompanied by a few whimpers. She hated the sound, hated the weakness it conveyed. If she were standing right now, her legs would quiver, unable to hold her weight.

"It's okay. You're going to be fine. I'm digging you out now." Though his eyes held an urgent and untempered concern, his smile reassured her. "My name's Cade, by the way."

That's right, keep talking in those soothing tones.

Cade, wearing the usual thick snow-country gloves, breathed hard as he expertly thrust the snow shovel in and around her, moving the iced powder almost as efficiently as a mechanical snowplow. He'd uncovered her torso and had started digging out her legs.

"What's your name?"

She wasn't sure what name she could trust him with. She didn't want anyone to know she was here, much less know her name. Telling this man could put him in danger, too. She'd been hiding in the remote wilderness cabin, in fact, when Detective Snyder had sniffed her out and come to kill her. Panic set in and she glanced around at her limited view. Where was he? Had he been buried, too?

Oh, God, please... But she hated herself for wishing him dead.

"It's okay if you're unable to give me your name," he said.

He probably thought she was in shock. And she was.

"Is there someone I should call? Friends or family?"

"No." Her cold answer iced over her heart. It wasn't a lie.

"Can you tell me if you have any pain—how bad it is on a scale of one to ten?"

She felt numb and cold at the same time; stiff, as though rigor mortis had already set in. Oh, no...was she paralyzed? Had the impact broken her back?

With the shifting snow she tried to move her body. Her legs responded. *Thank You, God.* And there wasn't any pain.

"No, I don't think I'm injured. I don't know." How could she be sure if something hurt until she was completely free? She felt so numb, she couldn't really tell.

His chuckle lightened the seriousness of her near death. By the look in his eyes, that had been his intention. She liked his laugh, but it was hard to trust, even in someone who had rescued her.

"Almost there." He threw the shovel aside and began scooping snow away from her back and legs.

Leah shifted and moved, and the sheer freedom of that act left her with the daunting awareness that she'd almost died on this mountain today—twice. The thought pressed in on her, suffocating her. This man digging her out only knew the half of it.

As she started to climb to freedom, Cade grabbed her and gently lifted her out as though she weighed nothing at all. He then set her to the side, away from the hole that had almost been her tomb.

"You sure nothing's broken?" He assessed her limbs with practiced skill.

Again she moved her arms and legs. "No, nothing's broken. Nothing's crushed inside or I'd be in pain, wouldn't I?"

He pulled something from a pack—a thermal blanket—and wrapped it around her. Crouched next to her, he wouldn't stop staring at her, until finally Leah had to look away.

"You're more fortunate than you know." The solemn tone of his voice pulled her gaze up.

She figured he'd ask her why she was skiing in the back country with the avalanche danger high, but he didn't even ask her what had happened to her skis. She hadn't been skiing, so didn't have any, of course, but she had no idea how she'd explain her presence here if pressured.

Cade frowned and stood tall, squinting as he skimmed the slope behind Leah. "What can you tell me about your friend? The man you were with?"

Leah's heart stuttered. She forced a calmness into her expression she didn't feel. "What man? I wasn't *with* anyone." True enough.

What am I doing? Why lie about Snyder now? Confusion crept over her like the cold trying to slip into the thermal blanket. She wasn't sure how to handle this. But one thing she felt all the way to her chilled core: she wasn't out of danger yet.

Snyder might not be working alone. That meant she had to stay on her guard and she couldn't trust anyone. Until she discovered why he'd killed Tim that night and what he wanted from Leah besides her life, she couldn't be safe. That meant she needed to disappear again somehow. And when she was gone, the less people in this area knew about her or what had happened to her, the better.

Cade stared down at her, his pensive gaze taking her in once again, wringing her insides as though he'd have the truth from her.

"Okay, then," he said. "There was a witness—someone who'd seen the avalanche and called it in. He reported seeing a man and woman go under. We have another victim out here somewhere, and I need to help find him. If you think you're not hurt, and are able, you can search, too. There's only me and my partner until another team arrives, but they'll take too long. And our witness seems to have disappeared after pointing me in your direction."

What? He had no idea what he asked of her. How could she make herself help find the man who only moments before had tried to kill her?

Cade must have noticed her reaction. She saw suspicion in his eyes.

"Are you okay to rest here, then, while I help?"

No. She wasn't okay. She didn't want him to go. She hadn't felt this safe, this secure, in so very long. And those things poured from this man. She'd never needed that before, and the realization stunned her. But she reminded herself she couldn't afford to need anyone. To trust anyone. "Sure, I'll be fine."

"Someone will be here soon to evacuate you."

Leah nodded and searched the canyon, reliving that moment only a few days ago when Detective Nick Snyder had shot and killed her boss, Tim Levins, in cold blood.

Tim was a lawyer and Leah was his legal investigator. She'd been leaving town that night for a three-week vacation. Tim had insisted she go and use the bonus he'd given her as thanks for her two years of service in his office. He'd bought her a present, too—a necklace that she'd forgotten on her desk in her rush to put everything in order before leaving. She'd stopped by the office late that night to pick it up, not wanting to hurt his feelings if he noticed that she'd left it behind.

Deep down, she knew she had wanted to stop by the office for more than just the necklace. She'd had a feeling something was wrong…that Tim had been trying to hide things from her. He'd been a little too insistent that she use the bonus to go on a long vacation. So she'd gone back to investigate.

She'd liked Tim, but thanks to the trauma of her childhood, she'd never met anyone she trusted, her lawyer boss included.

She'd arrived just in time to witness Tim's murder. And Snyder—a decorated, trusted police detective and the town's hero—had come for her.

So she'd disappeared on her own to figure it all out. It had seemed impossible that he'd find her in the remote cabin hidden deep in the Inside Passage of Alaska, hundreds of miles from Kincaid, the small town in the Seattle metropolis where she worked and lived.

Tim had recently inherited the cabin from a distant uncle. He'd wanted Leah to do some research for him regarding the man's daughter, who Tim thought should have inherited the place. But the woman had vanished. With their case loads, researching anything about the cabin had been put on the back burner.

And when she'd known she had to run and hide, the cabin had been the perfect choice because she'd thought no one had known about the place or had any reason to connect it to her. That is, until she'd spotted Snyder at the cabin.

Until she found out why he'd killed Tim, she couldn't be sure Snyder had been acting alone, which meant Leah didn't know who she could turn to with what she'd seen. There could be others in the department who could make her disappear.

Pulling the thermal blanket tighter, she tried to ward

off the double chill that told her she wasn't out of danger, even if Snyder died on the mountain today.

Cade and Isaiah were still fruitlessly probing for the other avalanche victim when the whir of an additional helicopter echoed beyond the spruce trees covered in white icing. The second mountain rescue team had arrived.

He glanced up the hill at Isaiah who gave a shake of his head. By this time, it was highly unlikely the second victim would survive.

Disappointment corded through Cade and pulled tight. He glanced over to where rescue team members were already preparing to evacuate the woman and reminded himself that he'd succeeded, at least, in saving her. This could have turned out much differently for her. They could be placing her in a body bag right now, as they might be doing in a few minutes when they discovered the other victim. His chances of survival after all this time were almost zero. But they would continue the search for as long as they could safely do so.

Cade's thoughts tracked back to the five snowboarding victims.

Five body bags.

Earlier in the week Cade and Isaiah had hiked into the backcountry to out-of-the-way paths in the higher elevations. On the north ridge they'd found packed cornices—heavy snow blown in by the wind and overhanging a ridge. After dozens of compression tests to determine the strength or weakness of the snow layers,

Cade had been ready to call it a week when they'd received the callout for the snowboarders.

Before the mountain rescue team had even been able to begin searching for the snowboarders, Cade and Isaiah had tossed scores of explosives to trigger the snow that remained above the avalanche—the hangfire snow. Stabilizing the area so that the mountain rescue team could go in. All part of their jobs as avalanche specialists. That, and forecasting and educating the public. While rescuers had shoveled several feet of snow to uncover the victims, their hapless friends or family watching from the sidelines nearly always asked why this was happening to them.

There was no one standing on the sidelines today for either this woman or the other victim.

David, Cade's older brother, was leading the second team. When he spotted Cade, he approached. "Tell me."

Cade pointed to the debris field and explained what the witness had said. "We figured with the victim's trajectory and where we found the woman, this would be the likely catchment area. But as you can see, we're still probing."

David grabbed Cade's shoulder. "You did good, man. You saved someone today. You can take that to heart. Now go home and celebrate. We got this. We're already setting up a probe line and shovel crew. Handlers are bringing the search and rescue dogs in, too."

As David jogged through the snow to dole out instructions to his volunteer rescue team, Cade spotted Isaiah hiking toward him.

"Let's get going. We need to finish our forecasting

work before the sun goes down so there won't be more victims."

Cade wanted to stay and help. Isaiah must have sensed his hesitation. "You're exhausted. *We're* exhausted. You did what you could, Cade, and it worked. You saved that woman. There are plenty searching for the guy now. Forecasting the avalanche dangers, which is your primary job, saves lives. You can't know how many lives, but you have to trust that it does."

Isaiah's words encouraged Cade. His friend was right. They had work to finish and he'd be in the office until late again, as it was. "I wanted it to be more."

"I know you did, man. I know you did. I parked the helicopter over the ridge. Let's go."

Cade grabbed his gear and followed Isaiah, trudging through the snow that less than an hour before had turned brutal and lethal. More often than not, they had to cart victims—or bodies—out of the area on snowmobiles and toboggans because there wasn't any helicopter access. This time they had two helicopters—though Isaiah's was a single-engine R22—and a survivor. The R22 could only accommodate two passengers, so Cade might have had to wait around or hike down on his own while Isaiah evacuated the survivor if not for the medevac.

Cade still didn't know her name. Strange that she'd seemed hesitant to tell him what it was. But she'd been through an ordeal and he'd given her the benefit of a doubt.

They topped the ridge and spotted the R22 and the medevac that provided both medical attention and transported mountain rescue teams as necessary.

The woman climbed into the medevac, her ash-blond hair with golden streaks half hidden under the blanket covering her shoulders. When he'd found her, tunneled through to her, he'd been stunned at the blue-green eyes staring back at him—the crystal purity he'd seen there. Like a tomb raider, he'd pulled her from the snow-laden crypt and it was then that he'd noticed the rest of her face. She had a clean, natural look. No makeup hiding flaws. She had an open, honest look—like someone with nothing to hide.

If only he could believe it were true. She'd winced when he'd asked her about the other person with her; denied she'd known anything about another victim. She'd been hiding something.

He hated the images that accosted him at that moment. Images of his fiancée with another man. They'd been caught in a situation that required a rescue, revealing her deception. Cade had been devastated that day. Even now his heart was still too strung out to think about loving again and he couldn't stop himself from looking at this woman with suspicion.

Normally he wouldn't concern himself too much with whether or not someone he'd helped was deceiving him. After all, it wasn't as though he usually knew any of them well. It wasn't until a victim teetered on the precipice between this life and the next that Cade met them, which only made sense. But then he never saw them again. He liked it that way. Better to keep his distance. He'd rescued them. End of story. They didn't need him anymore anyway.

His throat twisted tight. He couldn't understand why

he didn't want this to be the last time he saw this woman. Then again it had been too long since he'd rescued someone buried alive in an avalanche. Too long since he'd seen a positive outcome. Maybe that explained it.

With no relatives or friends to call, she had that proverbial deer-in-the-headlights look about her. Well, who wouldn't after being buried alive? But Cade couldn't shake the sense that she was afraid, scared of something or someone that had nothing at all to do with the avalanche.

He had a feeling he wasn't done with this rescue.

Cade trudged forward and chided himself. He was probably reading way too much into things. He was tired and distracted and too suspicious for his own good. He tugged his gloves off. At the very least, Cade would deliver her home. Wherever that was.

He grabbed Isaiah's arm as the medevac rotors started up. "Nothing personal, but you mind if I ride with them?"

"Instead of with me? Thought we were going to finish the assessments?"

"I think we've done all the assessments we're going to do of the mountain today. You have about enough time before dusk to fly back to the center. Anyway, the avalanche gives us a good assessment of the instability. I'll do the reports back at the center, so you don't have to."

Isaiah saluted and gave a crooked grin. "Have it your way. So, what *is* your evaluation of the instability?"

"The danger is high."

THREE

"I need to get a brief medical history, ma'am." The medic sat next to Leah inside the helicopter. "Take your vitals again. They'll do a full assessment at the hospital. Your name and age?"

"Twenty-nine." She didn't want to give her name; didn't want it surfacing in the computer system. She wanted to be invisible. To disappear. "But I'm fine. I don't need to go to the hospital."

He frowned, but didn't push her on that or her name. He went through a list of questions, which she answered, portraying a healthy medical history. When he cuffed her for blood pressure, Leah sighed.

Please, just leave me alone.

She needed space. Time to think about what had happened. About what to do next. She inhaled a breath to calm the turmoil rising inside.

I'm alive.

She should be grateful for small things. For this moment. That she was alive, thanks to God. And to the man who had believed he'd find someone beneath the snow on a backcountry strip of a lost canyon.

"Looks good." The medic packed his equipment away. "Still, you should go to the hospital for a complete exam. Make sure I didn't miss anything. Internal bleeding or a concussion could be serious."

"Thanks. I'm fine."

He promised to return in a few minutes and hopped from the helicopter.

Maybe he was going to check on the other victim. See if the helicopter was free to whisk her off the mountain. Had they recovered Snyder? Leah's heart stammered at the thought of Snyder, alive or dead. The whole situation filled her with fear.

She strapped herself into the seat, as though it would protect her from whatever would come of it all, the events of the past few hours—past few days—blowing through her thoughts and twisting into a tight knot. For this moment in time—this one moment—she was safe inside this helicopter.

She leaned her head back and closed her eyes.

The deafening whir of the medevac's blades started up. A familiar voice resounded over the obnoxious sound. Leah opened her eyes to see Cade—the man had stepped from her thoughts into the helicopter. He sent an assessing glance her way and spoke to the pilot, who nodded. Cade closed the door and took the seat next to her, strapping in. A few moments later the medic climbed aboard and sat next to the pilot.

Cade looked at her, that concerned yet calm, soothing

expression she'd seen when he was digging her out now gone, replaced by something she couldn't read. "Hi."

"Hi," she said.

Closing the helicopter's door had turned down the volume of the rotors, but not by much. Did the relative quiet mean she might have to talk to Cade? What did he want from her? Had he seated himself next to her to gather more information such as, say, her name? Or for some unrelated reason?

"You never told me your name."

Leah sighed and looked out the window, away from him. She would only make him suspicious if she didn't answer, didn't give him at least this much of the truth. "Leah. Leah Marks."

She would be forever grateful to him, but she reminded herself not to take his rescue too personally—that was part of his job. He was likely a volunteer as most were. Men and women from all walks of life who gave up their time and their own hard-earned dollars to rescue people who too often made life-endangering mistakes while hiking, climbing or skiing.

Her knowledge from her ski patrol experience had made her aware of the avalanche risk today, but she'd had no choice but to run straight into the danger zone. The way things had unfolded seemed surreal. The avalanche had prevented Snyder from harming her.

She wanted to relax and breathe, but she couldn't think she was home free yet.

The helicopter lifted up and away. Leah shifted in her seat to peer out the window, the sun beginning its dive toward the horizon. Darkness would overtake the rescuers soon. Cade leaned over her, a little too closely, to look out the window on her side. She smelled the faded remnants of a musky aftershave overshadowed by the outdoors—evergreens and mountain air and something entirely masculine.

It made her uncomfortable. She wanted him to move away.

He pointed out the window. "Look, you can see displaced snow from the crown and the path. That's the avalanche that took you down."

The width and breadth... The whole side of the mountain appeared to have caved in, flattened by snow. Looking like ants from this distance, people were searching for the other victim. For Snyder.

Her ribs contracted. Feeling her lips tremble, Leah slid her hand over her mouth. How had she ever survived that? She knew...she knew exactly how.

She knew exactly who.

Slowly she turned her eyes to look into Cade's. His face was still much too close, making it hard for her to remember to breathe. The burn started behind her eyes and she blinked at the moisture. That same look of concern she'd seen when he'd first pulled her from the snowy depths pulsated there again.

"Thank you." The whisper creaked from her lips.

His half grin spread wider. "You're very welcome."

The sound of his voice was comforting—too comforting. She knew better than to trust anyone, especially now. Besides, men were louses. She'd seen the way they'd treated her mother, learning that much at an early age. Every person was only out for themselves. Even someone like Cade.

He eased away from her and Leah breathed easier.

"About the other victim, what are his chances?" With this question, Leah's pulse thundered in her ears.

She already knew, of course, but she needed to hear it from Cade. Wanted to know that she was at least free from Snyder. And yet part of her knew she should hope and pray he survived. That she could somehow bring him to justice. But the thought of Snyder alive and well, tracking her down, plotting the best way to kill her and leave no trace, terrified her.

Her question had apparently affected Cade, as well. He leaned forward, dropping his head into his hands. Then, just as abruptly, he sat up, wiping them down his face. Obviously losing someone to an avalanche upset the guy. As though he felt he was somehow responsible.

Leah didn't know what came over her, but she slipped her hand over his. "You did what you could. Maybe they'll find him in time." Oh, why had she said that?

Though he left his hand in place under hers, Cade relaxed his head into the seat back. "His chances aren't very good. I'm sorry."

He *was* sorry—she could hear it in his voice, see it in his expression.

He didn't know what she knew. The victim was a murderer. How she hated to see Cade suffer through the agony of believing he'd let someone down because he hadn't saved a man today. Maybe she could ease that pain by telling him the man had stalked her, wanted to kill her. Then again, Cade didn't seem like the kind of guy who wanted to play God, deciding who should live and who should die.

Regardless of Cade's answer, fear that Snyder or someone involved with him was still out there waiting to kill her clawed across her thoughts.

For a moment Cade had felt like some sort of superhero or something, filled with elation that he'd rescued Leah. Her question had knocked him back to earth.

Leah finally took her hand back from where she'd covered his. Showing him compassion, she'd only meant to help, but she couldn't understand how her simple touch had moved him.

He didn't understand it. He didn't want to be moved. Didn't think it could happen.

And then he remembered looking into her crystal-clear eyes from the snow—a life hanging in the balance.

She'd moved him, all right.

For a million reasons he hadn't figured out yet and some reasons he might already know.

He'd been untouchable since Melissa's betrayal. And the pain of his father's untimely death while saving old Devon Hemphill, a man his father had quarreled with for the better part of his life… Cade had no words. Even at the thought of the loss, his heart recoiled.

He stared out his own window now, studying the terrain, looking at the cornices and the buildup of windswept snow after the storms. All death traps waiting to be sprung. The helicopter carried them away from the canyon and Mount McCann and would set them down at the Incident Command Center location.

Leah seemed happy that Cade had left her to her thoughts. She had to be exhausted. Did she have any idea how fortunate she'd been?

God had intervened on this one, Cade was sure. Something Cade rarely saw anymore, which made him wonder about God sometimes.

"We'll land at the Incident Command Center for co-ordinating the avalanche rescue and recovery," he informed her. "They'll want to take you to the hospital to get things checked out."

She shook her head.

Cade had expected that reaction. "Listen, when I was digging you out, you mentioned you had no family or friends for me to call. I need to make sure you get home safely. That is, after your visit to the ER. The hospital staff needs to thoroughly check you out."

"That's not necessary. You don't need to worry about me."

"You might be injured and not even know it."

"The medic already checked me out and said I was fine. I don't need anything else."

Cade knew what the guy had told Leah. Too bad he was up with the pilot, wearing a headset and oblivious to their conversation. Why didn't she want to go to the hospital? "Look, at least let me give you a ride home."

"Thanks, but I can get myself home."

"Really?" Dusk clamping down on them, Cade shifted in his seat to face her full on. "Because unless you parked your vehicle at the ICC, you'll need a ride somewhere."

Leah blew out a breath. "You're persistent, aren't you?"

"What kind of rescue is it if you can't get a decent ride home?" He was only being courteous. That's all this was, wasn't it?

Part of him liked Leah, sure—he'd admit that. He should stay far away from her on that reason alone, except that same feeling came back to him that he'd had before. He sensed that something was terribly wrong. That he shouldn't let her vanish into the night. He wasn't done with this rescue.

He almost wanted to roll his eyes at his own thoughts—he thought much too highly of his ability to assist people.

"Listen, Cade…"

Anything prefaced with those words couldn't be good. Had he given her the wrong idea? That had to be it. But he had a strange feeling that he'd given her exactly the right idea about his interest in her—and he couldn't be interested, not in that way. How did he protect himself and protect her? Especially when she clearly didn't want his help or protection.

"I'm listening."

"I like you." She paused, appearing to measure her next words. "It's just that I'm not in a place in my life right now to have friends, especially someone…"

She left the sentence hanging and Cade wondering what she had planned to say about him. She obviously had thoughts about him one way or another; she had been thinking about him. Even in the dimming light of day at only four o'clock Alaska time, Cade noticed the rush of color to her beautiful, nature-girl face. He'd be a jerk if he told her now that he wasn't interested.

Cade held up his hands in mock surrender. "Point taken. But I'm only trying to wrap up your rescue and leave you safe and sound at home. If not me, then let someone else deliver you there."

Passing her off to someone else to help her was for the best.

"I'm in a cabin up by Dover Creek. Not far from—"

"Dead Falls." Where the avalanche happened today. "I know the place."

All too well.

After her insistence that he stay out of her business, he was surprised she'd told him where she was staying. Acid burned through him. Though that explained what she was doing in the avalanche area, it didn't explain why she was in old Devon Hemphill's abandoned cabin. When Devon had died not long after Cade's father had saved him, he'd taken with him the chance for Cade to get answers to his questions as to why his father had given his life to save the man he'd always seemed to hate. Could the answers be hidden somewhere in that cabin? Was he supposed to meet Leah for that very reason?

"You said there was a witness who called to let you know about the avalanche." Her shaky voice weaved through his tumultuous thoughts and pulled him back to the present.

"Hmm?" He turned to face her again, her question sinking in. "Yeah. He pointed to where he'd seen you and the other man, and that helped me to pinpoint where to search for a beacon signal."

Which reminded him. "You wore a beacon. Smart girl. But you weren't wearing skies or snowshoes, unless the snow slide stripped them from you." He was probing, now, hoping she'd tell him why she'd been out there. People didn't usually hike or ski the backcountry in the winter alone. It was stupid and dangerous, even if she was staying in a nearby cabin. She'd told him that she didn't know the victim, so why had she been out there alone? For that matter, why would the other victim be out there alone?

Things didn't add up. Her story didn't fit. Maybe it wasn't his business, but he wanted to know what she was hiding.

"What else did he say?" She frowned.

Why would talking about the witness make her frown? Without that guy's efforts, she wouldn't have survived.

"His call about the avalanche and the information he gave us saved you. I guess you could say he was the real hero today, whoever he was," Cade said. "After he pointed me in your direction, there wasn't time for much small talk. I asked him to help find the other victim, but by the time my partner got there, the man had bailed."

"What did he look like?"

Cade stared, wondering why it mattered, if she'd been there alone as she'd claimed. Hadn't seen anyone else, as she'd said. What was she digging for? Her questions spiked Cade's curiosity even more.

"The witness," she said again. "What did he look like? What was he wearing?"

He scratched his head. "Black. Everything black, including his ski mask. I could only see his eyes."

Fear rippled across her face in a quiet shudder.

FOUR

He survived.

Everything tilted. Leah gripped the seat, unsure if Cade's unwitting confirmation that Snyder had been the "witness" had sent her world spinning or if the helicopter had simply angled sharply.

Or did he have a coconspirator? She doubted that, whatever he was up to, he was working alone. It seemed too hard to pull off a cover-up as a detective without someone else watching your back. But that remained for her to investigate. Before today, she had seen no one else at the cabin. No one other than Snyder had pursued her. Unless there'd been someone else dressed exactly the same that happened to be in a position to witness the avalanche and make the call. That would be far too coincidental.

Pulse throbbing in her neck, Leah looked out the window and away from Cade. He was too perceptive and would see her distress. She'd held on to a sliver of hope that Snyder had been buried in the avalanche today. That would have at least bought her time to investigate, discover why Tim had been murdered and who else, if anyone, was involved, before she went to the authorities—the ones she could trust, anyway.

But now…she'd have to keep running for her life. Her nightmare wasn't over, not by a long shot, and she doubted Snyder would give her much time before his next attack.

Images of him killing Tim in cold blood flashed through her thoughts. His words resounded in her head. "Give me what I want, Leah."

He'd called for a rescue team. That he needed her alive was obvious. She'd thought he only wanted to kill her because she'd witnessed Tim's murder, but his words on the mountain told a much different story.

No. He needed something from her first and then he'd kill her. An image of his knife flashed in her mind. Leah shuddered.

"Are you okay?" Cade asked.

What should she tell him? What explanation could she possibly give? The truth wasn't an option.

"Leah, is everything all right?" he asked again.

Leah rubbed her arms. "I'm fine." The events of the past few hours played through her thoughts, images of her icy tomb wrapping around her once again.

She'd come here to hide, to stay alive, to investigate Tim's murder from a safe distance. But now she had to add one more thing to that list: finding out what Snyder wanted from her.

Thankfully, Cade seemed to sense her need to process everything because he didn't ask more questions. The helicopter landed and Cade assisted her onto the pavement of the parking area swarming with emergency vehicles with flashing lights.

A rescue worker approached Cade. "A storm's moving in."

Cade frowned, eyeing Leah. "They're giving up the search for the other victim then?"

"The incident commander suspended the search. He'll reevaluate at first light," the guy said, then left Cade alone with Leah.

"There's no point in risking more lives." Cade's intense gaze studied Leah. "Unless they found something to indicate they were close to finding him. Skies, gloves or poles. Something like that."

Her throat constricted. Shouldn't she tell him that there wasn't another victim? Except, what if she was wrong? What if Snyder *had* been buried in the avalanche? The witness had said there were two people who had gone down in the avalanche. If Snyder had survived and made that call, then why would he lie about the number of people needing rescue?

To throw her off? Maybe he believed that if she thought he was dead, she'd let down her guard so he'd have the advantage again. Leah wrapped her arms around herself, wishing she could tell Cade everything. But it wouldn't help—they would still need to search for another possible victim if there was any chance someone was still trapped out there. Besides, she couldn't tell anyone about her predicament. Not until she knew who she could trust.

Dropping her hands, she eyed the man who had

pulled her out of the snow. He hovered over her as though he was afraid to let her out of his sight.

She didn't need some overprotective rescuer getting involved in her life, putting himself in danger for her any more than he already had.

She needed to find a way to get her things from the cabin and get out. But as Cade had pointed out, she didn't have her vehicle. It was parked in the shed at the cabin along with a snowmobile. Besides, the road would be treacherous and maybe unnavigable in the dark with the storm moving in.

At least Tim had paid some guy to keep the drive to the cabin plowed. There was only one way in and one way out and considering she had a killer after her, she liked it that way. But now that her hiding place had been discovered, she couldn't afford to stay there.

"If you're still willing to give me a ride back to the cabin, I could use that."

He nodded, as if he'd only been waiting for her to see the obvious. "I know the road well. I can get you there."

"I appreciate your help." She hung her head. "I hope it's not too much trouble."

"I like to finish the job. Make sure you're safe and secure, tucked away at home. The only problem is that with the storm coming in, I don't know if that cabin is fully secure. You sure it's a safe place to stay?" He lifted a brow.

No. But not for the reasons he might think. She held her hand to her forehead. "Look, I'm tired. I need to get back." She wouldn't call it home. Leah couldn't return to her real home—a small apartment a few miles from Tim's office. But one thing at a time. One day at a time. She had to survive this night first.

"Okay, then." He watched her for a few seconds longer than necessary. What was he thinking? Then he turned his attention to finding a ride. He spoke with a police officer, and Leah stiffened. She turned away, concealing her shudder. Snyder had driven home her reasons to fear people who were sworn to protect. But then, her past had already done that for her. She'd watched helplessly from the sidelines as people sworn to protect had put an innocent woman in prison. Put her mother in prison.

Someone agreed to transport Cade and Leah to Cade's vehicle. From there, he could take her to the cabin. She climbed into the backseat of the sedan, while Cade sat in the passenger seat. He and his buddy spent the drive talking about the avalanche. They didn't engage her in their conversation, which was just as well. But she knew that wouldn't last. Cade was all too clearly the inquisitive type. She couldn't really hold it against him—she was the same way. It was one small part of why she'd become an investigator. But any digging that Cade did into her situation was only going to cause trouble for them both.

Once Cade got her alone, she had a feeling his interrogation would start. He was perceptive, and she'd read in his eyes that he had questions. She wasn't sure how to evade them, but she had to try. She hadn't done a good job of hiding her emotions, but maybe she could convince him that her state of mind was all due to the avalanche. Involving someone else in her dilemma, possibly putting them in danger, wasn't something she would willingly do.

Leaning her head against the headrest, she closed her eyes. This brief respite, this was the first time in hours she could shut off what was going on around her, if only for a few moments, as Cade and his friend talked about the approaching storm. Another one. She thought that southeast Alaska, with the temperate rainforest, was supposed to be milder than interior Alaska. Maybe it was—but it sure didn't seem that way to her.

Ignoring the words, she let Cade's smooth voice wrap around her again, reminding her of when he'd spoken reassuringly to her as he'd dug her out. She couldn't ignore that the whole rescue-hero thing was more than attractive. Add to that, the guy seemed so selfless. His concern for her, when he had no reason to care about her at all, was disconcerting. So unlike any of the men she'd known. But there had to be some reason she couldn't trust him. Even if she didn't know it yet, she'd find it. Men couldn't be trusted—her boss and trusted hero Detective Nick Snyder were prime examples. This Cade guy had a secret, a side to him he kept well hidden.

Everyone did.

They arrived at the avalanche center, which shared space with other businesses in a five-story building along the main thoroughfare in Mountain Cove. Cade and Leah got out, and Cade thanked the guy for the ride before leading Leah to his vehicle.

It was only four-thirty in the afternoon in February, and the sun was already setting. She'd only had three days at the cabin, but had learned quickly how limited the daylight hours were in the dead of winter. Parking lot lights illuminated Cade's big blue truck sitting at the side of the building along with other vehicles. But his was the only vehicle with a plow attached to the front.

She glanced at him and he shot her a grin. "I live up a long drive. It's a little higher elevation than the town, and snows a lot more."

Leah couldn't help herself. She smiled back, the first genuine smile to cross her face in days. But she couldn't let herself get too comfortable with him. She needed to vanish. Once he took her to the cabin, she could pack her stuff and leave.

Disappear.

If only there was another place on earth farther away than a lone, off-grid cabin in Alaska.

Sitting in the warm cab of his truck, Cade glanced at his passenger. He hated the awkward silence, but what had he expected?

Snow filled his headlights as he drove away from Mountain Cove on the one road out of town. The only problem was that the thirty-mile road didn't go anywhere. Just came to an abrupt end. To say the town was isolated was an understatement, but this was southeast Alaska where "remote" took on a whole new meaning. The only way in and out of Mountain Cove was by boat, floatplane or helicopter.

At least Cade could get to the road to Devon's cabin this way. Accessing most off-grid cabins required serious trekking by snowshoeing, skiing or snowmobiling for miles.

Up in the mountains, sometimes even the cabins got buried in the snow. That's why uncertainty about Leah's stay in the place gnawed at him. Devon had known how to dig himself out of the snow up there, but Leah looked like anything but a mountain girl.

It didn't help that his protective instincts had kicked up a few notches after he'd pulled her from the snow, and they hadn't shut down. No. In fact, if anything, the thought of her staying in that cabin in the heart of avalanche country—especially with another storm rolling in—put his protective instincts on high alert.

He reminded himself he didn't know enough about her to make that kind of judgment call. She might be completely capable of handling a stay at the cabin during a harsh winter—and this one was certainly looking that way.

"You warm enough?" he asked. "Need more heat?"

"No, I'm good. Thanks."

That was all she said. His neck tensed. How did he get her talking? He wanted her to open up for a lot of reasons. For one, he wanted to know what she'd been doing out there today. She'd almost died. The panic and fear he'd seen in her eyes was because she'd been shell shocked from having barely survived an avalanche. But the natural disaster didn't explain all of her reactions. When she'd asked about the witness, and he'd told her, she'd all but freaked out. He'd seen her eyes before she'd turned her face from him in an attempt to hide her reaction.

What was that about? Cade couldn't shake the sense

that she knew something vital she had no intention of sharing.

He pursed his lips and watched the road, the glow of the dash lights contrasting to the darkness outside. He had to be honest with himself. Sure, he wanted to help her, but he also wanted to know whatever Leah could tell him about Devon Hemphill and why she was in his cabin.

More than anything, he wanted answers to the story behind his father's quarrel with the man. He wanted answers to explain the reasons behind his father's tragic death. Those were answers he doubted he'd ever get. But he had to try. Leah might know something. She might be able to give him a clue.

When Cade finally made the turnoff to the cabin, he was surprised to see the drive had recently been plowed, but snow was already piling up again. He glanced at Leah. Maybe she was more capable than he'd given her credit for. Still the new snowfall would make the drive long and tedious.

He stopped.

"What are you doing?" she asked.

"Have to engage the plow." He climbed out, lowered the blade and then got back in the truck, Leah watching him.

"So, I knew the guy who used to own the cabin where you're staying. Devon Hemphill. You related to him or something?"

Leah stiffened and grabbed the armrest. Whether from the question or the slipperiness of the road, he couldn't tell.

"A friend inherited the place. They are letting me stay for a little while."

Cade glanced over again. A friend, huh? She conveniently left off if the friend was male or female. Not that it mattered to him. All he cared about was finding answers to his questions and making sure she was safe. He had a feeling, a very strong feeling, her life was in need of rescuing again. Cade scraped a hand down his face—was he even up to that task?

More importantly, did it matter if he wasn't up to it? He couldn't abandon someone who needed help. He just wished she'd tell him what was going on. Maybe if he gave up something private and personal, she would, too. Reach out to her and then she'd reach back. He could pull her the rest of the way.

What are you doing?

"Devon Hemphill and my father knew each other well." Maybe a little too well. "They had an ongoing disagreement about something. I never could figure out what. It seemed to escalate as the years went by."

He'd tried to ask about it so many times but all his father would tell him was to mind his own business. Completely out of character, considering Cade and his father were close. So Cade had tried to learn more by digging for answers in other ways, but none of them had panned out. "My father and I argued about that the day he died."

"I'm sorry," she said.

He waited, hoping for more.

"I didn't get the chance to say anything else to him

before he got the call for a search and rescue. Didn't get the chance to say I was sorry."

He kept his eyes on the road, reliving that day. In his peripheral vision he saw Leah watching him, waiting for the rest of the story. He wasn't sure he could keep going, especially with a perfect stranger. But maybe that was exactly the person he could tell, say it out loud to. Face his battles head-on.

"The stranded person was Devon."

Leah gave a slight gasp. "What happened?"

"I never saw my father alive again. Devon walked away and my father died during the rescue mission to save that man. A man he detested. I still don't understood why." Cade blinked back the memory of pulling his father's body from the avalanche and pushed the rising anger down. "My father liked everyone, and was liked by everyone. Except Devon."

He felt as though he'd said too much. But maybe in the telling he could stir things up and get information. "I never got an answer from Devon about what had happened between them, and then he died, leaving me with nothing but questions."

"Now here I am, staying in his home," she said.

Cade didn't reply. It was her turn to talk.

When the truck's high beams illuminated Devon's cabin in the distance, Cade thought he saw someone in the trees behind the pile of old tires and barrels of diesel for the generator. Had to be the shadows dancing off his lights. Who would be out here at this hour in the middle of nowhere, especially with a storm moving in? Unless Leah wasn't alone in the cabin. But that couldn't be the case, could it? She'd told him there was no one he could call.

Stopping the truck at the end of the drive, he shifted into Park but left the motor idling. A soft glow emanated from one of the cabin windows. At least she wouldn't have to enter a completely dark house, although she'd have to hike the final twenty-five yards. He couldn't get the truck between those trees.

"And here we are at Devon's once-empty cabin, now your vacation home away from home." He repeated what she'd said earlier, thinking that might ignite more conversation on the topic. He hid a wince at the sound of his own gruff tone, which had been way more accusatory than he'd intended.

"Look, I didn't happen upon the cabin and find it empty and decide to stay."

Yeah, she'd heard it in his voice, too. "I didn't mean to insinuate otherwise." He blew out a breath, hoping she understood. "Thinking about everything that happened frustrates me in ways you can't understand."

"You're wrong. I do understand. You blame yourself for your father's death. You think you should have been with him that day."

Cade nodded, surprised at her words. "If I had been, maybe he would still be alive."

"Or maybe you would have died instead." She stared at her hands in her lap. "I know how you feel. I have my own regrets. Things I wish I had done differently. But we can't change the past."

"No, we can't."

"I can't help you find the answers, Cade, if that's

what you're thinking. My friend who inherited the place never said anything about the man who used to live here. I'm sure he…doesn't know. But I'm sorry you lost your father. I'm sure he was very proud to have a son like you."

Her words were clearly meant to heal and reassure, but instead they scraped across his wound.

"I don't know."

Cade strived to live up to the kind of man his father was, but always felt as if he fell short. An awkward silence filled the cab again. He'd gotten too personal.

She clutched the door handle, glancing back at Cade. "Thank you for saving me today and for bringing me here."

"Wait," he said. "Are you sure you should stay here by yourself after the rough day you've had? Especially with the storm coming?"

"I'll be fine, I promise." Something contrary to her words flashed in her eyes.

Cade was skeptical, but what could he do? "I'll come in and get the fire stoked."

He shoved on his door and the cold air blasted into the cab of the truck, swirling icy snowflakes around them.

"No," she said, the force of her words meant to convince. "No, Cade. Please, go home. You've done enough."

Cade nodded reluctantly, recognizing when he'd been dismissed. He shut the door as she opened hers and stepped out.

Headlights illuminated the cabin while he continued

to wait, thinking he'd watch her go safely inside. For the longest time, he'd been about saving people. She might have sent him away, but the anxiety lurking in the shadows of her blue-greens said she still needed his help.

How could he turn his head now? As long as he could keep his heart in a safe place.

Out of danger.

FIVE

His intense gaze softened, the accusation gone—but not forgotten. Though he came across as concerned and protective, she knew he didn't trust her. But he didn't have to. This was where they went their separate ways. Still, Cade made her wish she could trust people. Trust men. This one in particular. Take his help instead of going into that cold cabin alone. Even if she trusted him, she didn't want to pull him into the danger that was closing in around her. Smothering her more quickly than she ever imagined.

How could she live with herself if something happened to the man who had saved her today?

"Goodbye, Cade." She slammed the truck door and stepped into knee-high snow covering the path to the cabin.

Arctic cold swirled around her, chilling her to her bones despite her parka and down bib overalls, and stirring doubt deep inside about her next move. She hurried by the wood pile and chopping block, glad she'd already stacked more firewood next to the cabin door.

Yet another thing that didn't matter—she wasn't staying the night.

Snyder knew where she was hiding. He'd make his way back as soon as he thought it was safe and that meant her time was running out. Was he already there, inside the cabin, waiting for her? There was no way to tell. The headlights from Cade's truck kept the cabin in the spotlight and for that she was thankful. She'd told him to leave, but as she closed in on the cabin, she wasn't sure she'd made the right call.

Why couldn't Tim have inherited a hut on a tropical island? She made her way to the door and paused. What would she find inside? Would the place be torn apart, her stuff scattered everywhere because Snyder had come to find her and whatever he thought she had? One thing she knew, she hadn't had a chance to lock up before leaving earlier. She'd gone to explore one of several small buildings on the property and when she'd returned, she'd seen Snyder step out of the cabin and lock eyes with her.

At the memory, a shudder ran over her. How had Snyder located her? Whatever it was that had given her away, another mistake like that one could be deadly.

Taking a deep breath, she shoved the door open and stepped inside. Nothing appeared disturbed. And that confused her. But she could figure it all out after she gathered her things.

She wouldn't be here long enough to bother with stoking the fire, but the cabin was well insulated and remained relatively warm, considering she still wore her parka.

The kerosene lamp in the corner hissed, crackled and dimmed. Leah quickly added more fuel, brightening the small living area, shadows blinking in the tiny bedroom and the mudroom. Grabbing the lamp, she carried it into the mudroom to chase the darkness away from the shelves and the solar energy equipment, making sure she was alone.

When she'd first arrived, it looked as if Devon had been experimenting with solar power even with the limited sunlight in this region. But Leah had used the lamps and generator for the short time she was here. The oil stove in the corner caught her attention—she could use some coffee or hot tea after the day she'd had, but she didn't have time for that. On the kitchen counter lay the knife she'd used to cut an apple earlier that afternoon. It reminded her of when Snyder had flashed a knife at her today. She'd lost her handgun this afternoon, and would need another weapon.

Leah grabbed her laptop from the table. Had Snyder searched her files? Could be that was why he hadn't bothered ransacking the cabin. He wouldn't have found anything. For all her investigative prowess, Leah had failed to get the one photograph that would change everything. The photograph of Snyder murdering Tim in cold blood.

An image forever seared in Leah's mind, for all the good that did.

And that's why she understood Cade's anguish and self-recrimination—that feeling he seemed to carry that if there was anyone Cade should have been able to save, it was his father.

And if Leah couldn't save Tim that night, at least she should have taken that photograph.

Had she not been paralyzed where she'd stood, and instead taken the picture, Snyder would have been quickly put away with the evidence against him. She could have gone to the press or posted it on the internet for the world to see so that Snyder or his coconspirators couldn't bury the evidence. Without it, no one would believe her against a town hero and decorated police officer. Snyder was free to stalk and kill her, much as he was doing now.

If she hadn't seen it with her own eyes, she wouldn't have believed it—his actions were completely out of character with his public image. He must have been desperate to commit murder. Now he was desperate for something from her—and he was clearly willing to kill again

After stuffing her laptop into her briefcase, she carried the lamp to the bedroom to grab her duffel bag and pack her few belongings inside.

A sound stopped her. The back door? Panic engulfed her.

Was it Snyder? She stood stock-still.

Listening.

In this case, the light wouldn't chase the monsters away. Leah snuffed out the lamp. Keeping her location obscured was her only chance to get away if someone had broken in.

Utter darkness wrapped around her. Her heart pounded, needing escape.

Now she wished she had asked Cade to wait. She

could have followed him down the mountain in her own vehicle. If only she could have told him everything.

The floor creaked somewhere in the inky blackness of the cabin. Near or far she couldn't tell. Holding her breath, she listened to the footfalls that let her know she wasn't alone.

They grew closer, permeating the small dwelling with deadly tension. Fear surrounded her like hundreds of snakes slithering over her body, around her neck, arms and legs, paralyzing her.

The knife on the counter. If only she'd taken it the moment she'd seen it. If she could make her way to the kitchen.

Move. Your. Legs.

Leah's breathing ramped up. She was tougher than this. *Do something! Save yourself!*

"Leah." It was Snyder. His voice was low and threatening. "This can all be over. You can have your life back. Or disappear, I don't care. But give me what I want."

Liar. He'd killed Tim and would kill her, too. She wanted to tell him that, wanted to ask him what he thought she had, but said nothing. In the blackness, answering would give her position away. Instead, she stood in her prison of darkness and listened to his deadly threats.

Cade had only driven a short distance when he decided to wait and watch for a few minutes in his rear-view mirror, unsure of what he would see. Maybe he was crazy, but he kept thinking about the moment when he'd first driven up. He thought he'd spotted something in the shadows, but at the time, he'd disregarded it. Cade didn't like that Leah was staying in the remote and ill-fitted cabin to begin with.

And suddenly, the place went dark. Completely.

Leah was probably tired and had gone to bed early, and he was an idiot. If she knew he was out here, she'd think him a stalker. But hadn't she at least stoked the fire? If she had, Cade would be able to see the dim light through the windows. She couldn't blame him for checking on her. A person could die up here if they didn't know what they were doing. He should have insisted on going inside and stoking the fire. Check on things. He reminded himself that Leah was a grown woman perfectly capable of taking care of herself. She'd made it clear she wanted her privacy.

Perfectly clear that she didn't want his help. Didn't need him to rescue her.

Yeah, yeah. None of that eased his gut feeling—a feeling he'd learned to listen to when it came to avalanches, when it came to search and rescue. And he couldn't ignore it now. He steered the truck in a U-turn on the narrow drive, tires spinning and grinding through the deepening snow. Cade would never forgive himself if he didn't at least check on her one last time. Staying on the safe side was worth the risk of her thinking him an idiot any day of the week.

Hand lifted to knock, he stood at the door. All was quiet inside. Almost too quiet. Should he forget it and leave her alone? Except, he knew the lights from his truck would have disturbed her already.

He blew out a foggy breath. Here went nothing.

He pounded on the door. "Leah, it's Cade."

Three seconds went by before the door flew open and Leah rushed out. He caught her in his arms, buffering the sure collision. Gripping her shoulders, her face near his, he witnessed the fear in her eyes before she pulled away.

"What's wrong?" he asked.

"I need a ride down the mountain, after all. Can we get out of here?"

"Of course."

Leaving him behind, she hurried for his truck, carrying bags, trudging over the snow-covered ground like a fugitive fleeing in the night. This was getting weird. He was glad he'd hung back and waited. Glad he'd decided to check on her. He only had a degree in glaciology but it didn't take a rocket scientist to see something was wrong. Just as he suspected this afternoon as he'd watched her. Just as his gut told him while sitting in the truck. But what the problem was…he didn't know.

He glanced back through the door she'd left open, seeing nothing inside the cabin except darkness reaching out to him, and raising the hairs on his neck. Was it only his aversion to all things Devon Hemphill and the memories that accompanied him, the cabin included, or was there truly something sinister inside?

He shut and locked the door then hurried after Leah. She was already sitting in the truck. Cade climbed in on the driver's side and studied her, hoping she'd tell him what was going on, but she didn't even look at him. She wasn't wearing gloves and her hands trembled.

From the cold or something else? Cade had thought she was staying in the cabin, but a duffel bag and briefcase rested in her lap.

"I'm glad you came back to check on me." Her voice cracked. "But it's getting late. Snowing hard. Can we go?"

Cade frowned, disturbed to his core. The snowplow still engaged, he shifted into Drive and headed back to Mountain Cove. He'd ask her where she wanted him to take her, but there was only one way back to town and he had a more pressing question.

Tense and breathing a little hard, Leah kept glancing in the side mirror.

"Are you in some kind of trouble?" he finally asked. Might as well get right to the point.

"Why would you ask that?"

"I don't know. Something about the way you've acted since…well, since I pulled you from the snow. Like you're scared. Why are you in such a hurry to leave? I thought you were staying in the cabin tonight."

She huffed a laugh. "I didn't mean to mislead you. I never actually said I was staying tonight, just that I would be fine. I asked you to give me a ride back, that's all."

"Well, I must have misunderstood. It's none of my business if you stay. I just want to help."

Leah sighed. "I know. As for me not staying here tonight, the cabin isn't completely functional yet. I needed to grab my things, and with the snow really coming down, I realized I'm not sure I can make the drive down.

I don't have the plow like you do. I made a mistake in ignoring your concerns to begin with."

Her words made sense but Cade had a feeling they were only for his benefit, and meant to hide something else. His brothers would want to knock him in the head for digging into her business like this. For not taking her words at face value. And as for driving back to town tonight in the storm, Cade had a feeling she would have tried if he hadn't been there.

"I could help you attach a plow, if you want." They'd have to order one from Cooper's in Juneau to fit her specific vehicle.

"No." Her reply was too emphatic.

He glanced her way, trying to watch her and the road. To his surprise a timid grin broke through.

"Not tonight, that is," she added. She was trying to be friendly, to warm up to him, but still, it seemed forced.

He risked another glance over and caught her eyes—where he saw the truth. She was terrified and hiding something.

Who are you, Leah Marks?

She was in trouble.

He wanted to protect her from whatever evil was after her. Protect her even from trouble of her own making, if that turned out to be the case. He hated himself for that innate instinct that was in his blood, but as long as he kept his heart out of it, he should be safe.

He concentrated on the road and the driving snowfall, growing thicker by the minute. One wrong move on his part and they could end up down an embankment stuck in the snow or worse. When he made it to the intersection with the highway that led to town, he slowed to a stop at the sign.

"Where to?" he asked.

"What?" She turned from staring out the passenger window, the look in her eyes telling him her thoughts had been a million miles away.

"You left the cabin," he said. "Where were you planning to stay?"

"Could you recommend a quiet, out-of-the-way motel?"

Cade rubbed his scruffy jaw. Sure, he could think of a few. Mountain Cove might be out of the way and hard to get to, but people came from all over to hunt and fish and get away. The town counted on that money. There was a bed-and-breakfast, too, but it might be booked up. His family was friends with the owner, Jewel. Cade could give her a call. But another thought burrowed in as if coming in from the cold. "I have an idea."

Troubled eyes gazed into his. Strength, determination, the will to survive lingered in them as well. She blinked, waiting for him to go on.

"You could stay with my grandmother and sister tonight. Then figure things out tomorrow."

"I couldn't do that."

"No, really, you can. My grandmother would want me to invite you." Especially under the circumstances, though he wasn't exactly sure what the buried details of the circumstances were. But that shouldn't matter. Leah was in trouble, and he knew without having to ask that his grandmother would want to help.

Cade turned onto the road and headed home, won-

dering if she would take him up on his offer. He hoped
so. Leah could use the kind of nurturing only his grandmother could give. She'd come to live with them after
his mother died twenty years ago. Cade had been thir-
teen then, his brother David, seventeen, Adam, ten and
Heidi, eight. His father had been devastated after losing
his wife, and caring for four kids while working wasn't
an easy task. The arrangement had been good for Cade's grandmother, as well.

"Come on," he cajoled. "It's a cold night. You've been
through a lot today. Grandma cooked up a nice big pot
of beef stew and homemade rolls."

Leah's stomach rumbled. Cade almost laughed at
that, but he kept it inside.

She quirked a brow. "You're not playing fair. Besides,
how do you know what she cooked? You've spent what
feels like the entire day rescuing me."

"I know because she told me this morning what she'd
be making. She and Heidi, my sister, know I can't always make it in time, but they keep the food warm. Just
think. It's ready and waiting for us right now."

*What are you doing, man? Bringing her into your
life this way?*

Maybe he was trying too hard to be a hero, to live
up to his father's reputation. Yeah. Had to be that. He
couldn't let it be anything more.

"You live with your grandma and sister?"

"In an apartment over the garage. I like to stay close.
Be the man of the family, if they ever need a toilet un-
clogged or a sink fixed. That sort of thing. Not that my
sister couldn't do that, mind you, but why not ask me

to do it instead? What else am I good for?" He sent her a grin, hoping to disarm her.

Cade drove back through Mountain Cove proper where the snow had all but stopped. Rain was forecasted at the lower elevations later this week, which would make things a slushy mess. He waited to see if Leah would ask him again about a motel, but she stayed silent. Apparently she was accepting his invitation. Finally he turned onto the road that led to Huckleberry Hill, a subdivision above the snow line that overlooked Mountain Cove. A few hundred yards up and the snow started in full force again.

"Got any other family?"

He liked that she was engaging him in conversation. "Sure. My older brother, David, is a firefighter here in Mountain Cove, has his own place. He was at the rescue today but I doubt you met him. I have two younger siblings. Heidi, who you'll meet at my grandmother's tonight, and Adam, who has his own apartment. They both work at the avalanche center with me. We're all search and rescue volunteers." Following in their father's footsteps.

Cade turned into the steep driveway, steering through the twists and turns until he was in front of the two-story home. He parked his truck and looked at Leah. "What do you say? Are you hungry?"

If he could get her to eat, he could get her to stay. For tonight, at least, and then he'd sleep better knowing she was, for the time being, out of harm's way. But the way she kept looking at the mirror, watching as if someone might follow, he doubted she'd feel safe no matter where she stayed.

SIX

"I don't know." She weighed her options. Did she have any?

She never wanted to face Snyder alone again. Not on a mountain. Not in that cabin. Not in a motel she might pick to stay the night before fleeing again. She hadn't been able to escape the gripping terror brought on by the sound of his voice resounding in the cabin. His threats echoed through her mind, and her only relief had been Cade's reassuring voice as he tried to make conversation.

He'd rescued her again. Did he know? She wished she could thank him for that.

She eyed the thick snow that had started up again, swirling beneath the security light near the street, reminding her of the nasty storm. She wished she hadn't asked him about his family. This was getting too personal.

Cade turned off the ignition as though she'd already given an answer. Confident guy. But in this case, he had a reason to be—after all, she'd let him drive her all the way up here.

Leah had been on her own for a long time. Could
take care of herself. But right now, the last thing she
wanted was to face a cold, dark night alone. The images
he'd painted of beef stew, homemade rolls and a cozy
home with family waiting ignited the hunger pangs inside of her for more than just food. Sitting in the cab of
Cade's warm truck, in his presence, raised her awareness in other ways, too.

She'd always felt confident and secure in her inde-
pendence. The world she'd built for herself. Didn't want
to depend on anyone. Yet she was starving with a need
for exactly that. To trust. The need to feel safe and secure. She hadn't known the need was even there inside
her, but then, she'd never witnessed a murder before.
Never been hunted by an angry predator before.

Staying in the remote cabin hadn't worked. Out of
the way as it was, it hadn't been off-grid enough.

"Leah," Cade said, "you have to eat. I know you're
hungry. What's holding you back? Am I such a terrible guy?"

Why did he care what she did or what she thought of
him? That's what she didn't get. She read the questions
behind his intense green gaze—but also saw the protector in him. And maybe that was driving him. "Still
doing your job?"

"All part of a day's work." That grin she liked came
out again.

"Well, then, thank you. Beef stew sounds wonderful." She opened the door, the cold nearly slapping sense
into her, but not quite.

She'd eat and then decide whether or not she'd stay

for the night in his grandmother's house. Of course, that also depended on Cade and his family—if the invitation he'd offered on his grandmother's behalf still stood once the woman actually met her.

He escorted her to the front door of the light gray home and ushered her inside. The aroma of fresh-baked bread and beef stew—as promised—wafted around her along with something else she hadn't felt in a long time. If ever.

Love. It was palpable.

Hanging on the wall was a lovely framed cross-stitch that read, "Do not withhold good from those who deserve it, when it is in your power to act. Proverbs 3:27."

Yeah. Leah could see that in Cade. It was part of his upbringing.

The cozy atmosphere and inviting smells almost overwhelmed her. She and Cade took off their coats and dusted off the snow, leaving puddles on the floor. It was then that she noticed he carried a concealed weapon in a shoulder holster beneath his coat.

She felt her eyes grow wide as her gaze lingered on the weapon. She looked from the gun to Cade's face.

Noticing her surprise, he frowned and disarmed himself. Not that he owed her an explanation, but she wanted one all the same.

She never got one.

Two women entered the foyer that opened into a living room. One was obviously Cade's grandmother, her silver roots battling bushy auburn hair. The other woman—was that his sister? With big brown eyes, she looked nothing like him, except that she shared the same thick, coffee-brown hair.

"Glad you finally made it." The younger woman stepped forward and smiled.

Oh, wait. She had Cade's smile. A nice smile.

"This is Leah Marks," Cade said by way of introduction. "Leah, Heidi, my sister, and this is my grandmother. We call her Grandma Katy or just plain Grandma." He chuckled.

At Leah's name, recognition flashed in Heidi's eyes.

"Nice to meet you," Leah said.

She hoped they wouldn't ask too many questions. Maybe coming here had been a mistake. She was too exhausted to keep her guard up. Why hadn't she thought this through? "I hope I'm not intruding. Your brother invited me."

Cade's grandmother reached over and took Leah's hand. "Of course you're not intruding, dear. We're so pleased to have you. And you can call me Katy."

"Okay, Katy. Thanks," Leah said.

"This is a first," Katy said.

"A first?"

"Cade has never invited a rescue victim over for dinner before," Heidi said.

Oh.

Katy escorted Leah into the dining room where dinner plates were set out as though it was still only six in the evening instead of nearly eight o'clock. Cade had mentioned his grandmother kept the food warm for him, and some people ate that late anyway. She would die of hunger if she waited that late to eat, and that was probably why Cade had so easily talked her into this.

"Have a seat, Leah," Katy said. "I'll bring in the stew and heat up the rolls."

"Thank you." Leah slid into a seat at the dining table, feeling more awkward by the minute.

"I'll be right back." Cade disappeared.

Leah was left sitting alone in the dining room. She stared out the large window that was meant to take advantage of the incredible view during the day, but at night only darkness stared back. Leah stood and went to the window, hoping to see past her own reflection. Was Snyder out there now, watching her? She fingered the thick curtains, wondering if Katy would mind if she closed the miniblinds. If Katy knew the kind of person that might be out there, she most certainly wouldn't mind. Leah closed the blinds and peeked through. Someone touched her shoulder from behind. Leah jumped.

"I didn't mean to startle you," Cade said.

"No problem." Leah moved back to her seat, aware that Cade was watching. Funny that he hadn't asked her why she'd closed the blinds.

He probably knew she was exhausted. Vulnerable. Maybe he even knew she was terrified. And he'd brought her to his home so he could feed her well. She almost smiled at the thought. Things could have gone much differently.

Regardless of his thoughtfulness, she couldn't let herself be used and abused the way her mother had been. She would only trust Cade to a point, and never with the truth. Never with even a small part of her heart.

Just as Cade's grandmother set the stew on the table, a yawn overtook Leah. Katy ladled a big helping into Leah's bowl. Then Cade's. He said grace and thanked the Lord for Leah's survival today. Leah could swear she heard tears in his voice as he thanked his Heavenly Father for allowing him to save someone from the claws of an avalanche.

She heard the pain and knew it went deep. That couldn't be for her. There had to be much more to the story and she figured it had to do with his father. She yawned again before he even said amen. Considering the events of the day and the fact that since witnessing Tim's murder she hadn't been able to sleep, it made sense that exhaustion would catch up to her.

Her cheeks warmed. "I'm so sorry."

Katy patted her shoulder. "You'd better eat up before you fall over. Cade informed me you need a place to stay tonight. We have several extra rooms and there's one all ready for you."

Leah took in a breath to argue; she hadn't told him she was staying yet. Not wanting to endanger someone because of her predicament, she throttled him with her gaze for his presumption. But she couldn't blame him. He didn't know what she was up against. Who he'd brought into this house.

She'd find somewhere else to stay, somewhere safe.

Her mind scrambled to process this life he lived like something from the fifties. A loving grandmother to cook and keep meals warm for him in a nice, cozy home. A protective sister, too, and brothers. A family.

Or was this normal? Leah really couldn't say. She'd never had a real father. Only her mother's various abusive boyfriends. She could only watch other families from the outside.

Unable to disappoint his sweet grandmother, Leah knew that rejecting her offer wasn't the right thing to do. She couldn't hurt Katy's feelings by refusing to accept her kindness. And after what Cade had done for her today, after listening to his heartfelt prayer of thanks, she knew she had to stay the night. At least this one night.

She couldn't think of a safer place than right here where Cade Warren made it his business to watch over things like a sentinel.

With the decision made, relief washed through her, even though she hadn't exactly made the decision herself. But she was a free agent—could walk out at any moment. Stew and bread before her... A warm bed waiting for her upstairs... Safety. Security. For now.

Besides, she couldn't walk out when she was this exhausted. She wasn't free, after all.

"Thank you, really," Leah said. "I don't want to be any trouble."

"No trouble at all, dear."

But Katy couldn't know how far from the truth her words were.

Cade shared the details of the rescue with Grandma and Heidi while he ate. Leah kept quiet through most of it, not adding to his story. Not shedding any light on why she'd been on the mountain. Never mentioning who the witness was or the other victim.

Right now she was busy eating Grandma's stew. Cade was glad to see she had a hearty appetite after the day she'd had. He knew his grandmother would take care of Leah, as much or as little as she would allow. When Grandma had moved in with them, she had thrived as she'd looked after him, his siblings and his father before he'd died, making this house into a home again.

He chafed at the reminder he'd lost both his parents. But he had his siblings.

Heidi busied herself between the kitchen and the dining room, cleaning up and putting away dishes and hovering near the table. She'd been filing reports today at the avalanche center and not on call; otherwise she would have been involved in the search and rescue, as well.

When Leah attempted to hide another yawn, Grandma stood. "Leah, I'm happy to show you the bedroom where you can sleep if you're ready."

Leah smiled at Grandma, much of the tension and fear he'd seen in her face today, even moments before when she peered out the window, fading away.

"Yes, thank you," she said.

She grabbed her glass, dish and utensils, and made for the sink, but Heidi quickly whisked them from her. "I'll take those."

Cade was surprised that Leah didn't put up more

of a fight, insisting on doing her part, but she looked ready to collapse. Exhaustion weighed on him, as well.

Before she followed Grandma, she glanced in Cade's direction, the gratitude in her gaze meaning more than words ever could. He'd been right to bring her here, at least for tonight.

Cade stood, took his dishes to the sink and chuckled that Heidi didn't whisk his away, too. But, hey, this was an equal opportunity home and it wasn't as if he was a guest. He had as much right to wash a dish as the women. He rinsed his dish and stuck it in the dishwasher, then opened the fridge looking for something with fizz, aware of Heidi's gaze boring into the back of his head.

"What?" he asked. But knowing full well why she stared.

"What's going on?" At the sink, she worked on the rest of the dishes. "What's with bringing an avalanche survivor home?"

He turned around, popping the top on the can of soda he'd grabbed. "Is there a problem with that?"

She shook her head. "No, of course not. It's just not usually done. At least not something *you* usually do. You must have a reason."

"I'm not sure." Cade scratched his neck. "She seemed lost and dazed. She needed a place to stay."

Heidi crossed her arms. Tilted her head. Cocked a brow. "Really?"

"Yes, really. What do you think?"

"I think you're a softie. And here I thought you always threw those walls up, keeping your distance. But this one…she's pretty."

"Don't even go there," Cade growled. He leaned on the kitchen counter and weighed his decision to bring Leah home. He didn't think he'd really had a choice, but getting into all that with his sister wasn't something he was prepared to do yet. That was the problem with living in proximity to his family. Good thing he could escape to his apartment above the garage.

"Where's she from?" Heidi would persist until she had answers. "What was she doing on the mountain?"

"Don't know anything except she was living in old Devon Hemphill's cabin."

Heidi sucked in a breath. Cade wished he hadn't said that much.

The front door opened and shut. "Anybody home?"

They heard rustling sounds for a few seconds—someone slipping out of their winter wear—then David found them in the kitchen, his eyes scanning the counter and table. "You didn't leave me any food?"

Heidi popped him with a towel. "You don't live here. And you don't eat here. You wanted your cool bachelor pad, remember?" She batted her eyelashes. "But I could warm something up for you."

David shook his head at her antics. "Nah, I'm good. Grabbed a bite with the boys. Was just teasing you." He removed his wet cap and raked a hand through his disheveled hair.

"What have you got?" Cade asked.

"Nothing. You already know we ended the search.

With this storm coming in, we might not recover the victim until spring thaw."

Cade's gut twisted.

"The only thing we found was a knife," David said. "The good news is you were there in time to dig someone out alive."

Heidi gestured above them. "Not only did he dig her out, he brought her home."

David's eyes widened. "What? Why?"

"Why not?" Cade shoved from the counter, done with this conversation. He couldn't give them answers he didn't have. He didn't want his siblings getting too nosy, either. Spooking Leah. He didn't feel comfortable sharing that he believed something was very wrong. It could all be his imagination. He wished that was the case, but he didn't think so.

David and Heidi followed him into the living room. A step creaked. They all turned to see Grandma.

"Leah is tucked away now." She said it as though Leah were a small child. "I'm heading to bed myself. Oh, David…" She hurried the rest of the way down the stairs to give him a peck on the cheek. "I haven't seen you in ages. Why didn't you tell us you would stop by? We could have kept dinner warm."

Cade took that as an opportunity to leave. "'Night, Grandma. I'm heading up to my apartment." He leaned in to give her a quick hug and a kiss on the cheek. "The stew was your best yet."

He exited through the back door and headed up the steps to his over-the-garage living space. Once inside, he flipped on the lights and let the adrenaline drain from his body, though tension still coiled around his shoulders. Scared and possibly in trouble, Leah Marks was sleeping under his family's roof. Tomorrow, Cade would try to convince her to stay here until the storm passed and then he'd help her dig the cabin out. She'd said a friend was letting her stay there, but she hadn't said for how long. Still, Cade could check to see what repairs needed to be done, if any. If she was going to stay for any length of time, the place likely needed some work.

Yeah, and he was the guy to do it, too. Right. Why did he think she would even agree? Or that she needed or wanted his help? Leah could work at Home Depot, or be a handyman herself, for all he knew. But the churning in his gut kept him determined to make sure she was okay.

Cade didn't like to think that he had any ulterior motives for wanting to help. Never mind that it was Devon's cabin—and if Cade made a few repairs, he could get inside and look around for answers. Some clue to the feud between Devon and Cade's father. Never mind that Cade had had an entire year to do that while the cabin was unoccupied. Who would know or care if he'd gone to look inside? Except he didn't have a key and getting inside without a key or permission would be breaking and entering.

Not the actions of a hero. Not something his father would have done. But it would be worth it if it got him answers. Cade wanted to know why his father had died that day. It shouldn't have happened. It didn't make sense.

He'd shared the story with Leah, hoping that she would confess what she was doing staying in the cabin. What or who she was hiding from. But that had apparently been asking too much. He thought back to the moment when he'd knocked on the cabin door and it had flown open, Leah rushing out and into his arms.

The fear and panic in her eyes had nearly done him in. Maybe she'd simply been afraid of staying in a lonely cabin in the middle of a stormy Alaska night, especially after what she'd been through. Who wouldn't be?

Cade was reading too much into this whole situation. Had to be. But whether she was truly in danger or not, the real question he had to ask himself was, why did he care so much?

He couldn't lie to himself. The moment he'd pulled her from what could have been her grave in the snow, the instant he'd looked into her crystal blue-greens, he'd connected with her, formed some sort of emotional attachment. He should have walked away as he always did after a search and rescue. After he'd completed his SAR responsibilities, retrieved the lost or injured party—whether dead or alive—Cade Warren always walked away.

Never looked back.

What was wrong with him this time? Why had he gotten so attached, particularly to a woman who seemed unwilling to let him in? She was hiding things from him, which should have been warning enough to keep his distance. He'd been through that already. He couldn't let himself grow close, couldn't let this connection or whatever it was between him and Leah go any further. He'd never forgotten how it had felt catching Melissa with another man.

Rising, he moved to the window to twist the blinds closed, the thought reminding him of when Leah had done the same in the dining room earlier that evening. Looking outside, he saw that the snow had diminished to barely visible pinpricks. He let his gaze sweep over the snowdrifts between the trees and down the twisted driveway to the lights of Mountain Cove below the hill.

Thirty yards out something moved in the shadows beneath the trees.

Cade peered closer, stunned at what he saw.

A man dressed in black.

SEVEN

The soft bed conformed to her body perfectly. Leah rolled onto her side, the aroma of bacon wafting over her. She bolted straight up. Where was she?

Cade's face came to mind, along with Katy's and Heidi's. She was in their home. Safe. She breathed a sigh of relief, though she could never completely relax. Not with a killer after her.

The digital clock read 8:00 a.m. and only the faint, gray light of morning peeked through the blinds.

A Bible lay on the side table. She'd seen it last night but had been too exhausted to look through the pages. Instead she'd fallen asleep praying. God had brought her to this place of safety so she could at least catch her breath. She wouldn't question that. And He'd put her in a Christian home. After hearing Cade say the blessing before their dinner, she had no doubt his faith went deep.

But staying one night didn't mean she should stay longer. She climbed from the bed and dug for clean clothes in her duffel bag. She'd been too traumatized, too drained, to figure out what she would do when morning came. Nor had she thought beyond getting to the cabin when she'd first fled from Snyder—getting to Alaska and staying alive had been her first priority.

It had been difficult enough to find the place. She'd spent the first couple of days making sure she could survive there, stocking up on fuel for the generator and food in case she got snowed in. She hadn't progressed to investigating Snyder, which would have been hard to do anyway without internet at the cabin, not to mention far away from the city where the crime had occurred. She'd steered clear of civilization because being off grid was meant to have kept her safe, but it hadn't worked. How had Snyder found her? How could she keep him from finding her again?

She couldn't research if she was dead.

Was there wireless internet access here? Leah pulled out her laptop and set it on the small secretary desk against the wall. She flipped on the desk lamp. Her laptop booted up. Yes. Of course, Cade and Heidi would have Wi-Fi. Maybe Katy even enjoyed the social media sites. Again, Leah felt the pain of being utterly alone in this world, with no family except her aunt in Florida. And now she didn't even have a job. But those were selfish thoughts considering Tim had lost his life.

She focused her attention on her computer, finding a strong wireless signal. The family hadn't set things up to require a password, either. Her heart raced. Getting research time in could mean the difference between life and death. She hoped that connecting to cyberspace would help her find the evidence she would need against Snyder. Somewhere there had to be something that would give her the clues she needed.

And that was all part of Leah's job as a legal investigator.

She glanced around the quaint room, noting more cross-stitched pictures, some of them Bible verses. This was a well-kept and well-loved home. So opposite of what she'd known growing up. A person could get used to this. Well, any person that wasn't her. She couldn't put these people in danger.

Chances were good that Snyder had already searched the local motels. There weren't that many in the small town. Eventually he would have found her if she'd stayed in one of them. She would have been awake all night worrying about that. If the storm hadn't hit, and Snyder hadn't come back to the cabin to find her, she would have gotten in her SUV and driven…somewhere. Except she couldn't drive her way out of Mountain Cove. If she wanted to leave, she'd have to take a ferry along the Alaska Marine Highway north to Haines or Skagway, or south to Juneau where she could catch a flight out of southeast Alaska.

The truth is she had no idea where she could go to be safe since this plan hadn't worked. But Snyder had no idea where she was at the moment. How could he know that she was staying with a local family? And which one, at that? Though she couldn't stay here long, she should at least pray about staying long enough to get her bearings.

A scraping noise outside caught her attention.

She went to the window and peeked through the

miniblinds, morning light finally brightening the skies. Cade was shoveling snow below her. The sight brought a smile to her lips. She owed it to him to help with that.

But maybe she could help him in a better way…

Tim hadn't even known the cabin existed until a few months ago when he'd found out his distant uncle had died and Tim had inherited the property. It hadn't made sense because Devon had had a daughter. But she'd simply disappeared. Though Tim had made an initial trip to see the cabin, he'd hoped Leah could conduct further investigation regarding the disappearance of his distant cousin. He'd wanted to pass the cabin over to what he thought of as the rightful owner. So she really did have a mostly legitimate reason to be in the cabin, though she could tell Cade hadn't believed her story. Finding out more about Devon Hemphill could help Cade, too, if she could dig deep enough to discover the reason for a family feud that even Cade himself couldn't figure out.

Leah shoved all that aside for now and went back to the laptop, searching for information on Detective Nick Snyder. Head in her hands, she stared at the laptop. There was the story of Tim's murder and the ongoing investigation conducted by none other than Detective Snyder himself. Then another story the week before of Snyder's role in a sting operation to bring down a drug ring.

How did the guy do that? It was as though there were two sides to the man. Hero on the one side and villain on the other. He hadn't earned his position by being a lousy detective; he knew how to sniff out criminals.

So why had he killed Tim? If she could figure that

out, then she'd know what Snyder was after—and why he was desperate enough to have to follow her here. He had to know she hadn't taken a photograph of him because she would have already exposed his secret identity as a murderer.

She had to figure out what was going on between Tim and Snyder.

Closing her eyes, she thought back to the weeks leading up to Tim's murder. He'd acted strange. Had had a few too many private phone calls...had snapped at her and been irritable when she'd walked into his office... She was his investigator, and he'd never treated her that way, so she'd known something was up. But Tim hadn't been in a sharing frame of mind.

A creature of habit, he'd had protocols in place for everything. Leah knew all of those as had his paralegal, Sheila, who was out on maternity leave. Leah thanked God for that small kindness, otherwise Sheila might have ended up in Snyder's crosshairs, too. Tim hadn't wanted to bring in a temp, so filing was backlogged, which wasn't a good thing for an attorney's office. Letting the office run shorthanded was unlike Tim and she had wondered at it at the time. Now Leah understood—he'd known something bad was coming down and had wanted as many people as possible out of the way. Sheila on maternity leave... Leah on vacation... Tim facing down the oncoming danger alone...

Leah knew Tim's habits well enough that she knew where he put sensitive documents. Except this time. And he would have known that she might be in danger, too, if what Tim had planned turned south.

Her pulse ratcheted up as the image replayed across her mind.

Leah had gone back to the office and parked on the street. She'd spotted Tim from a distance in the parking garage when Snyder had showed up, railing, *"Think I'm going to take this from a scumbag like you?"* Snyder had whipped out a gun with a sound suppressor and shot Tim in the head.

Leah had taken her share of incriminating photographs in her role as investigator, but never of an actual murder in the making. She should have tried to stop him. Something. But it had happened too fast. She'd frozen and flattened her body behind the concrete beam, squeezing her eyes shut and praying for her life. *Oh, God, Oh, God, Oh, God... Let him not find me here.*

Snyder had gotten into his car and driven off. As he'd exited the parking garage, he'd glanced over and seen Leah. It was all over then. Like so many of those police chases she'd witnessed she expected Snyder to chase her down. To tell the police that she'd shot and killed Tim to cover for his deed.

But none of that had happened. It was insanity. She'd driven to the airport and parked, hoping to mislead him, and then she'd taken a cab to the ferry that would take her through the Inside Passage to Mountain Cove. To Tim's cabin.

She pressed her palms into her eyes, pushing back the tears, her breaths raspy. "Oh, Tim, what did you get into with that man?"

She replayed Snyder's words in her head. *Take this*

from a scumbag... Take this from a scumbag... Take this from a scumbag...

Take what?

Leah thought of all the possibilities.

Someone rapped softly on the door.

"Leah? Breakfast is ready," Katy said through the door.

Leah cracked it. "Thank you. I'll be right down."

Leah finished dressing, brushed her hair and grabbed her toothbrush for a stop at the bathroom, but right before she left the bedroom, the shoveling stopped outside. She heard voices and peeked out the window again.

Cade was speaking with a police officer, showing him the gun she'd seen on him last night as if it was a new toy.

Leah jerked back, her pulse jumping to her throat. Normally law enforcement would be a good thing to have around, but the fewer people who knew she was here, the better, especially given the police channels to which Snyder had access. With his reputation, he could easily turn the police force against her. She had a feeling the only reason she wasn't already a suspect in Tim's murder was that Snyder needed something from her. And the words he said before she'd heard Cade's voice at the cabin door last night flooded back to her.

"If I don't get what I want then I'm going to pin Tim's murder on you. I have all the evidence I need to do it, and you helped me when you fled the scene. The next thing I'm going to do is kill you."

Of course, Snyder's evidence would be circumstantial or planted. But it would be her word against Snyder's—if she was even alive at that point to speak in her own defense. If only she knew what he was after. Was it evidence against him—perhaps something Tim had found? Maybe that's exactly what Tim had been about to do—use the evidence he had against Snyder—but Snyder had killed him before he could do anything.

Now Snyder would do the same to Leah. He had her on the run and scared for her life, which was all part of his plan. She understood why Tim had sent her away now. She'd been suspicious of her own boss, knowing something was going on, but she'd been too slow in figuring things out. None of that mattered now.

In the end Snyder would kill her whether or not he got what he wanted because he couldn't afford to leave the one witness to Tim's murder alive.

Cade glanced at his watch and said goodbye to Terry Stratford, a close friend he'd grown up with who now worked for Mountain Cove PD. Cade had told him he thought he'd seen someone outside watching the house last night and he'd gone to investigate. Terry knew Cade would have a weapon, something to defend himself with, and then they'd started talking about Cade's new gun, a .44 Magnum.

He put the shovel away in the garage and glanced across the yard into the wood that separated this house from the next one. Last night, with flashlight in hand, he'd seen footprints that confirmed he hadn't imagined the person he'd seen outside. Someone had been watching the house.

This morning those footprints were gone, of course,

after the sky dumped more snow during the night. Funny that the guy had been dressed in black like the witness at the avalanche, though that could be simply coincidence. It didn't prove anything. But he didn't believe in coincidences.

Cade stomped his boots to knock the snow off then stepped through the back door. Leah sat at the kitchen table alone, eating a piece of bacon. Her cheeks warmed when she saw him watching.

"Hey. I don't want to track slush through the house, but I wanted to let you know I'm heading back to work at the avalanche center. Was in the office at six this morning already, working on the forecast. Heidi's there now. I came back to shovel more snow for Grandma so she could get out if she needed to."

That brought a half smile to Leah's pretty face. She should smile more often. Cade wished he could come all the way inside and sit at the table. Drink coffee with her. Get to know her better so he could help her get settled in safely. Find out what repairs she needed at the cabin. What she might know about someone watching the house last night. He struggled with whether or not to say anything about what he'd seen. If she knew, she might try to leave the safety of his home, and from what he could tell, she was all alone in whatever trouble she was in. He wished he knew what was going on. Guessing all the time was driving him crazy, but he was a patient man. He could wait for her to tell him.

"Your grandmother is on the phone," she said. "I'll give her the message."

"Listen," Cade said, "we got record snowfall here last

night, so that means even more for the cabin. I know I said I'd help you put a plow on your vehicle, but getting back there today is not such a good idea. Besides, I need to get the right attachment. When the weather clears up more, I can go with you to take a look at anything that needs repair in the cabin, too."

"Or fix a sink or unclog a toilet? Except there's no toilet unless you count the outhouse." She gave an exaggerated shudder to which Cade chuckled. "You're a real handyman, Cade, but I'm used to living on my own and taking care of myself."

"I'm sure you're completely capable of handling anything," he said. "I'm just offering some help. Hey, even I have to ask Heidi to hold a wrench once in a while." He hoped she heard the teasing in his tone.

Leah stood from the table and strolled toward him. Arms crossed, she leaned against the counter, a tan turtleneck hugging her slim body. "I saw you talking to a police officer outside. Any more news about the other victim? Did they find anyone else?"

"No. But my brother said they found a knife in the debris field."

She recoiled. "A knife?"

"That wouldn't have been yours, would it?" He injected the question with a teasing tone.

She shook her head too quickly. "Of course not."

"That wasn't an accusation." He'd been trying to make a joke, but he'd clearly chosen a touchy subject. Idiot. "Relax. I didn't mean to sound judgmental. People carry knives all the time around here, especially in the wilderness. They carry guns, too."

"Like the one I saw you with last night? The one you were showing the officer this morning."

"Yes, like that one. That's only one of several weapons I own." He cocked a brow. Took a guess. "You're not from Alaska, are you?"

"Uh. No."

Didn't think so. "Alaskans love their guns. In my case, I do a lot of work in the field and I'm always armed in case I run into a brown bear, bigger than grizzlies here in Alaska. And if you stay at the cabin, you should have protection, too. If you'd like I can help you learn how to fire one."

He took a step closer at the risk of letting the muck melt onto Grandma's clean floor.

"I know how to use a gun, Cade. I had one on the mountain with me when I got caught in the avalanche. I was actually hoping the rescuers found it." Her words surprised him, considering her reaction to the knife and to the sight of his holster.

The mystery Leah Marks brought was almost like the cornices loaded with too much snow, ready to bury him if he disturbed them.

Once again he wondered if he should tell her that someone had been outside the house last night, watching from the woods. He didn't want to scare her, though he knew she was strong. He saw a fire inside Leah. Determination. He liked that way more than he should. In the face of that strength, what right did he have to keep the truth from her? But he knew if he told her about someone watching the house, and if she believed it had to do with her, then she would leave.

His throat constricted. He admitted he didn't want her to go away for a far deeper reason than simply keeping her safe or because he wanted answers that he believed he might find in the cabin.

Leah slow-blinked and looked away. "Thank you for letting me stay last night. For saving my life. I appreciate everything you've done for me, but I need to get going as soon as I can—as you say, when the weather clears. We don't need to go back to the cabin until then. And I won't need repairs in the cabin because I don't plan to stay. I need to get my SUV, though."

Wait. What? "I asked you last night if you were in trouble, Leah. What's going on? I want to help."

When she looked back at him, her blue-greens locked on his gaze like crampons clawing into the glacier of his heart. He could hardly breathe.

A small laugh escaped, sounding forced. "You have an overactive imagination. I'm a legal investigator by trade, so believe me, I know how to take care of myself. The situations I can get into are pretty rough sometimes, hence the gun. So you don't need to worry about me, Cade. I'll be leaving the area soon, anyway."

Disappointment surged.

"Then you're heading back to wherever you came from. Where would that be?"

Leah smiled the kind of smile that told him he was asking too many questions. "I need to do some research before I leave Mountain Cove altogether. I was planning to go to a motel…"

The way she let her words trail off—was she asking

him what he thought she was asking? "You're welcome to stay here as long as you need."

What was he doing?

Relief washed over her features. "Are you sure? Because I don't want to take advantage of your generosity. It won't be for long."

"Of course, I'm sure. Grandma and Heidi will love another woman in the house." Cade didn't even want to think about how much he wanted Leah to stay. Or why. He only wanted to help. Uh-huh.

"While I'm here, I thought I could help you in your search for answers."

"Answers?" She was going to help him? He thought *he* was helping *her*.

"About whatever happened between your father and Devon Hemphill. Though come to think of it, if we're looking for insight into that, we might need to go back to the cabin for more than my vehicle."

Cade shifted in his boots, sweating under his collar. He didn't have time to take off his coat. He had to get going. And yet here he was, still trying to make sense of this bewildering woman.

He shrugged. "How could you help me? The quarrel was likely something buried and very personal. Not a legal matter at all." He said the words but still hoped she'd be able to find something.

"You do your job and let me do mine. I'm quite good at it, actually. I know how to find evidence to prove someone's innocence or guilt." Her eyes grew dark. "I know how to find evidence to put killers away."

A chill slithered along Cade's spine. What was that about?

EIGHT

Three days later Leah felt as if she was getting cabin fever. At least she wasn't stuck in the real cabin up the mountain practically living like a pioneer. Though she was grateful to Cade and his family for allowing her to stay, for not prying into her life, Leah grew frustrated that she hadn't been able to find out more about Snyder.

At least she hadn't been able to spot him in Mountain Cove. He'd likely had to travel back to Washington to show his face and do his real job instead of stalking her. She'd counted on the fact he couldn't know where she was, but he was a smart man. Sooner or later he would figure out she hadn't left Mountain Cove, after all. She only hoped that by the time he realized that, she'd have found evidence that she could use against him.

At least she'd made a few discoveries by accessing the files in Tim's online database. She had pulled up all the digital files of cases they had worked on over the past year, looking for something that connected them, starting with their ages and birthdates. Types of crimes. Those whom Tim had gotten off and those few who had ended up going to prison. Tim had been a great defense attorney, making a name for himself. Starting in alphabetical order, she had done an internet search on each of the clients in her files.

Obituaries for at least three of Tim's recent clients had showed up in the search.

Leah logged in again now, so she could cross-reference the client list, find out if she was on to something. Or at least she tried to log in, but her access was denied.

"No." She shoved from the desk and clenched her fists.

Tim would have assigned another attorney to close his office in case of his death. The first thing the new attorney would do is go through files to find out which ones needed immediate action. It would take time to close Tim's practice, and she doubted anything had been moved from his office yet. Clients would be contacted and must then decide on new representation. But apparently the attorney had already changed the password, not even bothering to talk to Leah about anything. But then...she'd made herself pretty unavailable. Maybe he thought her strange for not rushing back from her *cruise* upon learning of Tim's death. He'd likely talked to Sheila if he needed anything.

Looked as though Leah would have to access the physical files. Go back to Tim's office.

A noise downstairs startled her. Once again Leah wished the SAR volunteers had found her gun on the mountain. She'd made a few trips into town but always with Katy, and Leah hadn't felt comfortable buying a gun in her presence. At the sound downstairs, she thought of Cade's gun, wishing she had it in her hands right now. Wishing she had access to the other weapons he had mentioned but hadn't showed her.

She crept down the stairs and found Katy unpacking groceries. She hadn't even realized the woman had left the house. She'd let her guard down too much.

Katy's eyes grew wide. "Leah, I didn't realize you were still here. Cade mentioned wanting to take you back to the cabin now that the streets are clear. He's working at the center today instead of doing field work. I always worry about him and Adam or Isaiah, whoever goes with him. But I thought he'd already come by to get you."

Funny, Cade hadn't mentioned that to her, but he'd left the house before she'd gotten up. "Not yet. But don't worry, I'll be out of here soon enough."

"No rush, dear. None at all. You stay as long as you need. But we get things done while the weather allows. I expect it'll start raining. It snows one week, then rains the next."

So she'd be smart to get her vehicle while the weather cooperated. Once she had her ride back she would be free to leave this sweet family. But she wished she had something to give Cade in return before she left. She hadn't had much success in tracking down Devon's daughter—another missing piece of the Warren family feud puzzle. The daughter might be able to answer a few questions. One thing she suspected—the cabin itself didn't hold any answers for Cade as he hoped. No. If there were answers to find, they were probably in the box full of papers and letters that Tim had brought back with him from his one trip to the cabin after inheriting it.

Leah helped Katy unpack the groceries. What had Cade told his grandmother about Leah and why she needed to stay here? If anything, Leah was like a stray they'd taken in, and she hoped to remedy that soon enough.

"Oh, I can't believe it." The woman looked through the cabinets. "I thought I had pasta sauce. I hate it when that happens."

She shook her head and poured coffee from a carafe, then moved to a chair at the table. "Getting old isn't for the weak at heart," Katy said with a wink.

Leah chuckled. "I'm happy to go back into town for you and get the pasta sauce. Only, I don't have a vehicle."

And if she was on her own, she could buy a gun while she was in town. It would have to be a rifle or shotgun since she was from out of state, but it would be better than nothing.

Katy eyed Leah over the rim of her cup. "I wouldn't want you to go to any trouble, and Cade will be here at some point. I'll call and ask him to pick some up on the way."

"No, please." Leah tried to sound calm, but she realized how much she wanted some time away from the house. "There are a few items I'd like to get for myself while I'm there. I'll be back before you know it, and Cade can wait for me if he beats me home." She smiled, hoping Katy would agree.

She set her coffee on the table. "If you're sure, then. The keys are right there next to my purse, dear."

"Thank you." Leah took the keys. "Any particular kind of sauce?"

"Ragu. Two large jars of Ragu garlic and onions."

"I'll be back in a few."

With her hands on the steering wheel of Katy's sedan, Leah sucked in a breath, taking control of the unexpected sense of freedom that rushed over her. This wasn't her car, she reminded herself. She couldn't leave town in it. Besides, she had nowhere to go.

She steered carefully down the steep, curvy drive—surprised the homes were spaced this far apart—and through the small subdivision on the hill down into Mountain Cove. She relished the sense of safety that came from the fact that Snyder didn't know where she was this time, and he was likely back at his job until he could break free to track her again. That bought her some time.

But how much? A week? A day? Two hours?

She drove through town along the main thoroughfare until she found the first grocery store. She grabbed two jars of pasta sauce, then headed to the express line behind two others. The temperature was in the high forties today so Leah hadn't worn her parka but dressed in layers instead. She hoped the line would hurry because she didn't want to have to peel out of her layers just to put them back on again. Plus, the quicker she was done here, the more time she'd have to look into getting a weapon.

Pasta sauce bagged and in hand, Leah headed out the doors and into the parking lot. She was reaching for the car keys when someone bumped her shoulder, causing her to drop her grocery bag. Startled, Leah whirled around, but the man apologized and kept going. Nothing to be alarmed about. She reached down to grab her sack but didn't see the keys. Where had they gone? When she stood, she glanced across the street.

And locked eyes with Snyder, his face half-hidden behind the hood of his gray-fleeced hoodie.

Terror crushed her lungs, cemented her feet onto the sidewalk. She stood frozen as if time had slowed, and watched Snyder cross the street, moving toward her as though he expected her to stand there and wait.

Um. No. Leah shook off the chains of fear and searched for the keys to the car. She couldn't find them. Would he really come after her in broad daylight in front of all these people? She wouldn't put it past him. But no way would he want to call attention to himself. He would try to keep things low-key. She was counting on that.

Worst case, he could pretend to arrest her, cuff her and take her away. He could easily plant something incriminating on her. Or he could frame her for Tim's murder as he'd said. Her imagination ran away with all the possibilities.

But he would do none of that until he got what he needed from her.

What was it?

No time to think about that now. She glimpsed him push into a jog as he realized she was going to flee from him yet again. Leah got her feet moving and kicked the car keys. She scrambled to pick them up, but it was too late to drive away. Leah took off behind the building. She rushed through an exit door of the appliance store next door right as a worker came out, but unfortunately he called attention to her. She shoved him out and locked the door. No one was around to see so she strode through the employees-only section as though she belonged there, looking for an exit. Leah hurried out the front of the store and jogged down the sidewalk between alleys. If Snyder wanted to keep his apprehension of her low-key, he'd already made one mistake. People had seen him chasing her.

She didn't have time to contemplate all that could mean.

Breathing hard, she ran a good distance and then blended into the early afternoon crowd at the shopping center, finally slipping into a women's undergarment store. She pretended to shop for bras while she gathered her thoughts.

How did she get out of this? How did she escape this nightmare when she didn't have time to breathe, much less figure things out to save her neck?

Before Katy had come home, Leah had been researching Tim's deceased clients with the files she'd been able to access before getting locked out. The week before he'd left to check on the cabin, a client's ex-wife had come to see Tim regarding her ex-husband's death.

That was when Tim had scolded Leah for not taking her vacation time and become adamant that she take a few weeks off. Could it be related?

She glanced out the glass front of the store, watching for Snyder. Holding the keys in her hands, she knew she'd have to make it back to Katy's car. She could only hope Snyder didn't know which car that was, or he might sabotage it. She would get in and drive away and hopefully lose him before he figured out where she was staying.

Leah slipped outside; the clear skies a break in the gray, wintry, wet weather of the region. Birds chirped and flitted, cars filled the parking places along Main Street, the downtown bustled with people going about their business as though nothing at all was wrong.

Reversing her hoodie, she stepped in to the dance, joining the rhythm. She stared at the untraceable track phone she'd purchased when she'd first arrived in Mountain Cove and walked next to two teenagers, chatting with them as though she knew them. Admiring their boots had brought on smiles and conversation instead of the weird looks she might have invited. But could she do this all the way to back to the grocery store? She didn't know.

The girls moved across the street and Leah's gaze darted to her next target—someone to make it look as if she was with them. Walking alone, she was a far easier target to spot.

A hand twisted her arm and she cried out, tried to move away.

"Scream and I'll kill you here and now," Snyder whispered. "Keep walking."

Her legs were jelly, but she did her best. How had she missed him?

Oh, God, help me...

Snyder smiled and nodded to a couple that walked by. He pinched tighter, walking closer to her, making them look like a couple themselves. Her stomach roiled with nausea. She was weak, so weak. She only thought she was strong, but she'd lied to herself.

And then, to Leah's surprise, he yanked her into an alley, into the shadows. He held her from behind, his arm around her throat, his hot breath in her ear.

A decorated town hero. How could he do this?

"This isn't who or what I want to be, Leah, but your boss left me no choice. Here's what's going to happen. I'm going to hurt that family you're staying with if you don't give me what I want. You should never have involved them."

Leah had to be strong and think on her feet in her line of work, but never had she been in this situation. She called upon all the strength she could muster. "You wouldn't *dare* touch them," she snapped. "The more people you mess with, the dirtier your hands get and the greater your chances of going down. So. Stay. Away. From. Them."

His grip tightened. "Then give me what I want."

She struggled to breathe, to speak. "But… I don't… know…what…you…want." She could barely creak the words out.

"Don't lie to me!" His hiss revealed his own panic.

And in that moment Leah found strength in his weakness. She threw her head back into his nose, stomped on his foot and turned to kick him in the crotch.

She burst from the alley and crossed the street.

A honk blared in her ears.

A snowplow filled her vision.

Cade slammed on the brakes, his vehicle skidding on the wet street.

And Leah went down.

He tore open the door, fear and panic strangling him as he made it to the front of his truck.

There. She was on the ground, unconscious.

"Someone call 9-1-1!"

A crowd gathered. Concern over Leah along with questions about what had happened swirled around him. He bent over her, checking her vitals, thankful that her pulse was strong.

Sirens blared in the distance.

How had this happened? How had he managed to hit this woman when he'd been on his way to pick her up? "She…came out of nowhere," he whispered to himself. He couldn't believe that he'd rescued her earlier in the week only to take her out today. But had he actually hit her? He didn't think so.

Her eyes fluttered open and those blue-green irises dilated, focusing on him.

Déjà vu.

Her face contorted into an expression of fear as she scanned the crowd and tried to get up.

"Easy now," he said, holding her in place. "You're hurt. You shouldn't move. The ambulance will be here soon."

"No!" Her eyes were wide. "No…" Softer this time. "Please, help me up."

He couldn't resist her pleading eyes but the timing worked for him as the gurney rolled up with the EMTs. Cade moved away.

"No, Cade, stay with me," she said.

At this moment the confident legal investigator was nowhere to be found—there was just a scared woman looking to him for help. He moved to her side again and held her hand as the medics gently helped her onto the gurney.

"I'm not going to the hospital," she protested. "I'm fine."

Cade frowned and shared a look with Johnny, one of the EMTs he knew well. "I don't know what you have against hospitals, but at least let these guys check you out, okay?" If there was something serious wrong, they could insist on a hospital visit. But Leah had a strong opinion of her own. That much was sure.

She nodded and they wheeled her out of the street and over to the ambulance parked at the side of the road. Cade moved his vehicle over, too, and told Terry Stratford, the police officer on duty, what had happened from his point of view.

Another witness had already explained that Cade had stopped in time but Leah had either slipped or passed out, they weren't sure. She'd hit her head on the street, accounting for the knot. When he explained that Leah was the girl he'd pulled from the avalanche debris days earlier, and that she was also staying in his grandmother's house, Terry chuckled and gave him a hard time.

"Maybe you'd better ask her to marry you before you run into her again and something worse happens," his friend teased.

"It's not like that between us."

"Oh, no? The way you talk about her, could have fooled me."

"I haven't said anything."

"No. More like the way your eyes light up."

Cade glared.

"You could do worse," Terry said, then went back to his cruiser.

Yeah, but Cade knew nothing about her except his suspicions that she was in trouble. What would his police officer friend say if he told him that? Part of Cade wanted to, but not before he found out more himself. Besides, it might be nothing at all, and then Terry would really have a reason to harass him.

No. This was definitely something. Cade hadn't missed the terror on Leah's face as she'd run across the street without even looking. She wasn't going to talk her way out of this one. Cade wouldn't let her this time.

He scraped both of his still-shaking hands through his hair and crushed his eyes shut. He released his pent-up breath, creating a puffy cloud. Man, that had been close. He could have killed her. Once he found his composure, he headed toward the gurney now stuck halfway into the ambulance, and bumped into a sturdy man striding the opposite direction.

Cade glanced back at the man—caught his dark eyes and grim features tucked beneath the hood of his gray hoodie—and tossed out his apology, then kept walking. There was something familiar about the stranger's face, but he didn't have time to worry about it. He headed to where Johnny stood trying to convince Leah that she needed the hospital.

"It's a small bump on the head," Leah said, and climbed off the gurney.

Johnny saw Cade and shrugged.

When Johnny and his coworker had packed up their equipment and were out of earshot, Cade leaned in. "What happened back there? A witness said I didn't hit you, that you collapsed. Either way, you need to see the doc. Maybe this is something residual from being buried in the ice. You sure you don't need a hospital?"

Lights still flashed around them, but the crowd of people had moved on, although some rubberneckers still slowed traffic on Main Street. Leah rubbed her arms and blinked up at him.

"Can you take me home, er, to your house?"

"That's where I was headed when we had our collision," he said. "What were you doing? I had planned to take you to the cabin today." He gently ushered her over to his truck.

They climbed inside and shut the doors before Leah spoke.

"I went to the grocery store for your grandmother. Her car is still sitting in the parking lot." Leah frantically searched for something. "Where are the keys? And the Ragu?"

Cade started his truck. "Relax, I'll see if I can find the keys, but my grandmother has more than one set, and we can buy more pasta sauce. You wait in the truck and stay warm."

Cade was almost afraid to let her out of his sight. He held his hands up for cars to stop while he jogged to the middle of the road, lifted the keys, surprised that no one had picked them up. He nodded his thanks for the drivers who had slowed for him, waved goodbye to Johnny as the ambulance pulled away and headed back to his truck. The day had warmed up and the snow was turning to slush.

He glanced up at the clouds. Rain was predicted this afternoon, at least in the lower elevations. Up at Leah's—er, Devon Hemphill's—cabin, would be a different story.

Was that guy ogling his truck?

Cade stiffened. He glanced into the cab.

Leah was gone.

NINE

Leah tried not to panic as she hunkered down on the floorboard of Cade's truck. She was a legal investigator for crying out loud—how had she been reduced to slinking and hiding like some kind of criminal?

Of course she knew how—Snyder could make her a criminal, with the full support of a city that adored him. But somewhere...someone else had to know what was going on. Who Snyder really was. If only she could get the chance to find some evidence that proved it. But Tim had figured things out and he hadn't even been able to use what he found.

Leah was in over her head. Why didn't she admit it? Steadying her breaths, she prayed that God would help her bring Snyder to justice. That's all she ever wanted, to help defend the innocent, the falsely accused. She never dreamed she would be in this situation.

The driver's side door flew open and Leah's heart jumped into her throat.

Cade slipped inside. He started the vehicle as though she wasn't even there, glancing in the rearview mirror. "You want to tell me what you're doing?"

"I'm, um, I'm hiding. What does it look like?"

Leah hated that she'd involved his family in this. Hated that Snyder had threatened to hurt them, but was determined that she'd be long gone before he would get the chance. Besides—if he was the smart guy she knew he must be, he wouldn't want any more collateral damage than he'd already created with Tim's murder.

Cade steered his truck down the street. "That much is obvious. What sort of trouble are you in?"

Leah slowly climbed back into the seat and buckled herself in. "It's not what you think, Cade, I promise."

There was nothing she wanted more than for this man to think good things about her. But why did it matter? She'd never cared about what others thought before. That would make her too weak—like her mother who gave up everything to please people.

To please men.

Pain burning behind her eyes, Leah turned her face away from Cade and watched the quaint town coated in white icing pass by.

"You don't know what I think. And you can't know if you don't tell me what is going on. How many times do I have to ask you? Please let me help."

Cade thought he could fix the world. Or at least rescue it one victim at a time.

"I don't need some hero coming in to save the day. I've made it this far without anyone's help." Ouch. She sounded brutal. "I'm sorry. I know that's not completely true. I would have died on the mountain without your help." And maybe she'd already be dead if she hadn't had the refuge of Cade's home.

He and his family had extended kindness to her, and how had she repaid them? She'd endangered them all because she was weak and needy and let herself slip. Let herself depend on Cade a little. Never again. She wished she could tell him everything, but she shoved the thought away. Trusting someone that much, especially someone like Cade, could be dangerous to her life plan. To her heart. She wouldn't do it.

"And that night at the cabin..." he said. "Were you running from someone then?"

Telling him anything could end up endangering his life. But then again, it was probably already too late, considering Snyder's threat. Ignoring his question, she said, "I need to get out of town. To leave again. Please take me to your grandmother's car so I can follow you back. Then I'll grab my gear and if you give me a lift to the cabin so I can get my SUV, I'll get out."

She hated to run again before she'd found out what she needed to nail Snyder before he nailed her. But getting out of town was the only way to protect herself—and Cade's family.

"No. You don't have to leave," Cade said. "You don't think I knew something was wrong when I invited you to stay? You looked like someone who needed help." He pulled into the grocery store parking lot and idled next to Katy's car. "I can help you figure this out if you'll let me, Leah. If you're in danger, we can get help."

She pinned him with her gaze. "Why, Cade? Why would you do that?"

He scratched his jaw, appearing to search for an answer that would make sense to both of them. "I've never gone beyond the initial rescue with a victim. Not like this. Not until you. It's almost as if in that moment I pulled you from the snow, I just…couldn't let go." He chuckled softly. "Sounds kind of creepy when said like that. I want to help. It's what I do."

She frowned, staring down at her hands—she'd never seen such complete transparency in another human being and it almost physically hurt. Finally, she gathered enough strength to look back at him, to face him and the questions brewing behind his eyes. He'd never been anything but open and honest with her, and she was nothing but a liar who'd brought danger to him. She'd never needed another person. Not until this moment—and it was near impossible to reject his offer.

Reject him.

She placed her hand over his on the console and felt the strength there. Tried to absorb some of his goodness. Telling him everything—well, no, that would put him in more danger. "That's sweet of you, Cade. Very sweet."

He frowned. "I wasn't going for sweet."

"You were going for gallant, I know." She chuckled and clasped the door handle. "We'd better get the pasta sauce and head back. Your grandmother is going to wonder what happened."

"Oh, she knows. She always knows."

Cade got out with Leah and they made the quick purchase. Back at the vehicles, she climbed inside Katy's car and started it, looking up at him.

"You know your way?" he asked.

She nodded. "I think so, yes."

"Good. I'll follow you there."

Leah exited the parking lot and drove out of town and up the hill, the snowplow grille of Cade's truck in her rearview mirror serving as a reminder of her near-collision today. Feeling safe and secure had never been on her radar until now, when she was in Cade's presence. That man was the embodiment of safety and security and so much more. She was drawn to him for reasons that mattered, and reasons she couldn't entertain. But her mind was traitorous and her thoughts drifted to what it would feel like to have his strong, protective arms around her. To never live in fear again.

To be loved and cherished.

She shoved the crazy thoughts away. She couldn't afford to think that way, to let her edge slip. Instead she focused on her dire circumstances. It was clear that she wouldn't have any chance to escape if she didn't figure out what Snyder wanted and why he was so desperate. Why had he killed Tim?

Could she trust in Cade's words and let him help? The bigger question was could she trust him once he knew the scope of what she was involved in? It was too dangerous to share with another person, and yet, too dangerous to keep to herself. What did she do? What if something happened to her and the truth never came out? Telling one other person would remedy that—but if Snyder found out that Cade or his family knew, then what would happen to them? On the other hand, Snyder might think she had already told Cade. If that was the case, he needed to know what he was up against.

God, show me what to do.

* * *

On the short drive out of town and up the hill to the house, Cade watched the other cars to see if someone followed them. That man in the hoodie who had been looking at his truck—was he the same man Cade had seen watching outside the house? Or was Cade being completely paranoid?

Regardless, Cade hated that he'd brought trouble home to his grandmother and sister, but he'd never been one to turn his back if he could help. If Leah had some crazy ex-boyfriend chasing her down so he could abuse her, he'd have to go through Cade first. If there was one thing he couldn't stand it was abusers. And he'd be just as guilty if he stood on the sidelines and watched when he could do something about it.

His father had held to that. And Grandma had that scripture she'd cross-stitched and hung on the wall: "Do not withhold good from those who deserve it, when it is in your power to act." Cade saw it every day on his way out the front door after breakfast.

He didn't believe he was in the position to judge who deserved help and who didn't. When he saw Terry again, he would ask him about cruising by the house once in a while to scare the creepers away.

When they arrived at the house, he followed Leah inside to hand off the pasta sauce. Cade had called Grandma to let her know they were on their way.

"Finally." Grandma took the jars. "I'll start the pasta and brown the meat. Oh, and I'm making a new broccoli casserole."

Leah looked ready to run. "Leah, can you help

Grandma get dinner going? I need to check on something." Her eyes told him she knew what he was doing—keeping her there.

"Sure."

He hovered for a second longer than necessary until a smile finally cracked at the edges of her lips. He had every intention of getting the details out of her, but that might prove to be harder than he'd first thought, considering she'd held out this long. And with the way things were going, he'd probably get a SAR callout tonight at the exact wrong time, considering he was on call.

And anyway, why did he think he had a right to her secrets?

With his handgun tucked securely in its holster, he stepped outside and marched around the house to make sure he didn't see any footprints in the melting snow.

When he walked around the front, Terry pulled up the drive in front of the house in his cruiser and climbed out. "I'm off duty now and heading home. See anyone else this week lurking in the shadows?"

"No." Cade glanced back at the house. Somehow he had a feeling that Leah would be very unhappy to see a police officer standing outside. She hadn't gone to the police for a reason. "Just got home myself and was walking the perimeter."

Terry gestured toward the house. "She inside?"

Cade nodded.

"Who is she?" Terry asked.

"I don't know yet."

His eyes narrowed. "You sure know how to pick 'em. You want me to do some checking?"

"No, I think I'm good." Terry was only trying to help. "But maybe drive by once in a while. Maybe seeing the cruiser will keep the lurker away."

Terry agreed and got back in his cruiser to head down the driveway. Cade watched him go, thinking about his offer. He'd rather have Leah tell him, to trust him, than go behind her back that way. The thing was, he wanted to be able to trust her, too, but as much as he was driven to save people who needed saving, to protect Leah, he was hard-pressed to trust her too far. Melissa had forever cured him of trusting easily. But he didn't have to worry about trusting Leah with matters of the heart. She had no plans to hang around that long. Cade didn't want her to go, but considering how his pulse kicked up a few notches when he was near her, maybe that was for the best. But not until he was certain she was safe.

When Cade went back into the house, the aroma of Italian cuisine made his mouth water. Grandma was in the kitchen alone. Cade panicked.

"Where's Leah?"

"She went upstairs to pack, I think."

"What?" Cade grabbed the big pot of pasta from Grandma and put it on the table.

She pinned him with her gaze. "You were expecting her to stay, dear?"

"Yes," he said. "Yes, I was."

Cade ran up the stairs and knocked on the door to Leah's room. She opened it and glanced up at him, her eyes red. He saw the duffel bag on the bed, but her laptop was open on the desk. She moved from the door back to her computer.

"Don't go," he said. "I thought we agreed you would stay and I would help you."

She laughed bitterly. "No, you agreed. I said nothing."

Leah shut her computer and turned to face Cade again, pulling back her beautiful hair. "Look, Cade, I don't want to go, I'll be honest. I need a little time to figure things out and…" She glanced out the window then back to him. "And then I might survive this. But I won't risk your family. I won't. If you knew what was going on, then you wouldn't ask me to stay."

Cade held out his palms. "How can I help if you don't tell me?"

"I don't think you could help even if you knew." Leah sat on the bed, wringing her hands. "I don't even know where to start. It's so complicated."

Cade pulled the chair away from the desk and sat down, holding her gaze. "Start from the beginning."

"Why did I ever let you talk me into staying?" she huffed.

Her turmoil was evident in the twisted features of her face. Cade couldn't stand to see her this way. He wanted to take her in his arms, but instead took her hand in his. "Leah, it's okay. From the sounds of it, you owe it to me to let me in on what's going on."

She nodded. "You're right."

Tears slipped from the corners of her eyes and she wiped at them, sniffling. "I don't usually cry. This is embarrassing."

"Nothing wrong with crying. Don't be ashamed."

She gazed up at him, looking unconvinced. "I've seen too much of the world. So many bad things. More than anyone should see."

An ache coursed through him. He didn't know how to help her and that drove him crazy. "Leah...tell me."

"I—"

His pager went off. He grabbed it up and looked, pursing his lips. He'd been afraid this would happen.

Callout SAR for lost snowshoers. Staging point Taryn's Creek. Winter hiking gear needed.

Unbelievable. Cade glanced at his watch. It would be dark soon.

"Cade?" Heidi called from the stairs. "Cade?" Her voice drew near as she searched for him.

"In here," he answered.

She paused at Leah's door and looked from Cade to Leah. "You got the callout? I talked to David. They're lost somewhere in the Three Cliffs region."

Heidi waited for Cade to acknowledge that he understood. But he said nothing. He didn't want to desert Leah in the middle of this.

"They're going to need you to assess for this one," Heidi said. "You know that, right? We had all that snow last night." She searched his gaze. "I'm heading out. You coming?" She didn't wait for his answer.

Leah squeezed his hand. "Go, you have to go."

He frowned and shook his head. He didn't want to go this time. He was busy saving someone else.

"I'll tell you everything when you get back, I…promise." Her eyes confirmed her words.

Could he trust her?

"You never get to eat at normal hours, do you?" A soft smile played on her lips, breaking through her pain.

"Mostly, I do."

He liked her smile, the way her lips hitched up at the corners in that certain way. It gave him hope that they were making some headway. And then…then he couldn't help it. He lifted his hand and cupped her cheek. Shutting her eyes, Leah leaned into it, close enough for the lavender scent in her hair to wrap around him, teasing him. He could have stayed like that forever. No, he'd much prefer to pull her into his arms. Or maybe even kiss her.

Wait. What was he thinking?

He couldn't do this to her. She was vulnerable and alone. He'd be taking advantage. And he wouldn't do this to himself. He had to guard his own heart. If only he didn't feel the need to live up to his father's standard of defending and protecting.

Swallowing as if he could wash away the knot in his throat, he let his hand drop. Her startled eyes watched him now. In them, he thought he read that she hadn't expected to let her guard down, either.

"Listen, I have a friend who's a police officer," he said. "He's going to drive by the house once in a while to show there's a police presence nearby."

Her face visibly paled. "What do you mean? What did you say to the police?"

"Nothing." Her negative reaction was stronger than

he would have expected and hit him like a mountain landslide crashing down in his gut. She was hiding something from the police.

"Then why?"

He frowned. All things considered, he couldn't keep it from her. "There was someone standing in the woods the first night I brought you here. Watching."

Her eyes widened, but beyond that she didn't appear all that surprised.

"I have to get out of here now. I could have already been gone if you had told me. Why didn't you tell me? I never should have come here. I knew that. I've been such an idiot." She started to head toward her bag, apparently intent on returning to packing.

He stood and gripped her shoulders. "Leah, wait. Please, I'm begging you, wait until I get back before you do anything rash. You're safe here. Terry's watching the house."

"Me? You're the one who's not safe." Leah tried to break free. "I'm sorry I did this to you."

Cade held tighter. "Promise me that you'll wait until I get back before you leave. Tell me everything, and if I really can't help, then you can go. Besides, Grandma is expecting you for dinner. Please don't disappoint my grandmother."

The hint of a reluctant smile chased away the lines of frustration in her face. Well, most of them anyway.

"I could never disappoint your grandmother. All right. For her sake, and to make sure she is safe, I'll hang around here with her until you get back, but no promises after that."

She stepped closer, acting like she wanted to say more, but was measuring her words first. A battle raged behind her eyes as she hesitated.

Cade waited patiently, though he'd received an urgent callout.

Then finally, she said, "Go. Do what you do best—go save people."

To Cade's surprise, Leah gave him a quick kiss on the lips, then left him standing there and bounded down the stairs.

TEN

After Cade and Heidi left to find the lost snowshoers, Katy hovered over her cooking pots and chopped
broccoli—the woman seriously enjoyed cooking—and
Leah checked the locks on the doors and windows, hoping she'd come across the gun cabinet where Cade kept
his weapons.

Discovering a window in Katy's sewing room unlocked, Leah quickly secured it. She peeked through
the blinds into the darkness on that side of the house,
too far for the security light to do much.

A shudder crawled over her neck and down her back.

Snyder was out there somewhere. She could feel it.

She needed to flip on the outside lights. Was she
going crazy to think that he would be bold enough to
enter the Warren home? Continuing to check windows,
she suddenly realized Katy stood behind her.

"Everything all right, dear?" Katy smiled and adjusted one of her cross-stitched hangings that read
"Home is where the heart is."

"Yes, everything's fine." She didn't want to tell Katy

about Snyder. Not until she'd told Cade everything. Besides, Katy couldn't do anything but worry, and worry never changed a thing.

"We might as well eat. It could be hours before they return," she said.

Great.

Please, Cade, hurry back. Since when had Leah relied on someone besides herself to keep her safe? The answer was simple enough—since the first night she'd stayed in this house.

She followed Katy into the dining room and considered the best way to ask about the location of Cade's weapons. None of this was unfolding the way she'd thought it would.

Cade shouldn't have left, but lives were at stake. Leah should have gone, but she'd had to stay for Katy's sake.

Katy ladled a hefty portion of pasta onto Leah's plate. "I'm so glad you're here to eat with me. The kids are so busy with their own lives—jobs and friends and search and rescue—half the time all my effort to make a nice dinner is wasted."

"Oh, that can't be true," Leah said. "Looks to me like they enjoy all your meals."

They shared small talk as they ate. Leah wondered about Cade's brothers, Adam and David. Maybe they were also involved in the search and rescue tonight. Cade had been called out for avalanche assessment, too, but would help in the search and rescue no doubt. He was so driven when it came to his chosen causes—protecting people from avalanche danger, helping to find and rescue them. She'd never met anyone like him. Some toy maker should create a Cade Warren action figure.

Leah helped Katy clean up their dishes and the kitchen, but kept the pasta and broccoli casserole waiting as the hours seemed to tick slowly by. It had grown dark early, as usual, and was now almost eight-thirty. The SAR team wouldn't stay out there long in the dark, she didn't think, but what did she know about it? With each passing hour, the tension in her shoulders grew. She should never have promised him she would stay, but she couldn't leave his grandmother in the house alone. Not with Snyder out there somewhere. He'd known from the beginning that Leah was staying here, and the thought made her skin crawl. He'd probably wanted to get her alone but she'd never left the house until today.

Leah paced the living room, rubbing her shoulders.

"You worry too much, dear. They'll be all right. You'll see."

She smiled at Katy. The woman had misunderstood Leah's agitation, but Leah had to admit some of her anxiety was for Cade and his siblings. She'd seen first-hand how dangerous their work could be.

"I'm sure you're right." Leah forced a smile. Oh, why had she promised him she'd wait? Promised that she would tell him?

Should she write all the details out and send him an email? Somehow, that didn't feel right. He deserved better.

Standing at the dining-room window at the front of the house, Leah peeked out the miniblinds. Sure enough, a Mountain Cove PD cruiser crept up the drive and turned around to head back down. If only the sight could make Leah relax rather than remind her of the crazed murderous police detective on her tail. Today she'd intended to purchase some kind of weapon, but that plan had been foiled. Cade had guns in the house somewhere, but she hadn't discovered them yet. Maybe she should find them, and now.

"Would you like some tea, dear?" Katy stood behind her. "On evenings like this, I usually sip my tea and work on my cross-stitch."

"No, thanks. But I think I'll run up to my room to grab my laptop. I need to do some research. Mind if I join you down here?"

Katy chuckled. "Of course not. I'd enjoy the company."

Leah took one step on the stairs, intending to search for a weapon while she was upstairs. Would Cade keep his guns in his garage apartment? Or in the house somewhere? Leah hated to ask his grandmother, hated to upset her, but safety had to come first. Their lives could be in danger. She should come right out and ask the woman. She sucked in a breath—

The lights went off.

God, please, no. Not now. Not here.

"Oh, dear," his grandmother said. "I'm sorry. The power goes off sometimes. We might need to start the generator if it lasts too long. But the glow of the fireplace is light enough for now. Except you can't use the internet. Maybe I should—"

"No," Leah whispered. "Keep quiet."

What if that's all this was? A simple matter of the power going off and not something more. But no, Leah couldn't risk that this was nothing. Where could they hide? How could she protect this woman? In the dim firelight, she spotted the door to the basement. They could hide there and wait it out. Maybe.

"What's wrong?" Katy asked.

Leah rushed to Katy's side and grabbed her hand. She leaned close and whispered into Katy's ear. "Please, listen very carefully. I see you have a basement," she said. "Let's get down there."

"Tell me what's going on." Katy wouldn't move.

"Someone wants to kill me, and I think he might be here." Leah still whispered, but put force behind her words. "Now, let's hide."

"Oh, dear." Katy kept her trembling voice low.

She hurried to the basement door with Leah. Katy jiggled it open, making too much noise. Leah urged the woman through the door and quickly closed it behind them. Right inside the door, Katy grabbed a flashlight hanging on the wall and switched it on. They crept down the steps. At the bottom, Leah glanced up at the door, now in the shadows, wishing it had a lock on it.

Leah turned back to Katy. The woman's face revealed her concern, yet a sense of determination burned there, too.

Katy took the lead and shone the flashlight around. She pointed. "Over there," she whispered. "We can hide behind those plastic storage boxes."

They passed a wall of neatly organized tools and Leah grabbed a wrench. It would have to do. Leah helped Katy move the storage boxes forward enough for them to crouch behind. Then they waited.

And listened.

Above them, the floor creaked.

Katy flicked the flashlight off. "I can't call the police on my cell. There's no signal down here. I should have—"

"Shh," Leah whispered. She clasped Katy's hand. None of this was the woman's fault. Leah should have been much more prepared. Until this point, this hadn't been Snyder's MO—coming after Leah when she was with someone. Coming into a private home. But his patience had obviously run out.

How far the town hero detective had sunk. Leah squeezed Katy's hand, hoping the woman was praying silently as Leah was.

As soon as this was over, if they lived through it, Leah would leave whether or not Cade had returned. She had to lead Snyder away from Cade's family. Never again would she allow herself to be this vulnerable. The weakness had come when she'd let herself count on someone else. She should have only stayed one night to regroup and get her bearings, plan a new escape, but she'd craved the safety and security, and yes, even the comfort she'd found here. She'd justified her presence here to herself.

Now evil had pursued her, even here, inside what had felt like a fortress. Leah's presence had drawn it inside and put this kind woman at risk.

At the top of the stairs to the basement, the door-knob jiggled. Then the door opened. Pulse soaring,

Leah gripped the wrench tighter and held her breath. She suspected Katy held hers, too, instinctively knowing they shouldn't breathe. Shouldn't make even the slightest noise. But Leah thought she could almost hear both their hearts pounding in the silence.

A step groaned above them. He was coming down into the basement. Leah's palms slicked against the wrench. She'd only get one chance at this. She positioned herself for her surprise lunge. She'd have to hit hard.

God, help me.

A truck engine rumbled outside and lights flashed through the open door at the top of the stairs, throwing the shadowed silhouette of a man across the opposite wall.

Leah sucked in a breath. Katy grabbed Leah's arm.

Then the shadow froze, turned and ran out.

Katy started to move.

Leah held her back. "Wait."

They couldn't be sure Snyder had left, or even that the person in the truck was someone they could trust. But Leah suspected it was Cade and Heidi returning.

Glass shattered somewhere above them.

Oh, God, keep Cade and Heidi safe!

Leah jumped to her feet. If there was any chance that Heidi or Cade was in the vehicle she'd heard approaching, she had to warn them.

Exhaustion overcame Cade as he parked in front of the house.

They'd finally gotten a ping on a cell phone and located the snowshoer who'd gone for help and gotten lost. He helped the rescuers find his buddy who'd fallen and broken his leg. But through all of it, Cade hadn't stopped thinking about Leah. Hadn't stopped thinking about that kiss, though it had been nothing more than quick and innocent. Maybe he'd read more into it, but it had kept him warm the rest of the evening.

Only he wished he'd gotten the information out of her before he'd left, because he'd been distracted during the rescue. Heidi had sensed it, too, and kept grilling him about what was going on, distracting him even more.

She hadn't ridden back with Cade, preferring to hang out with friends. Isaiah had said he'd bring her home. Cade scraped a hand down his scruffy jaw, wondering for not the first time if something was going on between those two. Something more than the easy friendship they all shared with Isaiah. Cade wasn't sure how he'd feel about that if that were the case. Isaiah was a good man, but Cade suspected he had more than a few secrets.

He turned off the ignition. It suddenly hit him the house was dark, except for the moon peeking through the clouds. Grandma would have started the generator if the power had been out for long.

Cade tensed.

He grabbed his handgun. Quietly, he got out of his truck and approached the house, gun at the ready.

God, please let this be nothing but a power outage.

Where was Terry? He thought the guy was supposed to drive by. Probably had other police duties, and driving by Cade's house was unofficial business.

Lord, please protect my family. Please let them be okay.

Approaching the door, Cade couldn't decide whether to call out or to keep quiet. The stealth approach won out. He tried the front door.

He unlocked, then slowly opened it. Creeping inside the house, he prayed to God that he didn't fire his weapon at someone he loved. Though his eyes adjusted to the darkness, he could barely see a thing with all the miniblinds closed and curtains drawn. That would be Leah's doing.

What had he been thinking to bring Leah and her troubles back here with him?

When his boots crunched over glass, he heard more than saw someone swinging an object at his head. He ducked and grabbed the wielder in a death grip.

With the whiff of lavender hair, he loosened his grip and turned her around, gripping her arms. "Leah," he whispered.

A curtain whipped open and Cade jumped. Grandma stepped into the light of a moonbeam streaming through the window. "Now we can see. I lost the flashlight down in the basement."

Cade pulled Leah into a hug, relief flooding him. "What happened?"

"Someone was in the house," Grandma answered.

On pure impulse, he'd pulled Leah into his arms and now he wanted to shake her. He released her and stepped away, feeling the absence of her body and warmth to his core, all tangled up with his anger and frustration.

Didn't she have anything to say?

"I'd better check around," he finally said. "Make sure he's gone. I'll get the lights back on."

"He's gone all right. He was almost on us but then you drove up. Leah thought he was still here and that you were him, obviously." Again, Grandma did the talking.

"You didn't call out or say anything, just crept through the door. I'm sorry I tried to take you out," Leah finally spoke up.

"No harm done." What was Cade going to do with this girl?

"I'm calling the police." Grandma sounded shaken.

"No, please, don't," Leah said.

"Give me one good reason why not." Cade had been waiting for hours to hear what Leah would tell him. He was done waiting.

"I don't trust them, that's why."

"I've known Terry since I was in grade school."

"You trust him more than you trust me. I get that. Call him. But leave me out of it."

Oh, she was part of it, all right.

Cade called 9-1-1 and relayed to dispatch they'd had an intruder. He eyed Leah, who stared at him with her arms crossed. She rubbed them. Nervous or cold, he wasn't sure. If only he could have stayed to hear her story, these two women he cared so much about might not have been in danger. It didn't escape his notice that he'd lumped Leah in with Grandma as someone he cared about.

He couldn't deny that he'd grown attached to her in

a short time. But he might have to claim insanity on that one.

Cade finished checking the house and restored the power. A simple matter of flipping the main breaker. It might be a bit before a police cruiser showed up. There could be another emergency tonight, and the Warren household was out of danger at the moment.

While Grandma warmed up the spaghetti dinner he'd missed, he grabbed Leah's arm and dragged her out of earshot so they could speak in private. Grandma had given him the eye, meaning she expected him to find out what was going on. Not because she was angry with Leah. No, his grandmother didn't have an angry bone in her body. Grandma would want Cade to do a better job of protecting the girl his grandmother thought was "a dear."

But Cade was angry at himself. He'd known there'd been someone watching the house that first night and still he'd insisted she stay. He was angry at Leah for putting them all in danger. He shoved away his frustrations. No time for that. He needed details. Staying calm, being patient, would get him more answers. Maybe if he could disconnect his emotions from her somehow, he could think through this whole thing with clarity.

Looking at her now, he thought of her quick kiss again. And all his anger melted away. Not good. He was entirely too vulnerable.

"Tell me," he said.

Tears streamed from her eyes. In the short time he'd known her, he'd seen nothing but how strong she was— until today. He thought her knees might buckle, but then she bent over, and Cade tucked her in his arms, bearing her up. He brushed his hand down the back of her soft mane of blond hair.

When he sensed she had regained her composure, he urged her into a chair in the corner of the room.

"Tell me." He pinned her with his gaze. "I won't let him hurt you."

Men who abused women were the lowest creatures on earth, but to break into his house and send his grandmother into hiding in the basement along with Leah, the man had found a new enemy.

Leah wiped at her nose. He grabbed a tissue and handed it to her. "I'm sorry if I sounded angry, but I need to know what this is all about."

She hung her head. "You have every right to be angry with me. I'm such an idiot for staying here for even one minute. I thought... I needed a safe place to hide while I figured things out."

Cade couldn't stand it anymore. He crouched down to look up into her face. "If you need a safe place to stay, then you've found it. You can stay as long as you like, but I need to know what I'm dealing with here."

She nodded. "I'm sorry I didn't tell you before. I thought that I was protecting you because if you know what I know, then you could be in danger."

He grabbed her wrists, making her look at him. "You see we're already in danger."

She took in a shuddering breath. "I witnessed a murder."

Whoosh.

Her words were a punch in the gut. He hadn't expected that, but he remained where he was. Let her know he was there for her. He'd expected to hear she had an abusive ex tracking her down. But…a murderer? This was out of his league.

No matter. Cade would do the right thing. He'd do whatever was within his power to help her.

"Then why would you run? Why didn't you tell the police?"

"This is where it gets complicated. The guy who murdered my boss is a decorated town hero. A detective in the police department. Now do you see?"

Cade blew out a breath. "You didn't think anyone would believe you?"

She shook her head, shoved from the chair and paced. "Of course not. I didn't think I would survive long enough to tell anyone. I think that's what happened to Tim—my boss, the man who was killed. He found something on Snyder. That's why he'd insisted I leave for a vacation. Only he didn't tell me any of this. But when I saw Snyder kill him, I got out of town as fast as I could. Kept my travel low key. But he found me anyway. How, I have no idea."

"Okay. So you saw this guy kill your boss. Then you disappeared. Didn't you think the authorities would immediately suspect you killed him? Oh, wait. Is that why you avoided the hospital? You didn't want your name in their system in case the cops decided to look for you?"

"Obviously, I've been found out by the cop I'm trying to avoid, so it's too late for that. Snyder is overseeing this murder case from his end. Don't you see? He doesn't want anyone else to question me."

"How do you know he's on the case?" he asked.

Leah frowned. "He's a hero in Kincaid. If he wants a case, he gets it. I knew he'd want this one. Besides, I read his comments about the case online. He's the detective in charge." She managed a laugh. "He even commented about me, stating I wasn't currently a person of interest because I was on a cruise in the Caribbean."

"A cruise?"

"Yeah." Leah shuddered. "I was heading out of town for the cruise when I went in late to grab something. I saw it all in the parking garage."

"This is bad." Cade shook his head. "Very bad."

"But I didn't go on that cruise. I changed my plans to mix things up. Came to the only place I could think of where he couldn't find me. Tim inherited the cabin recently so I knew all about it. I took the ferry. Sure, the detective could pin me with the murder, but first he wants what he thinks I have. Then he'll dispose of me. It's easier for him if I simply disappear. He thinks if he threatens me, I'll give it up. That I'll believe he'll let me live."

Cade stood, too. She stared out the window now. He wanted to pull her into his arms again. "Does this have anything to do with the witness at the avalanche?"

"Yes. That was him. He was on the mountain. Threatened me with a knife. Wanted what I supposedly have. I was running from him when the avalanche hit. He was dressed as you described the witness. I can't know if he had someone with him or not. There may still be a victim under the snow, but I doubt it."

"What do you have that he wants, Leah?"

"I don't know. Maybe he thinks I ended up with the evidence against him that Tim had." She turned to him then, red and blue lights flashing across her face in the window. "Please, Cade. Don't tell the police any of this. I don't know who I can trust with this information. Do you understand?"

"How can I help you? What do you need to solve this?"

"I need to go back to Washington, to Kincaid." Dread flickered in her gaze. "I need to go back to Tim's office."

ELEVEN

Leah stared out the window of the floatplane Cade had secured through a bush pilot friend—a guy named Billy—to transport them. It had been two days since Snyder had broken into the house, but it had taken them that long to arrange everything. Leah was all too aware that she was running out of time.

Cade knew the people and had connections that Leah didn't. He'd become an asset she hadn't known she would need.

When Snyder had found her, she thought she'd made a big mistake in going to the cabin. But meeting Cade had changed her mind. Now she believed God had led her here, after all. With Cade's hand gripping the arm rest, she wanted to reach out and lay her hand over his. Let him know how grateful she was that God had sent him.

The small plane flew over a ferry like the one Leah had taken to get here. She wished she could have taken that amazing trip without the burden of the murder she'd witnessed. Without the fear of being tracked. As she watched the snowcapped mountains, rainforest islands and waters of the Inside Passage beneath them through the window, she wondered how she'd let Cade talk her into letting him come along. It was one thing to stay at his house a few days, but another for him to get involved in her search for answers.

For all practical purposes, she was a fugitive.

The night Snyder had broken into the house, she'd overheard Cade's conversation with his grandmother and sister when he'd told them he'd be going with her to Washington. They hadn't understood why he'd go this far to help Leah, a woman none of them knew well enough to trust. Leah wasn't sure why he was doing so much, either. At least Cade had insisted the two women stay with his aunt and uncle—his father's sister—for a few days. They'd left earlier, taking the three-day ferry to Seattle, which should put plenty of time and space between them and Snyder.

Isaiah and Adam, and even David if necessary, could handle the Mountain Cove Avalanche Center until Cade and Heidi were back.

Leah had no idea if Snyder knew they had left, or if he would guess where they were headed. He had a job to do, too, and couldn't afford to take too much time off to harass Leah. He couldn't afford to raise more suspicions. Maybe he would claim he was investigating Tim's murder. Of course, his methods were not sanctioned by any law-enforcement entity.

Regardless, there was a piece missing in the way Snyder was handling things. Why was he taking so long to make any real move against her? Why was he playing games?

In leaving Mountain Cove, she and Cade had made sure they hadn't been followed. Bottom line, she'd never be free of Snyder, nor would she survive, if she didn't find out what was going on. She'd made a few discoveries that left her with theories, but she needed hard-copy files from Tim's office to go through his client list for the past several years. See if any others besides the three had died. She had no idea if she was on the wrong track, but it was a start.

Shutting her eyes, she pinched the bridge of her nose. *Oh, Tim, why didn't you leave me a clue?* He'd thought he'd been protecting her by sending her away—she got that now—but in the end, by keeping her in the dark, his nightmare had become hers.

A hand brushed hers then grabbed two of her fingers. Leah turned to look into Cade's eyes. It reminded her of that day on the medevac helicopter when he'd ridden next to her. He smiled. She'd liked his smile the first time she'd seen it. He'd been looking down at her when he'd uncovered the snow from her face where she'd been buried in the avalanche. His smile had been meant to reassure, yet he'd done so much more. He was beginning to mean so much to her, and that terrified her.

"Are you okay?" he asked.

She blinked. Where did she start? She didn't want him to be involved. Hated that she'd put him and his family in danger. And yet, where would she be right now without him? "Sure. I guess I'm wondering why you would do this for me."

A frown crept into his smile. "Did you expect me to just let you go? To stand by and do nothing while you were in danger? You didn't ask for this to happen. And neither did I, but we're both in it now."

Leah nodded. She understood him better than he knew. "I know you're trying to be the hero again, but you can't control everything in life. Sometimes, you can't save people. Sometimes, all you can do is surrender."

Hurt flickered across his mountain-green eyes and Leah instantly regretted her words.

"You mean give up. I'm not willing to do that." Even his attempt at a smile couldn't hide his disappointment at her words. "It can't hurt to do some digging. And this way, I know you're safe. I don't have to worry that something happened to you."

That he'd worry about her that way—the idea made heat shoot through that cold, hard place in her heart. She had no idea how to respond. Besides her mother, no one had cared about her like this. No one had risked so much for her.

"Thank you," Leah whispered. Tears welling, she turned to look out the window so he couldn't see her cry.

Once they arrived in Juneau they took an Alaska Airlines flight to SeaTac, landing at the Seattle-Tacoma International Airport.

The next few hours would be tricky, if not harrowing, but the intense pressure of a ticking clock weighed on her. At some point Snyder would give up on getting what he wanted from her, and he'd pin Tim's murder on her and get a warrant for her arrest. Deal with her that way. And once he figured out that she didn't even have whatever it was he wanted, she was as good as dead.

As they disembarked from the jet, the truth finally hit her, stealing her breath. If it was evidence that Snyder wanted, then he had to know she didn't have it, or she would have already turned Snyder in.

Snyder wanted *her* to find it for *him*. How could she have been so stupid?

As they headed along the Jetway to the terminal, Leah slowed. Cade glanced back, worry lining his face. He reached for her, tugging her behind him as he moved with the flow of bodies.

Every airport security guard she and Cade passed sent icy fear through her veins. They followed the signs to baggage claim. In the distance, a man stood at a newsstand.

Snyder!

Leah grabbed Cade's hand and ducked into a nook. Heart in her throat, she struggled to breathe.

"What is it?" he asked.

"Snyder. He's here." Leah covered her mouth, holding back the panic.

"Where?"

"He was buying something at a newsstand."

"Leah." Cade tipped her chin up, his eyes locking with hers. "We have to act normally. Not draw attention. If he was waiting or watching for us, he would have been standing there when we walked out. My guess is he's getting ready to board the plane we exited and head back."

Cade leaned against the wall next to Leah and blew

out a breath. "Let's head into the store at the corner of this alcove. I'm going to buy a baseball cap, at least. You need something over your head, too."

"There," Leah whispered. "He's…over there."

Cade turned sideways, his back to Snyder, to shield Leah with his body and hide her. "We need to act like a couple until we get out of here."

When his gaze flicked to her lips, something warm surged inside. Leah remembered that moment she'd given him a quick kiss. She wasn't sure what had come over her, but she'd been overcome with emotion for this man. She still was, no matter how hard she tried to hold it back.

Cade ran his thumb down her cheek. He was only acting the part, she reminded herself, but when his gaze roamed back up and focused on her eyes, she knew she saw something more behind them. And that current had been there all along between them, but Leah had ignored it because she couldn't afford to fall for someone. She stepped away from him, disconnecting whatever flowed between them.

When they caught sight of Snyder walking away from the area, they entered the store to make their purchases and then headed to the terminal exit. Cade held her close, as though they were a couple. Other than dressing grunge, as if they were much younger, that was their only disguise. The funny thing was, she fit perfectly against him, his arm wrapped around her.

Her chest tightened. She couldn't let herself fall for him. She'd never met a man she could trust, and here she was trusting this man with everything. They walked right by baggage claim and strolled to the vehicle rental booths. Leah pulled away, wanting some distance. This was for show, she reminded herself, but her heart wasn't buying it. And she had to protect her heart at all costs.

Cade rented a vehicle for them. They decided she should leave her car where it was parked at the airport. Keep up whatever ruse was left.

"Which way?" he asked, the Seahawks baseball cap he'd purchased in the airport tugged low.

"For starters, I know an out-of-the-way hole-in-the-wall that makes great chili." She hunkered low in the seat. "We need to wait to go to the office until it's dark and quiet and nobody's around. As it was when Tim was murdered."

Cade didn't like it.

He didn't like it at all. They'd killed a few hours in Seattle. Eaten the chili. But now they were heading to the outskirts, into Kincaid, where they would get down to the dirty business of slinking into a murdered man's office.

He glanced at Leah, then turned his focus back to steering the vehicle as it crept along the lonely streets.

The conversation he'd had with Heidi and Grandma drifted back to him. He couldn't argue that he was out of his element with this sort of task, but he also couldn't leave Leah to do this on her own. He understood her reasoning—she had to find out what this guy was after other than her life. It was the only way.

Her only path to freedom.

"Ready?" she asked.

Nope. He nodded.

"We'll eat at the diner across from the office, wait and watch. Make sure Snyder doesn't have a flunky monitoring the building."

"Chances are he'll figure out we're not in Mountain Cove soon, if he hasn't already." Cade edged into a parking space and turned off the ignition. Shifted to look at Leah.

"Yeah, but will he think we came back here?" she asked.

"That's the billion-dollar question." Cade climbed out.

He ushered Leah into the diner, both pretending they were relaxed. Both likely failing. Ultra aware of his surroundings, Cade looked over the other customers. He hadn't ever hung out in a diner at two in the morning, but apparently it was the hopping place for night owls.

They chose a corner booth that afforded a good view of the street. Each ordered coffee and a short stack, but Cade wasn't hungry. He doubted Leah was, either. They tried to act normal.

Leah hadn't disclosed much more with Cade than that she'd witnessed her boss's murder and she was searching for answers. They'd had plenty of travel time to talk about things, but she hadn't offered any additional info and he hadn't pushed.

Now that he was here, sharing in this with her, he was almost beginning to second-guess the decision to come. He'd never in his life done anything so clandestine. But then he'd never met anyone in Leah's situation. He understood why she needed to get into her old office, Tim's office, during the middle of the night so no one would see her.

But Cade recognized that he needed to know more—such as details and a plan. His gaze darted around, making sure no one would hear their conversation. The diner was noisy and there wasn't anyone sitting near.

He leaned in. "What are we looking for, Leah?"

"He could have killed me already," she whispered.

That wasn't an answer to his question, but at least she was talking. "So what are you saying? That he doesn't want to?"

The waitress brought their breakfast, balancing the dishes like a plate spinner in a circus act.

When she left, Leah continued. "Oh, he wants to. But so far he can't afford to kill me until he gets whatever he's looking for. Then all bets are off."

"Right. You'd be the only loose end he has left." These were things Cade already knew.

Leah didn't act as though she'd heard him. Over the brim of her coffee mug, she was watching something through the window.

Cade followed her gaze. Someone in a dark overcoat jaywalked, crossing over to the old bank building that Cade and Leah would soon enter. He held his breath as the person walked by the parking garage and then the entrance and kept walking another block. Ignoring the flashing Don't Walk signal, he crossed without looking both ways. Cade took a sip of his black coffee. He was going to need it.

"You're a legal investigator. What's your take on

all this? You must have some idea of what he wants from you."

She dragged in a breath. "I worked for Tim for two years. It was my two-year anniversary in fact. He was keeping something from me, and I suspected he was sending me away for a three-week vacation to keep me out of it."

"To protect you?"

"Cade, you should know something about me. I don't…trust people."

No surprise there. Cade kept his thoughts to himself on that one.

"Life hasn't given me a reason to trust anyone except God."

Funny, she trusted God but not people. He had more struggles with God. Why He chose to save some people and let others die. Like his father.

"I was set to leave that night," she said. "I was going to Florida to visit my aunt, and then I planned to take a Caribbean cruise. I'd gotten a late start and stopped by the office on the way out. Tim had given me a necklace—sort of two-year anniversary, hooray-for-me gift—and I left it. Forgot it. I felt bad later when I realized I'd left it behind and thought I'd grab it so I wouldn't hurt his feelings. But the truth is, I also wanted to catch him in… I don't know, whatever he was hiding from me. I wanted to look around the office, to see if I could find something. I figured that if he thought I was gone maybe he'd relax and leave something on his desk."

Cade downed his coffee. "And you saw the murder instead."

Leah played with her fork. "Yeah, that. I have a theory about why he killed Tim, but maybe I'm wrong. Maybe Tim was involved with Snyder and double-crossed him."

"Is it impossible to think that your boss found something out about Snyder? Maybe he planned to expose him and didn't want you in the crossfire. Oh, wait. That's your theory, isn't it?"

"Yes. It's the obvious first choice of theories, if you want to take the high road." Her blue-green eyes studied him. "Do you always look for the good in people?"

"Why shouldn't I?"

"I don't have an answer for that," she said. "I'm with you, by the way. I think Tim had planned to expose him, and wanted to keep me out of it. Obviously that plan backfired. But to answer your question, I'm looking for anything I can find. Maybe I'll know it when I see it. More specifically, I need to look at files on all of Tim's clients. The ones who Tim got off, the ones who didn't go to prison."

A police cruiser crept down the street. Leah ducked her head and focused on her cold pancakes.

Cade tugged his cap lower and leaned back into the corner of the booth against the window. "This feels wrong."

"You can get out any time you want."

"No, I mean that we have to act like this. To hide from the police like they're the bad guys. But until we know more, unfortunately they are—at least in Kincaid."

She nodded. "Could be someone working with Snyder, watching the building on his orders."

"Then when he's out of sight we need to get inside."

"The good news is that Snyder is likely in Mountain Cove while we're here." She smiled this time.

One of these days, when this was over, he hoped to see her smile all the time. She was the strongest woman he'd ever met, and she deserved a few reasons to smile. Why was he thinking long-term? Maybe because part of him wanted something long-term with this woman. The other part remembered what Melissa had done to him.

The cruiser parked and the police officer strolled into the diner. He scanned the room then sat in a corner that gave him a clear view of the street.

Great. How were they going to get inside the building without him noticing?

"We should go," Leah said.

"No. Wait." Cade ordered more coffee. "We leave when we've finished with our breakfast. Act normal. You need to relax. Leaving now would look suspicious." Maybe. He didn't know. He hadn't done this before.

"What if he recognizes me?"

"Is there a warrant out for your arrest? Or is your picture circulating as a person of interest?"

The waitress poured them more coffee then took care of her other patrons. Cade leaned forward. "A better question is, do you recognize him?"

She shook her head. Cade had two more cups of coffee. He needed to be more alert than he'd ever been tonight. He already felt naked without a weapon, especially in this situation.

He glanced at the bill the waitress had left. "It's time."

Leah's look asked him what he was doing calling the shots. He shrugged.

She slid from the booth. Cade stood and dropped enough money to cover their breakfast and a few extra dollars for a tip. They continued with a fake conversation, blending in with the diner crowd that had unfortunately thinned.

Cade wished they had parked in a dark alley so they could walk away into the night. Instead the officer could look up the license plate of Cade's rental if he wanted to. Find something out. How had Cade so quickly fallen into this pattern of thinking?

But this was life and death. How he wished he could have told Terry. See what he knew—if anything—about this Snyder character. Cade shifted into Reverse and backed from the parking spot. With Snyder making frequent trips to Mountain Cove, someone had to have seen him. Struck up a conversation.

"Now where? If we park in the shadows, that officer is going to recognize this vehicle when he makes his rounds." Cade steered slowly down the street.

"Then we need to be quick about it," she said.

"What are you saying?" He seemed to be asking that question a lot, though oddly enough, he understood her all too well most of the time. Maybe if he hadn't connected with her so instantly, he wouldn't have sensed something was wrong. He wouldn't have offered her refuge, and he wouldn't even be here with her now.

"We need to get in and out before he's back to making his rounds," she said.

Whipping off his cap, he ran one hand through his hair while he managed the wheel with the other. If this ended badly, he would definitely never live up to his father's reputation. But somehow Cade doubted that his father would have let Leah down, either. And that thought brought a measure of relief.

Leah directed him to park a few blocks over. They headed back on foot, walking past dark nooks and corners. They crossed the street from the other side of the building, more difficult to see from the diner. Cade caught a glimpse of the parking lot, though.

"The cruiser is gone," he said.

"This way." She hurried into the parking garage. "Careful of the security cameras. They're at each corner."

"Why didn't the cameras catch the murder, Leah?"

"Why do you think? They can't cover the whole garage. It must have been a blind spot."

"But the police would have seen you there that night. The cameras would have caught you watching—very clearly not holding a gun or standing over the body, right?"

Her gaze speared him. "The police? You mean Snyder? He's the detective on the case, remember? He made sure of it so he could stay on top of the cameras and other details."

Her patience with him was wearing thin, but she'd had more time to think this through than he had.

Leah used a key card to enter the building and they got on an elevator. She pulled latex gloves from her pocket and slid them on. Looking at Cade, she shrugged. "They'll know I was here by the key-card log if they decide to dig that deep. My fingerprints are probably on everything, but they won't be on anything new, or anything Snyder might have planted to use against me as a murder weapon if I were to accidentally touch it." She handed a pair over to Cade. "Here."

Wow. She'd thought things through to the nth degree. He frowned, hating every minute of this. What other surprises could he expect? She touched the fourth-floor button.

When the elevator beeped and the door whooshed open, Cade's palms grew moist inside the gloves.

Leah grabbed his hand and tugged him out. "Relax, you're not doing anything illegal. This is my office. I work here, remember?"

Yeah, in the middle of the night wearing latex gloves. "At least, until your boss was murdered."

Cade wished he'd kept that thought to himself. He followed Leah down the hallway. He didn't see any security cameras. *What have you gotten yourself into?* The second elevator on the floor dinged. Someone had followed them up.

TWELVE

The office of Tim Levins, attorney-at-law, was only five steps away.

Pulse pounding in her ears, Leah focused on the doorknob. The keyhole. With the gloves, she fumbled with the key. What was wrong with her?

She could do this. Had to do this.

Come on, come on, come on.

Who would be here at this hour? The officer from the diner come to arrest them? Security checking each floor? She didn't recall someone doing that in the past, but that was before there'd been a murder in the parking garage.

Panic lodged in her throat.

Leah thrust the key in.

At the same time she opened the door, the elevator door opened, resounding into the silent hallway.

God, please make us invisible.

Cade rushed inside behind her.

He gently urged the door shut, managing to avoid the expected latching noise made when the tongue hit the strike plate. The door was mahogany but the wall on either side was glass. Cade and Leah flattened themselves against the door, hiding. Waiting for whoever was on the floor to leave. They saw a flashlight beam through the window on one side of the door and flashed around. Cade tugged Leah over and out of the way. Then the light shone through on the other side.

Had to be security checking the floors, especially after the murder.

Leah held her breath until the guard moved on.

"I thought you said we weren't doing anything illegal," Cade whispered in her ear, his warm breath cascading down her neck.

"We're not." She kept her voice equally low.

Was he messing with her? He knew exactly why she didn't want to be seen by the wrong party coming in or out of this office. Coming in or out of this city.

Finally the security guard made his way down the hall. They waited, listening until they heard the elevator once again. Cade stood close to her. Much too close. She looked up, his strong jaw mere inches from her face. His broad shoulders and muscular biceps were right there.

In her face.

Next to her.

Then she gazed up and caught him watching her with his mountain-green eyes. The man made her heart tumble over itself. When this was over...

When this was over—*what*? She and Cade could be together? Explore a relationship? What would it be like to be loved by a man like Cade? But Leah could never, *ever*, let herself do that. It was too hard to trust after everything she'd witnessed and been through. Too hard to take Cade at face value. She hadn't even known men like Cade existed.

She slipped around him to escape.

"I need to search Tim's office," she said. "But no lights. Those can be seen from the street. And we don't want that in case anyone is watching. I'll use the flashlight." She grabbed one from inside the receptionist's desk and held it up. "Sheila has a drawer full of everything."

"What do you want me to do?" Cade asked.

"Stand guard."

Cade frowned. "I could help you look. Get us out of here faster."

"No. You wouldn't know what to look for. Please, just stand guard for us. Snyder has probably cleaned everything important out of here already—that is, what he could clean up without raising suspicion."

That's one reason why he wants me searching for the evidence Tim found. But she wouldn't share that with Cade. He was already freaked out as it was.

"Then why are we here, risking so much?"

"In case he missed something or left what I need to figure this out." Leah left Cade in the reception area to watch the hallway.

He didn't look happy, but she couldn't help it. She slipped into Tim's office and flicked the blinds closed before turning on the flashlight. Tim had a set protocol for documentation and client files, both hard and digital copy. Inactive or active, copies had been made of all files so they could be quickly turned over to clients if needed.

First she scanned the room. Nothing looked out of place, but no doubt *Detective* Snyder had already been over it with a high-powered microscope. If she didn't find anything that jumped out at her in here, she'd move to the closed case files kept in the extra office, and she needed Tim's attorney notes. Tim had been in the process of securing a storage service company to inventory the files in case he needed the paperwork down the road, but it was currently all still in the office.

Leah sagged under the weight of it all. She didn't have the time she needed to figure this out.

"Come on, Tim, why did he kill you? What does Snyder want from me?" She'd wanted to think the best of Tim, but maybe it wasn't like that at all. Maybe Tim was involved in something illicit and that's why he'd wanted her gone—so she wouldn't catch on.

Leah strolled around the office, looking. Tim's laptop was gone, but the desktops remained. Snyder would have had his computer geek comb through the computers, but obviously, he hadn't found what he needed.

God, please help me to find out what is going on here.

She tugged file cabinets open and flipped through the files. She didn't have time to write all the names down. She rummaged through his desk. Even broke into two drawers that were locked. No doubt they'd already been sifted through. Frustration was getting the best of her.

On the top of one of the filing cabinets was the box filled with old letters, bills and scraps of papers Tim had brought from the cabin. She sifted through. Nothing important, except…wait. She skimmed a couple of the old letters. Arguments. Apologies. There might be something in here to help Cade with his search for answers about his father. She'd take this with her.

Setting the box on the desk, she flopped back in Tim's chair. She'd read through this first, so Cade wouldn't unnecessarily get his hopes up.

Cade stuck his head around the door. "Find anything?"

Shaking her head, she stood and walked by Cade, heading to her own office.

"Then we need to leave before we get caught even though we're not doing anything…illegal."

Leah ignored him and pushed the door to her office open. Cade followed her inside. Backing onto the conference room that spanned the outside walls, her office had no windows. She flipped on the desk lamp.

"Maybe we should talk about it," he said. "If you tell me what happened, maybe you'll think of something. Tell me about the cabin. Why did you choose the cabin to hide? First you told me a friend was letting you stay there. Then you told me Tim sent you to investigate, but neither of those statements is true. I'm not calling you a liar, don't worry, I understand you didn't know who you could trust."

Leah sank into her chair. Cade found the one in the corner next to her fake tree. "Tim inherited the place months ago. He wanted me to go check it out, and I was scheduled to do that, but he changed his mind and went to see it himself.

"When I saw him killed, I panicked. Didn't know

where to go. I remembered the cabin. There was no paper trail to tie it to me, so it seemed like the perfect place to hide. I went to the airport and parked my car in long-term parking as though I still planned to go to Florida. I took a cab to the ferry and then I took the ferry to Alaska instead where I bought a clunker SUV to get around. Paid cash for it all. I wanted to disappear."

She sank lower in the seat. She would never escape this. Never.

"Then what happened?"

"Snyder found me there and chased me up the mountain. There was an avalanche. You know the rest."

"No, I mean after Tim came back from the cabin. Did anything strange happen?"

Leah was an experienced investigator. She shouldn't need Cade's prodding, but then, her mind was messed up at the moment.

"He'd been acting strange all along, as though he was hiding something. It's my job to read people. To know when they're being evasive or deceptive. That's when he sent me packing for a three-week vacation." She opened the drawer and pulled out the necklace, holding it up. "Gave me this memento from his trip to Alaska. I got a bonus, too."

Tears crept from the corners of her eyes as she looked at the pendant of quartz etched in gold hanging from the silver chain. Leah wiped them away. She tried to put on the necklace, but her hands shook too much.

"Here, let me."

Leah stood so Cade could put it on her. She wasn't sure why she wanted to wear it now. It was a little late for that. But she hadn't appreciated it the way she should have, her suspicious mind running away with her, wondering why Tim wanted her out of his way.

"There." Cade had fastened the necklace.

"You shouldn't be here. You shouldn't have come with me." Unshed tears in her voice gave her away. "I'm sorry I involved you."

He turned her to face him and tipped her chin up. "I thought we'd been over that already." He cupped her cheeks.

Leah could swear he was going to kiss her.

How could she want him to kiss her so much? What was wrong with her? They were in the middle of finding the cure to a malignancy that was eating her alive and she wanted this man to kiss her?

"We're in this together and I'm not going to leave your side."

Stupid tears again.

She wiped them away and stared at this man who said he wouldn't leave her. And if she was as good at reading people as she thought, he wasn't lying. Oh, how she wanted to believe him. She'd never wanted anything more in her life, and yet, she had never trusted another soul with so much.

Her existence. Her life. Her heart... No, not that. Never that.

Cade inched forward and joined his lips with hers. Soft. Reassuring. Not taking. Only giving. He was a rock. A pillar she could lean on. And Leah took in all the strength she could. That a kiss could make so much difference astounded her. He'd known exactly what she needed.

How?

This was so much more than simple attraction. What, she wasn't really sure. Her need to find out battled with internal warnings of imminent danger.

Leah could never risk so much.

Beautiful Leah had somehow enchanted him. Drawn him into her cloak-and-dagger world. He pulled away, just a little. Her pliant body snapped to attention, her partially lidded gaze growing wide.

Cade sucked in a breath, expecting the worst.

If she slapped him, he would deserve it.

But he wouldn't lie to himself. He'd thought about kissing her from the moment he'd pulled her from the snow.

And here he was, kissing a girl in the middle of the best part of the espionage thriller their lives had become, turning things all sappy. But she'd needed reassurance, and for the first time in his life, Cade had no idea how to deal with it. How to give what was needed. Instead he'd just done what had felt right.

He took a step back and removed his cap, shoving a hand through his hair. He wouldn't apologize. Saying he was sorry would be a lie, too. If anything, he needed to get the kiss out of the way. He'd confirmed that she'd felt the connection between them, too.

In some perverse way, it satisfied his need to know that he was doing the right thing, even though he was getting in deep with a woman he barely knew.

"Okay." She cleared her throat. "I need to get the box I left in Tim's office and we need to get out of town."

Her sagging demeanor told him she was more than disappointed that she hadn't found what she was looking for, and he didn't know what else he could do. Wait— Yes. Yes, he did. It was time to pull his friend Terry into this. Terry would listen and know what to do. Leah wouldn't like the suggestion, so Cade would keep it to himself until he figured out how to present his case. Surely she knew she was running out of options.

Whatever happened, Cade knew he had to stand between her and Snyder. She leaned over to turn off the desk lamp. The necklace hung forward, catching the light.

Something strangely familiar drifted in and out of Cade's awareness.

The light off, Leah moved past him, bearing her flashlight.

"Wait," he said, catching her wrist.

"I don't have time for—"

"The necklace. Let me see it again." Cade turned the light back on. He examined the gold-etched quartz.

Standing far too close to Leah made it hard for him to focus on the necklace, considering the kiss they'd shared moments ago.

"What's the matter?" she asked.

"Let me get a closer look in good lighting. Take it off." Cade slipped behind her to unclasp it and thrust it beneath the light. "I see this every day. I know exactly what this is."

Her gaze rose up to meet his. "You see gold quartz every day? Where?"

"Not the quartz. I see maps every day. It's a topographical map. The contour lines, marking the elevations, is why I recognized that it was a map."

Leah gasped, covering her mouth with both hands, her eyes squinting to see the small markings.

Cade grinned. "I think we got what we came for."

She met his gaze. "If you hadn't come with me, I wouldn't have seen this. I wouldn't have realized what it really is."

"We can celebrate later. Let's get out of here."

"Wait. I thought of something." She stroked her forehead. "I can't believe I didn't think of this before. It could be something, but maybe it's nothing. And maybe Tim would have hidden this from me."

"Well, what is it?" Cade felt an urgent need to get out of this place. They'd found something. Now they had to go.

She weaved her hair back from her face. "We have a file check-out system we use so we know who has which file. Tim and I have handled everything while Sheila is out on maternity leave. She's due back to work next week. I'm so glad she was at home during all of this. Maybe all I need is to see what client files Tim has checked out over the past few weeks. Then I can cross-reference them with Detective Snyder, to see which cases he handled. See how it is all related."

"Sounds like a plan. Now let's get out of here."

They exited Leah's office and she grabbed the box from Tim's desk. "The check-out list is at Sheila's desk."

Cade grabbed Leah's hand, weaving his fingers with hers, and headed down the hallway into the reception area. Cade suddenly realized he had neglected to stand guard. They'd both gotten caught up in the search.

They stepped into the reception area.

A man pointed a gun at Leah's head.

THIRTEEN

"Don't move." The man flashed a badge. "Kincaid Police."

A silencer was attached to the gun barrel.

Leah didn't have time to think, to react, before Cade shoved her into the hallway. An instant later a bullet hit the wall somewhere behind them. Then another.

The muted gunfire still sounded like a weapon had been fired off, but at least it wasn't as deafening as it would have without the sound suppressor. And likely no one else in the building or on the street had heard the gunshots.

But a policeman shooting a gun with a silencer? *I don't think so.*

An officer shooting at them? *Nope.*

If they ran, he'd give chase, but he wouldn't shoot. They weren't even armed.

Cade practically carried her into Tim's office. He slammed the door, locked it and shoved the desk in front of it, before the guy slammed into the door from the other side.

"What are you doing?" she hissed.

"Get down." He pushed her behind the filing cabinets. "Stay there."

"Where would I go? We're trapped in here, thanks to you."

Pressed against the wall, he scanned the room. "I need a weapon. Don't happen to have one hidden away in here, do you?"

"No, I lost my only gun on the mountain."

He frowned, looking nothing like a man in control.

The threat on the other side of the door fired off several rounds, shredding the door.

"The fire escape," Leah whispered. Good thing they were in Tim's office and not hers.

"Make it happen," Cade said. "I'll take care of him."

Predictably the man thrust his fist through the door where he'd concentrated his bullets, creating a hole. He shoved at the desk then aimed his weapon at Leah. How many more rounds did he have? She ducked, Cade grabbed the man's arm and slammed it across the desk at an angle. The cracking sound and resulting wail sent a pang through her.

The gun slid across the desk.

She opened the window and peeked out. Where were the real police when you needed them? She glanced back at Cade who nodded for her to go ahead, and caught a glimpse of the man on the other side of the big gash in door. Not much of a look, but she could search the police department pictures. See if he was an officer working with Snyder.

Cade moved the desk, which brought Leah back through the window. "What are you doing?"

"Go!"

Leah slipped out the window again and onto the fire escape, for the first time grateful Tim's office was in an older building. A cold gust whipped around her body and she tugged the hood back over her head. She hoped Cade would hurry, because this was freaking her out.

She made it down the first flight of stairs and was halfway on the second. *Oh, God, please, let Cade be right behind me. Help us.*

Then she saw him, taking the wrought-iron fire escape steps much faster than Leah had and catching up with her. "Let's move it." His urgency snapped at her.

"What did you do to him?"

"I made sure he didn't have access to any more weapons. He was talking to someone on his cell."

"Snyder?"

"I don't know. Maybe he called more of his buddies."

"Police?"

"Keep going, we have two more stories before we hit the ground. I smashed his phone, too. I didn't lay a finger on him, but he was cowering, holding his arm."

Right. Because you already smashed his arm. But she couldn't hold that against him. The man was aiming to kill them.

On the ground, they hurried down the dimly lit sidewalk. Cade tugged Leah to him and she was grateful for the extra warmth. The memory of facing off with that man sent cold shivers all over her. If Cade had reacted differently, or taken even a millisecond longer to react, where would they both be now?

"How did you know he wasn't the police?"

"I didn't." The gruffness in his voice scraped over her.

"I thought the silencer gave him away," she said. "That couldn't be legal."

"Might depend on what law-enforcement agency."

"What law-enforcement agency would have him shoot at us like that?" She stopped walking and turned him to face her. "Cade. Are you telling me you were prepared to run from the police if it came to facing them head-on?"

His tight expression said everything and nothing. "Call it instinct. I knew he would kill you. Kill us. And that's not going to happen if I can help it."

Heat started in her stomach and spread around her heart, chipping away some of the cold. Breaking away at the part that didn't believe. That couldn't trust.

The magnitude of his willingness to sacrifice, especially after everything she'd dragged him into, slammed into her.

Shaking her head, she took off, walking fast. "I don't need you to do that for me."

Walking turned to jogging. Then to running. She fled from Cade. *He can't die for me. Can't die because of me.* As soon as she found the vehicle, she would leave him. It was the only way to keep him safe.

There.

Still parked in the alley, the vehicle Cade had rented waited in the shadows. For her. He was in this because of her. She ran, ignoring his calls from behind. She knew that with his long legs, he could catch her if he wanted to, but he gave her breathing room.

Leah made the car and leaned against it. Breathe. She had to breathe.

Cade clutched her shoulder.

"Come on, we're almost done with this. We have the map. Let's get what you need to put this man away and get your life back."

"I didn't get that list that would have told me the files Tim had checked out. I think that's the key here." But she knew there was no going back.

He unlocked the car and opened the door for her. She climbed inside. When Cade was seated, he started the ignition and turned up the heat.

She looked down at her trembling hands. Before this, nothing used to faze her. "You saved my life on that mountain. You saved my life tonight. I don't want you putting yourself between me and a killer again. Got it?"

"Got it."

His reply was out of character and surprised her. She hadn't expected him to agree. And it hurt. She hadn't expected that, either. Except that she didn't believe him. Not for one minute. He would, in fact, put himself between her and Snyder if it came to that. That was who Cade was. He had probably never told a lie until now. Until Leah. She had pushed him beyond his boundaries.

Cutting him free was for the best.

On the earliest morning flight to Juneau they could get, Cade couldn't help but notice that Leah had shut down. He didn't know if it was because of the kiss or the stress of being on someone's hit list, but she'd backed off from him, just when he thought he'd bridged the distance.

Exhausted from their night of cloak-and-dagger escapades, and surrounded by too many ears, they kept conversation to a minimum on the flight and didn't have a chance to go over their next step.

If it wasn't for the fact that she needed him to read the map depicted on the quartz, he had no doubt she'd disappear from his life. From a practical perspective, that might seem like a good thing, but pain zinged through him at the thought. He had no idea why he'd grown so attached to this woman.

Leah came with her own particular brand of problems. But Cade knew their time to figure this out, to uncover what her boss had hidden, was about to end. Snyder was closing in. Taking more extreme measures. They had to elude him long enough to find the evidence of his crimes and then determine what this was all about. He hoped and prayed Leah could buy her freedom with what they would find with the map. Cade feared it would only bury her deeper, Cade along with her. But as he'd told her, he was in this for the long haul.

Once in Juneau, they hitched a boat ride back to Mountain Cove. Leah stood next to the rail on the boat, wrapped in her layers. Red with cold, her gloveless hands grasped the bar.

Cadc took a risk and pressed his hand over hers. "You should put on your gloves if you're going to stand out here."

She pulled her hand away and thrust it in the pocket of her fleece hoodie.

"We need to talk," he said. He had to get her to open up. "When we get back to Mountain Cove, let's go to the house for a bite, maybe a quick shower. Get cleaned up. Then we can grab the maps of the region I need back at the avalanche center to compare to the necklace."

Leah didn't respond.

"What's your problem?" he asked. "I'm already in the thick of this. No going back. Now let's finish it together. I know where to find whatever Tim hid. You need me. I promise not to take a bullet for you. I think that covers everything. Satisfied?"

A half grin slipped in to her lips. Pretty lips. Soft lips. He recalled the feel of them against his, pliable and responsive, and it toyed with his concentration. "I need to know what you're thinking," he said.

Leah looked over the side at the cold waters of the channel rushing beneath the boat.

"I don't know what I'd do without you," she finally said. "I would be dead twice over, and I don't want there to be a third time. I don't want you to get hurt because of me."

"Remember, Leah, I risk my life for others on a weekly basis, if not daily, as a volunteer. I risk my life when I do field work for avalanche assessments. That can be dangerous, too. Don't think you're special." He injected a teasing tone. She was, in fact, very special to Cade, for reasons he hadn't figured out.

When she didn't respond, Cade watched the lush Tongass National Forest—the northernmost rainforest in the world—go by, looking as though it had seen days of rain on top of too much snow.

"Why do you do it, Cade? Rescue people? Risk your life for strangers?" Her blue-greens speared him, driving right through his heart with her question.

Where did he begin to answer that one? An icy breeze whipped over him and he jammed his hands into his pockets. "I don't know. It's a family thing, maybe. My dad served his community, served the people, for as long as I can remember until he died. Even then, he died saving someone." Cade paused. Swallowed against the thickness in his throat. "Dad...he was the best."

"You miss him, don't you?"

He nodded. "That's why I'd like to know what happened, you know? I'd like to know if Devon Hemphill set him up for that rescue. Set him up to die. And I can't know that until I know what they quarreled about, and even then, I still might not have the answers I want. Maybe those answers died with my dad and Devon."

"Then I showed up and brought the questions back to life." Leah looked away.

Maybe he'd been too harsh. But he'd been honest. "No matter how hard I work at my job, following in his footsteps at the avalanche center that he founded, or volunteering on the search and rescue team, I don't think I'll ever live up to the reputation my father had. Maybe that's why I work so hard, try so hard. I don't know. But I do know he deserved better than to die like that. He was a real hero."

She turned back to him then, pulled her hand from her pocket and thrust it inside his, wrapped her fingers around his, her foggy breath mingling with his own. "You are, too, Cade." Then her voice cracked a whisper, "You're my hero."

An invisible hand enfolded his heart and squeezed, lighting a fire in his chest. He'd do anything. *Anything* for this woman.

Not good. Not good at all.

Terrifying.

He would have done anything for Melissa. And she'd betrayed him.

FOURTEEN

Back at home, Cade searched the house to make sure there were no intruders lying in wait. The house was empty, which was good on the one hand. On the other hand, Cade chafed at how empty it was without Grandma's cooking and affectionate chatter. Without Heidi who loved to rule and reign over him. He'd never have thought he'd miss the sibling banter. But he did. He missed them both. He'd done this to them.

The sooner this was over, the better. Then again, he wasn't sure how any of it would end. Would he or Leah, or both, be killed? And if they survived, what would keep Leah in his life when this was over?

One thing at a time. He tried to tell himself that he didn't want her in his life after this was over. But he knew that wasn't as true as he'd like it to be. He'd gotten this involved because he couldn't let her go after pulling her from the snow. But he'd had his fill of this situation, and he was sure she had, too.

He needed to clear his head before the next phase of this ordeal.

"Why don't you take a shower, clean up, if you want?" he asked. "I'll make us some sandwiches, then we'll head out to grab the maps."

She hesitated. "Okay, but… Cade, we need to hurry. I have a bad feeling. As though things could get any worse. I'm not sure it's a good idea for you to go further into this with me, I mean, after you tell me where to look."

He frowned. Was she crazy? She wouldn't find the destination without him, even after he showed her on the map. This thing could be buried twenty feet beneath the snow for all they knew. "We'll talk about that after sustenance."

Cade opened the fridge to pull out the sandwich fixings.

She rubbed her arms. "I'm not sure it's even a good idea for us to be here. What if Snyder shows up?"

He perused the inside of the fridge. "So far, he always shows up at night. It's only eleven in the morning. If he sticks to the schedule, we have a few hours." They were so close to ending this. He could feel it.

Exhaustion evident in the dark circles under her eyes, Leah nodded and disappeared up the stairs.

He didn't want to scare her, but she was right. Snyder could show up at any time. The man had to know things were coming to a close. He had to be more than desperate.

Cade placed his weapon on the counter. He hadn't told Leah of his plan to get Terry involved, thinking she would only buck and run if he told her. He understood her misgivings about trusting anyone, especially the police, given Snyder was a detective himself, but she couldn't know how well Cade knew Terry.

He grabbed his cell phone and made the call.

Pain erupted in his head. Everything went black.

Head pounding, Leah opened her eyes.

She scanned her surroundings— The cabin? What was going on? She tried to sit up, but that sent a sharp pain through her head. Leah blinked, grabbed her head and shoved herself upright.

Boots clunked, catching her attention. Snyder stood in a wide stance, staring at her. He sipped from a mug. Warmth blasted from a fire and the percolator sat on the wood stove.

Leah rubbed her eyes. She couldn't believe it.

"What's going on? What do you want from me?"

"Sorry about the headache. It will wear off. Not that it matters."

He didn't want to answer those questions? Fine, she had plenty of others to ask him. "Why did you kill Tim?"

Are you going to kill me?

He set the mug down, as if he had all the time in the world.

Oh, no. Cade. What happened to Cade? Leah stiffened. Skimmed the room for a weapon. An escape.

Snyder crouched in front of her. "I didn't want things to end this way. But your boss should have kept his nose out of my business. He made it his career to free criminals, just like you have, while I've given my life to put them away. But Levins just couldn't leave it alone. So

I had to take extreme measures to keep criminals—the hardened ones, at least—from a life of crime."

"So that's your justification for becoming a criminal yourself?"

"I prefer to think of it as rendering justice when justice isn't served within the context of the law. You and your boss worked to free criminals."

Leah's mind swam back to what had happened to her mother. Why she'd become a legal investigator. "That's not true."

At least most of the time. Her mouth grew dry. What was he going to do with her?

Stupid question. Hadn't she known all along? Where was Cade? Was he still alive? Would he save her? Mentally, she scolded herself for relying on another human being to help her.

Only God could save her. But would He this time?

"I'm going to ask you one more time to give me the information you and Tim uncovered." He tossed the shoebox on the floor in front of her feet. "Thought it was in that. You seemed to think it was so important when you were in his office."

"Wha—?" Her mouth hung open. "How did you know about that?"

He smirked. "Set up a surveillance camera in his office that feeds back to my phone. I'd just gotten back into Mountain Cove when I got a hit. Called Marlow to grab you, but wait until you exited Tim's office with the goods. But the idiot bungled it." Snyder unfolded himself from where he'd been crouched in front of her and tossed another log on the fire.

"And that's how you knew to find me at this cabin? The camera?"

He chuckled. "Nope. I came to the cabin hoping Tim had hidden what he was going to use to call attention to my activities here. I couldn't be sure you had witnessed anything, but even if you did, it would just be your word against mine. Then I found you at the cabin, which made my day. And I knew you either had what I was looking for, or you could find it for me."

He blew out a breath. "I'm glad this is over. I'm tired of making all these trips to Mountain Cove and to this sorry excuse for a cabin. Been looking at rental property on a nearby island while I'm here. Have to justify my reasons for coming, in case someone else digs around. But I'll have all the loose ends tied up after I'm done with you."

He turned his gaze on her. "So. Where is it?"

"I swear I don't know. Tim sent me on a long vacation. He never told me anything about you. I guess he didn't want me in the middle of this, but that's how it's going down anyway. He didn't involve me."

"You're his investigator. You're the one who dug this up!" Snyder tossed the shoebox in the fire.

"No!"

He snatched it back out and blew out the flames. "What's in here that's so important? What am I missing?"

"Nothing to do with you. It's for Cade." Now Cade might never get his answers.

"Isn't that sweet. You've fallen for your rescuer." Snyder chuckled. "I'm out of time here. If you can't tell me, or won't, and I can't find it, then nobody else will, either. I've already disposed of anything that might incriminate me that Tim had in his files and on his computer. Your computer is sorely missing anything pertinent, so maybe you're telling the truth. But as of this moment, you're the only loose end. You're the only witness."

"What…what are you going to do?"

"There's a warrant out for your arrest that hit the wires two hours ago, in case I'd lost you. I was tired of hunting you down. Here's how it goes. You and Tim were involved in a love triangle. Tim was cheating on you so you killed him. You wrote a suicide note. Then walked off into the mountains to die of exposure."

"You're crazy, you know that?" Panic strangled Leah; she wanted to jump from the sofa and tackle the man. "I'll never write that note."

"It's already taken care of." Snyder turned her laptop to face her. "I typed it up myself, and I'll send the email as soon as the deed is done. Then I'll give the cabin one more look around before I burn it down. I'm going to take you so far and so deep into the mountains, nobody will ever find you. See, Leah, I'm a dozen steps ahead of you."

"Listen to yourself, Snyder. You've become like the criminals you took upon yourself to judge."

"You're a barrier, standing in the way of justice. That's how I see it." He grabbed the percolator from the stove and poured more coffee. He held it up, looked at her. "Want one last cup?"

Leah shook her head, closed her eyes, hating that this

man had gotten the best of her. She'd always thought she was so smart. So tough.

He must have killed Cade. That was why he wasn't here. The thought that he was dead because she'd taken refuge in his home, allowed herself to lean on someone, did her in. The will to fight seeped out of her. She slumped over on the couch, inhaling, exhaling shuddering breaths.

No!

Cade would want her to live. Would want her to fight until her last breath. Leah had her own brand of justice to render. She had to survive and make Snyder pay for his crimes. Make sure she found the evidence to put him away for a long time. Make sure that everyone knew he wasn't the hero he made himself out to be, but something dark and sinister.

Leah scrambled over the couch and lunged for the door. She'd rather face the brutal temperatures than wait for Snyder to mete out his own perverted form of justice.

His big hands gripped her, yanking her from the door. Pain shot through her arms, back and neck. Leah wasn't a screamer. She refused to scream. But Snyder ripped a scream from her all the same.

He covered her mouth, muting her cries for help. "What am I worried about?" He let his hand drop away. "Scream all you want," he said. "Nobody's going to hear you."

"Cade." The familiar voice broke through the darkness. "Cade, can you hear me?"

An ache ran through him. He squinted up to see Terry staring down in concern.

"Oh, thank You, God," Terry said. "I called an ambulance. Reed is searching the premises."

Cade sat up. "What happened?"

"That woman's what happened."

Oh, no...

"Leah?" Cade called, and tried to stand. Dizziness swept over him and Terry assisted him. "Where is she?"

"She's gone."

"Leah!" Feeling the knot at the back of his head, he stood, realizing he was in the basement.

His gaze landed on Terry who wore a knowing look. "She hit you over the head, dragged you down here and barricaded the door. You're fortunate your call to me connected before the line went dead. I came out here to see what was going on and found you down here."

Cade ran up the basement steps and made it to the kitchen before Terry caught up with him.

"Cade!" Terry grabbed him. Yanked him around. "Did you hear me? She's gone. She hit you in the head and left."

He thrust a sheet of paper in front of Cade. "See this? It's a warrant for her arrest. Did you know about this?"

"No, that's not right. She isn't guilty. She's been framed." Cade needed Terry to understand. To believe him. Leah had been right. They never should have come back to the house. Snyder was getting desperate. Cade had thought he'd be prepared to face the man if he showed up, but he'd failed again.

Utterly.

"That's what she told you?" Terry's demeanor made his skepticism clear. "Well, according to my sources, she's wanted for the murder of her boss, Tim Levins. Decided to do some checking on my own, and looks like I was just in time. She's been feeding you a pack of lies."

Head throbbing even more with the news, Cade shoved both hands through his hair and clutched the sides of his head. "No, Terry. Listen. Snyder must have her. He must have hit me on the head and taken her."

"Would you listen to yourself?" Terry paced the distance between the kitchen and the living room. "I don't want to think that one of my best friends has been assisting a fugitive, a murderer. Better to think that she fooled you. So tell me you didn't walk into this with your eyes wide open."

"She isn't a murderer."

An ambulance siren blared in the distance, getting closer. Emergency lights flashed outside the window. "No," Cade said. "No, no, no. I don't have time for this."

"Just where are you going?" Terry asked.

"I have to find her."

"You leave her to the law," Terry said. "That's our job. You're fortunate to be alive, Cade. Remember, she left you for dead in your basement. Now, I have to go out there and find her. But don't worry. She won't get far."

Terry opened the front door to let the EMTs inside. "I have to go to work. Once you have your head straight, I'll be back to take your statement. Do you get me, Cade?"

Cade nodded and watched Terry disappear. To the medic, he said, "I don't need you."

"Just let me check you over, and I'll decide if you need a trip to the hospital."

Shoving away, Cade headed for the stairs. "I promise I'll head to the hospital and get my head checked later. Right now, I have something else to do."

The man frowned, but he knew Cade well enough to know he shouldn't bother arguing. "Suit yourself."

Cade made it up the steps and burst through the door to Leah's room. She'd packed all her stuff. Her laptop and her duffel were both gone. He dropped to the bed, holding his head in his hands. Was he an idiot, as Terry had made him sound?

Was it true that Leah had been the one to murder her boss, and Snyder was simply a detective using unconventional methods to capture a killer?

No. Cade knew exactly why Snyder wanted her. Cade had seen a man try to kill her with his own eyes. Even if Leah was guilty of something, there was more to all this, and she was in danger.

He popped a couple of ibuprofens and grabbed his Remington stainless 870 and his .44 Magnum. Cade slipped on his winter gear and grabbed his pack, already loaded down with his survival and rescue kit, radio and satellite phone and a pack with climbing equipment—just in case. With only a few hours of daylight left, this terrible day could turn into a long and hard night. In his truck, he started the ignition and headed out.

Whatever her boss had hidden was near Devon's cabin. Snyder might have taken her there. At least, that's where Cade would start his search. He drove like a maniac, praying all the way.

God, please let me find her, save her. God had intervened on Leah's behalf before, but He'd let Cade's
father die. Cade had never understood why one person
survived and another died, but as much as was within
his power, he tried to keep people in the land of the living. He just had to hope God was on his side in this one.

If Terry wasn't going to listen to him—the only officer he felt he could trust with any of this—then Cade
was on his own. Nobody was going to stand in his way.
No way could he handle not being there again. He hadn't
been there for Dad.

Heart pounding his ribs, he finally made the driveway up to Devon's cabin. He steered his truck over the
road, bumping, swerving, sliding and plowing his way
there. There were fresh tracks to the cabin. Leah?

Or Snyder with Leah?

Cade parked a short distance away, not wanting
to alert Snyder if he was in the cabin with Leah. He
grabbed his .44 Magnum and slipped from his truck,
making quick time to the cabin. Smoke rose from the
fireplace.

Bingo.

Sneaking around, he looked in every window, but
no one was inside. Besides Leah's SUV parked in the
makeshift garage, there wasn't an additional vehicle
that Cade could see. His heart raced. Was she on her
own in this, after all? Or had Snyder driven her vehicle?

He shoved through the door of the cabin to look
around. Her laptop sat open on the table. Cade pressed
a key and it came to life. He read an email she'd written.

Suicide? A confession of murder? Could any of it be

true? No. This had to be part of Snyder's elaborate plan. In the distance, Cade heard the whine of a snowmobile. If Snyder had Leah, he was about to dump her in a place she would never be found. Within hours, another storm would be on them. Cade was running out of time.

He got hold of Isaiah on his satellite phone.

"Hey, bro, long time no hear. I have a quest—"

"Isaiah!" he interrupted, getting his friend's attention. "I don't have time. Listen to me. I need a big favor. It's a matter of life and death. I think Leah's been abducted. Can you fly over Dead Falls Canyon area around where Devon Hemphill's cabin is located, and see if you spot anyone? Relay back to me where I can find them."

"Sure. Adam and I'll go up. You want us to contact the Alaska State Troopers? Get a search and rescue on this?"

Cade hesitated. Did he? No one was lost or injured yet. But someone had been kidnapped, he was sure of it. And if he was wrong? According to that email, Leah was planning suicide. But it would take a SAR team too much time to assemble. "Yes, but I'm going in on my own. There isn't time to wait. Will you do this for me?"

"Sure, but I can't be up there for long with the weather turning bad."

"I know. And, please, make it quick."

"Cade, be careful."

"I will."

Cade needed a snowmobile, too, and he didn't have time to go back down the mountain for one. He found some snowshoes, retrofitted and strapped them onto his boots. As soon as he got through the door, his spirits sagged. This was crazy. He would never make it in time. He wasn't a hero. He wasn't his father. He would never be the man Dad was.

He should call Terry to let him know what he was doing. That he thought Snyder had Leah up on the mountain. And if none of it was true, if Leah had pulled one over on Cade, then Terry could find her and arrest her.

Then he spotted it. A snow machine half buried in the snow on Devon's property. Cade jogged in the snowshoes over to the machine and scraped the snow off. He had no confidence it would start, but not finding a key, hot-wired it anyway. It was as he had feared. The engine wouldn't turn over.

With a pleading heart, he glanced up at the heavy snow clouds.

A little help here, please, God?

His sat phone rang. "Cade," he answered.

"Spotted a man on a snowmobile, pulling a trailer full of stuff," Isaiah said. "Couldn't see what. He had it covered up. But I didn't see anyone else with him."

"Where?"

"Headed up Mount McCann. North side. Lots of ledges and drop-offs there so it was kind of weird."

Cade's knees buckled at the news.

Snyder was looking for a place to dispose of Leah. Had he already killed her?

"Thanks," he said. "Now get out before the storm hits. You know where I'll head if I can get there."

"You know the storm's expected to be harsh, dumping lots of snow. It's going to prevent any meaningful search and rescue. If you go, you'll be putting yourself in danger, risking your life. You know that, right?" His concern breached the connection.

Closing his eyes, Cade blew out a breath. "I know."

FIFTEEN

Nausea roiled in Leah's stomach.

Snyder had duct-taped her wrists, ankles and finally her mouth because he was tired of listening to her. He hadn't killed her yet. Said he wanted the time of her death, in case she was found, to fit in the scenario he'd concocted. That would end any further investigation.

Beneath the hefty blanket, wedged between his winter camping gear, Leah rocked and rolled in the cargo trailer towed behind the snowmobile. She'd heard a helicopter in the distance, but she couldn't know if that was Cade searching or his avalanche team assessing the danger before the upcoming storm. She couldn't know if they had spotted a man pulling a trailer on a snowmobile—but even if they had, it was unlikely that that would raise any suspicion.

How could anyone reach her in time? She was responsible for her own rescue in this instance. She and God, if she could convince Him to intervene.

Leah guessed she had only a couple of hours, if that, before Snyder shoved her off into some mountain gorge or crevasse in a glacier. He took a big risk himself, bringing her out here. Didn't he remember the avalanche that had nearly killed them both? If he unintentionally drove over a thin snow bridge, it could collapse and they would both die.

Whatever happened, he'd need to take care of her before it was dark and make camp if he couldn't make it back to burn the cabin before the snow hit.

God, is that all the time I have left? She shut her eyes, panic engulfing her. She had sensed all along that her time was running out, but she had no idea what that had really meant. Was she ready to die? In a spiritual sense, yes. She was right with God.

In an utterly human survival mode sense? No way. No how.

God, I know You're watching all this and that You're with me. If there's any way I can get out of this, please show me what it is. And if not, please send help. Send Cade, because that would mean he's still alive. He doesn't even know what a real hero he already is. The sacrifice he makes for complete strangers. Please help him to see that.

Leah's prayer turned to Cade and his family, and to her aunt who had raised her after her mother was incarcerated, and finally to Snyder, that God would open his eyes to the wrong he'd done. As her prayer ended on that selfless note, a sense of peace settled in her heart. No matter what happened, it was well with her soul, as the old hymn said.

The snowmobile stopped. This was it.

Oh, God, oh, God, oh, God... Please, help me.

Leah hyperventilated.

The tarp came off first, then the blanket was ripped from her and a gust of icy air whipped over her. Snyder loomed in her vision. He lifted her as though she were nothing more than a sack of Idaho potatoes and set her on her feet in snow up to her knees. She fell forward, but he caught her. He threw her over his shoulder in a fireman's carry. Leah kicked and struggled.

"If you don't settle down, I'll have to knock you out now, and you won't get to look me in the eye before the end. You won't get any last words."

Leah stilled, a million scenarios of how this would end running through her mind. A million possible ways she could escape. But that was all insanity. There was no escape to be found.

Hopelessness seemed to reflect in the heavy gray clouds and warred with her will to fight.

Finally, Snyder set her to rest on top of packed snow, next to a pair of lone spruces at the edge of the tree line. He secured himself to the tree with a climbing rope, standing on the edge of a jagged escarpment, as close as he could get without the risk of the snow collapsing beneath them. Hence, the rope. And there went her chance of taking him with her.

He brandished a knife and held it to her throat. "This is Suicide Ridge. Fitting, don't you think? I'm cutting you free, but any wrong moves and I'll have to end it with the knife."

The place looked more like a gash in the earth or a crevice than an actual ridge. Did he think she would agree to make things easier for him? To help him fit her murder into a believable suicide scene?

He ripped off the tape, pulling hair with it. Leah held her scream this time.

"Any last words?"

"Cade," she said, barely able to choke out the name. "He doesn't know anything. Leave him and his family out of it."

"I'm impressed that you're thinking about someone else instead of begging for your life. Warren is alive for now but don't think he'll get the chance to save you. Someone will have to find him first. I'm not going to kill him. I don't need more collateral damage. He only knows what you told him, which is hearsay. It'll just look like you duped him, lied to him. It would be his word against mine."

Oh, thank You, God. Cade would live. But if she'd learned anything about Cade in this short time she'd known him, the short time they'd had together—she knew the guilt that he hadn't saved her would eat at him every day.

Leah couldn't abide by that. She wouldn't fall down that ridge willingly. Snyder had the knife, so fighting against him was a risk, but one she was willing to take.

She'd been exposed to more violence at a young age than any child should ever have to see, and as an adult and a legal investigator, self-defense training had been a top priority. It hadn't worked so far in this situation, but it was all she had.

One more time…

Conscious of the knife he held, she took care not to

telegraph her intentions. Dragging in a breath, giving him the impression she had one last thing to say, in one swift move, she lunged away from the knife and kicked him in the groin.

Wrong move.

They both tumbled over the ridge toward the icy abyss below, Leah reaching for something, anything to grab on to, her screams echoing into the deep darkness beneath her.

Adrenaline punching through him, Cade gripped Leah's wrist with all his might, as she held on to the tree root thrusting out through the soil layered in broken rock.

"I've got you!"

Thank You, God...

Terrified eyes stared back at him. Though relief had infused Leah's face the instant he'd grabbed her, it was quickly dissipating. He tugged her upward and grabbed her other gloved hand when she reached for him. "I've got you," he said in that reassuring tone he'd learned to use, even when he wasn't feeling it.

But the gloves were slipping. Lying prone, he'd had no time to anchor a snow picket to secure himself. No time to grab a rope. He'd only had time to lunge and reach with everything in him as he'd come upon the scene just in time.

Hanging on his rope from below Leah, Snyder stared up as Cade pulled her from the ridge. She scrambled for traction on the snow-covered edge.

Leah climbed over the ledge and hugged him. For a

moment he let her hold him tight, relishing the feel of her safely in his arms, but finally he eased her away. "I have to save Snyder."

"What? Are you crazy?"

"I can't climb, my arm got caught in the rocks," Snyder called.

"I'll climb down and help you," Cade replied. The wind picked up, whipping around him.

He wasn't in a position to do a technical rescue from the rocky side of a ridge with an approaching storm. Nor could he expect any help that might be on the way to get here in time.

Pain pierced Cade's arm from Leah's fierce pinch. "He's a murderer. You're going to risk your life to save his?"

"She's the murderer," the man below yelled up. "Killed her boss, Tim Levins—my friend. I'm a police officer. I found her out here, trying to escape again."

"Right, that's why he dragged me out here to push me over the side."

He wanted to believe she was telling the truth, but what had Cade really seen besides the suicide email? He couldn't let himself dwell on that right now. The rescue needed his full focus.

Cade removed the equipment he'd need from his climbing pack and anchored his rope. All the while, Terry's words strangled him, keeping him from oxygen.

She's wanted for the murder of her boss, Tim Levins.

Leah grabbed him right before he descended, her eyes desperate, pleading. "You don't believe him, do you?"

His chest tight, Cade shoved back the images of Melissa saying the same thing when he'd come to rescue her and the man with whom she'd been cheating on Cade. The guy—Rob Garrison from Juneau—proceeded to tell Cade all about how Melissa loved him and not Cade. How she'd been spending time with him while Cade was working.

"I don't know what to believe. But I have to hurry," he growled. He could sort through this later. "A man could die if I don't act now."

"Cade," she pleaded.

He freed himself from her grasp. "This is what I'm trained to do. I'm prepared to risk my life, Leah, and yes, for a murderer, if it comes to that. It's not my place to stand in judgment like that."

But which one was the murderer?

Pain long and deep like the gash in the earth he was lowering himself into flashed in her eyes.

Maybe he was a sap, and would always be a sap for pretty eyes. Maybe she'd killed her boss—there was so much he didn't know about her.

"I'm coming. Hang in there," he called down to Snyder, hating his unintended pun. The man was more resilient than most, he'd give him that.

"Cade, be careful. You can't trust him. He brought me here to kill me. To throw me over!"

Cade glanced up but couldn't see Leah's face. "Stay away from the edge, it isn't stable."

Is this how his father had felt the last few minutes he was alive? When he risked his life for a man he'd hated? Cade's father was worth a thousand of Devon Hemphill. Cade squashed the thoughts—he wasn't God and shouldn't think like that. He wouldn't make that kind of judgment call. But even so, he hesitated rappelling the ridge for a millisecond. Was he willing to risk his life for Snyder?

He stared down at the man who was clearly in pain and who would die of exposure if Cade didn't do something. Of course, Cade couldn't leave him stuck out there, facing the approaching storm head-on.

Cade descended the rocky face of the ridge, grateful that snow wasn't clinging to the rock, to see what had snagged the man. Hoping he could help him, he tried to shove aside Snyder's identity. Tried to think of him as just another person Cade had to rescue. But as Snyder stared back, attempting to project an innocent look and failing, Cade recognized him as the same man who'd followed Leah in town. He'd know those dark and devious eyes anywhere. The same man who had claimed to be a witness at the avalanche. This man had been stalking Leah to find out what she knew and then kill her. This guy was the guilty party, not Leah.

His gut twisted that he'd doubted Leah even for a second.

"What's going on?" Cade asked, eyeing Snyder's arm.

"I was trying to get Leah. Trying to arrest her when she shoved me over. When I fell I tried to grab hold of something, only my wrist snagged between the rocks and the harder I pull the more stuck I am."

Cade sensed the duplicity in him, in the way he projected a warm and friendly tone. It was all a lie. But

Cade kept his thoughts to himself. Confronting the man
could wait until they were both on solid ground. For
now, he pulled a pickax from his pack, thinking this
could be a ruse on Snyder's part to get Cade down here
and incapacitate him. He'd never been in a position
where he needed to consider the possibility.

"Let's hope I can chip some of the rock away and
loosen your wrist. Then we'll see if you can climb up."
He hoped so. He'd need more gear if Snyder couldn't
make it up on his own.

Conscious of the heavy snow clouds, the dropping
temperatures and wind gusts that pierced like icy needles stabbing his face, Cade chipped away at the rock
that wedged Snyder's arm and wrist. The gloves made
the work clumsy, and he hoped he didn't hit Snyder in
the process. What would happen once the man was
free? Cade tensed as he chipped more rock, ready for
Snyder's reaction.

Ready to grab his weapon, already locked and
loaded, if necessary.

God, please don't let it come to that. He didn't want
to battle it out on the face of a ridge. Once Cade and
Snyder made it back to the top, then Cade had no idea
what would go down. But he did know that dusk would
be falling much too soon, and with a storm almost on
them, the three of them were about to get caught in
something dangerous and deadly that had nothing at
all to do with murder.

The rock fell away and, wincing, Snyder tugged his
arm free. His coat was torn, and Cade noticed the blood.

"Thanks," Snyder said. "For believing me."

Snyder didn't actually think Cade believed him about Leah, did he? Cade stared the man down, acid crawling up his throat at the thought that he was helping this murderer get to safety.

"Not my place to decide if someone is worthy of being rescued. That's God's job." He ground his teeth, wanting to say more.

Snyder gave him a funny look.

"You going to be able to make it back up with your arm?" Cade asked. "I can climb back and pull you up." He hated this.

"I think I can make it. If not, we'll do it your way."

Cade watched Snyder remove his gloves and ascend the cold ridge as though he knew how to climb, despite his wrist injury. And now, suddenly, it was a race to the top.

This, Cade hadn't expected.

Fear snaked through his insides. He had to make it up first. Had to reach Leah first. He'd counted on this man to cooperate with his rescue so that he and Cade could both make it up the ridge to safety. But what made Cade think he could trust the same guy who had been after Leah? The same guy who had murdered her boss.

Breathing hard, Cade scaled the rocky cliff, the sense of dread fueling him with adrenaline. Again images of his father with Devon flashed in his mind. Had Devon killed his father over their dispute in a scenario like this one? Cade reined in the deadly images bombarding him. He calmed his breathing. Focused on getting to the top.

What would happen once they both made it up? Cade

thought through every possibility. His weapon was ready to fire, tucked where he could reach it quickly.

He climbed over the ledge at the same time as Snyder. As Snyder untied himself, Cade freed himself from the rope, never taking his eyes from the man, prepared to reach for his gun.

Tension crackled through the air, raising the hair on his arms and the back of his neck. Like two men in an Old West gunfight, the moment was now.

Cade yanked his loaded weapon out and aimed it point blank at Snyder, who had done the same. Cade now looked at the muzzle of Snyder's weapon dead on.

"Put down your weapon," Snyder said. "I'm a police detective, and you've been harboring a fugitive. This woman is a murderer and I intend to take her back to Washington."

"You're lying." The words spewed through Cade's seething lips. "You tried to kill her. You don't deserve the title 'detective.'"

Leah approached Snyder from behind. Cade wanted to warn her to be careful with words or his eyes, but he couldn't telegraph to Snyder that she was there. She hit his gun-wielding arm with a log.

Gunfire rang out. He'd gotten a shot off and barely missed Cade. Cade tackled Snyder, determined not to shoot him if he didn't have to.

He needed to subdue Snyder until help arrived. The man punched him in the face and Cade returned the favor. Wrestling in winter wear wasn't easy. Snyder shoved Cade into a spruce tree, forcing the air from his lungs. He grabbed Cade and knocked his already injured head into the trunk of the tree.

Blackness edged his vision. He struggled to see clearly.

Snyder was getting away. Leah tugged Cade behind the tree.

Another shot rang out. This one hit the tree next to Leah's head. Cade shoved her to the ground behind a large boulder.

"Here." She handed over the weapon Cade has lost in the scuffle.

Snyder shot at them again. Cade returned fire. They wouldn't survive the night shooting at each other. The winter storm would kill them first. "I need my pack."

He watched in horror as Snyder threw the pack containing food and survival gear over the ridge, then climbed on his snowmobile. Snyder fired two more rounds and they ducked behind the tree. Cade listened to the sound of the snowmobile starting up and heading off.

"Great."

Wind and snow whipped around Leah, her teeth chattering. "What do we do now?"

"We get out of this storm. Nobody can get to us tonight."

"You were expecting others?"

"Not really. Not with the storm. They know where I was headed and that I'll be okay until tomorrow. But I need my pack."

He hiked over to the ridge, leaning into the high-velocity winds the storm was handing out. "Why'd he have to toss my pack? My radio and satellite phone are in there, along with food and water and survival equipment."

"I think you have your answer." Leah wrapped her arms around herself, tucked her head. "He doesn't want us to survive. What are we going to do?"

"There's a trail shelter not far from here for hikers to stop and rest, or get out of the elements."

"But can't we hike down to the cabin?"

"It's too far. We'll never make it."

"And you don't think Snyder made for the same place?"

"Doubtful." Cade couldn't be sure of anything anymore except they had to get out of the weather. Unfortunately he was also certain that Snyder would be back for Leah, and now Cade. "Maybe he went back to the cabin, or maybe he has a camp already set up somewhere because he expected the storm. But let's find the shelter."

Cade grabbed the snowshoes he'd removed to descend the ridge and hiked over to the snowmobile he'd managed to get moving. "Oh, no," he said. "Those last two shots killed the snowmobile."

Leah's desperate gaze found his. "He left us to die of exposure."

SIXTEEN

Even wrapped in her parka over several layers of clothing and her hood pulled tight around her head and over her mouth, Leah didn't feel as though she was wearing nearly enough. Her fingers and toes had grown numb. Leaning into forceful wind that pricked her face, Leah held on to Cade as he trekked through the snow. He wore one snowshoe and she wore the other one. It was the only way to keep from falling in snow that had grown too deep. With a chill that could steal her breath away and had already created tiny ice crystals on her eyebrows and lashes, this snowstorm terrified her even more than her experience in the avalanche had.

There was no choice except to focus with tunnel-like vision on Cade. No choice but to shove away the images of Snyder running up behind them and killing them both. Leah didn't doubt that he was crazy enough to take that chance in a blizzard.

"How much farther?" She yelled out the question so Cade could hear her over the snow and wind.

Glancing at her, his eyes peered through the slits in

his ski mask. He gave her a thumbs-up. Whatever that meant. Then he turned back to the task at hand—paying attention to the hike, leaning into the storm and, hopefully, heading to that shelter.

Please, God, let the shelter be there. Lead Cade in the right direction.

Without it, they wouldn't survive the next hour.

Cade turned on a flashlight they'd retrieved from his climbing pack, which seemed useless in the storm.

God, thank You for saving my life back there. For sending Cade. But I feel like I was rescued from one calamity only to die in the next one. I don't want to be buried alive again, don't want to die in this place.

Snyder had meant to use the approaching winter storm to his advantage—dump her with the certainty that no one would find her body until the spring thaw because this storm would bury her deep.

Her legs sluggish, she tripped over her herself, falling to her knees in the snow, but Cade never let go. He instantly turned and helped her up. That he knew his way in this seemed impossible. Maybe he was secretly lost and was hiding that from Leah.

"You okay?"

She nodded, not wanting him to spend time worrying about her. But no, she wasn't okay. Leah trusted him to find their way. To a point. There were a thousand ways they could die tonight, the least of which was Snyder. Cade flashed the light up ahead. Leah peered through the trees that served as a small barrier from the pounding snowstorm. But she saw nothing.

Tension melted from Cade's grip. He practically ran,

tugging Leah behind him. And then she spotted a small cabin—the trail shelter he'd mentioned. He pulled her up the steps and opened the door, tugging her inside. Cade shone the flashlight around the room and exposed a half cord of logs. "First order of business, start a fire." He shrugged out of his climbing pack, took off the one snowshoe and got busy making them a fire.

Leah wanted to make herself useful, but she was too cold to think straight. What was there to do until light and warmth filled the tiny cabin? What was there to do even when the fire was started? There was no stove to cook on. Nor did they have any food. But at least it was shelter from the storm.

In the meantime, Leah eyed the door, hoping, praying, that Snyder wouldn't burst through at any moment. She knew he wasn't done with them. Not by a long shot. He would stalk them and finish this before it was too late. Leah never dreamed anyone could be so tenacious, so driven, as though he would chase her to the ends of the earth.

She thanked God that Cade had showed up when he had back at the ridge. She wasn't sure how she felt about him saving not only Leah, but the man who was trying to silence her. Snyder had seemed almost as startled at the turn of events, but he'd disappeared to regroup.

Dim light and the crackle from the small fire caught her attention, filling the tiny room with warmth that had never felt so good. And hope. She stepped closer, wanting to shed her winter clothing, but she knew the room wasn't warm enough yet.

Cade turned to her, a grin on his face, but it couldn't cover the raw concern in his eyes.

"Come here." He reached for her. Pulled her to him and tucked her in his arms despite the bulk of their coats.

He was a pillar of safety and security. Leah closed her eyes and let herself lean on his strength. She'd never trusted anyone. Not with everything. But right now, what would it hurt to lean on him, if only for a moment? It wasn't as though she was giving away her heart. Her life.

Even though she wanted to do exactly that.

She'd meant to stay there in his arms for a mere minute or two. But she could have stayed there for an eternity and let all the fear drain from her. She might not be able to give her heart to Cade—not that he was asking—but she could trust him with her life. Deep down, she already knew that to be true.

He loosened his grip around her and stepped back. Positioned a chair near the fire. "Sit down and rest."

"What about you?"

"I'm good."

He pulled his gun out and set it on the small rectangular table that was shoved against the wall. Leah gestured with her chin. "Worried about bears?"

He arched a brow. "You could say that."

She blinked back unshed tears. "I didn't murder Tim."

"I know that."

"Back there. For a second. You doubted me."

"I've been lied to before. It was by a girl I loved." Cade busied himself with his pack. "You hungry?"

Letting the flames mesmerize her, she nodded.

"Here, catch." He tossed her a granola bar.

She caught it. "I thought you lost the food when Snyder tossed your other pack."

He grinned. "I forgot that I usually have bars stuffed in this for quick energy when climbing."

What had made him think he needed all this gear? He'd come prepared for anything.

She tore into the bar. "I don't blame you," she said.

"For what? Keeping energy bars handy?" After tugging off his coat, he positioned his pack and sat on the floor. His weapon stayed right next to him, pointed at the door.

"For doubting me...thinking that I could have murdered Tim."

"Oh." He stopped chewing.

"How can I blame you for that when I don't trust anyone myself? Distrust is second nature for me."

He leaned against the pack, the firelight making his face glow. The set of his rugged jaw and piercing gaze sometimes turned boyish. Like right now. Leah wanted to crawl onto his rudimentary pillow right next to him and snuggle. She wanted to trust.

To love.

The thought crushed her heart. She exhaled.

"Why is that?" he asked. "Why don't you trust people?"

That pensive gaze took over now, and he sat up, watching her with more intensity than she could handle. She was glad she could stare at the fire. When this was all over and she and Cade parted ways, she would definitely feel his absence from her life.

A pang crawled over her heart. She wanted—no, needed—this nightmare to end. But she didn't want her time with Cade to be over. Why did the two have to be tied together?

She sucked in a breath. Did she want to answer his question? Tell him everything? That would reveal a big part of who she was.

No one knew her. Not really. Tim had known some of her story. Maybe that was part of the reason why he'd worked to keep her from becoming involved with investigating Snyder.

Leah decided the room had grown warm enough and shrugged out of her parka. She'd keep the hoodie on a little longer.

Cade reached over and covered her hand. "Hey. You don't have to tell me."

She squeezed back, not wanting to let go. To tell him, she'd have to think about a part of her life she wanted to forget. "No, it's okay."

He let her hand slip away.

"But if it's too hard to talk about…" He trailed off. Leah understood he was giving her an out.

She nodded. If there was anyone in this world she wanted to tell, it was this man. They could die in the next few hours or days, depending on the weather, depending on Snyder. If there was anyone in this world she wanted to allow herself to love and trust with everything she was, it was this man. He didn't have a traitorous bone in his body.

She sucked in a ragged breath.

"I was only nine. My mom worked at a diner. I never knew my dad, or even who he was. She always brought strange men home." Leah shuddered at the memory. "Some of them were nice, but most were no good. Unfortunately sometimes they would stick around for a while. Maybe two of them stuck around long enough to think of themselves as my stepdad. She'd send me to my room to play alone while she entertained her guy friends."

Leah risked a glance at Cade, hoping she wouldn't see pity. Please, no pity. But there in his eyes she only saw compassion and concern for her. He didn't say anything, but waited for her to finish. She wasn't sure she could.

"Don't get me wrong, she wasn't a prostitute. Nothing like that. She was just…lonely, I guess. She took good care of me. Fed me, clothed me and gave me shelter. And in spite of everything, I know she loved me. It was on one of those nights when I was sent to my room to play with my stuffed animals and old Barbie dolls. Someone pounded on the door loud enough to startle me. I heard loud voices. Two men arguing. I was scared. Scared for my mother. Scared for myself. I didn't know what else to do, so I crawled down the hall and hid behind a chair."

Leah pressed her face into her hands. "I saw…everything."

Tears threatened, but she sucked in another breath.

She had to finish this. She had to tell someone. No one knew what she'd seen that night. At least no one who believed her. "My mother wasn't in the room. I didn't know then, but she'd gone to the corner store for cigarettes and beer. Her current boyfriend was facing off with another man. A stranger. I had never seen him before. Then my mother's boyfriend shot and killed that man and left. I didn't scream. I wanted to but I was too scared. So I sat there huddled in a ball. Frozen with fear."

"I'm so sorry, Leah." Cade's stricken voice broke through the images. "I don't know what to say."

She shook her head. "I'm not done yet. That isn't all of the story.

"My mother came back and found a strange man dead in her living room. She screamed and cried and shook me to find out what I had seen. I told her everything. But my mother didn't want me to tell anyone what I had seen. She was afraid for my life if the killer found out I'd witnessed his murder. Mom made something up about a burglar breaking in, but the police wouldn't believe her. The neighbors had told them plenty about her reputation, and they were convinced the murder victim was one of her boyfriends that she'd killed herself, during a fight. And even though I tried to tell them my story, they wouldn't listen. I was just a child.

"She was convicted of first-degree murder. My mother, an innocent person, was convicted and sentenced to prison…where she died."

Leah didn't say more, waiting for that to sink in.

They listened to the crackling fire and wind howling outside the cabin.

"What happened to you?" Cade finally asked. "Where did you live then?"

"I went to live with my aunt and uncle. They offered me a better life than my mother had, but I was a troubled child after what I'd seen. If the police and the lawyers had been doing their jobs, if they had been concerned about justice in the first place, my mother would never have gone to prison."

The mesmerizing flames of the fire took her right back to that night, and Leah let herself relive it. Finally, she blew out a breath, spent. "So you see now why I became a legal investigator and went to work for a defense attorney. If there is evidence out there to free an innocent person, I'm going to find it. So it seems beyond surreal that I witnessed another murder, and I could either lose my life for what I've seen, or be falsely accused, like my mother."

The look on Cade's face nearly did her in. No, it wasn't sympathy or pity, thankfully. Leah never wanted that. It was something visceral. As though he understood her in a way she couldn't even understand herself.

"I'm sorry you went through that," he said. "You're the strongest person I've ever met. Now I understand your determination to see this through on your own terms. Why you've been so unwilling to simply walk into a police station and trust that they'd take your word over Snyder's. You have good reason to mistrust the legal system."

His admiration, and the somber grin that bled into

his face, snagged her heart and caught on something deep inside. Leah wasn't sure how to handle the feelings this man ignited in her.

When she glanced back up and caught him studying her, she knew she had more to tell him. This time it wasn't about her. It was about him.

"There's something else I need to tell you. I…uh…"

Wow. This would be harder than she'd thought it would be. She wasn't sure if this was the time or if it was her place to tell him. But for the same reason she shared her story, she would give Cade the answers he needed. Then there would be no secrets between them—not on her part, anyway.

He sat up now, looking at the door. Had he heard something? What could he possibly hear over the storm?

He grabbed his gun and stood ready to shoot whoever entered. He motioned for her to get low, and slowly approached the door. "Stay here," he whispered.

"No." She wanted to stop him. "You're not leaving me here alone while you go out there and get yourself killed."

Cade managed to don his coat while keeping his weapon trained on the door. Finally he opened it, letting in a gust of wind and snow that rushed through the cabin, whipping around the fire and nearly blowing it out.

Then Cade disappeared.

With his back to the cabin, he walked the perimeter, gazing into the darkness, holding off shining the flashlight. He wasn't sure what he thought he'd heard, but he couldn't take any chances.

All his experience and various SAR training hadn't prepared him for what he would face when he'd pulled Leah from the snow that day. Hadn't prepared him to face off with a trained killer—an officer of the law, no less.

He couldn't see a thing, but instead listened, trying to hear anything unusual inside the storm.

Something cracked to his right. Cade pointed his weapon, unwilling to shoot until he could see what or whom he was shooting at. "Show yourself or I'll shoot."

Stupid. As if Snyder would answer that. If it was even him. How could the man have stalked them so effectively in this storm? He must have set up camp using an extreme weather tent and gear. But what kind of crazy would you have to be to do it in this weather? Regardless, the temperature had dropped severely, and Cade wouldn't stay out much longer. Whoever was out there was insane.

But then, he already knew the detective had gotten twisted somewhere along the way. He'd turned his back on the law he'd sworn to uphold without even realizing who or what he had become.

With the storm raging around him, Cade decided that he had become the crazy one. His paranoia was making him hear things. Snyder couldn't have followed them to the cabin. Not in this storm.

He turned to go back inside.

An arm wrapped around his throat.

Cade tugged at the strong grip, his need to breathe

and keep the man from crushing his trachea warring with his ability to fire his handgun.

Darkness edged his vision. But he couldn't free himself.

And if he didn't? Not only would Cade die, but Leah would, too.

It was now or never. Cade aimed and fired his weapon into the ground.

Snyder's grip loosened, accompanied by a shriek. Gasping for breath, Cade whirled to face the man. But he limped off into the darkness, likely leaving a trail of blood behind him. Cade aimed his gun, struggling not to shoot. He wanted to fire at him. But he couldn't shoot a man in the back. Not even a killer.

And Cade wouldn't go after him in this.

Leah ran outside, screaming. "Cade!"

He turned, grabbed her and pulled her back inside. Leaning against the door he soaked in the warmth, let it heat his chilled bones, his frozen cheeks. He had to stop facing off with the man this way. He was running out of ammo.

"Cade." Leah held his frozen hands between hers to warm them. "What happened out there? I can't believe you saw Snyder. How could he—?"

Cade shoved from the door. "He has to have a base camp set up somewhere nearby. The guy's a mountain climber and knows how to survive out here, too. That much is obvious. It's also clear that we're not safe here."

"But we don't have anywhere else to go in the storm. If we can't move, then he can't, either."

"If the storm lets up he'll be back."

Drained, he plopped in the chair and held tight to the handgun. *God, what do I do? How do I protect Leah?* A lifetime of saving and rescuing and protecting people flashed through his mind. First, his hero father and now him… What was it all for, if in the end he couldn't save himself, couldn't save the woman he loved?

He glanced up and caught her watching. He wished he could take her in his arms. Tell her everything would be okay.

"A team will be out looking for us first thing in the morning when the storm moves through. Isaiah will find us. He'll take the helicopter out. He knows where to look."

Leah's gaze held his, searching. He'd always put so much effort into reassuring people that everything was going to be okay. Though he'd given Leah his best, he knew his words had fallen flat. A rescue team arriving in the morning might be too late to save them. But he'd give his best, his all, do everything he could tonight. He would stay awake and watch. Protect Leah.

"Cade, before you went outside, I was going to tell you something. I want to tell you now, before it's too late."

Before it's too late. In case the worst happened, she meant. She didn't voice it, and he wouldn't, either.

She had his attention. "Go on."

"It's about the cabin. The box I found in Tim's office contained letters and receipts and slips of papers."

He stiffened. "What did you find?"

"You wanted to know about the quarrel your father had with Devon."

A knot grew in his bruised throat. "I still do."

"Remember, it's my job to look at the evidence, to figure things out."

"I have a feeling I'm not going to like this."

She looked at her hands. "I'm not sure I'd even be telling you this if it wasn't for the situation we're in."

He wished he didn't understand what she meant about not leaving things unsaid before it was too late. He'd always live with the regret of the argument he'd had with his father the day he was killed. Those last words between them would always be there, hovering in Cade's conscience. Gone unsaid were the things he *should* have told his father—that he'd loved and admired him and always would.

"I hope you're not upset that I looked through the box. But Tim believed the cabin should have gone to Devon's daughter and had asked me to look into this woman's disappearance. So, in a twisted sort of way, considering Tim is dead, I thought it was part of my job as an investigator. And to be honest, I was hoping to find something to help you. That's why I looked through the box on the ferry back to Mountain Cove."

"Tell me."

"Your father." Her eyes raised to meet his gaze and pinned him. "He had an affair with Devon Hemphill's daughter, Regina. It was years ago, like twenty or something. There's a few letters back and forth. But from what I could gather in the letters, Regina got pregnant. She left Mountain Cove when your father ended things between them because your mother was sick."

SEVENTEEN

Cade had no problem staying awake, given the news that Leah dumped in his lap.

It was all he could do not to call her a liar. He wanted it to be a lie, but Leah claimed there were letters between the two. Evidence such as that was hard to ignore. What he wouldn't give to get his hands on those letters. But if Snyder torched the cabin, the box and letters and Cade's answers would go up in flames along with it.

All he could do now was trust Leah. She looked into things like this for a living, so he had no excuse not to take her assessment for God's truth.

He leaned his head against the logs, watching the door, holding the handgun he'd reloaded with the last six bullets, while she slept in front of the fire, wrapped in her coat. The storm had blown through, and Cade heard nothing but the deep quiet that came after a blustering snowstorm.

If he heard the snap of a twig, or the crunch of footfalls in the snow, he'd know.

He would be ready.

But his mind and heart tripped over thoughts of his father cheating on his mother. Anguish engulfed him. All these years he'd spent looking up to the man. All these years he'd tried to be the hero his dad was, the man his dad would want him to be. He wanted nothing more in this world than to live up to his father's reputation, and Cade always failed. Or at least he'd thought.

But to hear that his father was an adulterer? That he'd lied and cheated on his wife and family? Cade struggled to wrap his mind and heart around it even as he drowned in disappointment, deep and cavernous.

And to think, if the pregnancy had gone to term, he had a half brother or sister out there somewhere...

Whop-whop-whop.

The distant sound of a helicopter jolted Cade awake. Ignoring the crick in his neck from sleeping in an awkward position, he shoved to his feet, angry at himself for falling asleep in the first place. Some protector he was—Snyder could have walked in on them. From where she lay next to the fire, Leah stirred in the cold cabin, the warmth from the embers nearly gone.

Her eyes grew wide when she recognized the sound.

She jumped to her feet and put on her coat, same as Cade. Then she rushed to the door.

Cade blocked her way. "We need to be careful."

"We need to let them know where we are." Leah tried to move by him. "That we're here and alive."

"That, too, but Isaiah knows I would have come to this cabin. A rescue team won't be far behind. But I'm going out first. Got it?"

Cade opened the door to a wall of snow, up to his chest. "Just what I thought."

He used the pickax from his pack to dig and clear enough of a path so he could climb out. Then he put on both snowshoes. Leah could stay here while he let the rescuers know where they were.

Gunfire echoed outside, the sound splintering through the timber of the rudimentary trail shelter and thundering through Cade's chest.

Leah stood frozen as another shot rang out.

The helicopter's rhythmic vibration of rotors shifted and slowed, and the engine gave a high-pitched whine. Something wasn't right. She saw anger and panic slice across Cade's face.

Standing in the doorway, he looked back at her. "Stay here." He ground out the words.

She knew he was afraid of what had happened. Afraid of what was *about* to happen. Most likely, he feared for his friend, if Isaiah was in that helicopter.

"But what if Snyder comes and you're not here? I don't have a weapon. No way to defend myself."

He shook his head as though shaking off a veil of confusion and crawled over the snow and out the door. This cold nightmare was getting to them both. She followed.

"Stay close." Cade tromped quickly across the snow, leaving Leah behind.

Without snowshoes, she couldn't keep up and stumbled as she waded through hip-high snow, deeper in some places, pushing through and taking big steps.

Breathless, she leaned against a tree, packing the white stuff down, fearing she would fall in a spot over her head and be lost forever.

A clearing up ahead caught her attention. Cade headed that way. Had Isaiah been trying to land?

But then she saw it all.

Time seemed to stand still. Cade stood fifty yards ahead of her. The helicopter was spinning out of control, not far from the ground.

And then.

Just like that.

It crashed.

Heart pounding, Leah caught up to Cade. He ducked behind a tree and pulled her with him, his chest rising and falling with his heavy breathing.

"Oh, Cade. Was that Isaiah?"

He turned her to face him, gripping her arms, sorrow and anger flashing in his eyes. "The snow was deep enough, he survived. He had to."

"What happened?" Leah couldn't believe any of this was happening.

"Snyder's still out there."

"Are you saying he did this? How?"

"Shot out the tail rotor probably."

"Why? Why would he shoot down a helicopter?"

"That was your only way out, away from him. Our only way out. He knows he has run out of time. He has to get rid of us now before the others get here." He tucked her behind him and fired his handgun. "He's in the trees. I have to get to Isaiah. See that? That's a snow cornice. We need to stay out of the path in case it collapses. It could trigger an even larger snowslide."

Avalanche.

A knot grew in Leah's throat.

"We'll make a run for it." He gripped her arm. "Keep low. Stay behind the trees."

Before Leah could react, Cade fired a shot off into the trees across the clearing. She could have used some warning. Her ears were ringing now. Cade ran to another copse of trees, tugging Leah behind him. When they reached the trees near where the helicopter went down, the dead silence made her heart sink. How could Isaiah have survived like Cade said? Of course, she knew he'd said the words to convince himself.

Cade looked at the Magnum. Made sure there wasn't any snow in the bore. Then he handed her his weapon, grip first. Leah took hold of the massive handgun. It was much heavier than hers. Why was he giving it to her?

"You cover for me. I'm going to pull Isaiah out."

Wait. What? "No, Cade. I can't do this. I can't be responsible for your lives." Any more than she already was.

"You can do this. You have to cover me."

He wrapped his gloved hand around hers on the grip. "Be careful you don't hurt yourself. It has a big recoil. It has a heavier trigger pull than you're probably used to so keep that in mind. And there are only four bullets left. Make them count."

Leah pleaded with her eyes.

"I have to go," he said. "You can do it. There's no other way."

Knowing he was right, she nodded. She dragged in an icy breath, then peered from behind the tree. Snyder was moving, but when he saw Cade heading toward the helicopter, he aimed his weapon. Leah fired a shot off, the blast knocking her on her backside. What she wouldn't give to have her own weapon right now. She crawled forward and looked for Snyder. He'd ducked behind a snowbank, out of sight.

Cade ran from the protection of the trees for the downed helicopter.

Leah's hands trembled, something she couldn't afford. Now there were only three bullets left. This wasn't going to work. She couldn't hold Snyder off with only three shots.

She watched for movement from the snowbank or in the trees across the clearing on the other side. Nothing.

And then Snyder was making his move again. He hiked down and away from the helicopter, crossing the clearing toward Leah. She fired at him, and he ducked again.

Two bullets left.

A glance at the helicopter showed her Cade assisting Isaiah out. He was alive. When Snyder took aim at Isaiah and Cade, Leah shot at him again.

He ducked and she missed.

She only had one bullet left and had to make it count.

As Snyder made his way toward her, both Isaiah and Cade were also in the line of fire—in Snyder's sights. This was all her fault. And it was up to her to resolve it. Cade hadn't meant for Leah to shoot to kill.

But that's exactly what Leah intended to do if Snyder took aim again.

Leah ducked behind trees and headed toward Snyder this time. Tired of being on the run, being on the defensive.

This time she was on the offense. This detective sworn to serve and protect wouldn't take down another person to cover his crimes if Leah had anything to do with it. She'd tried to find the evidence she needed to put him away—and it was still out there, waiting to be dug up—but she was here.

Now. Facing off with a killer.

She'd never killed another human being. Couldn't imagine what that felt like. Didn't want to know. She'd seen enough bloodshed to last a lifetime.

Footfalls crunched in the snow behind her. Cade and a limping Isaiah.

Ducking from tree to tree, Leah continued making her way to Snyder. The boldness grew inside her as she prepared to face him one last time. To end this.

With one bullet left, she intended to make it count, as Cade had said. For his and Isaiah's sake, if not for her own.

"Leah!" Cade said loud enough for her to hear him from behind. Hopefully not loud enough for Snyder.

But Cade was too far behind. He wouldn't catch her.

Leah spotted Snyder again. What was he doing? He moved and acted as though he'd lost sight of Leah, which meant she had the advantage.

Watching, waiting, Leah hid behind the tree until she saw him trudging in the opposite direction. To the trees across the clearing. Why was he running? What had him scared?

Oh, no, you don't. She didn't plan to live another day in fear that he would find her.

"Snyder!" she called.

Leah followed him across the clearing, stumbling. Almost falling face forward.

Then Snyder turned to face her.

There was something eerily familiar about this scene. About this moment. Then she realized. They'd faced off just like this before—when he'd first tracked her down. They'd both nearly died then. Would they die today?

EIGHTEEN

Snyder lifted his weapon and aimed at Leah.

Leah aimed at Snyder.

Cade couldn't believe his eyes. This could not end well. She had one bullet left, if he'd counted her shots right. But Cade had Isaiah's gun now and ran toward her.

"No!" Cade aimed and fired.

Snyder dropped before he could get off a shot. Then Leah dropped to her knees. Was she hurt?

But Cade had no time to think about that. Prickles ran over his skin. Dread churned in his gut. Three thoughts went through his mind at the same time. Snowstorm. Cornice. Danger. He looked to the crest of the mountain at the exact moment the cornice collapsed.

Blasting snow rumbled toward them.

Cade, Isaiah, Leah and Snyder. They were all in the path.

Terror gripped Cade.

He was an avalanche specialist. This shouldn't happen to him. Shouldn't happen to his friends under his watch.

Shouldn't have happened to his father, an expert, while out on a rescue.

But he understood now. Knowing the imminent danger didn't keep him from being pulled into this nightmare.

Cade's world.

Tipped.

Over.

Leah stood and whirled around in slow motion to look at him one last time.

Isaiah grabbed Cade, tugging him to run to the side and out of the path of the avalanche. But Cade pulled in the opposite direction to save Leah.

No way would she make it to safety. No way could Cade leave her there to go through it alone. He'd told her he would never leave her.

"Leah!"

The panic and fear written on her features cut through him like nothing before, but her eyes told him to save himself. Her demeanor said she was resigned to her fate.

"No!" He ran to her, reached for her.

Then the world collapsed in a wicked, fast-moving river of snow.

Cade tumbled in the crushing torrent, wild terror pulsing through him. For the first time he felt completely out of control. He could do nothing to save himself.

Nothing to save the others caught in the slide. Nothing…except…

Surrender.

Leah had been right all along. Cade couldn't control everything. Couldn't save everyone. Couldn't even save himself this time.

Though his terrified prayer was feeble—God was all he had in this moment.

Save...us...

In that instant the river of snow and ice stopped.

He calmed his breathing. He wasn't dead from impact with a tree or debris. Had made it this far.

God, help Leah and Isaiah. If You have to take someone, take me. Silence wrapped around him like the answer he expected.

You saved her once. I can't believe You'd save her to let her die in another avalanche.

Cade waited in the silence and the cold, hoping he wouldn't run out of air. Hope played with him. Toyed with his heart and soul. Hope that the search and rescue team that was already on its way would make it in time. Had even witnessed the avalanche. Would pull them all out.

But what were the chances?

Icy cold crept in, chilling his bones and his heart. He'd been involved in enough rescues that he knew their chances of survival were close to zero.

Why, God? Why?

Is this how his father had felt? Had he lived long enough to die alone? Or had he died instantly?

Then he heard it. The smallest of sounds, muted by the crushed snow entombing his body. Voices.

Voices!

God, let them find Isaiah and Leah. And, yeah,

maybe Snyder, too. If he survived, he should face justice for his crimes. Cade had his beacon on. Always
had his beacon on. But Snyder had intended for Leah
never to be found, so she didn't have a beacon. There
could be no doubt there.

Cade—idiot that he was—he should have made sure
she'd worn one. He should have given her his.

They'd found him. Were digging him out now. But
he wanted to die. How could they find Leah in time?

He hadn't been buried far from the surface and in no
time, he looked into his brother David's relieved face.
With help, he scrambled out of his tomb.

"You okay?"

"Leah. Where is she? Have you found her yet?" Cade
searched the area where rescuers were digging for one
person.

"We found another beacon."

"Isaiah." Had to be, by the trajectory.

Cade searched the area in front of him, concentrat-
ing on where he'd last seen Leah. "Leah!" he called,
knowing she wouldn't answer.

"Dig! David, get searchers with poles over there."
He pointed.

"Calm down." David grabbed him. "We'll find her."

Cade had said those words, those lies, enough times
himself to know they had little hope of getting her out
alive. The only saving grace was that the team was
here and onsite almost immediately after the avalanche
stopped.

But a fierce nausea roiled in his stomach and Cade

wanted to drop to his knees. To give in to it. But he couldn't do that. Not now.

Not with a life at stake. Leah's life. How could he be in this position? Saving her again? *God, please let us save her!*

A second team arrived. David and Cade instructed them where to search, and Isaiah—freshly released from the snow—joined Cade. Cade grabbed him in a bear hug, glad his friend was okay, though he'd need to get his leg checked after the helicopter crash.

Heidi appeared and hugged Cade briefly.

She and Isaiah looked at each other for the longest time, then she grabbed him, holding him close.

"Found something," another rescuer called.

Cade made his way over and started shoveling and digging for all he was worth. Leah's life depended on it. Then, slowly, he saw something in the snow.

It was a black ski parka.

For the second time nausea roiled in Cade's stomach. This wasn't Leah. This was Snyder. He stepped back to let someone else dig. Not protocol, but he had to find Leah.

"This isn't her. Come on people."

Desperate, he scanned the debris field. *God, why? Why did we find this murderer instead of Leah?* Cade had shot at Snyder to injure him, to bring him down before he killed Leah. But he hadn't fired to kill him. So he could be alive even now.

"Over here," a rescuer called closer to the tree line.

Oh, God, no. If she'd been pushed into the trees…

And even if she'd escaped injury from the trees, they

were looking at twenty minutes now, going on half an hour. He'd only thought he'd been out of control when the snow slide rushed over him. His inability to find the woman he loved crushed the breath inside from him. This moment would destroy him.

That is, if they didn't find her alive.

Cade was there, digging faster than anyone, his love driving him on. Hope and terror forcing the snow out of his way.

And then...there she was. Her beautiful face. Eyes closed; there was an expression of peaceful serenity captured on her features.

This time she didn't look back with relief in her vivid blue-green gaze, pleading with him to get her out. She stayed perfectly still. Cade staggered back, his heart splitting open.

"Keep digging." He dropped to his knees to work to free her.

Usually they would check for a pulse first, then proceed. But Cade would have none of that.

They pulled Leah out and laid her on the snow. "She's gone," someone said.

"No. Don't even say that." Cade's sharp tone cut through the tension. He couldn't believe she was gone. He wouldn't accept that. "See if you can find her injuries while I do CPR."

Cade immediately began compressions. Leah wasn't dead. He wouldn't allow it. All the frustration of losing his father rolled over him. He should have saved his father. He needed to be in control again, but all the control he thought he'd had over his life, or tried to have over his life and the ones he loved, had been a joke. He'd never once been in control. He could accept that, accept that it was in God's hands. But that didn't mean he couldn't try to do his part.

What use was being a hero if you couldn't save the people you loved?

"Come on, baby," he said between compressions. "Come on. You are not dying on me."

"Cade, she's gone, man." David's voice stabbed Cade.

He was required to keep doing CPR until the medical personnel arrived, anyway, so David could keep his mouth shut. Regardless, Cade would do this until Leah came back to him.

"She could have brain damage," someone whispered behind him.

He gritted his teeth. "No. She had an air pocket. She'll be fine."

Cade gripped her shoulders and shouted into her face. "I love you, Leah. Don't leave me."

Leah sucked in a breath.

Her eyes fluttered open.

She dragged in a cold breath.

Cade's face filled her vision. Were those tears streaming from his eyes? Her heart leaped at the sight.

Cade had made it. He was alive. And she was, too.

He cracked a grin. "You scared me half to death."

"And you saved me again."

"Ma'am, can you tell me if you're hurt?" another man asked. He wrapped a blanket around her.

Leah shook her head. She didn't know. Didn't care.

All she cared about right now was the love she saw streaming from Cade's eyes. She moved to sit upright. She felt a little dizzy maybe, but she didn't care. "Help me up."

A man approached as Cade helped her to her feet. She recognized him as Cade's police officer friend, Terry. "Detective Snyder is dead."

That should have been the most important thing to Leah. Relief that she would no longer be stalked by this murderous maniac. She wondered if it had been Cade's bullet that had killed him or the avalanche. But she couldn't keep her thoughts on that when the only person who mattered was the man in front of her.

"Thank you," she whispered.

"It's my job." He gave a teasing but shaky grin.

"You did more than your job. You rescued me from that killer." Leah reached up to touch Cade's cheek but hesitated.

"Why?" Now she felt her own tears sliding hot down her cheeks. She wanted to know if what she'd heard a few moments ago was true. "Why would you go that far? And don't tell me it's because of your job."

Was she reaching here? Asking for something she wasn't entitled to? Making a fool of herself?

Leah realized at that moment that the others had left them alone. They'd probably understood that she and Cade needed privacy. Cade stared at her as if he didn't want to let her out of his sight.

"I heard something," she said. "I thought I heard you say something."

He smiled then. Would she ever grow tired of that grin?

"I think my exact words were 'I love you, Leah. Don't leave me.'"

"I heard right, then."

"You heard right. What is your response to that?" he asked.

"I'm not going anywhere."

Cade *loved* her? Since losing her mother she'd never gotten close enough to anyone to let them love her. Or to love them back. And yes, she loved him back. At that moment her love for Cade overwhelmed her, in fact. Someone she could trust with her life and her heart stood right in front of her. She'd never intended to give so much away.

But, for the first time, Leah had found someone worthy of that risk. Cade was worth risking everything for, and maybe, just maybe, that was because he'd risked everything for her first.

Cade pulled her near, leaned in and kissed her, long and hard, until she was breathless. Warmth spread from her face down through her body, chasing away the numbing cold. He wrapped his arms around her, pulling her good and tight, in spite of their coats, and deepened his kiss, as though they weren't surrounded by rescue workers.

Suddenly nothing else mattered. Not the avalanche or her near-death experience. Not Snyder's attempt to kill her. Not the mountain or rescue workers. Only Cade mattered now. How had she found someone like him to love her, when she hadn't even been looking? When Cade eased away slightly, disappointment surged. Leah didn't want this to ever end.

He pressed his forehead against hers. "I thought I'd lost you today. And, Leah, I don't ever want to lose you, if that's okay with you." Cade tugged her a little closer. "Let's get you out of this cold."

He ushered her to the medevac where they were assisting Isaiah with his injured leg.

Leah sat in the helicopter, Cade next to her.

This was déjà vu. She still hadn't given him an answer, at least not the answer she knew he wanted, but there was too much going on around them.

Back at Cade's house, Leah sat next to her duffel bag on the bed. Her things had been retrieved from the cabin, but the authorities had retained her laptop for evidence, since Snyder had typed a suicide email for someone to find after he killed her.

It was hard to believe he was gone. But she wasn't sure this was over. She'd always suspected he couldn't work this alone—a suspicion proved by the man who had attacked them at the law office. There had to be others backing him, supporting him when he killed criminals that Tim had gotten off. And she'd held on to the necklace with the map. She hadn't handed that over yet.

She tugged it from where it hung beneath her sweater, surprised Snyder hadn't paid more attention to it. They needed to dig up whatever Tim had hidden, and she hoped it would include the evidence against any other guilty parties, as well.

She was still scared. Sure, the police were in on everything now and seemed to believe her story. Internal Affairs would be swarming soon. They would arrest

Marlow—the man who'd tried to detain them at Tim's office—but someone else could be scrambling to get away out there. They might want to dig up Tim's evidence, too, so they could destroy it forever. Or maybe they would want to silence the only witness to Tim's murder. The only person who'd discovered what was going on. Cade couldn't be counted as a witness in that regard.

He knocked on the doorjamb and leaned against it. "Hey."

"Hey." The word felt unnatural. Uncomfortable. Where did they go from here?

He'd told her he loved her. Leah hadn't said the words back to him yet.

He stepped into the room. "Terry needs the necklace. We're going for the evidence now. I trust him, Leah. He'll make sure the wrong people don't get their hands on it and destroy it, okay?"

She hung her head. "Okay."

Standing in front of her, he tugged her to her feet and slid his hands over her shoulders, around her neck and through her hair, cupping her head. Cade kissed her again, and she kissed him back. She'd never wanted anything or anyone more. They could take care of each other. That is, if Leah would only let herself be with him.

Cade eased away, and sighed. Clearly he was as concerned about what happened next as she was. "I never wanted to love anyone again. I actually thought I was immune to it, after the pain I'd gone through. I believed I'd never trust someone enough to love. But then

I pulled you from the snow and nothing has been the same since." His tone was calming and reassuring, as it had been that first time he'd dug her out of an avalanche.

But she also heard a desperation there she'd never heard before. Cade Warren was scared to death that she was going to hurt him. She understood what it had taken for him to love her, and for him to lay it all out there. She could tromp right over his heart. But he'd taken that risk with her.

She gazed into his intense eyes, remembering that first moment she'd looked into them. She'd never met anyone whose eyes conveyed so much emotion. So much passion. Leah might exist, but she couldn't hope to really live without this man in her life.

But he was the one to voice the words. "Life isn't worth living. Saving people has no meaning if I don't have someone that I love by my side."

Leah went into his arms, hoping and praying she could always feel this way, safe and secure in the arms of a hero.

EPILOGUE

Six weeks later Cade and Terry made another attempt to find the evidence Leah's boss had supposedly hidden. The weather had dumped more snow than they'd seen in years, preventing them from successfully digging up the buried evidence, though two police departments and Internal Affairs needed it. Cade wasn't sure how Tim had managed to bury anything, but if they had gotten the coordinates on the map correct, this was the spot.

Leah hung back and watched. She'd returned to Kincaid to assist in closing Tim's office and to pack up her apartment so she could move to Mountain Cove. She'd found a job with a local attorney, a friend of Terry's. She and Cade both needed to see where their relationship would lead them.

But Cade knew. He'd known from the first, though he'd tried to ignore the truth. Now he waited on her to realize they were meant to be together.

Until this was all behind them, Leah wouldn't be ready for anything from Cade. So to that end, Cade was determined to dig up the treasure, so to speak, and hope it was worth all the trouble.

The police had not been able to detain Marlow, the police officer who had worked with Snyder, after all. He had disappeared, which left them to believe he had gone into hiding. Leah might always have to look over her shoulder. But Cade wanted to be a part of her life regardless.

He trudged over to her and hugged her to him. "Let's get you back inside the cabin," he said. "You're getting too cold out here."

He glanced over at Terry, who nodded. "I'll be up in a minute," his friend said. "Need some coffee to warm my bones."

Leah followed him to the cabin where it all started. He took off his gloves and rubbed his hands in the direction of the fire, as did she.

"So what happens to the cabin now?"

"I guess someone should find Devon's daughter— or her child—"

Terry burst through the door. "I got something!"

Cade stiffened, unsure if any of them was ready to see what was inside the firesafe box that Terry held with gloved hands. He set it on the table and, after removing his winter gloves, he put on latex gloves. Terry pulled a camera from his pocket.

"Took pictures of it outside in the ground, too." He handed the camera over to Cade. "Hold on to that. Take pictures as you see fit."

Cade chuckled. He wasn't sure this was how things should go down, but they had a chance, a break in the weather, and they took it. Leah needed closure, and so did Cade.

Terry worked the lock and opened the lid. For a minute they all stared at the files and papers. More sludge to go through.

"May I?" Leah asked.

Terry frowned. "Put on gloves first."

After doing so, she flipped through the files and papers. "Tim's attorney notes on his clients that weren't convicted but that subsequently died in accidents. As I'd thought. But what's this?" She held up a recording device.

The three of them listened as Tim informed Snyder of his discoveries. They heard Snyder all but confess to Tim why he'd done what he'd done, as though he could convince Tim that he'd done the right thing. And he mentioned another name: Marlow.

The detective who had disappeared.

Terry got on his sat phone to tell his higher-ups about their discovery.

Leah appeared to buckle and Cade helped her into a chair. She pressed her face into her hands. "It's over now. It's all over. But Tim should never have told Snyder what he'd been planning. That cost him his life. Why would he do that?" She looked at Cade as though she hoped he would have an answer for her.

"Maybe he wanted to give the detective a chance to turn himself in. He wanted him to know that he'd turned into a criminal. Perhaps he hoped he would open Snyder's eyes to his crimes."

That was all Cade had, but he knew it fell short. She

was right. Doing that had cost Tim his life. He thought back to his father. Now he knew the quarrel he had with Devon Hemphill. For obvious reasons, Devon had hated his father, and maybe his father had wanted forgiveness. He'd obviously seen the errors of his ways and turned his back on Devon's daughter for the sake of his marriage, but what Cade didn't know was if his father had turned his back on the child he'd fathered with her. None of it mattered now. His father had risked his life for the man, and had died to save him, in spite of the animosity between them. Cade might never know the full truth of the rest of it unless he found Regina or her child.

When Leah said nothing, Cade lifted her chin. "Sounds like your boss was a good man. He didn't like having to turn in a detective like that, and wanted to do the right thing. Give Snyder a chance."

She nodded, a smile growing in her supple lips. Her vivid blue-greens locked on him. "And you're a good man, too, Cade. A man I don't want to lose. I never told you this. I'm sorry it took me so long…"

Cade frowned. Would she ever say it? "Tell me."

"I love you. Thank you for waiting for me to say those words back to you."

He scooped her into his arms and crushed his lips against hers, feeling her passion and love for him. Then he released her. "Marry me, Leah. You don't know how long I've wanted to ask you this. I've been waiting until…until you said the words or we found the box, whichever came first, and they happened together."

She laughed. He loved her laugh. Could listen to it until death parted them.

"Well? Are you going to make me wait on this answer, too?"

"No, Cade."

His heart tanked.

"No more waiting. I want to marry you as soon as possible. I've seen how quickly life can be snuffed out. I don't want to waste another minute living without you. I love you so much."

"Tell me how much." He was the one needing reassurances this time. But he knew their chances of survival were better than good.

* * * * *

UNTRACEABLE

For his anger lasts only a moment, but his favor lasts a lifetime; weeping may stay for the night, but rejoicing comes in the morning.
—*Psalms* 30:5

This story is dedicated to search-and-rescue teams everywhere, to men and women who volunteer their time, money and skills, and willingly place themselves in danger to find and rescue complete strangers. And of course, all my stories are dedicated to my family: my three sons, Christopher, Jonathan and Andrew; and my daughter, Rachel (and new son-in-law, Richard); and my husband, Dan—for giving me the time and space I need to create new worlds and characters. You guys rock!

Acknowledgments

Writers don't work in a vacuum, especially if they're novelists. I couldn't write without the encouragement and support I receive from my writing buddies—Lisa Harris, Shannon McNear and Lynette Sowell, and many more. So glad God brought us together on this writing journey!

I'd also like to thank my friends in Juneau who provided me with invaluable material regarding specific information—Doug Wessen, a community leader and SAR hero extraordinaire. And thanks to Teresa, a writing friend in Juneau who works for the US Forest Service. You're always available with just the right answer or photograph. Thanks to Bill Glude of the Alaska Avalanche Information Center for his assistance and for training search-and-rescue volunteers. Any mistakes are mine alone either by accident or on purpose in taking artistic license to create a more adventurous and appealing story world.

ONE

"Off rappel!"

Heidi adjusted her night vision goggles at her brother Cade's call up the rocky cliff face from below. The snow-covered, mountainous landscape looked green and black, but at least she could see instead of stumbling around in the dark and falling to her death. Even though the moon was out in full force, this side of the mountain remained in the shadows.

The helicopter had dropped them off as close as possible to the summit, but they'd still had to hike another two hours to get to the place where they would rappel down to the trapped climbers, at least one of them injured, or so the three rescuers—Heidi and Cade Warren and Isaiah Callahan—had been informed.

As a member of North Face Mountain Search and Rescue—like the other Warren siblings—this was only the second time Heidi had climbed at night, and she shoved aside the unpleasant memory of the first. There was enough tension between her and her brother Cade, and unfortunately their friend and coworker Isaiah—

who usually flew the helicopter—that she didn't need to tack on anything more to an already heavy load. And it wasn't just the emotional and mental burden. The pack on her back weighed her down, too.

Drawing in a cold breath, she hoisted the hefty pack—loaded down with climbing, medical and camping gear for spending the night—and rappelled the cliff. Cade, ever the protective brother, had insisted on going first, though Heidi was the trained technical climber of the three.

She'd made it halfway to the next rap station and paused for a rest, when gunfire ricocheted off the mountain. Heidi jerked and lost her balance. Her overfilled pack pulled her over, flip-flopping her. Now hanging upside down, her heart pounded.

She was the technical climber here.

She was the expert they counted on to assist in getting these people out.

She hadn't wanted to come. Not after what had happened last summer. But there'd been no choice. Two other daunting rescue operations were ongoing and they needed the manpower. If only she weren't out of practice.

All her fault. This was on her, and she knew it.

Heidi was a wreck, but she couldn't afford to give in to her emotions right now. Those climbers stranded in the saddle between the summits couldn't afford her messing up.

No way would she call for help, though. The last thing Cade and Isaiah needed was a rescuer who required rescuing. Besides, she'd assured Cade she could do this, but even if she hadn't, he'd pretty much insisted that she try. Isaiah had been the one to protest. He hadn't wanted her here. Whether because he personally didn't want to work with her after distancing himself for some unknown reason or because he didn't trust her abilities, she wasn't sure. Either way, his attitude stabbed her like an ice ax.

"What's going on up there, Heidi?" Cade asked over the radio.

"Nothing."

"You need help?" Now Isaiah. Great.

And the incident command center would hear their conversation, too. Over the years, they'd developed their own radio-speak, and didn't use the more technical terms. Cade always wanted them to talk plainly. Worked for her.

"Heidi, I asked if you're good?" Isaiah again.

At the very least, she would prove to Isaiah she was back. She could do this. "I'm rapping down. You're distracting me."

With all the strength she could muster, she grabbed the rope and inched her way up, righting herself. Then she breathed a sigh of relief.

But what about the gunfire she'd heard? Heidi used her night vision goggles to scan the mountain and the saddle below, but saw nothing of concern. Was it someone chasing off a bear somewhere? Cade and Isaiah hadn't mentioned it. Had she imagined it? Or was it simply echoing from miles away? She wouldn't bring it up. All she needed was for them to think she was hearing things. As always, Isaiah and Cade were packing weapons in case they came across a bear, so she wouldn't worry.

Following Cade down, she rappelled, careful that the unusually heavy pack wouldn't throw her off balance again. She met him at the second rappel. A glance down revealed a beaming flashlight and a small fire burning nearly four hundred feet below.

Voices resounded from the camp. The climbers must have spotted their rescuers. Cade rappelled again. Heidi watched and waited before she followed. She glanced up but couldn't see Isaiah from here. He was likely growing impatient to hear her call.

Heidi looked down at Cade and saw him swinging over, creating a new path.

"Be careful. There's a vertical ice wall and a sheer drop," Cade told them over the radio.

Negotiating the terrain would be difficult enough under the circumstances, but with the expected inclement weather, even in April, things could only get worse.

"Off rappel," Cade called.

Heidi clipped in and called up, repeating the words to Isaiah, and they were back in rhythm, rappelling and descending a snow-covered slope in the middle of a cold, wintry night.

Reaching the vertical ice wall Cade had warned about, she secured her harness and traversed the cliff face, following Cade's lead. She found the third rappel station and called up to Isaiah before descending the rest of the way.

The saddle where the two summits met formed a wind tunnel. Maybe that's why Cade hadn't mentioned the gunfire. He hadn't even heard it. The high-pitched wail of the wind harmonized with deeper tones making Heidi think of a lost lover singing a seriously morbid screamo song. Thank goodness she'd grown out of that phase a decade ago.

Dropping a few feet to the ground, the pack pulled Heidi back and she fell on her rear.

Thankfully, in this spot, the curve in the rock formations above and around them protected them from the harsh blasts of arctic gusts. She hoped that would remain the case.

"You okay?" Cade offered his hand.

She didn't take it, but instead slipped from the pack. "That thing is too heavy."

"I hear you," he said.

Isaiah joined them. He tugged Heidi around to face him, his touch surprising her. She tried to ignore the current coursing through his gloved hand and her parka to burn the skin on her arm. It was the first time he'd come close to acting as if he cared in months.

Still wearing his night vision goggles, he looked her up and down. "You okay?"

"Of course, I'm fine. We're here to help them." Heidi pointed at the group who remained huddled next to their small fire, a couple of them standing, expectantly looking in the direction of the rescuers. "Stop worrying about me."

She couldn't take his attention on her right now. It only confused her and she needed to focus. Besides, she hated to be coddled, and Cade's and Isaiah's concern was too much. Cade was right to insist she had to get back into search and rescue now or she never would, but after what happened, after she'd been part of a jaunt in the mountains with friends that ended in tragedy, Heidi second-guessed everything she did. Succeeding tonight in this rescue would serve as a rescue for Heidi, in a way. And she prayed that her participation wasn't a mistake, that it wouldn't cost more lives. She reminded herself that North Face needed her today.

Heidi helped Cade and Isaiah gather up their packs and equipment so they wouldn't end up buried in the snow once the storm set in. By the look of the dark clouds rushing in from the west, they didn't have much time. She led the way, hiking over to the climbers hunkered by the fire about a hundred yards in the distance. With a glance back she saw Cade and Isaiah pointing to a cornice loaded with snow, just waiting for a reason to bury them. Cade got on his radio and communicated their status and she heard something about the potential avalanche.

Just one of many things they'd have to watch for. In the meantime, a helicopter could drop more gear now that the SAR team had made it down. After assessing the climber's injuries, they'd relay their needs to the command center.

Only, Heidi noticed, they weren't dressed like climbers. Coats, sure, but jeans and regular shoes. How could they have hiked all this way this time of year without crampons or snowshoes? Heidi told Cade to request the extra gear and whatever winter hiking wear was available. He arched a brow, the question in his eyes confirming hers, and relayed the information.

What was going on?

* * *

Isaiah caught up with Heidi. She was too stressed for her own good. That could be dangerous. But he knew he was partially to blame for that. Or was he giving himself too much credit?

She'd had a rough time of things the past few months, and Isaiah had pulled away when he'd realized they were growing too close. He couldn't let himself get involved with anyone because of his own mistakes. He wanted to keep the past he ran from hidden. Heidi deserved better than him, and when he'd seen that look in her eyes—one of longing and admiration—a look that he returned too eagerly, he knew he had to withdraw.

And he'd hurt her.

Then came the accident. Heidi had been out for a hike with friends when someone had fallen to their death. Pain zinged through Isaiah. She'd blamed herself, and Isaiah could relate all too well to that feeling. How he wanted to be there for her. To encourage her and get her through it, but he'd already backed away. Let her family be there for her.

And they had been.

Except for when it came to informing Heidi that the man she was seeing, months after Isaiah had made his retreat, was married. Isaiah ended up with that grueling, dirty task. Why him, of all people?

But all that was behind them, and Heidi needed to focus on this rescue. Cade insisted that the only way for her to dig out of the dark place she'd crawled into was to get back into the thick of search and rescue.

While that made perfect sense, Isaiah had been worried it was too soon.

He swallowed the sudden knot that arose again as he recalled seeing her dangling on the rope through his night vision goggles moments ago. It was Heidi's decision to be here, and her brother's business to watch out for her. Not Isaiah's, other than as her SAR team member. No. He wasn't in the Warrens' inner circle. Not since he'd severed his emotional connection to Heidi.

And not since Cade had started acting as if something was eating at him. It was unusual for Cade to keep anything from Isaiah. He didn't know what was going on, but he feared his secret was out. Cade was brooding over something and he didn't appear to know how to share it with Isaiah. Now that Isaiah thought about it, Cade had tried to talk to him a few times about whatever was bothering him, but then he'd shut down. What else could it be except that Cade had found out the truth about Isaiah? That was too much to think about on an easy day, so he shook away the thought and concentrated on the rescue.

The moonlight had crept across the sky and into the gap between the two peaks so he tugged his goggles over his helmet and pushed past Heidi, leading the way to the group. They needed to establish that the SAR team was in charge from the very beginning.

As he approached the climbers, two of the men left the circle around the fire and hiked toward him, bundled up in their winter coats, though it was spring. But mountain summits didn't often care. Isaiah squared his shoulders and stood tall as he closed the distance to meet them.

When he reached them, one of the two stepped forward. The leader of this climbing party?

Isaiah thrust his gloved hand out. "Isaiah Callahan, and behind me, Heidi and Cade Warren. We're part of the North Face Mountain Search and Rescue."

"I'm Zach, and this is Jason. Rhea and Liam are by the fire."

Zach was trim enough, though he looked bulky with his coat, but he was about Isaiah's height at five feet eleven inches. Jason was both stockier and taller.

"Good you were able to make a fire." Isaiah noticed a bruise on Jason's forehead, a cut and smudges across Zach's temple and face. "How are you holding up?"

Jason huffed, and Zach sent him a glare over his shoulder. What was that about?

"Where's the injured party?" Cade asked, coming up behind Isaiah, carrying his pack and ropes.

"We were informed someone had taken a fall." A little breathless, Heidi finally joined them. She handed off the pack holding the medical gear to Isaiah. Though they were each trained to assist in all situations, Isaiah had the most medical experience.

"That was Robbie." Zach gestured to the shadows beyond the fire. "Over there. But he's already gone. No point in worrying about him now."

Was the guy in so much shock he couldn't render any emotion over a fallen friend? The cold words struck Isaiah. He glanced to Cade and Heidi. Did they sense that something was off here, too? He couldn't read them.

Zach led them over to the fire.

The radio squawked and Cade answered, discussing the coordinates and the extra gear the helicopter would drop. He left the group to position himself to receive the goods. Heidi began unpacking, preparing for an overnight stay that would include a winter storm.

Spring didn't mean anything up in the mountains in Alaska's Coast Range.

Letting his gaze skim the fire and the climbers' sorely lacking gear, except for one conspicuous green bag near the fire, he finally spotted the bundle, likely the body, about fifteen or more yards away in the shadows. Isaiah hated hearing they hadn't made it in time to save someone but it happened all too often.

Zach was suddenly at his side again.

"What happened to him?" Isaiah pointed to what he assumed was the body of the injured climber.

"He fell."

"But he was still alive when you called us." They'd gotten here as quickly as they could.

"I don't know, man, you know how these things happen. He fell and his injuries killed him."

Yeah, Isaiah knew. He trudged in the direction of the body, the thrum of a helicopter drawing closer. He glanced over his shoulder and saw Cade's silhouette in the distance as he made his way to gather the gear being dropped.

Something didn't add up. None of the climbers were equipped to climb the summit or traverse the cliff side. How did they get here? Confusion along with an unwelcome sick feeling that something was definitely wrong crawled over him like a sudden, drastic drop in temperature.

"Where are you going?" Zach followed. "I said he was dead. There's nothing more you can do for him. We need to get out of here tonight. You're wasting time."

Isaiah kept walking. "None of us are getting out tonight."

"What?" The guy jerked Isaiah around.

"A storm's coming. Life Flight is planning to hoist the injured man out of here in the morning, that is, after the storm clears out."

"We don't need to wait."

"The logistics of getting everyone out tonight are a nightmare. In the morning when the storm clears is better. It's safer. And it's the only option."

Isaiah proceeded to the body. He knelt down to examine the man, pulling out his flashlight. Had he died of hypothermia?

Then he found the blood and...a gunshot entry wound. When he was up top, he thought he'd heard a gunshot ring out in the distance behind him, too far to be related to the group in the valley. Had he been wrong about that?

Stiffening, Isaiah slowly pressed his hand inside his parka, covering the weapon in his shoulder holster. He was here to rescue people, not hurt them.

"Don't even think about it." Zach pressed the cold muzzle of a gun against the back of Isaiah's exposed neck.

Closing his eyes, Isaiah sent up a prayer and calculated his next move.

The gun pressed harder, digging into his flesh. "Put your hands up where I can see them and slowly stand up."

Zach backed away from Isaiah as he turned to face the guy, his hands up. Too bad. He could have wrestled the weapon from him.

"He's dead because he'd only slow us down," Zach said. "Are you going to be next?"

TWO

Heidi unpacked the tents and synthetic insulated blankets, tossing them to the wary climbers by the fire. Jason, Liam and then Rhea. The woman, face pale, lips a little blue, wore a dazed expression and shivered. It appeared she might be getting hypothermic. None of that came as a surprise considering the climbers had been waiting for hours for the SAR team to arrive.

Heidi must have let her gaze linger on Rhea too long because the woman blinked and looked up from the fire, regarding Heidi with an odd expression. Heidi hated that Rhea gave her the creeps. She was here to assist Rhea and her climbing buddies, so Heidi didn't like thinking that way about anyone. Yet she almost wished the moon wasn't shining on the woman's face. Soon enough, she'd have her wish as the light in the sky shifted behind the mountains or the storm clouds hid it from view. Unfortunately, she didn't relish working in the dark, either.

Heidi focused her attention back on removing the needed equipment from the various packs. The snow flukes to help secure the tents against the heavy and wet snow, along with the high winds that would come with the expected storm. The small camping stove and fuel they'd mostly use to melt snow for water. Sleeping bags. Now all she needed was some help to get the tents set up.

A blast of icy wind swept over her. It was definitely picking up. She shivered at the thought. Heidi hated to weather a storm like this, but the good thing was they'd gotten here beforehand and these people would have ample protection now. Cade had been right to insist she help. The swell of satisfaction she received when helping others was returning.

"You should wait," Rhea said.

Heidi looked up from the pack—stuff now strewn around. "Wait? Why would I do that? The faster I can get you warmed up the better."

"Because we're hiking out tonight."

The woman wasn't making any sense, didn't know what she was talking about. Yep, her core body temperature was too low. The quicker Heidi got Rhea inside a tent, the better. Heidi glanced at the two men who only stared into the fire. Obviously, they had experience in dealing with Rhea. Heidi would follow their example. She kept her thoughts to herself and focused on setting up camp. No need to further antagonize Rhea.

Cade had gone off to grab the rest of the supplies the helicopter dropped a few hundred yards from them to keep it safe, and Isaiah went to check on the deceased climber. Not so far away, but they couldn't get back fast enough for her.

"Did you hear me?" Rhea's tone grew belligerent.

What was this all about?

"That was never the plan." Heidi stood tall, facing her. "The plan was that a helicopter would hoist anyone who was injured out in the morning. It's too dangerous tonight."

Cade came from the shadows and tossed more packs and sleeping bags toward Heidi, where they plopped in the snow. Heidi shot him a look.

"What's the problem?" Cade caught his breath, then focused on Rhea. Jason and Liam stood up as if they were answering a challenge.

"No problem," Rhea said. "I told her not to unpack. We're hiking out."

Cade frowned.

Isaiah came into the circle of light, Zach right behind him. Zach shoved Isaiah forward.

What was going on?

Zach held two guns and pointed one at Isaiah and one at Cade. "I'll need your weapons and all communication devices." He glanced over at Heidi. "You, too, sweetheart."

Heidi gulped for air. This couldn't be happening. What would Cade do? She watched him, willing him to hear her pleading.

Don't try to be a hero now, Cade. Please don't.

"I don't have anything on me," Heidi said.

"You're going to have to prove it." Zach waved the gun. "Take off your coats."

"What?" Cade said. "It's too cold out here! We have to stay the night on this mountain."

Zach pressed the gun into Isaiah's temple. "I don't need all three of you."

"Yes, you need us all." Heidi didn't hide the desperation in her plea. "Whatever you're planning, to hike out tonight like Rhea said, you definitely need all three of us. You'll never make it without our help. We are the bare minimum required."

Angling his head, Zach studied her, considering her words.

The way Isaiah slightly shook his head, as though he was ready to die for them right here and now was too much for Heidi. She couldn't allow that. Cade could not get his weapon out in time to do anything for them. Isaiah had to know that.

"Do as he says, Cade." Heidi took off her own coat and arctic cold swirled around her. She shivered.

Wind rippled over the small fire and almost snuffed it out, but Heidi knew the darkness wouldn't help them.

"You should listen to her," Zach said.

Cade quickly stripped from his jacket, revealing his shoulder holster and the weapon inside. He handed it over to Jason.

"Radios and SAT phones, cell phones, everything."

Cade's expression turned dark and menacing as he handed over everything that would connect him to their brother David, who was monitoring this rescue mission from the command center at the base of the mountain. Adam, Cade and Heidi's other brother, had been called out on a separate search and rescue. The Warren siblings were spread out tonight.

"Is that everything?"

"We came here to help you," Isaiah said. "A storm is approaching, so we don't have time for this. Why are you threatening us, pointing those guns at us?"

"If you don't want our help, we'll just be on our way," Cade said.

"I like to hear that, because that's exactly what's going to happen. We're going to be on our way. All of us. You're going to lead, and we're going to follow you out."

Isaiah looked at the cliff face they'd just scaled. "We're not equipped to help you back up that cliff, not in the dark. Not with a storm closing in. There's a reason we brought supplies to make it through the night and longer, depending on the weather."

"Why did you call us? Why do you need us?" Heidi asked the question, but she thought she already knew the answer.

"The supplies you brought, and we need you to guide us out," Jason said.

Finally, someone besides Zach spoke up. Maybe if they could somehow take him out, the rest of them could be overcome.

"Our small plane crash-landed up there." Jason pointed behind them. "Two people didn't survive, the pilot died. Another guy, too. The rest of us…we made it this far, but knew we needed to call for help or die in the mountains."

But why the guns? Obviously, there was much more to this than they were being told. They were desperate to get out tonight, which was also a risk. So desperate that they would hold a search and rescue team at gunpoint. Why were they in such a hurry? What were they running from?

Fear gripped Heidi at her next thought.

Were they fugitives?

She didn't watch the news enough to know anything.

Heidi wanted to ask, but her brother gave a slight shake of his head. Knowing too much about this group in need of help could be deadly. But sooner or later the SAR team would learn the truth, and Heidi feared that truth, when it came, would cost their lives.

"Look, I don't know why you think you need to hold us at gunpoint. This whole thing is some sort of crazy." Isaiah regretted the words as soon as he said them. "You asked for help and you got it. That's what we're here to do, but you have to trust us. And believe me when I say we can't guide you out of this saddle tonight."

Isaiah's heart battered his insides. He thought he'd already seen enough trouble to last him a lifetime. But he needed to try to talk their way out of this.

Zach didn't appear to like to be challenged, especially in front of his friends. He stepped toward Isaiah, waving his weapons around, his thick gloves raising the threat of him accidentally putting too much pressure on a trigger guard. Isaiah didn't think Zach had the safety locked on either weapon.

An image of a woman covered in blood suffused his mind. He shook the memory. A vise gripped Isaiah's chest. He wanted to grab the guns and stop this insanity.

"Didn't I already warn you that if you slow me down,

I'll get rid of you?" Zach aimed both guns at Isaiah, point-blank.

"No!" Heidi screamed.

Zach made a mistake, standing too close. Isaiah could grab him, disarm him, but with Cade and Heidi so near and Jason holding the other weapon, that would gain Isaiah nothing. He couldn't risk someone else's life, but then again, if he didn't take the chance now he was risking all their lives.

To Isaiah's regret, Heidi put herself in the line of fire and pulled on Zach's arm. "Please, don't."

"Get back, Heidi." Isaiah skewered her with his gaze. He didn't need her risking her life for him.

"To get out of these mountains, you need all three of us," she said again.

Zach's gaze slid to Heidi. It was all Isaiah could do to keep from wiping that leer off his face. But he didn't have to worry about it for long. Zach slammed his weapon into the side of Isaiah's head, just under his helmet. He fell back into the snow, dizziness engulfing him.

"Isaiah!" Heidi's scream sounded as if it was coming from the other end of a tunnel.

She appeared by his side. "Isaiah," she whispered. "Talk to me."

He tugged off the helmet and grabbed his head. "These things don't protect against raving lunatics."

What had he expected from Zach, anyway?

"Heidi's right," Cade said to Zach. "We can help you climb out tonight, but it's going to take all three of us."

Ignoring his pounding head, Isaiah focused his vision. He had to stay with it. Heidi scrambled over to the medical kit a few feet away.

"I'm not convinced," Rhea said. She looked at Heidi.

What? That woman expected Zach to do away with Heidi?

Cade's tension was palpable. "In addition to our equipment and expertise, you'll need us to physically assist you down. There are four of you. You need all of us."

Something ran down Isaiah's neck. He pressed his gloved hand against the side of his head where he felt a knot and drew it back. Blood. Zach had given him a gash.

This was an absolute nightmare.

"That settles it, then," Zach said. "Now that we're all in agreement, let's get this stuff put away and get geared up."

Heidi dropped next to Isaiah. She examined his head and swabbed it, then looked him in the eyes. He wished she wouldn't do that. Give him that look that showed him how much she cared, and yet how much she couldn't care. How much he'd hurt her, on top of everything else that had happened.

"You shouldn't challenge him like that," she whispered. "Just do as they ask. We'll make it out of this. We have to."

She moved to stand, but he grabbed her wrist. "Don't put yourself between me and anyone like that again."

Shaking her head, she tried to stand, but he kept his grip on her. "Do you hear me?"

"You'd do the same for me," she said.

Yes. Yes he would, and more. But he couldn't have her risking her life for the likes of him. He didn't deserve the sacrifice.

Heidi stood and offered her hand. Of course, Isaiah could stand without her help, but he took her hand anyway. Felt the strong, sturdy grip beneath her gloves. Maybe Cade had been right. Heidi needed to get back into climbing and helping people. Search and rescue. Only Isaiah was certain she didn't need it to come at her like this, with crazy people waving guns around.

The moon finally dipped behind the north summit, and the silhouette of thick clouds edged into the sky from the west. Isaiah put his helmet back on.

"Hey!" Zach directed his attention to Isaiah and Heidi. "What are you doing? Let's get the gear packed up and ready to go."

Isaiah growled under his breath. This guy had no idea what he was getting them all into. He bent down to help Heidi pack the tents and stuff the equipment back in the pack. The helicopter had dropped more gear. How were they going to carry all of it down? He watched Cade studying all their supplies, probably wondering the same thing. If they were really going to do this, hike out tonight, at least until the storm prevented them from going farther, there were few items they could do without. Added to that, they had no idea how long Zach and his crew were going to need their assistance.

David monitored their activity from the command center and would want an update soon. Isaiah had no idea what they would tell the man. Did Zach even have a clue about that? And did he have a clue that it might be mid-April but up in these mountains it might as well be the dead of winter? Well, except there was more daylight. The thing was, if they went tromping off into this mountain wilderness and survived, at some point, another team would be sent to search for them when they went missing.

Oh, yeah, someone would look for them.

But the storm could very well prevent that search from happening anytime soon, and with Zach pressing them they could be far from here by then. They might never be found.

How far was Zach planning to push them?

Isaiah finished zipping the last pack, itching to ask Zach exactly that. Just how far were they intending to hike? How long would they need the SAR team's assistance?

How long before Zach killed them?

THREE

Heidi decided to wait until the last possible moment to tug her heavy backpack on. As overfilled as it was, it would weigh her down and tire her out before they made whatever unreasonable destination Zach had in mind. They'd yet to learn where exactly it was he wanted them to guide him other than off this saddle between the summits. All she knew was that leaving tonight was a potentially lethal idea.

Regardless, she couldn't afford to slow them down. By killing the other man in the group, Robbie, Zach had already shown he didn't have patience. Didn't care about others. A radio squawked somewhere. Heidi stiffened. They had to update the command center. That had to be David calling.

Zach approached her. *Why me?* Heidi wanted to be invisible.

Her nerves slid down her back and into the snow at her feet. *Please, God, make me invisible.* She didn't want this man to look at her. To talk to her.

But somehow she knew it was already too late.

He'd...*noticed* her. The look in his eyes confirmed it. He tugged her tight and leaned in close, his breath warming her cheek. She could fight him with everything in her and even wound him, but she knew that would only end up hurting Isaiah or her brother in the end. So she stood her ground instead.

Then Zach smirked at Isaiah while he kissed the side of her head. She tried to move away, but Zach held fast. A shudder crawled over her.

Even in the firelight, she saw the murder in Isaiah's dark hazel eyes. She could see Cade's jaw working from where he stood behind Isaiah—the very reaction Zach was going for. This was it then. Zach would use her against them until this was over. She was their weakness. She hoped that his actions meant nothing more than taunting Isaiah and her brother, and had nothing at all to do with an actual attraction to her. *God, please, no.*

Holding her close, Zach pressed the gun against her well-insulated coat. "Say anything wrong, and she pays for it."

He jabbed her rib cage and she winced. With his other hand, he lifted the radio from his pocket and tossed it to Isaiah.

"What do you want me to say, then?" Isaiah's scowl deepened. "What about the body of the guy you shot?"

"Say nothing about him. Tell them everything is going as planned. You're settled in for tonight. But tell them you'll hike out tomorrow. We don't need the helicopter to hoist anyone out, after all. We're all fine here."

Heidi couldn't help but think that was good. David

would probably suspect something was wrong but, then again, maybe not. It wasn't as if he could imagine this scenario they'd walked into. He would have no reason not to trust their assessment.

Eyes flashing, Isaiah replied on the radio, relaying all that Zach had demanded. Isaiah's pensive gaze never left Heidi. Something fierce and protective burned there, and it took her breath away. Now she couldn't help but fear for Zach. What would Isaiah do to the man once he got the chance?

She didn't want Isaiah to put himself in harm's way for her, or to do or say something he'd regret later. Finally, Heidi was able to withdraw from Zach, and she noticed Rhea watching her with those crazy eyes.

"Well, then, we're wasting time. Let's gear up and head out." Cade tossed the heavy packs, along with the bags dropped by the helicopter, to each of the climbers, since they apparently didn't have their own gear except for the one green bag.

Jason, Liam and Rhea stared down at the stuff and back up at Zach.

"What's all this?" Rhea asked. "We can't carry this stuff."

Zach shrugged. "We have to make it as far as we can tonight. Do the best you can."

"We'll need as much of that as we can bring." Isaiah tossed headlamps to them.

Heidi almost smiled at that. He always thought of everything. And it was a good thing, too, especially for this unexpected situation because these people wouldn't be able to see their way down. Maybe if the SAR team could show them what exactly they faced rappelling, Zach would change his mind. But he appeared to be a man on a mission and nothing would stop him.

The big question of the day: What was driving him?

This was insane. She didn't want to be anywhere nearby if one of them fell or got hurt. She couldn't go through that again. She had no idea what kind of shape this motley crew of criminals was in, but she'd guess they had no clue what they were in for.

Cade folded up the map he'd been looking at and tucked it in his coat. He started off, heading southwest. "Let's go, then."

Unmoving, Zach cocked his head.

"Wait," Isaiah said. "Why that way?"

Are you kidding me? She wished he'd stop talking. Zach looked irritated anytime Isaiah said anything, making her more scared that he would be the first of them to go. Something inside whimpered at the thought. But…how could this end any other way?

"Isaiah," she said, hoping she didn't have an audience. Everyone seemed preoccupied with their gear.

When he gazed at her, she willed him to understand, read her thoughts. *Don't stir up more trouble for us. Just follow Cade.*

But she knew Isaiah and Cade hadn't been getting along the past few weeks, and that would probably play into this whole mess. She hoped she wasn't the cause of the rift between them.

Isaiah directed his next words to Cade. "We need to talk about the best way down. If we choose the wrong way, we could all die."

* * *

Isaiah knew what Heidi wanted. She wanted him to follow her brother, like always, but maybe neither one of them was thinking right. Maybe Isaiah was the only one capable of thinking this through.

Cade got in Isaiah's face. He sure wished he could use this to his advantage like he'd seen in the movies. He and Cade distract the bad guys and then punch them. Take them out. But no. That wasn't going to happen tonight.

Fury rippled in Cade's overstressed face. "We hike out through Rush Gulley. It's the only way."

"Not with the storm coming. We'll be too exposed and get the brunt of it on that side of the mountains. Our whole purpose in bringing this gear is to make it through the night. Protect them from the storm. The deadly temps."

Cade worked his jaw and looked away, breathing hard, pondering Isaiah's words.

Then Zach was in the middle, playing with his gun again. "Do I need to kill one of you so we don't have to waste time arguing on the best way out? We hike out the safest and fastest way to the ice field."

"What?" So there it was. Zach's destination. "Why the ice field?"

"Because that's my only ride out of this frozen world. I have four days to get there."

"We'll never make it," Cade said. "That's too far."

"It's only thirty miles. We're that close. So we take shortcuts if we have to. Go over the mountains instead of around them. You can do it. You're mountain climbers." Zach grinned.

As if that would appease or charm them into agreeing. Isaiah wanted to punch him. They didn't have all the gear they'd need for such a trek. Or the food or supplies. It was a death wish at best.

In this weather and terrain, they'd be fortunate to make five or six miles a day, tops, and that wasn't counting the added burden of inexperienced climbers. Isaiah wanted to inform him there was no possible way, but he'd already done enough damage.

"Safest and fastest don't go together," he said.

The temperature dropped as the storm pushed arctic air deeper into the mountains. Isaiah sometimes wondered how it could get colder. They needed to keep moving or they'd get hypothermic right here. They needed to get the blood pumping. Sure, he wanted to take Zach down, but first and foremost, he was part of a search and rescue team, and he'd see this through. He'd get these people out and to safety, and then let the authorities deal with them. He didn't want to hurt them.

Unless he had to. He would do whatever was necessary to protect Cade and Heidi. His heart staggered at the thought of harm coming to her.

Hands at his hips, he looked at the ground, waiting for Cade to say something. He didn't want to get into it with him, but he'd needed to question Cade on his decision. He doubted any of them were thinking as clearly as they could under the circumstances.

"Isaiah's right," Cade said. "The north face will be tough going down. But it's the quickest way to your destination, so you should be glad about that. You'll have to stick very close to us, but I figure we have an hour, maybe two before we have to set up the tents to weather the storm."

"No. We keep going," Zach said.

"We won't make it if we don't stop. The storm will be a blizzard. A whiteout. Do you get that? We won't be able to see where we're going, even with night goggles and headlamps. We couldn't even if we were in broad daylight. This terrain is deadly all by itself. Be realistic, man."

Still looking at his boots sunk in the snow, Isaiah shook his head, mostly to himself. There was no good way out of here in the dark during a storm. But if he put himself in Zach's head, maybe he could imagine why the guy was so desperate.

"I got it," he said. "You want us to be gone by morning, so if the storm clears out, we'll be untraceable."

Zach nodded to Isaiah, respect in his eyes. Isaiah couldn't say he returned the sentiment.

"So tell me." He was going to do this thing. Ask the forbidden question that he knew Cade and Heidi wanted the answer to, too. But they were afraid to know the truth. The way Isaiah figured it, their lives were already forfeit. Might as well know the whole of it. "What or who are you running from? What did you do?"

The guy's eyes narrowed.

"Come on, man. We're risking our lives for you out here. Tell us what this is all about."

"Isaiah, no. We don't need to know what's going on." Cade glared at Isaiah, then directed his words to

Zach and the others. "It's none of our business. All we care about is getting you out of here and to safety, and we want to be left to make our own way. Let's agree on that."

Cade was right, and Isaiah had proven himself a bigger idiot than he thought possible.

Jason stepped up next to Zach, his headlamp blinding them.

"Armored-car robbery," he said. "That's what."

Cade's form deflated as he blew out a big breath. The look of pained disappointment he gave Isaiah hit him in the gut. He'd pushed things too far, he saw that now. Cade was right. They didn't want to know what this was about. Isaiah had just sealed their fates.

"We escaped," Jason continued. "Made it out. Nobody had a clue where to look. Then we hit a snag in Zach's big plans when our plane crashed. You want to know how much money?"

Jason opened his mouth and sucked in a breath, but Zach punched him in the face.

Grabbing his nose, Jason howled and cursed Zach. "What'd you do that for?"

With a single look, Zach silenced him. Too bad that couldn't have worked to begin with, before the punch to the face.

"Now if we're done with the small talk, lead on." Zach gestured ahead of him.

The wind picked up and the snow clouds slowly crept across the sky. Once the clouds blanketed the region and hid the moon, this clan would depend completely on the goggles and headlamps. And once the storm hit, their feeble lighting would be of little help.

Before he turned to lead the way, Cade gave Isaiah one long shake of his head. Isaiah hoped Cade could see the regret in his eyes, but he was sure it wouldn't matter. This wasn't the first time Cade had given him that disappointed look lately, but at least this time Isaiah knew the reason for it. Now wasn't the time to try to figure out what had been bothering his friend, especially since he likely already knew the answer to that. He tried to shove the unwelcome thoughts out of the way.

They would have to work together as a team in a way they never had before. This would require all their energy and focus and trust.

Trust. Why had this particular search and rescue scenario hit them when the trust between the three of them was at an all-time low?

Let it go, man. You don't have time to worry about that now.

Carrying the heavy packs and gear, everything they'd need to survive, the group trudged behind Cade as he led the way off the saddle, careful to stay out of the path of the avalanche that could spill from the cornice above at any moment.

Zach hiked next to Isaiah, pulling up the back, and pointing his gun at Isaiah for fun. "Don't forget that I have guns. Will kill."

"Well, Zach, I'm intimidated by you, sure," Isaiah said. This guy felt big and strong with the weapons he didn't handle all that well. "But facing off with nature in this part of the world scares me more. If you're not scared yet, you will be."

FOUR

Heidi struggled to keep up with Cade. With his big strides, he covered the ground quickly, even in the snow-covered saddle. None of the SAR team members had removed their crampons yet, and they hadn't tasked the climbers to wear them or snowshoes until required. The snow wasn't loose enough that they sank into it here, but the terrain indicated that they were approaching a sharp drop.

That was only one problem they would eventually face. Added to that, they'd have to be sure this group knew how to use an ice ax for self-rescue, or a technical ice ax if required. *Argh.* Did they even have all the equipment they would need? She doubted it. Heidi's breathing hitched. She wanted to pull her hair out. This wasn't going to work.

Straight ahead, on the other side of the peak across from them, she could see the silhouette of Devil's Paw, the highest point on the Juneau Icefield, which marked the border between southeast Alaska and British Columbia. And just below that, though she couldn't see it,

Michael's Sword thrust upward from the ice field, like its namesake blade.

Even if Heidi couldn't see much through the night vision goggles, she knew they were about to face their first taste of terror. Cade knew that, too, and likely feared how much worse it would be if they didn't make good time and find a place to hunker down in their tents. All because they had to please the madman who'd called them in to rescue him.

Clouds crept forward, the edges reminding her of pointed fingers, creeping toward the moon. With the summit looming above them to the north, Heidi wished she had her camera to capture this amazing image. But even if she did, she couldn't fathom stopping to enjoy her hobby.

Once the moon finally died a silent death behind the sword-clouds, Heidi would lose sight of Cade without her night vision goggles. Zach's gang had been instructed to wait to use their headlamps until absolutely necessary to save the batteries.

Heidi felt as if she was in a space suit again, her clothing thick, her movements slow—only she'd never wanted to be an astronaut. Never wanted to go to the moon. This might be exactly how it felt to be there, except, of course, her steps would cause her to bounce instead of sink.

Snow swirled as the wind picked up. Oh, no. Were they walking right into the screaming wind tunnel again? Or worse, was the storm on them already? She thought her space suit might be running out of oxygen.

Though her breaths came fast and hard, dragging in the frigid air, she still couldn't get enough of it.

Oh, Lord. Not here. Not now.

Breathe in, breathe out. Her lungs screamed. An iceberg of pressure weighed on her chest. And her head.

Heidi stopped and ripped off the helmet and goggles, grabbing her head. Would it explode?

Cade had always been there for her, but no—he trudged ahead as if he was the only one who mattered. Isaiah's face filled her vision. He'd removed his goggles and helmet, revealing his thick brown hat-hair, the moonlight caressing enough of his face that she could see the undeniable concern in his eyes.

He gripped her upper arms. "Heidi, what's wrong?"

"I—" she gasped for breath. "I—"

"Slowly." Isaiah pressed his gloved hands to the sides of her head. "You have to breathe slowly."

How did he know? Heidi focused on his gaze and the emotions she couldn't read swirling there. She had the sense that he was barely holding back a torrent of them. She calmed a little, her breathing easing, but the reason for her panic hadn't dissipated. Everyone stood around her, watching her as if she was some kind of mental case. What if Zach decided to kill her because of it?

"Are we really going to do this?" she asked. "Are we really going to hike down with inexperienced climbers in the dark and—"

"Shh." He pressed a finger against her lip, and it was surprisingly warm. When had he removed his gloves? "This is a search and rescue mission just like any other. You've trained for this, you can do it."

Zach pulled Isaiah away from Heidi. She hated him for it. *Isaiah, whatever happened to us?*

Oh, no, here it comes. He's going to kill me now. She and Isaiah never even had their chance, or rather, a second chance.

"You know I like you, sweetheart, but if you're not careful you might outlive your usefulness. Let's get moving."

Heidi saw Cade ahead of them watching her, but then he turned around and hiked forward at breakneck speed. Isaiah gave her a reassuring nod and tugged his helmet and goggles back on. She followed his example and hiked next to him, drawing strength and confidence from him. She had strength, too. She just had to dig down deep and find where it had hidden and pull it out. *This is a search and rescue mission just like any other.* She could do this. And as for anything else, like escaping? As long as Zach, Jason and Liam, and possibly Rhea, carried weapons, there wasn't much else they could do except follow orders.

Wait and pray.

A new team would be sent to search for them at some point when they didn't show up. But Heidi dreaded how long that would take. SAR volunteers were already stretched thin due to two ongoing rescue operations before Cade, Heidi and Isaiah had been delivered to the drop point near the summit.

How long before David began to worry? How long before they could even send a team to search for them? And if they did, she'd bet David and Adam would both be on that team. But the farther they trekked into the deep mountain wilderness, the less chance they had of being found, especially with a man like Zach, who would do everything within his power to keep their whereabouts hidden.

No. She couldn't count on being rescued. They were on their own.

No one knew they'd sent the search and rescue team to face a killer. Or killers. No one knew they were headed to the ice field. Making it there in this weather? That was another story altogether.

Cade stopped and held up his hand, signaling for the rest of them to stop.

Heidi closed the distance to stand just behind him. She sucked in a breath. Rush Gulley, Cade's initial suggestion, would have been so much easier than this jagged, angular descent into the lower ridge on this side of the mountain. She wouldn't want to do this on a good day, much less a stormy night. What would Zach's cronies say when they saw this, though their view would be limited?

"Looks like I'm up," she said. She had more experience in multipitch technical climbing, though both Isaiah and Cade could hold their own.

"Wrong. I'll go down first, make sure there's no loose rocks or hazards. And I'll untie them once they're lowered to the bottom. That's all we're doing here, lowering them down."

Heidi wanted to argue, but giving him a spiel about working as a team right now would be pure bad timing. Cade had always been the team leader, and that's just the way it was, so she held her tongue.

He shook his head. "I don't like this. Why did I listen to Isaiah?"

"He was right, that's why." She steadied her breathing, reining in the panic that threatened beneath the surface again. "We're a team, Cade, so we have to start acting like one. Granted, this is the worst possible scenario, but we pass this test tonight, and we can't face anything worse."

Except maybe a bullet to the head.

There. She got in her spiel after all, and reassurance for the both of them, too.

"Whatever we do has to be quick, or we're going to get caught in the jaws of something driving, cold and wet. I don't like keeping these people, no matter their crime, out in the elements any longer than necessary."

Isaiah stepped next to them. "Let's get busy then. We can rig a seat harness for this, and anything else we face. No point in risking their lives by letting them attempt to climb."

Even Zach looked a little daunted as he peered into what, for him, with only a headlamp, would be a bottomless abyss. "What's the plan?"

"You're forcing us to go on a suicide mission, that's the plan," Heidi said. "We need to set up the tents and wait out the storm. Not climb down some insane multipitch terrain at night."

It was worth a try anyway.

Isaiah dumped his pack and began setting up everything to lower them down.

A creepy grin slid onto Zach's face. "But here you are, preparing to do exactly that. You're turning out to be useful, after all. I'm glad, because I wasn't ready to leave you behind. Not yet."

Frowning, Isaiah motioned for Heidi to join him and help. She was grateful for the excuse to get out from under Zach's gaze. But his words clung to her just the same. Isaiah set up an anchor around a rock, and Heidi clipped a carabiner—a small oval ring used as a connector—to hold the belay device, which was used to create friction on the rope, in place for lowering the climbers.

"So, um, what should we do to get ready?" Jason asked. "We don't have climbing gear."

Very perceptive.

"Pray. That's what you should do." Isaiah worked with the tubular webbing they always carried to create the right seat harness.

Depending on the situation and injuries, they could create whatever kind of harness they needed for the person or persons they rescued.

"That is," Isaiah said, looking up from his task, "if you consider yourself a praying man, Jason. We need a lot of prayer if we're going to live through the night."

Two hours later, Isaiah knew someone had been praying.

Shivering at the bottom of another ridge cutting between the mountains—which kept them in the upper elevations—they quickly assembled the three tents, all geared with the required flies, sealed seams and enough extra snow flukes to withstand the approaching blizzard. Then supplies of water and food were dispersed among each shelter. They'd only brought one cooking stove with fuel, though.

Regardless of their predicament, relief coursed through Isaiah that they'd been successful in lowering their charges and setting up a camp, all in the middle of a frozen night. All as the storm closed in on them. Still, he wasn't sure he could ever shake Rhea's shrieks as they lowered her.

Zach had finally agreed to stop but only after Rhea's terrifying experience down the terrain had left her crying and pitching a fit. She demanded they stop and wait until daylight. Isaiah could see that she would freeze to death if they kept going, as it was. Inside the tent, she could get warm in a sleeping bag and then get into the better winter wear they'd brought with them.

Isaiah finished building a snow wall around the last tent to protect it from the gale-force winds, and couldn't wait to climb in and warm up. Rest his weary bones and mind. Except, depending on how fast the snow accumulated, he'd have go back outside to dig them out at regular intervals. Too much snow could collapse the tent.

Zach approached and shoved him with his foot, his headlamp flickering. "One of you sleeps with each of us in a tent. Rhea and Heidi are together."

Isaiah stood to face the man. "There's nowhere for us to run."

"Get in." Zach held his weapon.

Did Zach know how to clean the snow and weather out of the bore so it wouldn't malfunction? Just before Isaiah climbed into the tent, he saw Cade and Heidi, and shared a look of regret with each of them.

Isaiah had a feeling he knew what they were both thinking. Once they got Zach and his men and woman to safety, they would likely be killed. They knew more than they should know about the armored-car robbers and killers. Knew their faces and their names. He squatted and crawled into the tent. What a weird twist of fate, to save people knowing they would kill you when you finally delivered them to safety. Isaiah crawled over to the sleeping bag to the right, making it his own. He dropped down and didn't bother taking off his coat. Not warm enough inside yet.

At least tonight he would be warm and dry, despite the nefarious company.

Their supplies were limited because they hadn't expected they would be hiking through the frozen Alaska wilderness. They were all too exhausted tonight to use the small camping stove they'd brought to warm up their water. But if they were in this very long, they'd need to conserve the fuel to melt snow. For now, keeping warm was a matter of bundling up in the sleeping bags and combined body heat to warm up the inside of the tent.

Zach and Liam crawled inside, too, looking as haggard as Isaiah felt. He guessed Jason was with Cade and he knew Rhea was with Heidi. Why did they have to be separated in the first place? He wasn't sure he could sleep for worrying that he would be killed in the night, or that Cade or Heidi would face the same fate.

He pinched the bridge of his nose and squeezed his eyes shut. *God, help us.*

"Praying again?" Zach asked.

Isaiah didn't have the energy for this. "You might try it sometime."

Zach and Liam laughed, though Isaiah consoled himself with the fact it was tired and weak.

"I'm starving. What have we got to eat?" Liam dug through the pack inside the tent.

"MREs and energy bars. I'd recommend the energy bar. Quick and simple." Isaiah was too bushed to eat one. He'd get one in the morning.

"They might try to contact us again, you know. So be ready to toss me the radio." Isaiah prepared to slip into the sleeping bag and prayed he could actually sleep. This was going to be a long night. A long, hard journey to the ice field.

"Don't give me orders." Zach held up a rope, then proceeded to tie Isaiah's wrists. "I won't bother tying your ankles. You're not going anywhere."

Now it was Isaiah's turn to laugh, and his wasn't so feeble. "Now that I'm all tied up, you get to go outside and scrape the snow off before it gets too heavy or buries us alive in the tent."

Liam stiffened. He looked to Zach for answers. When he got none, he studied Isaiah. "How often do we have to do that?"

Isaiah shrugged. "Depends on the storm. I'd say every hour for starters. Then if it snows hard enough, maybe every fifteen minutes."

"How will we know?"

"You'll know." Isaiah lay back down on the sleeping bag, grateful for small things. He wouldn't have to dig them out tonight. He could actually sleep, maybe, and trust God to make it peaceful.

"I say when. Remember, you're not in charge. I am."

A raging retort surged to Isaiah's lips, and he tried holding himself in check but failed. "Really? We just saved your lives tonight. And we delivered you down to this ridge under impossible circumstances. You couldn't have done that on your own."

"Whatever."

Isaiah sat up, adrenaline coursing through him once again. He needed to say the words. Get them out. He pointed a finger at Zach, holding up both tied hands. "That was the hardest thing I've ever done, *we've* ever done, as a team. Don't expect us to do anything like that again. You're fortunate that we all survived. But don't push it."

"You guys are as good as it gets, there's no doubt there. I know what to expect from you now. How hard I can push."

Isaiah believed that God had protected them. Answered their prayers. But as to how hard Zach could push them? Isaiah didn't bother answering. Zach wouldn't listen anyway. He had nothing to lose by pushing them.

Liam turned the flashlight off. They lay in the darkness, the storm beginning to rage around them. Isaiah couldn't stand to think about what tomorrow would bring, and hoped he would drift quickly to sleep, but escape plans exploded in his head.

If they'd retained their weapons, they could have won the day. Maybe. But they'd been caught off guard.

And... Heidi.

A pang stabbed through him. Why did she have to be the one to come? Isaiah couldn't stand that it was Heidi with them. Not on this mission. But he'd better not say that to Heidi. Still, she had to see that Zach appeared intent on using her against Isaiah and Cade.

Isaiah thought back to the good times they'd shared since he'd met her. He'd run from Montana to hide in Mountain Cove, Alaska. Even changed his name to start a new life.

He'd been struck by her soft, kind and huge brown eyes and that dark mahogany mane of hers. But the most beautiful part of her was on the inside. What man wouldn't be attracted to her? He'd done well enough, keeping his distance. They worked together for one thing. Or used to before he'd changed his schedule around. But he'd been able to keep his relationship with her as an easy friendship, that is, until that day not quite a year ago.

The sunset had dazzled them with the most amazing hues of orange and pink as they stood looking out over the channel, waiting for Cade and Leah to return from another trip to Seattle. Isaiah's gaze had veered from the sunset to Heidi, and he'd made the mistake of letting himself take her in for a little too long. When she looked at him—something happened between them. Something and yet nothing at all. He couldn't put words to it. But they'd connected. He'd felt it. She'd felt it. He *knew* she had. Maybe it had been building for a long time.

He also knew that he'd hurt her by backing away.

But what else could he do? He couldn't let himself get

close to anyone like that. Not after everything he'd been involved in. He was almost thankful the wind howled outside the tent as it drowned out his sullen thoughts. On the other hand, it brought him back to their deadly predicament.

FIVE

Heidi opened her eyes. Something had jarred her awake.

She couldn't see her hand in front of her face. The storm wailed outside. What could she have heard over the din? Was Rhea still asleep, or moving around in the tent? Maybe she planned to smother Heidi in her sleep.

Or was it one of the guys scraping the snow off their tent? Liam had informed them earlier that he and Jason had been tasked with the job.

Wary, she shifted inside the insulated sleeping bag, grateful for the smallest of comforts, but concerned about sleeping in the tent with Rhea. Thank goodness they had both collapsed with exhaustion, or at least Heidi thought Rhea had conked out first. The woman had creeped Heidi out from the beginning of this ordeal, and she hadn't relished the idea of sharing tent space with her, but better Rhea than one of the others in Zach's mangy troop.

Rhea was a weird person, and had to be more than a little disturbed to be with a guy like Zach. To admire him. Heidi sensed Rhea's pure and lethal hatred toward her because of Zach's unwarranted attention. Couldn't the woman see that Zach was simply using Heidi against Cade and Isaiah?

Except that wasn't completely true, either. There was something about Heidi that Zach liked. A girl just knew these things. A chill scuttled over her, even though the inside of the tent was relatively warm.

Why had she let her mind take her down this path? She needed sleep, and thinking about the crazy people who could kill them at some point didn't help. They had to get out of this.

Heidi repositioned herself and sighed.

"What's with all the racket over there?" Rhea asked.

"I'm not doing anything. It's the storm."

"I hear you sighing and huffing and puffing. Every time you move in that sleeping bag, I hear it."

Maybe Heidi had been the one to make the noise and had woken herself up. "I'm sorry."

"I don't know why I had to be in here with you instead of with Zach."

"Do you love him, Rhea?" Now, why had Heidi asked the woman such a question? Why *else* would she be with a man like that?

"Why? You think you can have him? Well, he's mine. All mine."

"That's not why I asked. I can't sleep. I'm just trying to figure out why this is happening to me, Cade and Isaiah. I can't figure out why you would love a criminal." Or maybe Rhea had been in on the heist. Heidi had better keep her mouth shut. Rhea snorted. "Zach is bril-

liant. He needed money to get started, that's all. Wealthy
people aren't going to miss two million dollars."

Two million dollars? Heidi held her breath. Did
Rhea realize she'd just shared that information? Zach
wouldn't be happy to hear that, but Heidi wouldn't be
the one to tell him so it probably didn't matter that she
knew.

But…two million dollars. *Oh, God in heaven, help
us out of this.*

"Now that I told you about the money, don't think
you can steal Zach away from me. I'd kill you first."

Heidi frowned. What kind of person thought like
that? Had Rhea been institutionalized at some point?
She sounded like some sort of female Praetorian Guard,
an elite bodyguard for her emperor, Zach, whom she
worshipped. Besides looking and acting crazy, she
sounded crazy, which meant Heidi was in even more
danger. They all were.

"You don't have to worry about me. I have no interest in Zach. I've learned the hard way that people can't
be trusted when it comes to relationships. I don't want
to love anyone."

First, Isaiah had distanced himself. Then Lon… Pain
knifed through her heart—he'd been a married man, for
crying out loud. She could never get over the fact that
she'd been romantic with a married man. How his wife
must feel about her. She turned in the sleeping bag, not
caring if she made Rhea mad. A hot tear slid down the
side of her face and right over the bridge of her nose. It
dropped to the bedding below. Then she'd learned that

her own father, whom she'd loved and adored and admired, had cheated on her mother.

She swiped at the tear then thrust her hands back in the bag.

Rhea didn't say anything to Heidi's comment about relationships, so she added, "Be careful, Rhea. Zach could break your heart."

Heidi should be more concerned about living through this than whether or not Zach would break Rhea's heart, which he would undoubtedly do. She didn't want to trust or love again or feel that pain, but every time she looked at Isaiah, she wished she could feel a different way. Wished he hadn't hurt her.

What had happened between them?

Earlier tonight, he'd been right there, helping her through her panic as if he'd never left her side—physically or emotionally.

"You're a liar," Rhea said.

"What have I lied about?"

"There is someone you want to love."

Heidi held her breath. What had she done or said to give Rhea that impression? "You're wrong."

Rhea's laugh was deep and raspy, a sick, mocking sound. Where had Zach found her? Heidi's pulse ratcheted up, although it was already near racing. Would Rhea tell Zach, causing him to use Isaiah or Cade—both of whom meant everything—against her?

Wait. Isaiah meant everything? "I don't love anyone. And I don't want anyone. But I'll make you a deal."

"What's that?"

"Remember when Zach punched Jason in the nose because he almost told us how much money you stole?"

Rhea was silent, but Heidi knew she remembered. They all did.

"Zach doesn't want anyone to know how much, but you just told me that he stole two million dollars. That can be our little secret. So I'll keep your secret, if you'll keep mine. Do we have a deal?"

"Yes." Rhea's voice cracked. Was the woman that scared? "Zach will kill me if he finds out."

Tension crept back into Heidi's body. She wouldn't fall back asleep now. Heidi had some power over Rhea, but she could never use it because then Rhea could tell Heidi's secret. Not that she'd admitted to anything.

But the images of what Zach could do tormented her like the howling wind outside.

The radio squawked. Funny the places those things would pick up, and then sometimes when you needed them the most, they failed. But that's why the SAR teams carried a couple of different kinds as well as a SAT phone. Isaiah also took his cell on rescues, which would give off a ping if kept on. Zach had commandeered all their communications equipment except, well, the avalanche beacons, but those weren't exactly communication devices unless you were buried in the snow. Isaiah had turned on his beacon to transmit, anyway, but where they were, nobody was near enough to pick up that signal. No one even knew to look.

Snuggled inside the sleeping bag with his hands tied, he bolted up, oriented himself to his surroundings and spotted the radio on the floor next to Zach's sleeping bag. Didn't the guy hear that? Admittedly, the noise had to burrow into Isaiah's head to get him to wake up.

David was calling to check on his team. Isaiah figured it might be better if he didn't answer, let them start worrying sooner, except there was no getting them out of this place with the inclement weather and gale-force winds still screaming outside. At least morning had broken. That was an advantage they hadn't had last night, and yet somehow they had survived.

He'd give God the credit.

David sounded agitated. Maybe…maybe Isaiah could somehow let David in on what was happening. Give him a clue, if nothing else, but only if Zach and Liam slept through this.

Isaiah worked his way free of the bag and scrambled over to pick up the radio with his hands tied. "I'm here, David!"

The next thing he knew, Zach sprang from where he slept and pressed his gun against Isaiah's temple. Tension corded around his throat and tightened. He couldn't speak.

"Isaiah! Finally. I thought you ran into trouble."

He found his voice. "You could say that."

Zach shoved Isaiah's head with the gun. A clear warning.

Isaiah quickly added, "We're still weathering the storm. But you can be sure we're going to deliver the climbers down the mountain into the right hands."

He wasn't sure why he added those last words, but he had every intention of doing just that. However that played out. Whatever Zach thought he would pull off here, wasn't going to happen if Isaiah—and he knew Cade and Heidi would be with him on this—had anything to do with it. He'd think of something before this was all over. Something before Zach killed them.

"How's Adam? Did his team make it back yet?" Isaiah knew that Cade and Heidi would want to know about their younger brother.

"Yeah. Last night. Found a little boy who'd gotten lost hiking with his parents."

"That's good to hear." At least someone had found success.

"I need your updates more frequently."

"Sure, every hour?"

Zach snatched the radio from him. "If you do that again, you can say goodbye to the woman."

When Zach put the radio to Isaiah's mouth, his eyes narrowed.

"I'll try," Isaiah said, "but we're getting buried here and we're busy."

Zach leaned in and whispered, "Heidi."

Isaiah closed his eyes at his next words. "Don't worry about us. You know we'll be fine. I'll contact you with coordinates for an extraction point. We'll hike as far as we can first. Could be tomorrow maybe."

"Is Cade around? Why doesn't he answer his radio?"

What? Didn't David trust Isaiah? But then Cade was his brother. Isaiah should understand that. "He's outside, brushing snow off. Heidi's in another tent."

"Okay, then. You guys take care."

"Tell him over and out." Zach nudged him with the gun again.

Huh? They never used that. But Isaiah could use it now. The radio at his mouth, he said, "Over and out."

Would David hear that for what it was? Would he pick up on the clue that Zach had forced Isaiah to drop?

The radio conversation over, Zach shoved Isaiah to the ground. He couldn't stop the fall with his wrists tied. "You ever try that again and I won't kill you. I'll hurt you and leave you to die a slow death."

"The radio had been squawking for a while, and you guys snored through it. Next time I'll just let the command center wonder what happened to us. Let them think we need our own rescue team, if you prefer."

Zach studied Isaiah, considering his words and that outcome. The tent shuddered, fierce wind breaking through the snow wall.

He growled. "It's April, for crying out loud. Why is this happening?"

"This mountain range has some of the roughest weather in the world. That's why. Your plane had the great misfortune of crash-landing here." Isaiah wanted to know where they'd been heading. Had they come from the Alaska mainland running from an armored-car robbery there? Or were they leaving the Lower 48 on their way to Alaska or Canada? But he wouldn't make the same mistake he'd made before and ask.

"Let's pack up. We have to get going."

"No. We have to wait out the storm."

"There's no time. I have four days, now three, to get where I need to be for my ride out of here."

"If you wanted to go on a suicide mission, why did you call for our help? Huh? Tell me that." Isaiah didn't bother to rein in his temper. "You called us to help you out of here. Hear those winds out there? It's a whiteout. We hike out there now and we won't be able to see a thing. It'll be worse than last night. At least we had the night vision goggles then."

"Maybe he's right, Zach." Liam rubbed his tired eyes like a three-year-old. "Let's at least wait until there's a break in the storm. We could make some headway then."

"I need to talk to the others on my team," Isaiah said. "Figure out the quickest and safest way to the ice field. Believe me, I want this to be over with as soon as possible. Just like you." Isaiah held out his hands. "Mind untying me now?"

Zach nodded to Liam. "Untie him, then go get the other one."

Liam's eyes widened. "You want me to go out there?"

"If you don't want me to leave you behind when we leave, then yes, go and get him."

Backing down, Liam shook his head. Zach trained his weapon on Isaiah as if he expected Isaiah to try something as soon as his hands were free. And when Liam left, he just might. But then he thought of Cade and of Heidi.

Liam grabbed his coat and put on his gloves. The tent was small, but at least it was warm.

Isaiah rubbed his hands and wrists. "I'm going to need Heidi, too. She's part of the team."

"It'll get too crowded in here." Zach shifted on his sleeping bag as if he was already feeling claustrophobic.

"Well, I'm sorry about that, but I need her help to plan our next move." He needed her to be here with him. Needed to know she was all right after a night with Rhea, although he knew that Heidi could win that battle, if it came to that, hands down.

"All right." Zach glared at Liam.

The guy unzipped the tent and cold and snow rushed inside. Liam hesitated and Zach kicked him the rest of the way out. There was a chance, though slight, that Liam would get lost altogether and wander into the blizzard, missing the tent. "The next tent over is to your left, Liam," Isaiah shouted.

He wasn't sure Liam heard him. He should be the one to go out there. "I don't know if Liam has it in him to find the other tents in this storm."

Zach scrunched up his face. "He's not an idiot. He was out moving snow off the tents half the night. I think he'll be fine."

"Have you been out in that yet? Do you even know what you're talking about?"

The man shrugged.

Isaiah sent up a prayer.

"You praying again?"

"Yep. Praying that Liam doesn't lose his way."

Zach's face paled. "How could he? The tents are right there."

"You've never been in a blizzard like this. It's called a whiteout for a reason. You can't see where the sky meets the ground. You can't see where you're going. You can even get vertigo."

"That sounds like a bunch of bologne to me."

Was that the answer? Should they just let Zach have his way and try to lead him and his crew out during the whiteout? No. Then they would all be at risk.

A few minutes passed. "Let's pull out the food, get it ready for the others."

Isaiah busied himself starting up the small camping stove. He opened the vents in the tent.

"What's taking him so long?" Zach raked his hand through his hair. "How hard could it be?"

"You should have been the one to go." Isaiah decided he took a little too much pleasure in taunting this guy. "I can go check on them if you want."

"No. You stay right here."

"Okay, then we're both left to wonder if he even made it." Planting the seed of fear in Zach had worked out better than Isaiah thought.

Zach was suddenly in Isaiah's face, pressing the muzzle of his gun under his chin. "You'd love that, wouldn't you? One down, three to go."

Should he wrestle with Zach? Take the gun from him? It was now or never. Squeezing his eyes shut, he reined in the images of taking the gun from Zach. What would that gain him? Jason still had a weapon trained on Cade. He wasn't sure if Rhea had one, as well.

All he knew was that this wasn't the right moment.

Someone unzipped the tent and stepped inside.

Heidi.

Isaiah's heart jumped.

Cade followed.

Isaiah had made the right decision—wrestling with the weapon could have set it off and killed her or Cade.

Liam tried to come inside, too.

"Go with Jason," Zach said. "There's not enough room here."

Heidi sent Isaiah a soft smile, the strain of a restless night in her face. She crawled over next to him, took off her gloves and shrugged out of her coat. "It's warm in here. How are you holding up?"

"Good."

She slid her hand over his and squeezed.

Isaiah tried to ignore what her touch did to his heart. He pulled his hand away.

God, I have to get her out of here.

Maybe if he could save her—and Cade, too—then Isaiah could redeem himself. Although he knew that wasn't true. Only Christ was the true Redeemer. But maybe if he could right this wrong, it would be something. Although he hadn't been arrested or convicted, hadn't killed anyone, he knew in some roundabout way, he'd played a role in that murder.

SIX

Bundled in her winter gear, Heidi exited the tent.

They'd stared at the maps long enough.

Conserving what water they had, Heidi had used the camping stove to melt snow to drink, and portioned out the energy bars. When the wind had died down, the quiet drew them outside to assess the damage.

Cade, Isaiah and Zach stood next to the snow wall. The tents were nearly buried again, even though the men had taken turns scraping off the snow. Liam, Jason and Rhea were still eating their energy bars, their gazes drawn to the exquisite splendor surrounding them—a pristine but deadly beauty that had threatened their lives.

Indescribable.

The clouds thinned enough that the sun tried to break through. Heidi wanted to celebrate, but she knew the lull in the storm might not last.

"Let's get going." Zach started taking down the tent closest to him.

Everyone followed his lead, that is, everyone except Isaiah.

"I don't think this is the end of the storm." Isaiah followed Zach. "We could get stuck out there, in the thick of it, and this time we could all die."

Zach turned on him. "Do your job, man. Pack up the camp and let's move."

Unfortunately, Heidi had made the mistake of watching the exchange, and caught Zach's attention. Isaiah must have noticed, too, because he looked ready to take Zach down. At some point, they should definitely do that, but not like this. Not without a plan to overpower their captors. She had to intervene before Isaiah did something stupid.

"Isaiah, help me pack the sleeping bags. You know we need to hurry." She searched his intense, fury-filled gaze, pleading with her own.

Rhea approached and leaned into Zach, kissing him and turning his head. Heidi sighed with relief and gestured for Isaiah to join her.

Isaiah climbed inside the tent with Heidi and they started packing up the bags and gear as quickly as possible.

"What were you doing back there?" Heidi hissed.

"You know we're in the best place to wait out a blizzard for miles. This isn't over yet. Not by a long shot. That's why we brought the tents and food and water. We knew it was coming. So what are you doing, giving in to him?"

Heidi stopped rolling up the bag and looked into Isaiah's eyes. Something pinged in her heart—she'd missed seeing him at the Mountain Cove Avalanche Center ever since they had traded shifts and no longer worked together. Especially his eyes. The contrast of the striking hazel color with his dark brown hair, and the essence of all that was Isaiah in the depths of his gaze, stirred a crazy longing. But it also stirred other emotions like sadness. Regret.

She shoved those unbidden and unwelcome thoughts aside. "We have to pick our battles with Zach. We can't just survive the storm. We have to survive him and his friends. I don't know about the others, but I know Rhea is crazy. My guess is a person would have to be a certain kind of irrational to commit a crime like that. I wouldn't want to risk setting any of them off."

Her throat constricted. She reached toward Isaiah, pressing her hand against his heart. "Please, I couldn't bear it if something happened to either you or Cade. Keep your head down and do what Zach asks us to do. Get them through the mountains so we can go home."

Remorse burned in his eyes. He pressed both hands over hers on his chest. "I didn't mean to scare you. You're right." He grinned. "You always are. I shouldn't cause any trouble that could get you hurt."

Heidi returned his smile, wishing they were any-where but here. She had so much to say. So many questions. But the side of her heart that had gone dark over the past few months rebuffed her for giving a possible romantic relationship with Isaiah another thought.

He inched closer. "As much as I hate scaring you, I need to say this. You know they're not going to let us go home. They can't let us go."

Tears burned at the back of her eyes. She hated them. "But they *can*. All we have to do is convince them!"

"That could be a tall order, Heidi, even for you." Isaiah reached up and ran his thumb down her cheek. "You have always been full of hope and life, and able to persuade others to do the impossible. It's what I've always admired about you."

He admires me? How could that be when she'd lost her hope, her love of life? More than anything Heidi wanted to deserve his admiration. She wanted to get back what she'd lost, but how?

Her questions faded with the sear of his touch. She couldn't breathe, but this kind of panic was something much different than her anxiety attacks.

One side of the tent collapsed in on them, jerking her back to reality.

"Hey!" Isaiah yelled.

"What's going on in there?" Cade peeked inside. "Get the bags and get out. You're wasting time."

Heidi didn't recall ever seeing Cade that haggard, well, except after Dad had died in an avalanche. That had been tough on all of them. But Cade had been through something terrifying before when Leah, who had since become his wife, had been stalked by a police detective.

Exiting the tent, Heidi realized everyone had already packed up—and they were waiting on her and Isaiah. Had everyone been listening in on them? Isaiah's words of admiration still burned inside her heart—he was talking about the old Heidi. That person was long dead.

Still, Isaiah made Heidi want that person back. She wanted her old self to live again.

She wanted to survive this and somehow, someway,

she had to convince Zach to let them go. He watched her, an uncanny look in his eyes as if he knew what she was thinking.

An arctic gust rippled across her, reminding her that she would only get the chance to convince Zach to let them live if they survived nature's worst.

Isaiah's gut churned. The deep snow became an obstacle course even with snowshoes. A person had to be in great shape to negotiate this terrain and the journey was quickly wearing on their so-called climbers as they all tried to keep up with Cade. They'd descended the ridge without incident and now hiked through a snow-filled gap. At least they were heading into the lower elevations, but not fast enough.

Isaiah expected the weather to worsen again before it got better. Jason followed Cade, then came Liam and Rhea. Heidi hiked behind them, and Isaiah was right behind her.

Zach followed them all, never letting them forget that he was looking for a reason to shoot someone. Anyone. Isaiah tried to keep his head down and simply follow through with the task, but he was constantly formulating escape plans. He bet that Cade and Heidi were, too. If only they could get the chance to strategize together. He'd bet that was why Zach kept them apart.

In front of them, Rhea stumbled and sank several feet into the deep snow, letting out a yelp.

"Cade!" Isaiah called for him to stop and come back to assist. That far ahead, he wouldn't be aware of Rhea's stumble.

When he saw Rhea, Cade scrambled back to help Isaiah pull her out.

"Get back." Zach shoved Isaiah. "Liam and Jason will help her."

Rhea flailed in the snow. "Someone help me out of this." She refused Liam and Jason's help. "Zach, help me!"

But Zach ignored her plea for help. He held his gun ready, presumably in case Cade or Isaiah tried anything. Breathing hard, Rhea finally crawled far enough to lie flat on a section of packed snow.

Then Heidi reached forward and helped Rhea back to her feet. When Rhea was steady, she shoved Heidi to the ground. Eyes wide, Heidi gazed up at Rhea. What kind of person accepted help, then returned the favor with a vindictive act? Isaiah figured Rhea had simply taken out her disappointment and frustration with Zach on Heidi. Weird and perverse.

Isaiah reached for Heidi and assisted her back to her snowshoed feet. He didn't know why, but he tugged her to him and held tight. "How are you holding up?"

Stupid question.

Wearing a deep frown, Cade headed back to the front of the pack.

She squeezed harder. "I'm okay."

Zach pulled her away from Isaiah and gestured for Isaiah to get going. "Go on. I'll watch over her."

Heidi's eyes narrowed, and Isaiah couldn't stand the dread he saw there. But she gave a subtle shake of her head. She wanted him to comply so there wouldn't be more trouble.

He grabbed the bag he'd dropped, as did Heidi. All the gear and packs they carried, and some they pulled, made their journey sluggish in the loose snow. They were all loaded down like packing mules. It couldn't be helped.

What he wouldn't give for a pair of skis right now.

Or even better, for his weapon back.

"Get going." Zach started forward, and Isaiah took his place in front of him. He didn't miss the murderous look in Rhea's gaze as she watched Zach with Heidi.

Was that for Zach or Heidi?

In the foreboding environment, time seemed to stand still, making it appear as if they hadn't made any progress at all through the gap. But they pressed on anyway, finally reaching a wide opening where they could see for miles. Then, just as Isaiah feared, the wind picked up to a fierce tempo, swirling blinding snow in their paths, and all around them. Isaiah couldn't see in front of him or behind him.

They were going to lose each other forever.

At one point, Isaiah looked up to see nothing but blinding white erasing any sense of sky or earth or horizon. Vertigo knocked him to his knees. Zach and Heidi stumbled over him into the snow. He gripped Heidi's hand. If they made a run for it, even if they couldn't see where they were going, at least they would be free from Zach.

Pulling her to her feet, Isaiah took off. But Zach toppled him, and even in the blizzard the man wouldn't give up his fight, pressing his weapon into Isaiah's temple. "I should shoot you right here."

"Do it. Go ahead and do it! We're all going to die

anyway," Isaiah yelled over the storm. "We can't see where we're going. I told you this would happen. You're insane."

Cade pulled Zach off and got in Isaiah's face. "We don't have time for this. We're going to die if we don't stick together through this storm."

"What should we do?" Heidi yelled. "It's a complete whiteout!"

"We stop here." Cade grabbed Zach by the collar. "We'll never make it through this."

"How do we put up the tents now?" Zach stumbled back, snow sticking to his cheeks and eyebrows. "What about a snow cave?"

"No!" Cade and Isaiah said at the same time.

"You and your men build snow walls like I showed you last night," Isaiah said, "while Cade, Heidi and I set up the tents. We can do it quickly."

Zach shook his head. He wasn't buying it.

"Look, every second you wait we're all getting closer to death. Hypothermia is a real threat. Rhea looks like she's already there. You have no choice."

The man had to admit Isaiah was right. The group huddled together in a circle while the blinding blizzard that left them unable to distinguish anything, causing them to lose all sense of balance, roared around them. Jason fell to his knees.

"Where's Liam?" Zach asked.

"Liam!" Isaiah called.

Zach started to walk away, but Isaiah grabbed him back.

"No. You'll get lost, too, if you go after him. We'll

shout his name and if he's out there, he'll find us. Start building the wall right here, which is probably not the best place, but it's all we have."

"Everyone, pile your bags and packs right here in one place so we don't lose anything."

"Heidi and Rhea, you guys dig us out as we go."

As long as they kept moving and built the tents and then stayed inside they had a chance.

"With Liam gone, we don't need that extra tent," Cade said. "Let's just put up two for now so we can get inside and get warm and out of this storm."

A half hour later, Isaiah lay on top of a sleeping bag, exhausted, knowing he would have to exit the warmth of the tent every few minutes—although they would take turns—to dig out the shelters to keep from being buried alive.

"I can't feel my toes," Jason said.

"Get out of your boots. Your sock could be wet. We'll get you warmed up," Heidi said. "This small stove, along with our bodies, will raise the temperature inside."

Isaiah opened the vents to release any carbon monoxide. Though it was a low-output stove designed for this kind of usage, he dug around in the pack for the CO detector.

So far no one had gotten frostbite, but that could easily change. Getting inside and warm would go a long way toward preventing those kinds of injuries.

As Isaiah watched Heidi melt snow in a pan on the little stove, his heart filled with warmth. He was relieved to be sharing a tent with her and Jason this time.

Rhea had insisted she stay with Zach, and he wouldn't allow the rescue team their own tent, of course, leaving Jason to guard Heidi and Isaiah, which meant Cade was with Zach and Rhea.

Isaiah wouldn't try anything. He didn't have the energy to fight the man. He had to conserve everything to battle the storm. To keep Heidi alive. He didn't care about himself or anyone else. Cade could take care of himself, and likely Heidi, too, but making Heidi his mission would keep Isaiah going.

There was a time he thought he could have something with Heidi, but he didn't deserve her and now it seemed it wouldn't matter. Except he'd come too far, moving to a new place and changing his name, to lose it all now to this insanity. But he'd do what it took to keep her alive, even if no one else survived.

She glanced up at him, that small smile he loved on her lips. His pulse jumped. He hadn't seen that in so long, and hadn't realized how much he'd missed it. He hated that she was in the middle of this nightmarish rescue, but in her smile, he saw some small part of the Heidi he'd known before the ordeal of last summer that had changed everything for her.

The thought of how he'd distanced himself after they'd grown close slashed his insides. And then she'd needed him after the accident, but he'd failed her. He should have been there for her, but getting close again would only risk hurting her in the long run.

"Here, drink this. It'll warm you up." She passed the cup to him.

Their fingers brushed. "Thanks."

He was all too aware of their proximity. Did she feel it, too? And even if she did, he wasn't sure what difference that made. He'd already decided she was off-limits to him. Had already put the wall up between them. He could almost be grateful for the raging blizzard outside, and the unintentional chaperone and criminal sharing the tent.

He sipped the warm liquid from the cup, but Heidi did much more to warm his insides. Maybe being in the tent with her hadn't been a good idea. A guy could only control his emotions so much. But he felt better knowing she was safe for the moment, and that was in line with his mission.

Jason drank up as well, and dozed in the corner, barely holding his weapon within reach. Some kind of guard he was. Still, this wasn't the optimal situation for any of them to perform well in. And what did it matter if Isaiah wrestled the gun from him if they all died in the blizzard?

Finishing his drink, Isaiah pulled his gloves back on and shrugged into his coat, tugging the hood over the knit cap he'd switched out with his helmet. "I'm going to dig us out."

Isaiah stepped outside, the shock of cold and snow jolting him as though he hadn't been prepared for it. He began the laborious task of removing the snow and caught a glimpse of Cade doing the same for the tent next door. Any other time, this would have been fortuitous—the two of them outside and alone. They could make plans. But there was no way to do that now.

Over by the snow wall that buffered the wind, the

snow had already piled high over their bags. Another bag lay a few feet away, an odd look about it.

Isaiah trudged over. Grabbing the bag, he tried to tug it back with the rest. It rolled over. Liam's stone-cold frozen face stared back.

SEVEN

Stretching, Heidi blinked, her mind slowly registering the gray of morning filtering through the tent.

And something else.

It was quiet. The wind had ceased to snarl around them. The storm had stopped.

Sitting up, she glanced about the tent. Jason stopped snoring and shifted, but Isaiah was gone. He'd already gotten up and out without disturbing the man guarding him.

Peeling out of the sleeping bag, Heidi crawled over and unzipped the tent.

"Where do you think you're going?" Jason grumbled. "Hey, where is everybody?"

Heidi hesitated, then turned to look at him. "I think everyone is packing up. And I think the storm might be over."

Relief washed over Jason's face. He blew out a breath. "Almost dying in a plane crash was bad enough. I don't want to go through any more of these storms."

Compassion kindled in Heidi. "I'm sorry you had to

go through that. You know, this probably won't be the only storm we wait out, but we'll try to get you to the ice field as fast as we can."

He nodded, and got out of his sleeping bag.

Heidi zipped the tent completely closed. If she couldn't persuade Zach, maybe she would bring Jason over to her way of thinking. He seemed to have warmed to her. "And if we do that, Zach is going to let us go, right? I mean, a deal is a deal."

Shrugging, he averted his gaze.

Disappointment swelled inside her. She'd try another tact. "How did you get involved with him anyway?"

Jason swiped his light brown hair from his face and narrowed his eyes. His cheeks were puffy and red, and his expression reminded her of a young child. "I didn't wake up one morning and decide I wanted to rob an armored car, if that's what you think. But I'm in it now, and Zach is calling the shots. He's just crazy enough that I have no intention of offering up information like I did before. You can quit with your interrogation."

So he wouldn't be so easily persuaded to share what he knew about Zach's plans.

Heidi ignored her disappointment. "No interrogation. But even though you somehow got in with Zach, it doesn't mean you have to keep going down this road. You have choices, you know?"

"That's easy for you to say. I got no more choice right now than you do."

"Why do you say that?"

"I'm not talking to you anymore." His gun within

easy reach, Jason pulled on his boots, shuffled around, found his coat and gloves, and donned them, as well.

When he started for the tent exit, Heidi moved aside and let him go through first. Well, it had been worth a shot. Still, she'd seen something behind his eyes. He wasn't as hard-hearted as he wanted her to believe. Everyone, even bad guys, had something good inside of them. Maybe Heidi was crazy to believe the way she did, but she hoped to find Jason's soft spot and connect that way. It might be their only chance.

Heidi started out of the tent only to face Isaiah on his way in, his nearness taking her breath, like always. She scooted out of his way.

"What's going on out there?" she asked. "Where did you go?"

"The sky's clear for now." A grin crept into his somber expression. "It's going to be a sunny day."

"Oh, Isaiah." Relief swept over her. But they weren't out of this yet. "I'm amazed we made it this far. But that still doesn't answer my question."

He started rolling up the bags. "I went to explore what we'd face next, see where we've been and where we need to go. I didn't go far."

"And nobody saw you? Stopped you?"

He shook his head. "Everyone is too exhausted. These guys aren't accustomed to this much exertion. Frankly, neither am I."

He sent her a wry grin, along with a chuckle.

"Why didn't you try to get a radio and make a call for help?"

Pausing, he looked up at her. "How do you know I didn't?"

Words caught in her throat. She studied him, her heart pounding. "Did you?"

He focused on the sleeping bags again. "I tried. Couldn't get through."

"Isaiah, what if Zach had caught you?" She crawled closer. "He'll kill you if he finds out."

He started to speak, but she pressed her hand over his mouth. "Don't say he's going to kill us anyway. I don't want to hear it. There has to be another way. I talked to Jason this morning."

Isaiah scowled. "You're not going to talk us out of this. Jason is not going to help us."

"Then why don't we overpower them, get the guns back? Something." She hated the trembling that crept into her voice along with a rising panic.

"If we get the chance, we will. But I need to tell you something." Isaiah gripped her shoulders.

"What is it? Is it Cade?" *Oh, God, please no…*

"No, no." He hesitated, then, "I found Liam's body yesterday." Another pause, then, "I haven't told anyone yet."

Heidi shrank back, tears surging. She'd presumed he'd died. They all had. How could he have survived out there? But to find his body…

Covering her mouth, she sobbed softly. Isaiah pulled her to him and held her. His arms felt strong around her, and she could easily sink into his chest and soak up his confidence, his reassurance. Everything about Isaiah that she admired. And Heidi wanted so much more from him, but she couldn't bear the thought of getting hurt again. Isaiah had been the first one to hurt her. He'd been the one to start her spiral away from trusting in forever, and he'd done it while they were only friends. She couldn't imagine how hard it would be if she let herself love him.

She moved away from his embrace.

"I know the point of search and rescue is to save people," he said. "I don't want to sound harsh, but he might not be the last person to die as we make it through these mountains. Do you understand what I'm saying?"

Heidi nodded. The harsh environment would pick them off, one by one, despite the best efforts of the search and rescue team. Then they could worry about fighting whoever was left. But she didn't get the chance to voice her thoughts.

Outside the tent, someone shouted.

Gunfire resounded through the mountains.

"Stay here." Isaiah scrambled from the tent, praying Zach hadn't suddenly decided to shoot them all now.

Zach stood a few yards away from the tents where Cade and Rhea had paused from digging out the bags. Had he found the body?

The man holding the weapon turned, spotted Isaiah, and the game was over. "There's the man of the hour."

Uh-oh.

Zach strolled toward Isaiah looking as if he would toy with him, maybe even kill him. Isaiah stiffened when Zach looked from the gun to Isaiah. "Rhea said she saw you leave the camp this morning."

"Just scouting around to see where we need to go, that's all."

"With a radio."

"She was mistaken." Isaiah kept his face straight. "Radios don't work out here." Depended on the radio, of course.

Zach shot a look at Rhea. Isaiah feared she would argue with him, try to convince Zach that Isaiah was the liar, but terror filled her eyes instead. The control this guy had over his people should be more than terrifying, but Isaiah hoped to use it to his advantage.

Heidi tromped up behind him.

His gut clenched.

I told you to stay in the tent.

He wanted to whirl on her and send her back, but he stood his ground. Didn't move. Didn't flinch. Didn't act as if he cared.

Unfortunately, that wasn't enough to fool Zach. The smirk that Isaiah was growing to hate filled out Zach's face as he studied Heidi.

"What was with the gunshot?" Isaiah hoped to distract him.

"I fired off a shot to bring you back from wherever you'd gone, and to remind everyone who is in charge. And it worked. You showed up, and everyone is shaking in their snowshoes."

"Come here, sweetheart." Zach motioned for Heidi to come closer.

Isaiah almost threw his arm out to stop her. Push her behind him. But doing that would only put her in more danger. Zach was becoming drunk on his sense of power and the money he lugged around with him. Isaiah had to bide his time until he could take Zach down for good.

Though he hated that someone had died, there was one less person for him to fight. When would Zach bring up his friend? Mourn his loss? Did he even care?

Heidi hiked over to Zach, and Isaiah didn't miss Rhea's hateful look.

Zach snatched her to him. Cade flinched at the same moment Isaiah stepped forward, reacting before he could catch himself. And that was the worst thing he could do. Zach would take that and run with it. Toy with them in painful ways Isaiah didn't want to imagine.

The man pulled her even closer and smelled her hair in an overly dramatic fashion. "I love the smell of lavender."

Zach's gaze stabbed Isaiah. It took everything inside him not to take the bait.

Isaiah clenched his teeth, squeezed his gloved fists and stared Zach down. They would have their moment to face off.

"Rhea, bring me the radio."

Rhea glared at Zach and Heidi, but did as she was told, handing off the device.

Isaiah thought he'd been as discreet as possible earlier when he'd tried to establish radio contact with the command center. Everyone had been snoring. He'd taken a risk, yes, but what else could he do? He'd lied when he'd said the radios don't work here. Sometimes they did. Same with the SAT phones. It all depended on a lot of factors. But he still hadn't been able to reach anyone.

In the silent winter wonderland around him, in the terror of the scenario unfolding, his heartbeat resounded in his ears. Isaiah prayed hard. *God, please. I know what I said earlier, begging You to let the radio work, but I want to reverse that request now.*

Zach tried the radio.

They all listened to the static as the sun peeked over the mountains from the east.

"If we have any chance of making the ice field, we don't have time for games." Cade dug their bags and packs filled with supplies and gear out of the snow. "Like Isaiah said, radios don't always work out here. We're in the mountains in a dead zone."

"Why'd you take the radio, then?"

"I told you, I didn't." Okay, so that was a lie, but it was unavoidable. He stood his ground.

Cutting Zach's interrogation short, Isaiah ignored him and hiked over to help dig their gear out, keeping his head down. Cade was right to bring Zach's focus back. Another storm could come through and bury them for good this time. They had to make it all the way out of this gap between the mountains that created another ferocious wind tunnel before it began all over again.

When Isaiah knew that Zach had lost interest in grilling him about the radio, or using Heidi to taunt him, he blew out a breath. In his peripheral vision he saw Zach, Jason and Rhea breaking down the tents. He and Cade should do it, to make sure they didn't destroy their only protection against this environment, but he needed a moment to steady his nerves, rein in his anger.

Cade grabbed a snow-covered bag near Isaiah, leaning in. "I'm surprised you held it together."

How well Cade knew him. "Thanks for jumping in when you did."

"The radio wasn't the issue. I jumped in to protect all of us, but especially my sister. It's obvious that Zach has picked up on your affinity for Heidi."

Isaiah shrugged, digging another bag out. "I haven't done anything to encourage him, Cade. You have to know that. I haven't responded to any of his taunts. I wouldn't do that to Heidi. He just doesn't like me. That's all."

Cade's eyes were colder than the air. "You're going to get her killed."

"What do you want me to do? Walk off the next cliff?" Isaiah wished he could take the words back.

Breathing hard, Cade straightened to his full height. "Just keep your head down and stay out of trouble. Don't leave the camp again. Don't try *anything* again."

"Have you got a plan then? Because I'd sure love to hear it."

"Sure I do. I plan to get the group to safety. We're taking them to the ice field. We have to believe a search and rescue team will find us by then. David will figure out something has gone wrong soon, if he hasn't already."

Isaiah wanted to believe in Cade's plan. He really did. "This guy isn't going to let them find us, and besides, we have to warn them, Cade. We can't allow more people to be put in danger."

Since Cade was clearly delusional, finding a way out of this mess was up to Isaiah.

EIGHT

They hiked in snowshoes throughout the morning, but at least the sun broke through the clouds and warmed them, though Heidi knew that another snowstorm was on the way. And when it came, the inclement weather would be like a recurring nightmare. Torturing them during the day, too.

Facing the harsh Alaska environment was one thing, but she'd never imagined herself in this predicament. Not in her worst nightmares, recurring or not. This journey couldn't end soon enough. And yet she almost dreaded the end, especially after Isaiah's words.

They can't let us go.

Would she face her death, then? Watch Cade and Isaiah be executed?

Heidi shoved aside the foreboding thoughts, though they stayed at the edge of her mind. She wished she were hiking closer to Cade and Isaiah. Instead, Zach kept her near him at the back of the line so he could use her to control them. Cade led the way as they hiked out and down toward the base of the mountain, followed by Jason, Isaiah, Rhea and then Zach with Heidi.

Rhea tried to hang back so she could be near Zach, the man she claimed to love, but he kept urging her forward. If only he would pay attention to Rhea and reassure her of his affections. After her talk with Rhea, Heidi hoped she'd convinced the woman she had no plans to steal Zach away. The very idea made her shudder.

"What's going through that pretty head of yours?" he asked.

His question repulsed her. Rhea glanced back and glared at Heidi.

"I'm thinking about what's up ahead. We got a short reprieve from stormy weather and from any serious climbing. But there's more to come. And we're all exhausted." How would they survive this?

"Those energy bars don't stay with you long, do they? I'm hungry again. Aren't you?" Zach's attempt at a normal conversation fell flat. What did he think? That he could change the way Heidi thought of him?

"Yeah, I'm hungry, too," she admitted. They were burning up their energy reserves quickly, and running out of supplies.

Rhea slowed and hiked next to them, and this time, Zach said nothing about it. "Do you think we'll need to use your climbing ropes again?" she asked. "That was the worst experience of my life."

Heidi nodded, pleased that Rhea's thoughts were now turned to the dangers ahead, and not Zach's misconstrued interest in Heidi. At least she hoped Zach had no real interest in her. She ignored any warning thoughts to the contrary, burying them deep.

"Mine, too. But we won't have to climb at night during a storm if Zach doesn't force us to."

She hoped Zach wouldn't push them, if it came to that.

At her comment, he scowled at Rhea. "Get back up there, you're slowing us down." Once again he urged Rhea ahead.

By the time the sun had crawled to late morning, almost lunch, Heidi's stomach had been rumbling for over an hour. They only had a few energy bars left and would need to save them, or else start on the MREs. David would be expecting them to show up where Isaiah had said they would be hiking down, but he'd been forced to misdirect the rest of the team who presumably waited back at the command center. How long before David sent helicopters out to search for them? Would they look for them in this region, and could they even spot them if they did?

She felt Zach's eyes on her. She had no doubt he would force them to hide. But maybe a helicopter would spot their tracks before the next storm came through.

Please, God...

Ahead of them, Cade stopped, his rigid form reminding her of their traumatic scale down the ridge two nights ago, only this morning they wouldn't have to use their night vision goggles. The group crowded together near the edge of a jagged escarpment.

No one said a word, but their shared dread was palpable.

"Why did you lead us this way?" Zach shoved Cade.

"It doesn't matter which way we go, we're descending from the mountain summit. That will involve a combination of hiking and rappelling. No way around it. You wanted to make the ice field, this is the only way. It was your decision to put fast over safe."

Venom filled Zach's laugh.

"Look at it this way." Isaiah dropped his backpack. "It will be a breeze compared to the last time we did this."

Exactly the way Heidi saw it. The only difference was these guys could now see what they were facing and they might panic or cause problems.

Whimpering, Rhea covered her mouth. "I can't do that! Not again. Please, don't make us do this, Zach."

Heidi's heart went out to the woman. She had panicked the first time she'd been assisted down a ridge, and she hadn't been able to see into the dark abyss beneath her. Now she had to be a hundred times more terrified.

"Shut up. We don't have a choice."

"The burden is on us," Heidi said. "We're the experienced climbers, so you don't have to do anything but trust us. Just like last time."

In a way, the power now shifted back to the search and rescue team. A tenuous smile crept onto Heidi's lips. She hadn't meant for the words to give her any sense of power, but they had all the same. She dropped her backpack and gear and moved to stand next to Cade and Isaiah. Unfortunately, Zach didn't let her stray too far from him.

"So what are we doing? Same as last time?" Isaiah asked.

"No other choice." Cade searched for an anchor point. "Anything else and people die."

That odd sense that things were not right with the world dinged her thoughts. They were working hard to assist this group safely down a mountain—a group that had every intention of killing them when it was over. Insanity ruled the day.

Heidi sighed and gazed down the gash in the valley of the mountain fold they'd been following. They were tiny, insignificant creatures in this wild topography. "It's going to be close. That's a long drop. Our rope needs to be twice that length."

Isaiah flicked his gaze to Zach. The look in his eyes chilled her more than the icy landscape. "Doesn't matter. We're going down."

Dropping his backpack and gear, Zach shifted uncomfortably. Had it occurred to him that the SAR team might attempt to deliver him down the escarpment in a risky fashion, ensuring their own safety?

"I'm heading down and will receive the packages." Geared up to rappel, Cade dropped out of sight.

Rhea's face paled. Maybe she didn't like being referred to as a package.

Isaiah pulled out the seat harness they'd created from the tubular webbing. They would then lower Zach and his friends the entire distance, though, like Heidi said, it was going to be close. Heidi set up the anchor point for the operation and clipped in the carabiner for the belay device. She was vaguely aware of Jason, Zach and Rhea watching as she and Isaiah prepared everything to lower them. Were they aware of the fact they were putting their lives in search and rescue team's hands? The very team that they had abducted? The whole thing was surreal.

Heidi barely registered that Rhea had meandered over to where she worked. She glanced up and something in Rhea's eyes made Heidi take a step away from the staggering, jagged-edged drop-off.

Rhea bumped into her.

Hard.

More like shoved.

Heidi teetered before stumbling into a granite boulder that broke through the snow. Her heart jumped to her throat, lodged there and pounded. She could have gone over the edge, falling hundreds of feet to her death.

Had that been Rhea's intention?

Her knees screaming, Heidi wanted to cry out, too, but stifled her reaction. She rolled away from the rock into the soft snow, praying she wasn't too injured to hike out, or else Zach would kill her. Of that she had no doubt.

She'd slow them down, and he wouldn't accept that. He'd made that plain enough when he'd killed one of his own people.

"What was that for?" she asked.

Rhea leaned over her. "I warned you to stay away from him. Next time, I'll make sure to shove you off a cliff."

Heidi gasped. "I've already told you I have no interest in him. He's a criminal, and he's all yours."

Rhea's frown deepened as though she considered

Heidi's remark an insult. Heidi hadn't intended it as such; she was simply stating the facts. Rhea could take it however she wanted.

Gripping her knees, she glanced up to notice Zach watching the two of them from where he stood at the ledge. She forced a straight face, hoping to hide her pain, and attempted to stand, but fell back in the snow. His face pale and drained, he hiked over. Maybe that was from watching Jason being lowered down the ledge. Served him right.

"What are you two doing over here?" He directed his harsh tone at Rhea. "You need to pay attention to what's going on, so you don't get yourself killed. Got it?"

Rhea shrank away from him, then glared at Heidi as if Zach's scolding was her fault. The woman opened her mouth to speak, but then Zach grabbed Heidi's hand and assisted her up, a concerned smile on his face. Was he for real?

Not good. Not good at all.

Heidi hadn't done anything to garner his attention or smile. Couldn't Rhea see that? But his beam didn't win Heidi any points with Rhea. And this time, he didn't appear to be using her as a way of taunting Isaiah or her brother. But she'd buried her fear that he might actually be attracted to her and instead hoped and prayed he was simply using her as a pawn.

Back on her feet, Heidi saw that Isaiah had turned from the edge of the escarpment and spotted the three of them. The power of his dark gaze crossed the distance and held her.

Oh, Lord, please don't let him interfere. Or try something that would get him killed. She wouldn't put it past him to risk it all to save her. Funny to think that even though Cade was her brother, and an overprotective one at that, it was Isaiah who was acting this way. And something in Isaiah's fierce watchfulness ignited her feelings for him—emotions she'd tried to keep buried. She missed their easy friendship, and wished he hadn't pushed her away. But even if he hadn't, Heidi couldn't trust anyone with her heart.

She'd keep telling herself that. Except, as she watched Isaiah moving toward them, she knew if she could trust anyone with her heart, she'd want that someone to be Isaiah. Good thing her mind reigned over her heart.

And then he stood there in the mix—between her and Rhea and Zach. Heidi admitted his presence brought a measure of relief.

"Isaiah." She exhaled his name.

Her mind and heart battled for control.

Now she understood how Rhea had known Heidi cared for Isaiah. Hopefully Rhea would see that again now, just a little, but if she recognized it, then unfortunately, Zach would, too.

As if he answered Isaiah's unspoken but tangible challenge, Zach stood taller, the exhaustion in his features morphing into aggression.

Somehow Heidi had to defuse the explosive tension, and fast.

"What's going on here?" An idiot could see that Heidi was hurt. "You guys need to get ready for the ride down."

Isaiah knew not to draw attention to the fact that Heidi was somehow injured—if Zach didn't already know. Heidi succumbing to an injury could lead to the criminal-in-charge putting her out of her misery. Isaiah had every intention of facing off with the maniac right here and now if that's what it came to. After all, half the men were at the base of the cliff. Isaiah could take Zach down if he could separate him from his weapons.

True to form, Zach tugged the gun from his pocket and pointed it at Heidi. Would he do this every time?

Isaiah threw up his hands in surrender and took a step back. "Whoa! Whoa! What are you doing?"

He'd caused Zach's reaction. Why did he always have to be the reason a woman suffered? Heidi blanched, her eyes pleading with Isaiah. Powerless, there was nothing he could do except back off. But more than anything he wanted to take Zach down and bury him deep in the snow, then wrap his arms around Heidi. He wasn't worried about Rhea. As a threat, she was a nonissue.

"Just reminding you who is in charge." Zach's smirk grew broader.

"Put the gun down." Palms down, Isaiah slowly lowered his hands. He knew he'd come on too strong in his attitude. "We need to get going so we don't get caught in another blizzard. We won't make your rendezvous if we do." Isaiah wasn't sure they would make it in time even if they *didn't* catch another storm.

Deep inside, Isaiah wanted to hope, as Cade did, that making the rendezvous would be their freedom. But no matter how hard he tried, he knew it couldn't be true. Weird that they had to rush toward this one goal that would only end their lives. They were running toward death itself.

He glanced at the blue sky. Ominous clouds were building in the distance once again. Why couldn't he hear the welcome sound of rotor blades? David had to suspect something was wrong by now. But then what would Zach do? Hold them hostage?

"Let's do it then." Zach lowered his weapon, though he kept it at his side, and marched to where they'd rigged the ropes. "Just remember, your man Cade is being held at gunpoint at the bottom, should something happen to any of us." The man chuckled. "We're in control. We're always going to be in control. Don't think you can pull a fast one."

Isaiah blew out a breath. He was right, of course. The way things were, they could never gain an advantage. It was too risky to try something that could end in harm to one of them. Right now, guiding these creeps through the mountain wilderness was all they could do. Until their chance for an escape came.

Rhea tossed one last glare at Heidi, and even one at Isaiah, then followed her man to the edge. That's how it would be with her—that is, until Zach had a reason to leave her behind. Isaiah shook his head, and when he thought it was safe—Zach and Rhea were caught up in a conversation of their own—he turned his attention to Heidi. Cade was probably wondering what had happened to Isaiah. They needed to bring the seat harness back up for the next rider.

But Isaiah had to make sure Heidi was all right. Really all right.

She took a limping step toward him, and he closed the distance. Caught her up in his arms. For the briefest of moments he allowed himself to savor the embrace, then he put an arm's-length distance between them, gripping her shoulders.

"Are you okay?" Isaiah pinned her gaze. Searched it. He wanted the truth.

She nodded. "I will be. My knees are bruised, that's all."

He glanced over his shoulder to make sure Zach and Rhea were still occupied. He had to hurry. Cade was waiting on him to manage the rope at this end. "What happened?"

"Rhea. She tried to push me over."

The news stunned Isaiah. So Rhea wasn't a nonissue, after all. Isaiah had to make sure that Heidi wasn't left alone with that woman for even one minute, especially when they set up camp again. He'd make sure he was in the tent, too, to keep them apart.

"Get over here," Zach called, reminding Isaiah that he wasn't in charge and couldn't control if Heidi was left alone with Rhea.

"You know to keep your guard up around her, then."

The words sounded completely lame when all he wanted was to reassure her that he was there for her. But why would he do that now when he hadn't been there for her when she'd needed him those months after the accident? Why would she believe him?

But that's all he could say. He shouldn't make promises that he couldn't keep.

"I know. If I hadn't stepped back when I had then

she would have been successful in her attempt." Heidi looked down, sucking in a quick breath. Then another.

Okay. So Isaiah would make those promises now. He couldn't let her fall prey to a panic attack in front of everyone. But he'd made promises before. And someone had died in the end, and all because of him. Isaiah closed his eyes for a split second and buried those thoughts—they wouldn't do him any good here. Wouldn't help Heidi now.

He opened his eyes. "Look at me."

Her gaze drew up to his. Beautiful dark brown eyes, the color of black coffee. He'd been drawn into them the moment he'd met her. What was the matter with him? He couldn't think about that now. "Breathe, just breathe slowly and calmly. I'm here for you. I won't let anyone hurt you."

Pain flickered behind her eyes and knifed through him. He'd caused that pain, and he wouldn't deny his own guilt. "Do you believe me?"

His pulse slowed as if with time—he hadn't realized how important her answer to his question would be. Reluctance surfaced behind those dark irises. Doubt, heavy and suffocating, swirled in them.

Heidi nodded slowly. *She nodded.*

Isaiah couldn't believe it. Why was she lying? But maybe, just as he *wanted* her to trust him, she *wanted* to trust him, despite his actions in the past. Despite the fact that he'd severed their emotional connection just as it had grown strong. Maybe she was simply taking a leap of faith.

"We'd better get those two down the cliff before Zach

gets crazy and does something stupid." She stepped away from Isaiah, freeing herself from his grip and standing tall despite her injury.

Good. She was breathing okay now, too. Heidi was a strong woman, and Isaiah didn't doubt that for a minute, but this situation pushed each of them to the edge, and would likely test their limits before it was over.

NINE

Isaiah grimaced. Rhea screamed all the way down as they lowered her. Just like last time, only much worse. Her screams echoed through the mountains. Were there any searchers out there to hear her?

Cade and Jason signaled from below when Rhea was safely at the bottom, and Isaiah pulled the rope and harness back up. He glanced at Zach.

"You're next."

"What, and leave you and her here to run off? Not going to happen."

The last time, Isaiah and Heidi had rappelled after the last person was lowered. But Zach wasn't willing to trust them this time.

"Look, man, we're not going to leave Cade behind. We're not running off. You don't have a choice, unless you can climb."

"I can."

Suspicion crawled over Isaiah. As if he needed another reason to be wary of this man. He shared a look with Heidi. Zach had kept silent about his skills, keeping it from the SAR team and his partners. What was the man up to? "Why didn't you say something before?" What other skills did he possess? Maybe he really knew how to handle that gun.

"There was no call. I couldn't scale the mountain that night without goggles anyway."

True, all true. That had been one of the toughest mountain-climbing experiences of Isaiah's life. But he suspected the man had other reasons for keeping his climbing skills to himself. Whatever his reasons, the others would find out now.

"So you're next, and I'll rap down with Heidi last."

Isaiah's chest squeezed. Maybe this is how it felt for Heidi when she couldn't breathe. No way would he let that happen. He stepped in front of her, blocking Zach's view. "That's not how it's going to be. I don't know how strong of a climber you are. It's you and me."

On that point Isaiah wouldn't give. Setting his face like flint, he made sure Zach felt it in his gaze. Zach fingered the weapon in his pocket, but his hesitation was evident.

Heidi moved from behind him, and Isaiah instinctively knew she wanted to protest. She, in fact, was the better climber. He thrust his hand back and gripped her arm, willing her to stay still, to understand.

"You and me then."

"But—" Heidi stepped forward.

"You take the harness and we'll drop you down, Heidi." It was quicker and Isaiah didn't want to give Zach a chance to change his mind.

Heidi's expression told him she didn't like the way

he'd handled this, but neither of them wanted to argue in front of their mutual enemy. After she was secured in the harness, Isaiah and Cade worked to lower her. There just wasn't enough rope to do it any other way. This was what it felt like to not be in control of your life. He'd much rather cling to the mountain—feel the grip of solid rock beneath his fingers. Somehow, he was sure Heidi felt the same way. Especially when he caught her glance up at him, the fear tracing across her face.

Then it was time for Isaiah to see just what skills Zach had to offer. And it was time for Isaiah to ask the question that had been burning in his gut from the beginning.

He reworked the ropes so he and Zach could rappel, bringing the rope down with them as they went.

"Why'd you do it? Why'd you commit a robbery?" And how much money had he robbed? Had to be a lot if it was an armored car.

Zach looked surprised at his question. "Why do you want to know?"

They started down, Isaiah first, setting the rappel stations, and Zach following. This might be the only time he had the guy alone. "I'm not sure how to explain that."

Despite the temperatures and the snow and ice, the sun warmed him beneath his coat. "You'll be on the run for the rest of your life," he added.

As he rappelled, he gained clarity in his thoughts and emotions. The fresh air and exhilarating climb pushed adrenaline through him. He found the reason and held on to it. He wanted to understand because, in a way, he was like Zach. Isaiah was running, too, only he hadn't committed a crime. But that hadn't seemed to matter. People were suspicious of him all the same, and it had been enough to ruin his life. Make his neighbors and friends wary of him in the small Montana town where the murder had occurred.

He would never have chosen to leave, if not for those circumstances out of his control. And yet, it had been within his power to stop. He'd veered slightly and that small tangent had taken him far off track.

Zach grunted above him, making his way down. He hadn't answered Isaiah yet. Maybe he'd never considered the question, or never thought that it would be asked. But when he drew near so Isaiah could hear, he answered.

"I was a nobody from nowhere, that's why. Nobody paid me any attention—that is, until I started planning the heist. Now I have Rhea, a beautiful woman, by my side. And she's jealous of Heidi."

Now Isaiah understood. Zach was using Heidi for more than leverage against him and Cade. But the way he said it, Isaiah knew the man believed that Heidi returned his attraction.

Isaiah would never purposefully harm someone, though he'd been questioned by the police for the murder of a woman he loved, but anger burned so deep, and protectiveness ignited so bright, that he could almost imagine himself causing Zach to fall to his death. He reined in the thoughts, knowing that God was watching. Always watching. And that wasn't the way to handle their predicament.

He hadn't been able to prevent Leslie's murder. God help him, but he wanted to protect Heidi.

He should have done something to protect Leslie when it became clear that her fiancé had a violent history. But what? The police hadn't listened when it mattered.

And this time, even with God looking on, would he have to actually kill someone to protect another?

At the bottom of the cliff, Heidi watched Isaiah and Zach scale the cliff face, grateful that snow and ice hadn't clung to the rocks on this side. She'd been as stunned as Isaiah at the news that Zach could climb. But right now, her pulse thrummed in her neck—would Zach do something to harm Isaiah? The man had seemed to look for a reason to hurt Isaiah from the beginning.

Not to mention that Isaiah had stood up to Zach moments ago and Zach had backed down. Would he want to exact some sort of twisted revenge?

Cade discussed their path to the ice field with Jason, while Rhea sat on the bags, nursing her imaginary wounds from the trauma of being lowered to the bottom. She ranted, going on about how she hated amusement parks. Could never ride the roller coasters. That this had been the worst day of her life.

Granted it was quite a breathtaking drop, and Heidi understood Rhea's pain. But, though Heidi hadn't liked sitting in the seat harness either, she couldn't help but harbor some satisfaction in Rhea's discomfort, and smiled to herself before glancing back up to Isaiah.

Even in April, the days weren't that long, and especially up here, the sun dipped below the mountain range far too early. High in the sky, the sun now prevented her from seeing Isaiah, so she moved closer, into the shadows of the cliff he rappelled.

Isaiah and Zach. What an odd pair they made.

They were moving at a good pace and worked together as though they'd been doing this for years.

"Come on, Isaiah, slow and steady," she whispered under her breath.

I'm here for you. I won't let anyone hurt you. The moment he'd said those words they'd wrapped around her and squeezed, sending her heart and mind back into a raging battle. Oh, how she wished those words were true, that she could count on him, could trust him. He cared about her—she'd seen it in his eyes—and yet he'd been the one to sever whatever connection they'd had together. And Heidi had experienced too much heartbreak since then. There was enough hurt and pain in the world, and she wouldn't subject herself to it ever again.

Hot tears surged in the corners of her eyes.

Oh, not now. Not now! She refused to swipe at them and give herself away. In her peripheral vision, she saw Rhea push from the bags and meander toward her. Not again. Heidi didn't want to talk to the woman. Why did she have to be fixated on Heidi? For that matter, why did Zach have to be fixated on her? Heidi kept her focus on the two men almost down the rock-faced cliff.

Zach had made Rhea hate Heidi with his smiles and attention. If only there was a way that Heidi could avoid interacting with either of them, but Rhea had given her those creepy eyes from the first moment she'd seen her. That should have been warning enough. Now she was making her way over to Heidi.

"How are your knees?"

The gall.

"They're fine. I'm fine."

"Could have been worse." Rhea laughed her deep, hoarse laugh. The laugh of a smoker.

Yeah. Thanks for nothing. Heidi didn't appreciate her facetious jab at almost killing her. *God, what do I say to this woman? What do I do?*

Hiking in this terrain was no easy task, and if Rhea was a smoker she had to be struggling. Even though she'd wanted to avoid Rhea altogether, Heidi turned to her. "How are you holding up? This has to be really hard for you."

And she meant the words. Would Rhea see that? The woman studied Heidi, searched her gaze as though she wanted to believe her. Heidi recognized the questions in Rhea's eyes. How could Heidi sincerely care about Rhea? How could she be sympathetic or wish her well? In truth, Heidi struggled with those same questions, but she reminded herself that Rhea was misguided. How would she ever make it off the wrong path if no one stopped to show her the way?

For an instant, Heidi thought Rhea trusted her, had received her kindness. But if she had, even for a moment, Rhea hid it behind her narrowing gaze.

"Oh, you're good, really good. Trying to make me think you care." Rhea hiked away from Heidi toward

Zach, who'd finished his climb down. She glanced back at Heidi. "You watch your back."

Why had she wasted her breath on that woman? Bile rose in her throat—she hated her reaction to Rhea's threat, but couldn't overcome it.

Carrying the ropes and gear, Isaiah hiked toward Heidi, his tall frame and lithe form filling her vision, and unfortunately making her heart swell. Heidi imagined they were in another time and place and Isaiah caught her up in his arms. But that was in a world where people didn't cheat on each other, didn't forsake each other. That wasn't this world.

I'm here for you. I won't let anyone hurt you.

But you *hurt me, Isaiah. You.*

Even though Isaiah's look begged her to believe in him, she allowed the sound of Cade's voice calling her name to cut through the power that held her there, and she turned her back on Isaiah.

TEN

With only a few hours left in the day, they pressed on, making as much headway as they could while light remained. Isaiah leaned his head back, gleaning a little warmth from the sun as it broke through one of the few clouds skittering across the heavens. It almost seemed strange to finally see deep blue sky after the bombardment of storms they'd been through. So far the clouds had abated, and the group was left to trudge toward their ominous destination without any hitches.

Once again, Cade led the pack, not that Isaiah resented him. Cade had grown up in the region, knew everything there was to know about it, even the coastal range that bordered with Canada.

Isaiah thought back to his disagreement with Cade, who wanted to deliver this group to the ice field and hope for the best. He wasn't up for risking an escape or going for the guns. He believed David would send a SAR team to find them, and would probably be among the searchers himself. Adam, too. Isaiah prayed for the best outcome, too, but he wasn't one to do nothing if there was another way. At least he and Cade could search for that way out, but it looked as if Cade was given to his own plan. The guy hadn't said two words to Isaiah since their disagreement. Not that there was much opportunity for conversation with a killer pressing at their backs. But Cade had been more aloof with Isaiah, tossing him cold, accusing stares. Willing Isaiah to follow his lead and not stir up trouble for them.

He had a point on that. Isaiah didn't want more trouble.

Sounded as if Zach had enough trouble within his own ranks, though. The killer, who was pulling up the rear, was engaged in a disagreement with his cohorts.

Unfortunately, Heidi trailed Isaiah, forcing her to walk closer to crazy Zach and his girlfriend, who looked a little off, too. But a glance behind him told Isaiah that Heidi no longer walked next to Zach, who had slowed even more to argue with Rhea.

Isaiah had made Heidi a promise. He had the gut feeling it was a promise she didn't want, maybe didn't need, but he was more worried it was a promise he couldn't keep. Regardless, he'd made it—and Heidi had no idea what drove him to want to protect her. She could never know.

Isaiah suspected the reasons went much deeper than the trauma of his past. Even if he hadn't been close to a murder victim, blamed himself for her death and been considered a person of interest, he would have made the promise to Heidi.

There. He admitted it. Felt good, too.

He'd forced emotional distance between them to protect her from him, and to protect himself. But more often than not, he wondered if that had been a mistake. He couldn't deny he was drawn to her and every time she looked at him he saw the hurt in her eyes, though it decreased every day.

She was getting over the hurt. That was a good thing, wasn't it?

Yes and no. Isaiah couldn't help but feel the pain of loss. But none of that mattered in this insanity. What mattered was that Isaiah would protect Heidi. He'd never doubted that, but now he'd voiced the words to her, and that made her even more vulnerable because she might just trust him enough to follow through.

Sure, she could hold her own, and true, her brother Cade would do anything it took to keep his sister safe, but Isaiah wanted her to know he was there for her, too. He would make a difference when it counted. He *had* to make a difference this time.

Isaiah had been hiking fast enough to keep up with Cade's relentless pace, but Isaiah slowed, letting Heidi catch up with him. She kept her head down for the most part, focusing on putting one foot in front of the other. This was an endurance test they would all have to pass.

Behind them, Rhea continued to argue with Zach. Jason grumbled, as well. When Heidi looked up at Isaiah, he recognized the concern in her eyes over the discontent among the criminals. He felt it, too.

What would their grumbling mean for Cade, Isaiah and Heidi?

Isaiah slowed down even more to see if he could make out their conversation. If there was something other than a field of snow ahead of them, he might suggest that he and Heidi and Cade make a run for it. They could hide. But Cade would likely argue that they might be gunned down before they could ever find cover.

Soon enough, Zach would realize their formation had gone awry and Heidi would likely be in the back with him again, but for now, Isaiah needed to know what they were saying.

"If you can't get ahold of him how do you know he's going to be there?" Jason asked. "He's dumped us, that's what he's done. We're on our own."

"Shut your mouth, do you hear me?" Zach again.

"I'm so tired now. How are we going to make it?" Rhea whined. "Can't you have him pick us up somewhere near here? Get a helicopter or something."

"Both of you, shut your traps."

The pause in conversation implied that they feared Isaiah was listening. Time to redirect things. "Tell me about your photography?"

"Huh?" Heidi stumbled a little.

"We want them to think we're engrossed in our own discussion," he said under his breath.

"Oh, yeah, well, I think photography has kept me sane these past few..." Heidi let her voice trail.

"Months?" he finished for her. He hadn't meant for the conversation to turn serious, but she'd opened that door. "Heidi, I'm so sorry about everything that happened to you." *Including any part I played in it.*

"I didn't think I'd ever get over the day Jenks fell and died. I should have done something to keep it from happening. Some search and rescue team member I am."

"Hey, it wasn't your fault, Heidi. Never was." He knew others had told her that repeatedly, but she'd been unwilling to accept it.

He wasn't sure he would've reacted any differently had he gone hiking with friends and someone fell to their death. After all, they both assisted people who'd made poor judgment calls and were trapped or lost or injured in the wilderness. To have that happen on her watch had crippled her.

"No point in arguing about whose fault it was," she said. "It happened and it changed me. I'm coping better now. But then came Lon and the fact that he was married."

She conveniently left out that before the accident, and before Lon, Isaiah had stepped back from their growing friendship, hurting her. Nor had it helped that Isaiah had been the one to tell her about Lon.

She cut him a look. "I resented you at first, but you told me the truth and I should thank you for that. I just wasn't thinking clearly at the time."

"I know." His voice was husky.

"And then to find out about Dad cheating on Mom, and that we have another sibling out there we don't even know, made me think I could never trust again." She shrugged. "It all seems so trivial now with being abducted like this. Forced to lead these people through dangerous terrain, risking our lives for them. I don't know if we're going to live through this, Isaiah." She glanced up at him then, her lovely brown eyes that could coax anything out of him caressing his face.

Isaiah's heart floated. He shouldn't react to her this way, but how could he stop?

"These are big mountains," she continued. "We've made enough headway and we're far enough off our original path that I don't know how we'll ever be found."

"Your brother believes all we have to do is deliver these guys, and we'll be on our way. I hope it's that simple, but I don't see things happening that way." Isaiah wished he could take the words back. He needed to reassure her, not scare her more.

"We don't have much choice, except to hope that helicopters are searching for us already," she said, "but they have a lot of ground to cover before the next storm erases our tracks. So the coming hours, days, could be our last."

"Don't talk like that. You have to believe we'll be okay. You have to trust God. I know you do." Now listen to him, trying to convince her to trust God when Isaiah was struggling with that very issue. He believed they'd have to make their own way out of this. He wasn't even trusting God himself.

"You're right, I do. But people die every day."

She was right.

Leslie's face drifted across his mind. He hadn't known she was engaged at first. He'd fallen hard for her, and he'd thought she returned those sentiments. Then when he found out about Aaron, he'd thought he could change her mind. Why would she want to marry a man with anger issues? A man that would hurt her like that? When it became clear that she had every intention of going ahead with her wedding, and that Isaiah had only put more strain between her and her fiancé, he'd finally decided to back off. Should have done it much sooner. He'd gone to break things off for good, but he never got the chance. He'd been the one to find her body.

No matter how far he'd moved away, no matter how much distance he'd put between himself and his past, and how much effort he'd poured into starting a new life, those images would never leave him. His knees buckled and Isaiah caught himself, brushed the images aside. At least his past was nudging him to do the right thing now—tell Heidi while he had the chance.

"Heidi... I'm sorry for pulling away from you. Sorry if I hurt you." There was so much more to it. So much more he wanted to say.

She stared at him. "You didn't."

She'd lied.

The clouds resurfaced again and finally moved in, as though reinforcing her somber mood. Stomping along behind Isaiah as the snow fell thick and hard, wiping away their hope of someone spotting their tracks, Heidi couldn't get the look in his eyes out of her head. He'd hurt her all right, the moment he'd gone all nonchalant on her. She'd never forget that day, a defining moment in her life.

She wasn't sure when their relationship had started exactly, but she'd been sure when it ended, at least for her. Isaiah began giving her rides home after search and rescues. After work at the Avalanche Center they'd hang out together. Get dinner, or a soda, or catch a movie. Just friends, all along. Neither of them ever crossed that invisible line. But over time, they shared a few looks. Three years of that and Heidi's heart grew attached to Isaiah in ways she could never explain. His friendship meant the world to her, and his presence wrapped around her, protecting her and making her feel cherished.

Should a girl feel that way about a guy who was nothing more than a friend? They never talked about it, but she had a feeling he understood what she was thinking. She felt the attraction and suspected Isaiah did, too, but stepping over that line, becoming more than friends, would mean they'd risk losing what they had.

Maybe having more with Isaiah was worth the risk. And that's why that one evening while they waited on Cade and Leah to return from Seattle, she'd found herself looking into Isaiah's eyes and letting herself wish for more. Found herself wanting to trust him completely. She'd seen something similar in his eyes. Her heart had leaped at the possibility of freely loving him.

And her head had spun when the longing behind his gaze had shuttered closed, hiding his feelings from her. Everything about Isaiah had changed that day. His smiles weren't personal and special and just for her anymore. She could have been a stranger off the street, the way he treated her, though he was never unkind.

But he'd been scared that day. Apparently something more with Heidi hadn't been worth the risk to Isaiah, and yet his fear had shut down the friendship they shared anyway. He changed his work schedule so he no longer worked the same shift.

Nothing had been the same between them. After the

hiking trip that ended with the loss of her friend, Heidi had needed Isaiah and he'd failed to be there for her. His choice. After that everything had spiraled downward and sent her into a darker place.

She couldn't stand to let Isaiah know that he'd held enough of a place in her heart to hurt her. But if he knew anything about her, he'd know she had lied. Still, her words had cut him all the same. She could see it in his eyes.

Her pain.

His pain.

But none of what she'd gone through compared to this nightmare. *Oh, Lord, please give us hope. Help us out of this somehow. Use us to show these people Your love and grace. Just...show up.*

The prayer lifted from her heart, but she'd never felt so alone. God was there. She knew He was, but why couldn't she feel Him? Get a sense of His presence?

What about all those verses in Psalm 139? She'd meditated on them, used them to help her get through her most painful moments, and yet here she was hiking through the wilderness and slipping back into the darkness.

She whispered to herself, "'If I say, "Surely the darkness will hide me and the light become night around me," even the darkness will not be dark to you; the night will shine like the day, for darkness is as light to you.'"

Where are You, God?

No answer.

But Heidi knew that her heart was too strung out. God's answer always came in the form of a still, small

voice in her heart. And she always recognized His voice.
No matter that the situation seemed hopeless, she would
cling to Him the best she could.

And, as if He'd answered, the snow stopped falling,
and the sky peeked through the dense clouds, if only
a little. After her hurtful words to Isaiah, he'd left her
behind, hiking on ahead, but he glanced back now and
caught her gaze. He remained every bit the pillar to her
that her brother was, and that made no sense.

Isaiah stopped.

He stood at attention and peered into the sky.

Heidi heard it, too.

A helicopter!

SAR had finally found them.

Oh, thank You, God!

The sound grew louder as the bird flew closer. Heidi
couldn't contain her excitement. She searched the skies,
waving her arms up and down. Jumping, too.

Something slammed into her, knocking her into the
snow. Yanked her up by the arm. She gasped for breath.

Zach.

He dragged her, waving his gun around. If Heidi
could have managed it, she would have knocked it out
of his hands. But his grip on her was too strong, and his
brutality intimidated her. He'd had the exact opposite
reaction to the sound of a rescue helicopter.

This helicopter would not be a friend to him.

"Run to the rocks and hide there or I swear I'll kill
her!" He jammed the gun against her head and dragged
her through the snow as if she weighed nothing.

Heidi only caught a glimpse of the terror on Isaiah's

face, but they all ran for cover. No waving or catching the helicopter's attention. And the snow had covered most of their tracks from earlier. The mountains were beginning to eclipse the sun and whatever fresh tracks they'd made would likely go unnoticed from the air.

Running for her life through the deep snow, stumbling and falling, being snatched back up and dragged, Heidi felt her strength, her willpower melting. She operated on autopilot, keeping up with Zach and the others in order to survive. How had her life of saving and rescuing people twisted into this perverse experience that sucked the life from her?

If she made it back to Mountain Cove, life would never seem hard to her again. She would celebrate and be thankful. She would count even the smallest of blessings. She would connect with people she missed, she'd bridge the gap between her and Isaiah. Somehow. Someway.

They made it to the shadows of a spire that thrust high into the gray sky. The helicopter wouldn't fly nearly close enough to see them crouched behind where rocks sprung from the spire and other outcroppings, which had escaped being buried by snow and remained a dingy gray themselves. Only Heidi's bright fuchsia jacket could draw attention from the sky, and Zach had her tucked behind the rock to prevent discovery.

"Anyone make a wrong move and I'll kill you all." The words seethed from him, his hot breath a shock against her cold cheeks. How she hated feeling him this close to her.

Squeezing her eyes shut, she tried to calm her racing heart, slow her panicked breathing.

You are my Rock, God. You are my Rock, God.

The helicopter drew near. It was right there. If only they could jump out and wave. David had to be worried sick about them and must have contacted the Alaska State Troopers for a new search—one sent out for the search and rescue team themselves. Maybe they even knew about the armored-car-robbery fugitives. Knew what was going on. Then again, maybe they didn't have a clue.

Regardless, she, Cade and Isaiah were powerless to signal their would-be rescuers.

Zach had her pinned against the rock so hard, the gun pressed against her temple, she gasped for air.

Breathe in. Breathe out. An image of when Isaiah had said those words to her as this nightmare had only begun flashed in her thoughts. That seemed like an eternity ago. She opened her eyes.

Isaiah and Cade leaned against the rock opposite her, Isaiah's eyes locking with hers. In them, she saw the promise he'd made.

I'm here for you. I won't let anyone hurt you.

How she wanted to believe him. But right now, with Zach pressing his body over her, preventing her from signaling for help and rescue, Isaiah's promise fell flat.

It was dead to her.

ELEVEN

His gut twisted. The helicopter moved away, skirting the mountain in search of them.

He should have risked it. Should have fled the safety of cover and waved them down. So what if Zach shot him? That would be an even bigger mark against the guy. Didn't he know that? But Isaiah couldn't risk Heidi's life.

In fact, he was done watching Zach hurt her. He jumped to his feet, envisioning the instant he'd yank the man away and maybe take the gun from him, too. Cade held him back, but Isaiah shrugged free. It didn't matter.

Isaiah didn't have to get in Zach's face.

Jason beat him to it. He pulled Zach to his feet, the surprise clear on Zach's face.

"Why did you make us hide? That helicopter could have been our way out!" Jason's face grew even redder than it already was from the cold.

"What are you talking about?" Zach shoved Jason. "We can't let them know where we are, or who we are. Can't let them see us."

Jason jabbed Zach's chest with his finger. "You said that no one would know who we are. No one would know where we're going. What makes you think the helicopter pilot would? Or was it all a lie?"

Rhea appeared confused by the whole thing, unsure which guy she should side with.

"Watch your mouth or I'll give you another bloody nose. I didn't lie to you. We just can't risk it. Even if the pilot didn't know, these guys would tell them."

"You could just hold them hostage, threaten to kill them and hijack the helicopter."

"Yeah, at least we'd be out of this frozen wilderness." Rhea added her opinion.

Zach's own people were ganging up on him. Isaiah shot a glance at Cade. Was this good or bad for them? The conflict would definitely grow worse as they continued their trek, and they would need to be prepared to take advantage of it, but only when the time was right.

Heidi had crawled away from Zach and stood up near a rock. Isaiah didn't think that Zach would see or care that he went to Heidi at the moment. Cade joined him, and took his sister in his arms. Isaiah had wanted to do that, but Cade had more right than he did.

"You okay?" Cade asked.

Her smile tenuous, she looked at Isaiah around Cade's shoulder. "Of course. How are you holding up?"

Cade released Heidi, and she stood there awkwardly, staring at Isaiah. Did she want him to hold her? No, he was reading her wrong. She'd made it abundantly clear, at least with her words, that she had no real feelings for him. And that was the way he wanted it. It was best for the both of them.

Then why was his heart pounding against his ribs, fighting for a way out?

He'd let her down, letting Zach manhandle her like that. But the man with the gun ruled them all, at least for now. The two men were still arguing, but Isaiah only cared about Heidi. She hung her head.

She was strong. Didn't need Isaiah to hold her together. But maybe he needed her. He was the one with trembling knees at the moment. He needed her to keep him strong. A pang zinged through him at the startling reality.

Isaiah ignored all the warnings inside his head and stepped forward, dragged her into his arms and held tight. *God, when will this be over?*

He wanted, oh how he wanted, to kiss the top of her head. To tell her how much he cared. But what would that accomplish in the midst of this chaos except to leave them both confused? So Isaiah said nothing at all. Just held on to Heidi, soaking up her goodness, willing her to know that next time he wouldn't let Zach get away with any of this.

That was another promise he couldn't keep. No, Isaiah wouldn't stand in Zach's way until he knew he could win without Cade or Heidi getting hurt.

Zach finally punched Jason, and they got into a scuffle on the snow-packed earth. Heidi and Isaiah parted to watch. Cade took a step forward. Maybe they could grab the guns.

On the other hand, maybe the weapons would go off

and kill an innocent bystander. Before Cade or Isaiah could react, it was all over.

Zach hovered over Jason. "I don't care if you're my brother. Challenge me like that again and it will be the last time."

He crawled off the whimpering man.

His brother?

Now, that was news, though it made sense. Zach hadn't cared about Robbie, the man he'd shot back at the saddle. He hadn't mourned Liam's death, nor did he seem to care a lot about whether Rhea was around, but Jason—he cared about Jason, despite his threat.

And maybe they could use that fact against Zach. Unless Zach cared more about the money, more about his survival than he did his own brother.

"Let's set up camp here. The rocks will protect us from the weather and it will be dark soon." Cade barked orders at them, his gaze landing on Isaiah.

Isaiah understood that Cade wanted to diffuse the tension to keep crazy Zach from shooting off his gun and his mouth again. They set up the tents, used the camping stove to melt snow for water and prepared the MREs. They'd run out of energy bars and would now be subjected to the food Isaiah detested. He'd hoped this would all be over before it came to that.

What's more, they were quickly running out of fuel. Zach stomped around the campsite with a scowl, and Rhea whimpered, afraid of the man she loved. Jason was in a rotten mood, too, leaning against the supplies and eating the last energy bar. He held a weapon now, charged with guarding his rescuers.

Heidi crawled into the tent she would share with Rhea, reminding Isaiah that he needed to figure out how he could protect her from a woman who wanted her dead. He hated to think of Heidi lying awake all night on guard for her life.

But with their captors at a distance and preoccupied, this was his chance to strategize with Cade. "What's the plan?" He kept his voice low, focused on melting snow for water.

Cade only grunted.

"Look, I know something has been eating you for weeks now. Just put that aside. We need to figure out our escape. Whatever reason you're mad at me can wait."

"I don't think that it can."

"What?" Surprised at his response, Isaiah poured melted snow into a cup and handed it to Cade.

"I see how you are with Heidi, so it can't wait."

Isaiah stiffened.

"I know about your past, Isaiah. I thought I knew you pretty well, considering the amount of time we spent together, but even then I always thought you were hiding something."

Isaiah sat back in the snow. "What do you know?" And he could guess how he'd found out. Had to be Leah, his legal-investigator wife, sticking her nose where it didn't belong.

"I know that you were a person of interest in a murder that was never solved. You changed your name and moved here to assume a new identity." Cade's look of betrayal filleted Isaiah.

Was Cade accusing him of the murder? If he felt that

way, how could the guy even climb with Isaiah? How come he'd waited so long to confront him? "Please tell me you don't think I'm guilty."

Isaiah needed to hear that Cade trusted him.

"I don't want to think you're a murderer. No. I can't make myself believe that. So no, that's not it. It's that you hid all that from us, from me personally. You hid who you are. It's a trust thing with me. I thought I knew you, Isaiah. Thought I knew who you really are. But then I find out I didn't know you at all."

Isaiah absorbed Cade's words. He had expected to hear them at some point. He drew in a breath then dived in. "Cade, I meant no harm. You have to understand…"

Isaiah didn't say more. What could he say? The man had serious trust issues after learning of his father's infidelities. But Isaiah had to try. "Look, I'm innocent, but having people—a whole town of people—suspicious of you is like being guilty. I might as well have been guilty as far as they were concerned. So I wanted to start over. Is that so bad? I'm sorry that I didn't tell you sooner, but it wouldn't be much of a new life for me if I brought my past with me, would it? What if every time I looked at you, I saw that same suspicion in your eyes?" And in fact Isaiah had recognized it in Cade— he just hadn't wanted to believe it.

"Can't say that I would have done things any differently, but you're not the guy for Heidi so stay away from her."

Back when Isaiah and Heidi were growing close, when something was happening between them, Cade hadn't been happy about it. In fact, he'd been relieved when Isaiah had stepped away from Heidi. Maybe that was because of the secret he thought Isaiah carried, and now he knew the full of it.

As if Isaiah could stop caring about her here and now, especially in this situation. He'd really tried, but who was he kidding? He'd tried and failed miserably to not be seriously into Heidi Warren. Fortunately, that didn't matter—Heidi was definitely not into him, and he couldn't bear to break her heart after she heard about his past. Cade was sure to tell her if he hadn't already.

Isaiah couldn't look at the man. Resentment burned in his gut. "How did you find out?" He already knew, but wanted to hear it from Cade.

"Leah."

"I can't believe you had someone look into my background." Had Cade done it because he was worried about Heidi?

"It just…happened. A connection to another case she was investigating that took her all the way to Montana."

"I don't get it. Why now? Why did you wait until this moment to confront me?"

Cade exhaled long and hard. "I've trusted you in every way that counted, since we're on a SAR team. I tried to give you the benefit of the doubt that you had your reasons for keeping this a secret, and frankly, I just didn't know how to bring it up. I thought it was a moot point because you and Heidi weren't as close anymore, but this predicament seems to be pushing all those feelings to the surface. And seeing how you are with her, seeing that look in her eyes, has forced my hand."

Spoken like the overprotective father of a young girl. Did Cade even see that?

"I'm still the same Isaiah that you've known for almost four years now. Thanks for digging up the past I wanted to forget. Thanks for not trusting me." Isaiah stomped off into the darkness that edged their circle of light, feeling the isolation to his bones.

As soon as her tent was set up, Heidi crawled inside to rest on the sleeping bag. She was too tired to be hungry, and while she lay there, she could barely make out Cade and Isaiah talking. It didn't sound as if things were good between them. If only she wasn't so exhausted she might have edged closer to listen in on their conversation.

One thing she had heard clearly was Cade's warning to Isaiah to stay away from her.

Anger churned inside. She didn't need or want him to protect her. At least, not like that. Who did she think he was anyway? He wasn't her father. She could take care of herself. But he was her brother. Her heart softened a little. What kind of brother would he be if he didn't at least try to protect her?

She was capable of defending her heart from Isaiah. At least she thought she was, but all she could think about was the moment earlier—after the helicopter had come and gone, when Cade had finished hugging her. Isaiah had stood there, watching her. It was as if they'd both wanted to embrace each other, but each had held back for their own reasons. It had been kind of awkward and silly and so obvious. But Heidi had refused to give in to her crazy need for him.

That is, until she'd seen the longing and the desperation pouring from his gaze. All pretext washed away in the harsh reality of this dangerous adventure. Heidi almost had the sense that maybe it wasn't about Heidi needing him, but that Isaiah was the one in need.

Big strong Isaiah. Hard to grasp that he needed anything.

That image still dancing in her mind, Heidi rolled on her back and stared at the tent ceiling in the growing darkness. She heard footsteps outside and saw the silhouette of a man passing between the tents.

Isaiah. He'd left the unpleasant conversation he'd had with Cade. She had a feeling it was about more than her. She allowed her thoughts to drift back to that moment when Isaiah had taken the step forward and grabbed her arms, tugged her to him. She'd gone willingly. And yes, she needed him, too. Not as a person who would watch her back on this journey, but as something much more. Something she couldn't even define, but she sensed its light in her soul growing bigger, kindling, instead of being snuffed out completely. With everything she'd been through, she thought that light had all but died.

She savored the memory of being in his arms for no other reason than just being there, and she'd allowed herself to soak him up. Frankly, she was too exhausted—both emotionally and physically—to keep fighting what she felt for Isaiah, even though he'd hurt her.

But something told her that he'd had his reasons.

Good reasons. She'd never known Isaiah to do anything without thinking it through, and that was something she could take to the bank.

Ugh—the thought of the bank brought her back to the robbery and their predicament and, oddly enough, at that moment Rhea crawled into the tent. Heidi didn't relish the prospect of trying to survive the night with Rhea. She'd likely have to stay awake to keep from being smothered or strangled in her sleep.

"You don't have to worry." Rhea tugged out her own weapon. "Zach gave me orders to watch you. Keep you from running away. He said I'd better not hurt you."

Heidi considered threatening Rhea with their little secret about the money. Then again, that might give Rhea more of a reason to kill her. "I'm too exhausted to go anywhere, aren't you? Besides, where would I go? Without the protection of the tent, I'd just die of hypothermia." Like Liam.

"Zach said you might run after the helicopter if it comes back."

Zach would be right. Heidi rolled over, putting her back to Rhea. She'd had enough of the woman. But maybe she'd give it one more try. "Rhea, remember that first night in the tent?"

"What of it?"

"Remember how you said you thought I was interested in someone?"

Rhea grunted.

"I thought you understood that I have no interest in your boyfriend. None. I thought we connected and had an understanding. You weren't going to tell my secret and I wouldn't tell yours." She thought they'd shared a common bond after their initial heart-to-heart, but Zach had destroyed that.

"I don't have a secret on you anymore. Everyone can see what's going on."

Heidi's pulse raced. She wanted to know what Rhea meant. Hear all the details about it as if they were silly schoolgirls, but she kept quiet. She'd tried to deny it for far too long and that must be why Cade had warned Isaiah away. He saw it, too. Heidi blew out a breath.

"So I got nothing on you. But don't worry, I won't kill you for it tonight."

"Thanks." Heidi didn't bother to hide her sarcasm. She had a few surprises for Rhea if the woman thought she could take Heidi out so easily.

TWELVE

The next morning they packed up the tents and prepared to hike on.

Before Cade led the group out, Isaiah held his gaze. "We're out of fuel."

"We'll be at the ice field in a few hours." Zach stepped close to Heidi.

Isaiah couldn't wait for that moment at the end of this ordeal when he would get some personal face time with Zach. He couldn't know for sure that he would get that chance, like the good guy did with the bad guy at the end of an action-adventure movie, but he could hope.

"We're not going to make it, sorry." Cade pulled on his pack. "At least not today. Not even by tonight."

"What are you talking about?" Zach ground out the words.

"Like Isaiah says, we're out of fuel, which means we don't have water. We'll get dehydrated. We need supplies."

"So we eat the snow."

"No. We have to melt the snow and heat the water or die of hypothermia," Isaiah said, catching Heidi's gaze.

She had that fire in her eyes as if she was about to knock Zach's nose into his brain. With Zach holding the weapon, Isaiah wasn't so sure now was the time, but any other time, he'd say, sure, go for it.

"What are you saying, exactly?" Jason inserted himself into the conversation, but with obvious caution. "Sounds like you know where we can get supplies."

Cade nodded. "There's an off-grid cabin just a few miles out of our way, but in the same general direction. A summer cabin, but maybe it will have items we could use. We should head there and stay tonight. Get what we need, then we can make it to your destination tomorrow, alive and well."

"It's a trick," Rhea said. "Zach, they're playing us. They're going to take us into an ambush."

"Shut up." Zach tucked his weapon way. "This isn't the Wild West."

His reaction confused Isaiah. "It's no trick," Isaiah said. "Without basic necessities our chances of surviving decrease exponentially. I don't think we'll make it otherwise."

A severe frown creasing his exhausted features, Zach studied Isaiah as though weighing whether or not to ignore their advice. "You don't *think*? There's a small window of time for me to make that rendezvous."

"You, Zach?" Rhea asked. "What about us? We're all going to be on that plane out, aren't we?"

"We, I meant to say we. How many times do I have to tell you to shut up?"

From the look on Rhea's face, it appeared Zach certainly wasn't good at keeping his friends. Isaiah wondered why she continued to take it. Unfortunately, they were all stuck following Zach for the moment.

"Zach, we're not going to meet the plane if we're dead." Jason kept his distance from his brother. "Call him up and tell him what's going on. Put him off a day. I don't want to die over money. Not even…" Jason caught himself before sharing the amount.

Zach probably thought Cade, Isaiah and Heidi wanted to steal the money and that knowing the amount would make it even more worth their while. Right. The only thing important to the three of them was their lives. Zach could have his money, no matter if it was a million dollars or more.

While Zach, Jason and Rhea argued over risking the rendezvous point and stopping for supplies, Isaiah looked from Cade to Heidi. They each harbored their own brand of conflict with him, it would seem. But despite the tension between them, Isaiah hoped they could put their differences aside and work through this problem, which was quickly heading toward a fatal ending. Still, the future was unwritten. It could be changed.

Heidi gave an imperceptible nod, then Cade.

For years, they'd worked together on a SAR team, so they had that going for them. They knew each other well, and Isaiah knew then, they all shared the same thought—they had to make a move soon. The cabin would have to be it. But what would the move be? What could they do that wouldn't get one of them killed?

Though Isaiah didn't want to die anytime soon—he was only human, after all—he definitely wouldn't stand by and watch Cade or Heidi come to that end. Not while he had breath in him.

He'd racked his brain a thousand times to try to think of what he could have done differently, that is, besides not becoming involved with Leslie. Hindsight did him no good. What could he have done to save her? Too many questions with no answers, questions he couldn't afford to leave unanswered this time.

Zach was talking. Isaiah hadn't been listening.

"We're getting supplies at this cabin, but I don't think I need to remind you what's at stake if this is a trick. All you have to do to make it out alive is deliver us to the ice field and to our ride out. Don't try anything or I'll have to choose which one of you will live to lead us out. In case you're not any good at math, that means two of you will die in these mountains."

When Heidi spotted the cabin tucked behind a thick copse of evergreens, hope surged, and she picked up her steps. They all did. The trek through the mountains without any real shelter other than the tents had been long and arduous. No surprise there, but she'd always believed she was in top physical condition. Yet this experience challenged her beyond belief—and she was already stretched thin emotionally.

Maybe spiritually.

The snow wasn't as deep here, and they all hurried toward the cabin.

Isaiah got there first and appeared to jiggle the lock, Heidi wasn't sure. But he finally kicked the door in. Breaking and entering? But it was survival. Palpable relief poured from each of them as they filed into the dark, rudimentary cabin.

Cade got busy making a fire.

Isaiah found a kerosene lamp and lit it, then shone it around the cabin in search of supplies. Heidi wanted to follow but Zach closed in on Isaiah, maybe afraid Isaiah would come across a weapon of some kind.

While she helped Cade build a fire, she eyed the woodstove in the corner. Could they get that going, too? She could really use a cup of hot tea. Even coffee would do. Would it be possible they could find hot chocolate? She almost laughed at her racing thoughts. She was wishing for too much.

A frown under his brows, Cade was focused on his task.

"How did you know about this place?" she asked.

"Isaiah and I came across it while we were in the helicopter making our avalanche assessment rounds."

"Is it government property?"

"I don't know, but I doubt it would be stocked if it was. Likely private. Maybe even shouldn't be here."

Interesting. "How did you *know* it would be stocked?"

Cade glanced up at her. "I didn't. Still don't, but a fire like this, the warmth of a cabin, of a roof over our heads for even one night is enough, isn't it?"

She nodded. "It is."

For the first time since this ordeal began, she started to think maybe they would survive, despite the odds—though Zach remained their greatest threat.

Jason whooped across the small cabin. "Food. It's like we hit the jackpot."

"Never thought I'd be excited to see a can of beans." Rhea pulled cans off the shelves, letting them fall to the floor.

Heidi blew out a breath. "You don't have to make a mess of things. This place doesn't belong to us."

"Hey, you're the one that broke in." Jason stumbled around the room.

The fire blazed, drawing everyone closer. Cade stood and faced the enemy. "I'm sure the owner wouldn't mind us using the cabin if it's a matter of survival. But we don't need to take advantage of or abuse his or her property. And I plan to repay them for anything we use, and include an explanation and a thank-you note."

"Aren't you thoughtful?" Zach ogled the canned food, uninterested in the debate.

"Can we get the woodstove going, too?" Heidi asked. "Warm up some food. I see a water pump, so we might not need to heat snow for water."

"Already on it." Isaiah stepped out from the bedroom and started to work on the woodstove, a smile on his lips.

Heidi worked the pump, hoping she'd get water.

"Listen up." Zach raised his voice. "We are not here to get cozy and comfortable. We are here for those supplies, then we move on."

Rhea moaned. "I thought we agreed to stay tonight. Hike out tomorrow."

"I couldn't make contact."

"Well, try again," Jason said.

His own crew was ganging up on him again. Zach toyed with his weapon. Heidi wondered if he'd consid-

ered cleaning it while they were here. After their journey, the weapon might even malfunction. She'd watched
Cade cleaning his weapons often enough, heard him
talk about it. As for Heidi, she didn't like guns. Hadn't
needed to use one with so many brothers packing.

Zach growled and frowned. He was losing control
over his partners-in-crime and had to be exhausted, too.
He left the warmth of the cabin to try to make contact
with their ride on the SAT phone. Rhea and Jason followed, leaving Cade, Isaiah and Heidi all alone.

For a second, they stared at each other. "Should we
make a run for it?" Heidi asked. "We could flee out the
back. They wouldn't see us. Wouldn't know until it was
too late and they'd never find us."

"Don't kid yourself," Cade said. "We have no way to
protect ourselves if they find us. They have their weapons *and* ours. Two of them are carrying, maybe three,
though I haven't seen Rhea with one."

"I have." A pot of hot beans and what other real food
she could find might keep them distracted longer. If
only Heidi's mouth didn't water at the thought. She used
a can opener she found in a drawer and opened several
cans of beans, then poured them into a large pot. She
searched the cabinets for salt, seasonings and spices.

"The risk is too high," Cade said. "I don't want anyone to get hurt."

"Three of us couldn't make it." At the stove, Heidi
kept her voice low while she warmed the beans. "But
one of us could break free. Go for help."

Oh, why had she said that? She couldn't stand the
thought of losing either Cade or Isaiah. What if one of

them escaped but didn't survive? Or what if Zach killed whoever stayed behind? "Scratch that. I... We should all stay together. It's the only way."

"I think she's on to something." Isaiah spoke to Cade, didn't even look at her.

He was trying to cut her out of the decision. Heidi fumed, but kept her thoughts to herself. She knew they had little time, if they could even pull off an escape at all. The others would come back inside too soon. She swallowed the knot in her throat.

"Then it has to be her. She can be the one to get away."

The two men stared at each other long and hard. Heidi felt as if she wasn't even in the room.

"Guys, I'm here, right here. I need to be part of this conversation, and no, it's not going to be me. I wish I hadn't said anything." No way could she leave anyone behind.

Cade left the fireplace and stood behind Heidi. He turned her around. "I think Isaiah was right when he said that Zach isn't going to let us live once we get to the ice field. Why should he? We know who he is. It would be days, weeks, maybe even summer thaw before anyone found our bodies. The only way out is now. You have to leave. You have to be the one. We'll sneak some supplies into your pack and you go for help."

"But if I leave, then he'll kill you."

"No. He still needs a guide to the pickup point."

Isaiah stood too close. "You're burning the beans."

"Oh!" Heidi gasped. She removed them from the stove.

This time it was Isaiah who turned her to face him. "Your brother is right. Someone has to live. Someone has to call for help somehow. We'll cover for you."

"You're in the outhouse or something."

Heidi frowned.

"I have a better idea," Cade said. "Two of us go. Zach won't kill the one who stays behind, which will be me. I know my way around. I'm the only one who really knows how to get him there anyway," Cade said.

"Then why don't we all just leave now?" Heidi shook her head, hating their few options.

The cabin growing warm, Isaiah shrugged out of his coat. He scraped his hands through his hair. "I don't like any of this."

Her thoughts exactly.

"My idea is the strongest." Cade moved to the fire and warmed his hands. "But I hear voices outside and they're coming back in. We missed a chance to run, but we had to talk it through first. At least we had an opportunity. Let's agree on this. It's tonight or never."

"This evening, after they've eaten and they're tired, I'll take Heidi and we'll go for help." Isaiah slumped. "Are you sure about this, Cade?"

"It's the only way."

Like Heidi, Isaiah didn't appear convinced, but it was too late to discuss it further. Zach trudged inside, followed by his cohorts. His eyes grew wide when he saw the bowls of beans laid out for them. Heidi busied herself opening cans of tuna, as well.

"Who would think beans would ever look and smell

so good?" Jason sat at the table and started eating as if he was famished.

"Did you reach your person?" Heidi asked. "I mean, are we staying tonight?"

"Why? Are you planning an escape?" Zach sneered.

"No." Heidi answered too quickly, she knew. Her pulse raced.

"Because let me be perfectly clear." Zach stepped closer. "Surviving the wilderness in tents while a blizzard is blasting away is one thing, but this cabin is much different. I'll need to tie you up tonight. If even one of you escapes, you'll hear the screams of whomever you left behind echo through the mountains."

Shaking, Heidi stared at the floor. She didn't dare glance at either her brother or Isaiah. But Zach's threat rendered her helpless. It seemed strange that they were reduced to this…groveling to a maniac in order to survive.

THIRTEEN

Warmth from the fire suffused the cabin. Isaiah noticed everyone growing sleepy as exhaustion took hold, especially after filling their stomachs with the beans and tuna. If they made it out of this alive, he and Cade would make sure to replace all the group had taken from the cabin. Could be that the owner had left the supplies for just such an occasion.

Zach had not bothered to tie them up like he'd claimed, but Isaiah figured at some point he would get to that. Isaiah would do the same, if he were in Zach's position. Though in this warm and cozy cabin stocked with food, he and his gang seemed less intimidating than the dangers one could meet with if exposed to the elements outside, which made fleeing a less appealing option at the moment.

If they were bound, it would mean their chance of escaping according to their plan was dead. As he helped Heidi clean up the dishes in the small kitchen, only the dim light from the gas lamp and the fire across the cabin to illuminate their chore, he wondered what she was thinking.

Her lush chocolate mane fell forward, though slightly askew and tangled, and hid her face as she cleaned the bowls. Hiding her thoughts from him. As if he could read them if he could see her face—but there was a time, months ago, when he had felt that close to her.

The moment overwhelmed Isaiah.

The guard he'd put in place shifted. His resistance falling away, he surrendered and pulled her curtain of hair back, exposing her flushed cheek. Heidi slowly turned toward him and looked up, emotions he couldn't read pouring from her eyes. Well, one of the emotions he read well enough. Like a magnet it compelled him forward, tugged him closer, until his face was mere inches from hers. Her breath warm and soft against his skin, Isaiah did something he'd longed to do for months, maybe even since the moment he met her almost four years ago.

He covered her lips with his own, only the quiet and dim lighting protecting them from unwanted spectators. He felt her sweet and tender response, and beyond that, the flutter of confusing emotions that mirrored his own. Regret and loss mingled with longing, hopes and dreams. Isaiah held passion and desire in a well-guarded dungeon. This wasn't the time or the place, but now that he'd done the forbidden and kissed her, he wanted to somehow convey that she was a precious treasure that he cherished. The fierce protectiveness he'd always harbored for her washed over him, even in this moment.

He cupped the silky skin of her cheeks, and her response nearly undid him. If only he could wrap his arms around her and unleash all his buried emotions, show her everything she meant to him.

The thought jarred him as if he'd fallen through a frozen lake.

Isaiah severed the connection, tugged away from her lips.

Heidi's eyes were soft at first, then widened when realization hit her, just like it had him. The rogue environment had washed away his guard. Made him weak and he'd given in to it.

"Heidi," he whispered, his voice throaty. He should apologize for taking advantage of her and the situation. But he couldn't apologize for that kiss. Why hadn't he kissed her long before this? If he had, maybe everything would have been different between them. And now this moment had been their first kiss, shared at the worst possible time and place, under the watchful eyes of criminals and killers.

What did that say about Isaiah and Heidi's relationship? Did it mean that nothing else could ever break them apart, should they choose to build something between them? Or did it mean they were doomed to fail from the start?

By the fire, Jason struck up a conversation with Cade. Jason's words pulled Isaiah completely back into reality. Something about looking for rope to tie them up for the night. Isaiah wouldn't bother helping him. All Jason had to do was dig around in the mountain-climbing-gear packs.

Isaiah and Heidi continued with their chore, as though the kiss had never happened.

Had Cade seen them? Had anyone else noticed? Maybe they were all too overwhelmed with their own worries.

Once again their predicament weighed on Isaiah and he realized he wasn't thinking clearly. He shouldn't have kissed her, after all, letting his deepest feelings for her surface. His weakness appalled him. He shouldn't have any feelings for her. None. Even if he allowed himself to love again, he didn't deserve her.

Heidi reached for a dish, her fingers brushing his, then reached over and covered his hand with her own. She didn't look at him, just kept her head down, but her action conveyed more to him than he could have asked for. The kiss was much more than a moment of weakness for her. She spoke to him in a silent language that sent his heart and mind scrambling to find traction. Maybe he'd been wrong to think that keeping his past a secret was the only way to move on with his life. In order to move on, he had to open up and tell all. Cade and Leah already knew the truth, but Heidi was the most important person in Isaiah's life. He'd admit that much.

And maybe he needed to reveal his past to her.

She glanced up at him, a soft smile inching across her face, and he knew…he *knew* that once he told her—with everything she'd been through—she would be lost to him forever.

Heidi worked to put the dishes back, tucking them into the cabinet nice and neat, doing the best she could to respect the owner's property. She'd also picked up the cans Rhea and Zach had thrown on the floor haphazardly when searching the pantry. Acid burned her insides at their disregard for others, but she shouldn't be surprised, considering they had abducted a search and rescue team and forced them to guide them through the mountains.

The last bowl clinked and, before she closed the cabinet door, Isaiah's face filled her vision.

"Heidi." The way he said her name, the same husky way he'd said it moments before, after he'd kissed her, crawled all over her. She could live on that sound for months.

She thought her trust in love and happily-ever-after's had been tarnished for good—destroyed, more like. But Isaiah made her want to believe in good things again. Was he the right man? Could he make her believe in the possibility of a lasting love? Heidi sucked in a breath. How could she possibly think about a future with Isaiah when they were in survival mode?

"Are we still on for tonight?" he asked, keeping his voice almost too low for her to hear.

His question confirmed she needed to focus back on their reality. She shook her head and whispered, "They're looking for rope. We can't escape."

"I think I can get us out of it."

Another, more vigorous shake of her head. "Didn't you hear Zach's warning?"

"He won't harm Cade. He's his only way out."

"Maybe not right away, but eventually he would."

"That will be all our fates, Heidi, if we don't go for help. This is our chance."

"No. I can't leave my brother alone with the guy who is going to hurt him. We just have to trust God for another way out." *Where are You, God?* Her heart sent up the silent prayer once again.

Isaiah's gaze held hers, the disappointment in his eyes running deep, but mixed with fear and concern for her safety. Fear for his closest friend, her brother Cade. She knew he cared about Cade but both of them were basing this nonsensical plan on protecting Heidi, and she wouldn't have either of them risking themselves on her account. There had to be another way.

"The three of us should stick together. I wish I had never said anything."

It had been her initial idea, after all.

"Then we can all go. We'll all escape together," Isaiah suggested.

"Talking Cade into this won't be that easy, but that's the only way I'll go."

It would increase the chance of Zach following them, but how far could the guy make it without their help?

The seconds ticked by slowly with Isaiah standing far too close. Heidi could hardly breathe. For the longest time she'd known her feelings for this man ran long and deep. Any woman would find him attractive with his broad shoulders and strong, trim physique. Thick hair she wanted to run her fingers through. Deep, penetrating gaze that could see right through her. She'd been caught up in all that was Isaiah at some point, no doubt there. But it was more than that now.

The guy knew how to listen, really listen. She'd never met a guy like that. Or maybe it was just the way his eyes watched as though he lived on every word she said. But he was easy to talk to. All that had changed between them when he'd pushed her away. Not so much with words but with actions, and because he'd stopped looking at her with that penetrating look.

For a while Heidi had thought he couldn't look at her because he cared too much and didn't want her to know it. Or at least she'd lied to herself, convincing herself that was the reason. She couldn't bear to think of it any other way because it was much too painful to think that Isaiah would willingly push her away. That he didn't want her anymore—though they'd never before crossed the lines of friendship, not until moments ago when he kissed her, giving her what she'd dreamed about all those months ago.

But why here? Why now? Heidi thought she might know. Somewhere deep inside, the fear that their lives were coming to an end wouldn't leave her. Maybe Isaiah sensed it, too, and wanted to show her what he hadn't been able to reveal before.

She closed the cabinet, pulling them both out of their imagined private moment, hidden away behind an open door. Heidi wasn't sure why Isaiah had pushed her away in the past.

But that didn't matter because she had reasons of her own to keep her heart far and away from Isaiah or any man. Her head ached. She regretted that kiss, but her heart would never ever forget it. Still, she'd do well to remember the reasons she must try to forget Isaiah and his kiss—even though by tomorrow evening that all might not matter. They could all be dead and buried beneath a field of ice.

FOURTEEN

Isaiah watched Jason tie Cade's hands and feet to a chair. He huffed. If Cade wanted out of that, he could easily break the old rickety chair apart and be done with it. Instead the guy went along with these miscreants like he had no other choice.

Isaiah grew tired of playing this game. They had choices, all right. They could take control of this situation. Should have done it long ago. With Zach and Jason showing severe signs of exhaustion, now would be the perfect time to gain the upper hand. Maybe that's what Isaiah had been counting on all along—that he could outlast these rookies.

Unfortunately, Cade's eyes slid to Isaiah as if he could read his mind. His frown and narrowed gaze were a warning to Isaiah. They knew each other too well. Isaiah had never imagined himself in this situation. Of course, who would? But he never thought he'd be this torn about what to do. He'd never been so indecisive in his life except, well, where Heidi was concerned. But he slammed the door on those thoughts. Nothing mattered except surviving this ordeal.

Even if he managed to break free from the rope and untie Heidi as well, she would likely refuse to go with him as they had planned. Apparently, they still hadn't agreed on what to do, especially after Zach's threats.

There were trees here, plenty of cover if they ran this time. It wasn't as if they would be running across the snow—easy targets for Zach to shoot at—which had been the terrain for their entire trek until the cabin.

But the thought of Cade or Heidi taking a bullet rocked him. Should they try to escape or not?

God, what is the right thing to do?

Silence.

Not knowing the answer drove him up the wall.

But Isaiah did know one thing: even Cade had finally realized that their fates were sealed if they didn't find a way out. And Isaiah couldn't take the kowtowing anymore, not when he and Cade were both far stronger than their male captors. All they needed was to grab the weapons.

All Isaiah needed was a chance.

God, just give me a chance.

He eyed the situation. Zach looking on as Jason did all the dirty work. He didn't see Rhea. She must have been exploring the other room in the cabin. Jason finished tying the knots on Cade's ankles. He'd laid his weapon over on the hearth, easy enough for Isaiah to reach. Zach played around with his gun as usual, but leaned back in his chair like a kid.

Once Jason tied Isaiah up his chance would be gone.

He kicked the leg of Zach's chair and it fell back. Isaiah knocked the gun from his grasp, then reached for Jason's weapon on the hearth just as Jason clued in and lunged for the gun. From the chair where he was bound, Cade leaned over and onto Jason, doing at least that much to help.

Isaiah had the weapon. He motioned for Jason and Zach to stand against the wall.

"Heidi, get Zach's gun. Then untie Cade. We need to make a call on Zach's SAT phone. Call for help. Get the Alaska State Troopers here." He didn't want to guard these guys any longer than he had to. In fact, he considered just leaving the three criminals here. It wasn't as if they could make it through the mountains themselves. They would be trapped until someone came for them. A SAR team backed up by Alaska State Troopers this time. "And then we're getting out of here. We're taking all the camping gear and the weapons with us."

Heidi's eyes grew wide and she lunged toward Isaiah. She didn't agree with him? "Watch out, Isaiah!"

Pain sliced through his head. Darkness edged his vision.

Shards of a vase tumbled down his shoulders and hit the floor. Isaiah fired the gun into the ceiling to gain control, but Zach and Jason tackled him to the ground. Behind them, he saw Rhea.

She'd been the one to take him down.

"I'm going to kill you." Zach flashed a knife in Isaiah's face. Isaiah believed him. The man had done it before to one of his own.

Isaiah had been an idiot, but he'd been desperate.

"No. Please don't, Zach." Heidi sounded more desperate than Isaiah.

He didn't want her begging for his life, putting her own in danger. Why hadn't he paid more attention to Rhea? He hadn't really considered her a threat. Jason kicked Isaiah in the kidney and pain erupted.

Zach stood up, getting off Isaiah and letting him breathe. "Did I tell you to kick him?" He stared his brother down.

Come on, Jason. Stand up to the guy for once.

Heidi was suddenly next to Isaiah, her face in his. "Are you okay?"

"You mean other than being an idiot?"

She smiled, the kind of pained smile that came from a situation like this. Zach yanked her away. Isaiah tried to stand but Jason shoved him back down with his booted foot.

"Get your hands off me." Heidi twisted from his grasp. "The only way you'll make it to the ice field is with our help. Haven't you noticed it takes all of us to help you rappel the cliffs, guide you and set up the tents? You'd better not lay a finger on him, or you can forget about going anywhere."

Zach just stared at her. So did Isaiah. Really? Heidi had blown up in his face. He'd never seen her do that. He wanted to cheer her on, but this was a nasty situation. She'd just faced off with a killer.

Zach smirked, a lascivious grin of the worst kind. "I like your spirit. You've got real fight in you. I haven't seen that in a woman in a long time."

Isaiah caught Rhea stiffen at those words. That did

not bode well for Heidi. Only put her back in the cross-hairs of Rhea's imaginary sniper rifle. Or maybe even a real gun.

Heidi stiffened and took a step back. Drawing Zach's attention to her hadn't been a good play, but she'd done that to protect Isaiah. He found himself the reason someone was in danger. Again.

Wanting to stand and protect Heidi, he shoved Jason's boot away and stood, dizziness making the room tilt. This was all his fault, after all. He'd gambled with their lives and lost.

Zach inched closer to Heidi. "I like you. So this time, I'll let your friend live. But I have to hurt him."

Isaiah didn't have time to think about what those words meant. Stabbing pain in his head rendered him helpless just before darkness took him.

Her wrists and ankles bound, Heidi lay on the floor on a sleeping bag near the fire. Tears flowed freely and she wished she could wipe the salty moisture that stung her cold-reddened cheeks away.

Unconscious, Isaiah rested against the wall on the other side of the room without a blanket. His hands and feet were tied as well, and blood oozed from a gash on the back of his head. Another one. She couldn't stand to see him like that—big, brave Isaiah incapacitated. Hurt. She wanted to go to him and patch up his wounds. Make sure he was okay.

He'd tried. She'd give him that. It was more than either she or Cade had done. He'd wanted to escape and maybe if she had agreed to go, they would all be in a different situation.

"Don't cry, Heidi," her brother whispered.

He was still propped up in the chair. An uncomfortable way to sleep. But they weren't in a position to make demands after what had happened. They were happy to let Zach and the others sleep in the bedroom. There wasn't any chance of escape with Isaiah incapacitated.

"Why is this happening?" Heidi kept her voice low. "Why can't we get away?"

"I'm sorry that I let you down. I just thought if we saw this through, we'd be better off than taking any risks by trying to overpower them. I admit I made a mistake."

"It's not your fault, Cade. You're probably right. Isaiah tried tonight and see what happened? Zach was going to kill him."

"You saved him. But I can assure you he wouldn't want you to put yourself at risk. And I don't want you to risk your life for either of us. We're big boys and can take care of ourselves. So if it comes to that, don't try to save me. Understand?"

Heidi shook her head. No, she didn't understand. She could take care of herself, too, and was tired of being overprotected all the time. So what if Zach liked Heidi and she'd used that to persuade him not to harm Isaiah? Though, she knew she'd better watch out for Rhea. She didn't doubt the woman might try to shove her off a cliff again, simply because Zach had paid her a compliment.

"And Isaiah…he isn't the guy for you."

Where had that come from? Heidi struggled to find a response.

"When we get out of this, and we will, just keep your distance. You don't really know him."

"What?" Why was Cade saying this? The words wounded her. Isaiah wasn't awake to defend himself.

"He isn't who you think."

"Just shut up, okay? This isn't the time." She didn't want to hear Cade saying negative things about the man she'd kissed earlier. About a man he called his friend. Cade only stirred the tumult inside her heart all over again.

Isaiah groaned. Had he heard Cade's negative words?

Heidi could protect herself. And she could protect her own heart, thank you very much. She wasn't afraid of Isaiah or whoever Cade thought he really was.

Another groan and mumble from Isaiah was all it took to have Heidi squirming in her restraints.

"Help," Heidi called. "Somebody untie me. I need to help Isaiah."

She'd admit that Zach's reaction to her had given her a measure of courage she wouldn't have otherwise felt.

"Heidi, no," Cade hissed under his breath.

He might be her older brother but he couldn't control her. She could make her own decisions.

"Hello, anybody?"

"What's the racket in there?" Jason called from the bedroom.

"I need you to untie me," Heidi yelled.

Jason lumbered into the living room, the firelight

barely illuminating his lumpy hair and worn face. "What's the problem?"

"Untie me, please. Isaiah's hurt. I need to make sure he's okay."

He rolled his head back, turned around and walked from the room.

"Hey!" Heidi's call was loud and sharp. Zach had to have heard that time. A tremor of fear rolled through her. Was she making a mistake? Would she only cause Isaiah more harm?

Jason turned, a scowl spreading over his face. She had to try another tactic.

"You want to make it to your rendezvous, don't you?"

He straightened.

"Then I need to make sure Isaiah is going to be well enough to help us tomorrow. We have to make good time, do you understand?" Now she sounded as if she was talking to a child. But maybe that's what it took to get it through Jason's thick skull. Anyone who would follow a person like Zach around, even if it was his brother, had to be a little dense.

Scratching his head, he nodded. "I suppose you're right. But try anything and I'll kill both of you before Zach can intervene. Don't think I won't."

Heidi wasn't sure, but she had a feeling Jason wasn't a killer. Just his brother. But now that she thought things through, maybe Zach had only shot his buddy after he was already dead to scare the SAR team. But did any of that really matter? It wasn't as if she could count on her theory.

After Jason untied her, she crawled over to Isaiah.

"Can you get me a first aid kit? There's got to be one in the cabin somewhere."

She wished Zach would have let her take care of Isaiah from the beginning, but she and Cade had been duly terrified, and didn't want to push the man into killing Isaiah, or either of them for that matter. Jason returned with the kit and Heidi made fast work of cleaning the lacerations beneath Isaiah's thick head of hair. She bandaged where needed, wishing she had an ice pack for the knot.

Rolling him gently onto his back, she was surprised to see his lids blink, then slide open. His hazel eyes stared back.

"Are you okay?" she asked.

A weak grin split his lips. "I am now."

FIFTEEN

They left the cabin at first light and lumbered through the snow-laced woods, wearing their regular boots this time. No snowshoes required, since the snow was packed. The most expeditious route to the ice field meant hiking over an intermediate peak, though Isaiah might refer to it as more of a swell. They'd made it over, but were now hiking down a steep slope into a slim gorge.

If Isaiah remembered this region correctly, the gorge should widen into a lake where they would find the glacier that would lead them to the ice field. He ignored the sledgehammer pounding his head. Probably had a concussion, but who cared. They were already in a death trap, so a concussion was a small price to pay for his lame attempt at an escape. At least they had all gotten plenty of sleep, food and water, and for whatever it was worth, were reenergized.

To a degree.

Today they were on the last leg of this nightmarish trek. He hoped this experience wouldn't forever scar the way he looked at the mountains. Only God could create such splendor.

Dizziness threw him off balance. At the wrong moment, that could be deadly. Isaiah leaned against the iced-over rocky wall that morphed from the slope, grappling for traction.

Heidi called out from behind him, too far away to be of any help. Zach had him isolated, hiking alone. None of them would be close enough to strategize an escape again. Their job was simple. If they kept at this pace, they would make it by late afternoon, just in time for his rescheduled rendezvous.

Isaiah couldn't stand the thought of Zach getting away. And Zach probably couldn't stand the thought of anyone identifying them or telling their strange story. Zach would not allow them to live, even Heidi whom he liked. He couldn't afford to keep them alive. But there was no sense in Isaiah rehashing what he already knew. Maybe deep in his subconscious he was looking for the remote chance, the possibility of a reason to hope that Zach would let them live.

Isaiah's failed attempt at freedom last night churned in his gut, adding to his painful headache. The blinding white expanse of snow only made the pain worse. He should never wish for clouds or a storm, but he prayed for one right now. And he would take the risk they'd been unwilling to take earlier and flee with Cade and Heidi into the elements. Dying at the hands of their captors couldn't be their fate. Somehow they would survive. They had to.

God, I feel so weak now. I've failed too many times.

Help me to not fail this time. Please be strong where I am weak. Maybe I acted last night without praying first, and I'm sorry, but make a way for us. Help me protect Heidi. If she dies, if I don't do enough, I don't know how I can live with that.

Isaiah trailed along next to the snow-patched granite edging their hike down the slope, though it really wasn't a slope anymore. It was a rocky ledge allowing them access to lower elevations, but also providing a quick suicide jump for anyone who so desired one.

Pebbles mixed with snow trickled from somewhere above.

Uh-oh.

He pressed himself flat against the wall. Looked behind him at Heidi and Zach, who followed his lead.

Rhea was closer to Cade up at the front of the line this time. Something rumbled above. More pebbles, rocks and bigger boulders poured down. On top of that, a rush of snow piled high. A rock slide.

Isaiah couldn't see Cade. Heidi was at Isaiah's side, trying to push past, but Zach pulled her back.

"Cade!" Her scream echoed in his ears, in the mountains.

Isaiah held tight, stopping her from rushing forward. Not yet.

"It's not safe. Wait until we're sure it's over."

"Let me go!" She tugged.

Isaiah released his grip. Who was he to control her? She moved past him.

But he'd try with words anyway. "Heidi...please, wait."

She paused and glanced back at him, dread pouring from her eyes.

"Let me check on them," Isaiah said.

Heidi covered her face and nodded, sobs racking her body.

He didn't blame her for a moment of weakness. It was a hard thing to see someone you loved mangled, bloodied. A memory iced over him. He shook it off. Creeping forward, Isaiah gave a wide berth to the pile of rocks and snow in case more followed.

His heart hammered at the thought of what he might find. He hoped that Cade wasn't caught beneath the rubble somehow. Even if he were alive, Zach would kill him now, finish the job.

"Over here," Cade called.

Hearing Cade, adrenaline galvanized Isaiah and he carefully maneuvered a slim path between the drop-off and the debris. On the other side of the massive pile, Cade stood next to the rocks, removing them, tossing them aside. He glanced up at Isaiah. "It's Rhea. Help me."

Fear and pain streamed from Rhea's golden eyes as she looked up from where a boulder had pinned her legs—crushed, more like. *Oh, Lord, help us.* This was not good. Not good at all. He never wanted to see anyone injured or in pain, even if that person had made the wrong choices. Everyone had made a bad decision at some point in their lives. Hers had simply been to fall for the wrong person. Not as if he couldn't relate to that.

He dropped to his knees to brush the smaller rocks

and rubble away from her body. "I'm so sorry. Just stay calm. We're going to get you out."

Then Zach appeared. "Rhea…"

His voice conveyed everything. His disappointment that she'd been hurt. That she was pinned. His resignation that she wouldn't be making the rest of the journey with him.

The sound was heart-wrenching.

Zach fell to his knees, too, next to Isaiah. "Rhea, how did it happen? Did Cade push you?"

Surprise registered in her eyes, and for a moment, Isaiah wondered if she would lie and blame someone else for her misfortune. But Rhea had been reduced to a person who depended on others for her life, and she knew Zach well enough to know she couldn't count on him to defend her or help her. The SAR team was her only hope now.

"No, no. Cade is helping me to get out. I'm going to be fine." Desperate, she lied to herself now.

"You're not going to be fine," Zach said. "I don't have time to wait for these guys to dig you out. And then what? I'm supposed to carry you? Your legs are crushed. You're going to…"

Die.

He was about to say it, but even Zach had enough human decency in him he didn't want to throw another stone on Rhea.

"She'll be all right. We're digging her out," Cade said. "I'll carry her. Do you hear me?"

Isaiah and Cade tossed rocks. Heidi, too. The boulder crushing her legs was the one to worry about, and

Isaiah wasn't all that certain that removing it without the prospect of immediate medical attention was a good idea. She could bleed out, depending on the damage. They weren't prepared to treat such a traumatic injury.

Lord, please show us what to do. How do we save her?

Zach leaned in and kissed Rhea long and hard. Isaiah recognized it for what it was.

A goodbye kiss. The brute. So much for his sense of decency.

"If you love me, you'll let me go. Isn't that how the saying goes? If I don't leave now, then I'll miss my rendezvous. You know you're not going to make it anyway. Do you love me, Rhea?"

"How can you be so cruel?" Tears rushed from Heidi's eyes. The compassion she felt for Rhea, a woman who wanted to kill her, moved Isaiah to the core. "You are a sick, brutal creature. You're not even human!"

Zach stood and gathered the gear he carried. "You can't save her," he said to Cade. "We need to go."

Cade didn't stop digging the rubble away from Rhea. Isaiah and Heidi kept digging as well, wanting to save her, yet realizing how futile their efforts were.

Zach tugged his weapon out and aimed it at the injured woman. "Let's get moving. We don't have time to dig her out and she's going to die anyway."

Rhea moaned and whimpered from her pain, and the sheer terror of watching the man she loved, the man she'd followed, prepare to kill her.

Isaiah, Cade and Heidi stepped in front of Rhea to prevent Zach from shooting. "No!"

"I'm not leaving without her," Cade said.

"Have it your way." Zach pointed the weapon at Cade's head.

Heidi thrust herself in the path the bullet would take, breathless desperation emanating from her. "Please, Zach. Cade isn't a threat to you. Let him stay to comfort Rhea. Help her if he can. Maybe they can even catch up."

The determination behind Zach's eyes relaxed into indecision. He definitely had a soft spot for Heidi. Maybe Zach was even a little glad Rhea wouldn't stand in his way now. That tore at Isaiah's insides. He couldn't stand for that insane murderer to look at Heidi that way. But his protests would only put her in more danger.

"We all know they're not going to catch up to us. I should put them out of their misery now."

Time for Isaiah to step up. "Save your bullets and leave them here. They'll die from the elements anyway. Hypothermia, another storm. But you never know when you'll need your ammunition. A rogue bear. Something." Convincing Zach they were as good as dead anyway was the only way to save Cade and Rhea. He hoped Heidi understood this.

He shared a knowing look with Cade. God willing, he would survive and get them help. Cade's eyes urged Isaiah to take care of his sister. Protect her. Odd, considering he'd warned Isaiah to stay away earlier, but Cade had been reduced to raw survival instincts, just as they all had. Cade would stay behind to help Rhea and entrusted Isaiah to protect Heidi.

Isaiah used that knowledge to steel himself when

Heidi suddenly refused to leave Cade's side. Cade hugged her, then gripped her shoulders, whispering something only she could hear, then he looked to Isaiah for help.

But it was Zach who yanked her away. "We have to go, sweetheart."

She ripped from his grip and rushed back to Cade. Isaiah thought she'd lost her mind. She'd been the one to suggest he stay with Rhea to begin with, but that was out of necessity. Now the realization that this could be the last time she saw her brother caved in on her. It caved in on Isaiah, too. He tore his gaze away and worked up the courage to do what he had to do.

Drawing in a deep, ragged breath, he wrapped his arm around Heidi and hauled her away from Cade, practically carrying her as she kicked and screamed. She'd hate him for this, and might never forgive him.

Heidi screamed Cade's name, an ear-shattering, gut-wrenching sound. Isaiah questioned if he was even doing the right thing, and the resulting anguish nearly crushed him.

When she finally calmed down, resigned to Cade's fate, he released her. She shoved away, unwilling to look at him. Now it was up to Isaiah and Heidi to lead the way, but it appeared she wanted no part of sharing the task with him. As he hiked forward into the widening gorge, he realized something—carrying Heidi, the chaos that ensued after Rhea's accident, had prevented him from grabbing his backpack and the other gear. Had prevented Zach from noticing.

That meant that a pack with supplies and a tent had

been left behind for Cade. Isaiah glanced over his shoulder at Heidi. Still brooding. He doubted she was putting on a show to intentionally keep Zach from noticing the pack.

All the same, Cade had what he would need to survive.

Thank You, Lord.

Despair hovered over Heidi, a dark cloud blocking the blinding white of the snow—maybe not from her eyes, but certainly from her thoughts. And her heart.

Rhea gone.

Cade gone.

Persuading Zach to let them live seemed the only answer, but then what? How would they survive the night when the temperatures dropped? Clouds hedging the mountains to the west told her another storm chased them. Nothing new. Nothing surprising. The Coast Range of southeast Alaska was one of the most inclement places on earth.

Frankly, she was surprised they had survived this long. Heidi fought the dismal feelings snowing heavily down on her, burying her deep. Smothering her. It was all she could do to simply shove one boot in front of the other and trudge on. At some point, the terrain had changed and Isaiah had made them don their crampons, but she couldn't remember when.

She still reeled from Cade choosing to stay with Rhea, who would likely die within the next few hours from her injuries. Her big, brave brother—always looking for a way to help and serve. To do what was right when he had the ability to do so. That had been his mantra, ever since Grandma Katy had hung up the cross-stitch that displayed it. What would Grandma think today, if she knew that Cade had given his life to keep that scripture alive and true in him?

And Leah. Poor Leah! A whimpering groan escaped Heidi and she stumbled. Cade didn't even know yet, but Leah had purchased a pregnancy test the very night they'd started on this rescue mission. Heidi came across Leah at the drugstore, asking the pharmacist about the ones kept behind the counter. So much for privacy in a small town.

But why, oh why, didn't Cade put Leah, his own wife, above Rhea—a woman who'd given her life to following a criminal and murderer? A woman who had wanted to kill Heidi.

Zach grabbed Heidi's arm to assist her. "Hey, sweetheart. Too bad about Rhea and your brother."

As if he cared. She wouldn't respond to him. Wouldn't say a word, though a million accusations blasted through her mind. If she opened that gate, she might never get it closed again, and the force of her words might crush Zach. On the other hand, maybe she should lay into him after all. But it was his reaction she feared.

Zach leaned in closer. Jason walked on the other side of her. Isaiah was up ahead. She was furious with him. Couldn't stand to look at him, even though she understood his actions. She hadn't tried hard enough to save her brother, either.

"Get away from me." She freed her arm from Zach and pushed ahead of him.

He caught up. "I hated to lose Rhea. She was a good woman. But now that she's out of the picture—"

Oh, that was it. "Are you insane?" Heidi stopped now, spitting mad. "I could never ever be interested in a murderous, backstabbing—"

"Hey! Look up ahead!" Isaiah's shout drew everyone's attention to him.

Zach and Jason all but forgot about Heidi and scrambled to meet Isaiah. They left her gasping for breath, to suffer in her own misery. She gazed behind her. How far was it again to Cade and Rhea? Could she simply leave now and take tents and supplies to them?

"Heidi." Isaiah was next to her then. "Come see, we're near the glacier that will take us to the ice field. It will still take us hours we probably don't have, but we have to try."

The pain in his eyes raw, she knew she'd tortured him, helped to drive in the nails of guilt even deeper.

"I don't care about that. I only care about getting back to Cade." She realized then that Isaiah had given Zach and Jason a distraction before Heidi lost complete control.

She wanted to thank him for that, but the image of Isaiah hauling her away and holding her against her will, her screaming and clawing, played across her mind. She had no words for him. The whole thing was an awful picture she would never forget.

But something was missing in that picture. What was it?

Her chest squeezed. "Isaiah, your pack with supplies. The tent."

A half grin slid onto his cheek and he nodded. He didn't have to say more because that was all Heidi needed to know. Cade would survive, and maybe, if he could get them help, Rhea, too.

But even more important—she had cried out to God, asking where He was.

And now she knew. He was here. Watching over them. Guiding them. And she also knew that while she'd been struggling with her faith, Isaiah had been praying every step of the way.

There wasn't anything she wanted to do more at that moment than step into Isaiah's arms. But with Zach's state of mind now about Rhea being out of the way, Heidi couldn't let her feelings for Isaiah show, or Zach would quickly dispense with him. They were near enough to the ice field that Zach might believe he could make it there on his own.

"We have to make sure Zach understands about the dangers of crossing the glacier and the ice field. About the danger of falling into a crevasse. We still have miles to go. He still needs us." She hated the knot in her throat.

Isaiah touched her chin. "Don't worry. We're going to make it."

But he had forgotten how well she knew him. How easily she read him, and his eyes told a much different story.

SIXTEEN

Isaiah saw hope flicker to life in Heidi's eyes. She would be okay, but for a while there he'd been worried, seriously worried, about her state of mind. They had to see this through to the end, whatever that meant. Isaiah had to keep praying, too. He couldn't stop. This was a battle in all senses: physical, emotional, mental and spiritual.

Heidi had to stay focused. Keep it together. And for his part, all Isaiah had to do was keep her alive until they were rescued, or he and Heidi could escape. He was afraid for Cade as well, but that was completely out of his hands. Cade had a better chance of survival than he and Heidi at this point. Cade wasn't facing a bullet from Zach anymore. He had a chance to get away and flag down the searchers. At least the helicopter had given them confirmation that a search for them was already under way.

God, please let them find us in time. Help me to keep Heidi safe and alive. Help Cade and Rhea, too.

They approached the moat, or the wall that signaled

the start of the glacier, which towered above them. Isaiah looked over at Heidi, who watched him, gauging
his reaction. With everything that had happened, he'd
pushed this moment to the side.

He blew out a breath. By their expressions, even
Zach and Jason seemed to understand the enormous
task ahead of them. At least Heidi had made sure they
had enough crampons for everyone before they even
began this ordeal. Without them he wasn't sure they
could have tackled the glacier.

But that was the only positive. How did Isaiah tell
Zach that there was simply no way they could cross the
glacier and make the ice field in time for his rendezvous
after this big push? How long would it take for Zach to
realize that on his own? And then when he did, what
would happen next?

He wished one of the glacier tour guides was here
with them. Those guys spent plenty of summers guiding visitors on such terrain and knew everything there
was to know. Isaiah, not so much. He preferred to look
at the beauty of the beasts from the air.

He blew out another breath and started to formu-
late a plan.

"What are you doing?" Zach asked.

"I need to find a safe entry point to get on top of the
glacier." What would it look like?

An hour and a half wasted away before they were
on top of the glacier. The sight was awe-inspiring. He
could imagine a glacier guide talking to the tourists.
*This is one of several glaciers that flows from the Ju-
neau Icefield.*

In the summer, Isaiah could have hoped to run across one of the tour groups. He wasn't sure if that would be a good thing or a bad thing. On the one hand, he might have been able to signal them to get help. On the other, anyone crossing their path would be in danger.

But it wasn't summer yet, and spring in this part of the world might as well be winter. He'd remained cognizant of the approaching storm clouds that would likely dump more snow on them. They were in a race against time now, and Isaiah wasn't hopeful they would win this.

He eyed the clouds once again and then gazed out over the river of ice ahead of them. He'd give it to Zach straight now and hopefully his brother, Jason, would make him listen.

"Crossing this glacier isn't going to be easy." As though navigating anything so monumental would be easy. "By far, it's the most treacherous thing we've faced. In the summer, maybe we could see all the dangers, but right now, there are plenty of crevasses and snow bridges hidden by layers of snow. That means we'll need to rope ourselves together, loop and hitch them for self-rescue, if required, and if that doesn't work, if one of us falls, the others can pull him or her out. But everything has to be tied right. We all have to be positioned a certain way, spaced apart as we cross, and there has to be tension in the ropes. Please listen very carefully as I give the instructions." It would take them some time just to get the ropes and harnesses and belay knots, for friction, tied just right.

This was going to be complicated. Isaiah squeezed

the bridge of his nose. He couldn't get enough air, and he knew Heidi could relate.

"So what?" Jason asked. "We tie knots and rope ourselves together. Big deal."

Isaiah thought about what he'd read and learned about glaciers, and gave them the spiel, everything he knew and could remember, so they'd at least picture in their minds exactly what they were up against. Then he instructed them on roped movement across glacial terrain, fearing it was too much information at once.

He glanced at Heidi. "Did I forget anything?"

A nod accompanied her tenuous smile. "Our biggest danger is going to be crossing the snow bridges. It's when snow piles up over a crevasse so you can't see it. You could fall through. The glacier is filled with crevasses, so let's make sure we understand how to do this from the start. We cross crevasses we can see at right angles, unless they're small cracks, and then we just jump over them. And if we suspect a snow bridge is too weak to support us, then there's another technique we use."

Heidi sighed, and Isaiah knew she understood his concerns, as well. This was beyond technical for Jason and Zach.

"And then we cross carefully, one at a time."

Now did Zach see how long this would take them?

"Everyone needs an ice ax," Heidi added. "I think we have extras in the bags."

"Let's gear up then, and tread carefully, spread out and rope up." Isaiah got the rest of the gear out.

Though he wanted to tell Zach they weren't going

to make it to the ice field in time, not before the storm rolled in, and not for his rendezvous, maybe it was best to let Zach see for himself. Isaiah didn't care to have Zach threaten Heidi's life yet again if he voiced his doubts.

When Isaiah started to tie Heidi on the rope, Zach yanked it away. "No. It's you, then me, then Heidi, then Jason. What's to keep you from dropping us into a crevasse and simply cutting the rope?"

Good point. Isaiah wished he'd thought of that himself.

The rope connecting her to Zach in front of her and Jason behind fully extended, Heidi put one foot in front of the other as they kept tension in the line.

Heidi was in top physical condition, and yet she wondered how much more of this she could take. Still, they were near the end of this nightmare. That both terrified her and kept her going. She had no idea what they would face once they actually made their destination and Zach's ride came to pick him up.

From where they were, as the glacier wound through the mountains like a big river of ice, she could see where it opened up into the Juneau Icefield. One of the largest in the world, it was the source of not only this glacier but forty larger glaciers that flowed outward, and scores of smaller ones, too. Funny to think the ice field encompassed hundreds of square miles and was rimmed by a temperate rainforest.

Where was Zach's rendezvous anyway? Crazy.

None of them had worried too much about where he

planned to meet his buddy in the ski-plane before, but if it was on the other side, he'd need to change the location. Especially with the threat of inclement weather. The sky began turning gray, clouds moving in over the sun as it started an early descent behind the mountains.

The wind whipped around Heidi. How she wished for a rescue today. She didn't want to spend yet another night with Zach, or another night in a tent surrounded by roaring wind and driving snow and arctic temperatures.

Zach yelled at Isaiah to move faster. He broke their line and moved ahead of Isaiah, tugging and yanking Heidi and Jason forward. Zach would get them all killed, including himself.

A sound broke through the wind. At the low whir of a single-engine plane, Heidi wanted to jump up and down. Wave her arms. But then she remembered.

Zach was expecting his ride. And they hadn't made the rendezvous, just as she knew they wouldn't.

In the distance, where blue sky met the clouds rushing in from the west, a ski-plane circled. Heidi couldn't know if it was the plane for Zach or just someone else.

But he was the one to jump up and down and wave and scream at the top of his lungs. The airplane circled back and flew away, growing smaller.

He cursed and kicked and shoved Isaiah into the snow. Then he drew out his SAT phone and cursed some more. He couldn't get it to connect.

Isaiah stood and made his way to Heidi, stuck between Jason and Zach on the rope. "We need to find the safest place to make camp. We're too exposed out here, and the storm won't be forgiving."

"I know. But what about the ropes? Should we keep them on?"

He nodded. "For now."

"Zach!" Isaiah grabbed the man, gaining control over the situation.

Heidi's insides squeezed. She hoped Zach wouldn't react in a fit of rage and shoot Isaiah.

"He'll be back! You'll get your chance to call him. But right now, we have to set up the tents or we are going to die. You need to get your act together and focus on living through the night."

Jason nodded his agreement. "He's right, Zach. Let's prepare to weather another storm. If I never see the mountains or snow again it'll be too soon. But we're almost there. We almost made it. He can come back again for us later."

As far as Heidi could tell, this spot was as good as any for a camp. Isaiah assembled an avalanche probe he had with him to hopefully detect any hidden crevasse beneath them. Heidi, Isaiah and Jason worked to set up the tents. Jason tugged as much gear as he could into one. The wind began to howl and the snow pricked her face like needles. Now they were down to two tents and four people. Would Zach notice the missing one?

God, please, I don't want to be stuck in a tent with Zach. He's crazy. She could only imagine in her worst nightmares what he might do to her.

Someone nudged her from behind. Heidi panicked and fought back. Then she realized it was Isaiah urging her inside the tent. She glanced over and spotted Jason watching. He gave a slight nod, as though he approved.

Zach was nowhere to be seen. Maybe he'd already climbed inside his own tent. With the storm and his need to make contact with his only ride out of here, he probably wouldn't think of Heidi until they were all buried in the storm.

When Heidi took too long to move inside the tent, Isaiah practically shoved her in.

"Stay there." He zipped the tent up.

God, please let Isaiah be the one who climbs into this tent. I don't want to weather this storm alone, but I don't want any of the others here. Isaiah was a good man. She'd always believed that, even after he'd hurt her. And she'd seen nothing but the best from him throughout this ordeal. He'd been strong enough to make the tough decisions, even when Heidi herself wasn't sure she could have done the same.

The wind whistled and the tent fluttered. Heidi's heart jumped around inside her, but she had enough experience that she shouldn't be so frightened. Her nerves were wearing thin, mostly because she didn't know what would happen next. She did know that she should only live one day at a time. One breath at a time, even. No one knew when their last moment in this world would be. In that way, everyone on the planet was terminal. Was it wrong to have so much left to do in this life? She didn't want to die. Not yet.

The zipper moved. Heidi held her breath.

Please, don't let it be Zach.

Isaiah crawled in and Heidi's head swam, dizzy with relief.

"This is a blizzard all right. A whiteout. I'm going to have to crawl out every so often and dig us out. By the looks of it, maybe every fifteen minutes, half an hour. You know the drill. I reminded Jason about it. He's the only reasonable one over there."

"And… Zach?" Heidi couldn't voice the words, but she hoped Isaiah read her concern in her gaze.

"The storm will be too brutal for him to bother crawling out. That's why I convinced Jason to help keep the tents from getting buried." His gaze softened. "It's going to be a long, tough night. But trust me when I say, I will kill Zach with my bare hands before I let him lay a finger on you."

Guys had a way of talking bravado like that, but Heidi wanted to believe in Isaiah's fierce protective stance. She wanted to believe in him. Maybe he was the one guy who could save her, from more than just the likes of Zach. Maybe Isaiah could save her from her heartbroken world, even though he'd been part of it. But there had to be a reason he'd pushed her away. What was it?

He positioned himself on a sleeping bag, but didn't appear to get too comfortable. He must be exhausted, just like Heidi, but he couldn't afford to fall asleep. He'd need to dig them out. Heidi wouldn't let him shoulder that burden alone. She'd trade off with him.

But right now, only one thing burned in her mind and heart. "What happened to us, Isaiah?"

SEVENTEEN

The question knocked the breath from Isaiah.

Why did she think of that now, when they would battle for their lives tonight, and then tomorrow when they would come face-to-face with Zach, meeting either their destiny or demise?

His shoulders dropped as he deflated completely. How did he explain to her what had happened? He took off his gloves and raked his hands through his hair.

She stared at him, waiting.

"Now. You want to know all that now." It was a statement, not a question.

"I'm facing my mortality. I want to know if there could have been something more between us. And why there wasn't. Why did you pull away from me?"

Okay, so she was serious, and he understood her reasoning. He'd wanted a chance to tell her, to open up about his past so he could move on. But now he was chickening out.

"It's a long story."

"I've got all night."

He liked her spirit. But this night would drain him in more ways than one. He'd sort of hoped for an evening spent in her company just going over the trauma they'd been through. Working through it all. Making a plan for the big escape tomorrow. Then again, he had her full attention now. She couldn't run or walk away from what he had to say. She'd have to face him, and he'd be able to read her reaction.

"I know I'm asking a lot, being that we're in this tent and you're exhausted," she said. "And this is going to be awkward, but I'm a big girl. Right now, with everything that happened before and now this, I'm sinking fast and I need to climb out before it's too late. If I could just understand what happened, that would bring closure for me. Was it me? Or something completely unrelated?"

Intensity spilled from her big brown eyes. Soft eyes that were the windows to a soul full of love and compassion. No wonder Isaiah had struggled to let her go.

He wouldn't be holding anything back tonight. And Heidi would hate him when he was done.

"Okay, then. Here goes." Isaiah stared at his hands, wondering if he'd have to pull on the gloves and his coat and get outside before he could finish his story. "You need to know that all I've ever wanted to do was prove myself worthy of your family. I just wanted to move on and leave my past behind. I didn't want to make another mistake, especially with you."

He glanced up from his hands to read Heidi's face. Slightly flushed. She'd understood him, then. She'd been right to suspect that this was all about his feelings for her.

"It's okay. I'm not going to judge you. Just tell me." Her voice was gentle, pleading.

Isaiah wished for another time and place in which to tell her. He prayed for the chance to have more with her, maybe even the rest of his life. The thought made his breath hitch. He couldn't wish for more.

"I have to dig us out first, then I'll tell you the rest."

"What? You're kidding, right?"

"No, I'm not. You hear that?" He pressed his hand against the side of the tent. "It's heavy with snow. But don't worry, I'll be right back."

He put on his gloves and the rest of his winter gear and scrambled from the tent into the blasting whiteout, darkness quickly falling. He had barely enough battery power in his headlamp to assist him, but at least he still had the night vision goggles. He'd loaned a pair to Jason, too.

But more than needing to scrape away the snow piling over the tent almost faster than he could dig, he needed time to think through his response to Heidi. He knew he'd have to explain one day, but he hadn't expected her question tonight.

Brutally cold wind blasted him, making it hard to stand against the force. Driving snow quickly buried both tents. Where was Jason? Isaiah risked a hike over and yelled against the tent, "Get out here and dig yourself out if you want to live!"

In all his time living in Montana and in Alaska, he'd never weathered anything like this.

He hiked back to the tent where Heidi was cocooned inside. *God, help me keep her alive, help protect her*

*from the forces of nature, and from the evil in the tent
next door. I don't know what tomorrow will bring, and
tonight has enough troubles of its own, as You say in
Your Word. And Lord, please help me give the right
answer when I speak the truth. Let it not just be more
hurt for Heidi.*

The anguish in his heart and his prayer made the
time he spent digging pass fast. Too fast, actually. Now
he had to head back inside and spill his story, the full
of it.

As quietly as he could, he slipped back into the tent,
snow blowing past him. Heidi's eyes blinked open. Had
she been asleep? He regretted waking her. She needed
the rest and besides that, he didn't relish telling her what
she wanted to know.

Heidi sat up, looking disheveled

"Why don't you get some rest?" He settled on the
sleeping bag at the far side of the tent. He couldn't afford to close his eyes or he might never wake up.

"It's my turn, you know. I'm going out next."

Isaiah shook his head. He couldn't be certain that
only Jason would dig his tent out. "I don't want you to
run into Zach out there. I don't want him to have a reason to think about you."

"You can't do this on your own all night. I'll wear
your coat, make him think it's you. How about that?"

He scratched his jaw. "That might work."

She smiled. "Don't think you're getting out of telling me the story. So give."

He sighed. Might as well dive in. "Before I moved

to Mountain Cove, I fell in love with someone, only I found out later that she was engaged."

Isaiah heard Heidi's quick intake of breath. He wouldn't avoid her gaze now. He would watch her with every word he said. The story would sound much too similar to her own betrayal, and he could hardly bear it. But let the blame fall where it may.

"When I found out, I confronted her, of course. She said she wasn't sure she wanted to get married after all and, well, a guy could hope. I guess I thought maybe she loved me and would break things off with her fiancé. Still, she saw me in secret. He knew nothing about us, and for that..." Isaiah hung his head. Shame filled him. "It was wrong. I know that now. Because then Aaron found out about us."

Heidi kept perfectly still, but her eyes grew wide.

"I thought it was over between them, and I would have a chance with her. I should have backed out of the situation completely from the beginning. I kept telling myself they weren't married so it wasn't cheating. She didn't leave him, and she didn't break things off with me, either."

"What happened?" Heidi's soft voice broke through the images Isaiah had fought hard to leave behind.

He wasn't sure he could answer. He needed to dig them out again. Find the words. "I found her body."

Heidi gasped, pressed her palms against her mouth.

Isaiah stood and left the tent before she could gather her thoughts. She was supposed to go out next and scrape the snow drifts away.

"Oh, Isaiah," she whispered. And that poor girl. What could have happened to her? She couldn't imagine how awful that must have been for her family, and for Isaiah to find her like that. And to have been part of a betrayal…

Memories of her own experience with Lon surfaced. He'd made her feel as if he cared about her, during one of the lowest times of her life, and assured her they were going somewhere in their relationship. Of course, she knew now she'd only been on the rebound from Isaiah. She hadn't even kissed Isaiah yet, but there was just something so powerful between them that it far outweighed her relationship with Lon. But she'd tried to run from the pain. And then the day Isaiah had told her that Lon was married had nearly been the worst day of her life.

It didn't help matters that the Warren siblings had learned the devastating news of their father's infidelity in recent months. Heidi's anger burned against Lon, as it had against her father, though it was through her father's death that Cade had uncovered the news that he had cheated on their mother, and that they could have a half brother or half sister out there somewhere.

How could Heidi have been so stupid? Why couldn't someone have told her before she'd gotten involved?

Still, Lon wasn't from Mountain Cove and didn't live there. He'd been camping at his cabin on an island along the channel, and she'd met him when he'd aided the SAR team on an island rescue.

She could hear Isaiah scraping the snow off outside, and the tent shuddered, pulling her thoughts back.

To find out he'd been part of a similar betrayal—no wonder he kept that to himself. No wonder he didn't feel he could ever share that with Heidi. Still, he'd pulled away long before Lon had stepped into her life so there had to be more.

He unzipped the flap and stepped in, bringing the cold and snow in along with his drawn features. Isaiah didn't even look up at her, just went to his place on the sleeping bag. And said nothing.

"I need to know the rest, if you don't mind."

"What do you think happened? I was devastated, of course. I loved her." He pressed his hand over his eyes.

An ice ax dug into Heidi's heart.

"But she'd hurt me, by stringing me along. I'd been an idiot. So I went to her to tell her we were over. I was afraid for her life, too. I learned she had doubts about her engagement because her fiancé was a violent man. I didn't want him to hurt her because of me. And in the end, that's exactly what happened. But did they arrest him? No. I was the one who became a person of interest. Almost a suspect then."

"And now?" *Oh, Lord, please don't let it be that he is in hiding. That he ran away.* She couldn't bear to hear that.

She studied him. He wasn't a murderer. No. Never. She wouldn't believe that.

"The police were never able to find enough evidence to pin things on me or her fiancé, though I know he must have murdered her." Finally he looked at her. "But you see, it doesn't matter that I'm innocent. I live in the shadow of those events. I feel like I helped her betray her future husband, and because of that, she's dead. Because of me. I didn't pull the trigger on the gun, but what's the difference? I played a part in her death. Maybe I could have prevented it. Could have been there when he shot and killed her. Taken the bullet for her instead."

"You don't mean that, Isaiah." As horrified as Heidi felt from hearing that story, her heart went out to him.

"Yes…" He nodded. Searched her eyes. "Yes, I do. And even though I didn't kill her, as far as the town was concerned, I might as well have. They were suspicious of me. The gossips couldn't just drop the story. The newspapers and media wouldn't leave me alone. I had to change my name and start over. I thought that I could leave it all behind and make a new life."

Heidi hated the tears brimming in her eyes. But she wouldn't swipe them away. She wouldn't look away from Isaiah. But she said nothing. There were no words to comfort him. There were no words to express the battle that raged in her soul.

"Now you see why I never told you. I thought I had to keep it all hidden away to move on. Then as we got closer, I knew that I couldn't keep that from you. After what I'd been through I didn't want to make another mistake when it came to love. I wanted everything to be out in the open. But how could I tell you? I knew you would be hurt. And you deserve much better than me. I had to pull away from you to…"

"To protect me." Because he cared. He'd even said the word *love*. Had Isaiah loved her? Did he still, even now?

"And then you were so devastated when you learned

about your father's infidelity, and after what happened between you and Lon, well, that only confirmed to me that I had done the right thing. After hearing all that, what do you think about us now?" Isaiah huffed, clearly disillusioned.

As she was. "I think it's my turn to dig."

Without looking at Isaiah, Heidi pulled on her gloves, hat, coat and boots and crawled from the tent. The hurt she'd inflicted on Isaiah by giving him such a lame response backfired and zinged through her. She was more than heartbroken over his story. She was hurt for him. Hurt for herself.

She'd held on to the slightest hope that he could make her believe in everlasting love again. But no. He'd only confirmed that love would eventually fail her, if she ever chose to risk her heart again.

"Why, God?" she shouted into the storm. She'd wanted an answer from Isaiah, but she hadn't in her wildest dreams been prepared for this.

As if leaving Cade to survive on his own in this storm wasn't enough. Watching Zach leave his girlfriend behind wasn't enough. As if being abducted like this wasn't enough.

Emotionally obliterated, Heidi wanted to lie down and let the snow bury her. It would only take a few minutes, tops.

Despite the frigid temperatures, she worked up a sweat beneath her thermal coat while digging the snow away with the pack shovel. Of course, she'd forgotten to switch coats with Isaiah, but she could care less about Zach seeing her anymore.

Her muscles burned. Lungs screamed. How had she even for one second allowed herself to think that Isaiah could be the man to pull her out of the abyss, to help her trust in love again? He was the absolute last person she should ever care about. He'd participated in the very thing she loathed, been party to cheating on a loved one. Sure, the woman had only been engaged, but it had all been a lie. Heidi couldn't begin to imagine the pain her fiancé had felt.

Had that driven the man to kill his intended?

She thought about her own father cheating on her mother. And she could have another sibling out there somewhere. The tears were freezing on her cheeks. Heidi had to stop freaking out.

She threw her arms up and looked into the raging storm. "Why, God?" she cried again.

Once she scraped snow from the other side of the tent, she would be done, at least for a few more minutes. But she wasn't sure what purpose that would serve. The cold reality of their situation churned inside her once again, and this time, she couldn't shake it off. They were going to die. She could feel it in her bones. If not by Zach's hand, then because of this storm.

They'd come this far, yes, but Heidi's strength had drained away to almost nothing, then Isaiah's story had taken the rest. She was broken and freezing. Her limbs grew numb with cold. She could barely dig anymore, her efforts having no effect. Growing more sluggish by the second, she fought hard to care.

She was frozen with pain and could not bring herself to cry out for help, or even pray anymore. Yes, she knew

God had been there with them, leading them, guiding them. But how much more could she take? It was one thing to battle the elements and Zach, but it was quite another to also fight the emotional and spiritual onslaught that threatened to topple her.

Heidi tumbled into the deep white stuff.

For a moment, she sat there, letting the driving snow pelt her, pile on top of her.

Bury her.

"God, I can't do this. I can't deal with this anymore. What do you want from me?"

Suddenly, a sense of calm came quietly into her spirit, even as the storm raged around her.

That was just like Him, she knew.

Eyes closed, lashes sticking to her moist but soon-to-be frozen cheeks, she nodded. "Okay, Jesus, I'm all Yours. I can't do this alone."

She couldn't lie to herself again, either. Despite her best efforts to protect her heart, she loved Isaiah. Even after everything he'd told her and knowing he wasn't the right man for her. She couldn't count on someone like him for a love that would last forever, but still, she loved him.

Isn't that kind of like You, God? You love us even though we fail You time and again. I want to love like that, God, You hear me? I don't want to care about Isaiah's past.

But she did. God help her, she did care that he'd been involved in a betrayal with someone. That the police thought he might have murdered her. And she wouldn't let herself love him. But none of that mattered as Heidi grew sleepy and the snow blanketed her. Somewhere inside her tormented psyche, she knew she had to get up or she would die.

But she couldn't move.

EIGHTEEN

He hadn't wanted to let her dig. Too many dangers out there. But he couldn't stop her, either. Truth was he'd fall over with exhaustion if he didn't have some help. But this hadn't been the way he'd wanted it.

He felt the furrow between his brows all the way to his toes and back up to his heart.

These past three, nearly four, years that he'd lived in Mountain Cove, he'd never looked back to his hometown in Montana. Well, except to phone his folks once in a while. Fortunately, his parents had bought a ranch and retired on the other side of the state before any of the "happenings," as they referred to it. Though they'd never made him feel unwelcome, he couldn't let go of the fact that he'd brought shame to them. All the more reason to change his name. But he was their only child and having him take another name had to hurt, as well.

He hadn't been back to see them until this past Christmas. Being with his family, and away from Heidi and hers, had given him some perspective. Time to come to grips with the fact that she deserved better than a guy who'd made the ugly mistake he'd made. A mistake that had cost a life. Ultimately, the police hadn't blamed him, but he blamed himself. If he'd never met her, never become involved with her, she'd still be alive.

And then Isaiah had to go through the pain of closing himself off emotionally from Heidi—he'd never known that kind of pain, watching her hurt, and being the cause of it. She never said much, but he'd seen the torment pouring from her eyes as hard as the driven snow. But it was for the best. For her, he'd kept telling himself. The knife only twisted deeper when she took up with a new guy. The entire Warren family was wary of the relationship, but Heidi had already been through so much that no one dared to say anything. That is, until Isaiah overheard the man on his cell phone talking to his wife one day. Isaiah had been the one to tell Heidi.

Nothing could ever be worse than finding the body of someone you cared about. Nothing. But hurting Heidi had come close. Watching her go through it all had only confirmed to him that he should keep his distance, and he should keep his secrets.

He glanced at his watch. She was due back about now, and he needed to be prepared for whatever she would dish out.

Raking his hands through the hair at his temple, he squeezed, pressing in hard. He wasn't sure how things had come full circle, and he'd somehow been persuaded to tell her everything.

But he did know that her reaction hadn't been a surprise. He'd deluded himself into allowing an ounce of hope that maybe things could work between them.

Maybe this fierce love that burned inside wasn't for nothing. People lied to themselves and would use any excuse to justify something they really wanted. Isaiah was no different.

He sat up. Heidi was taking much too long.

Zach...

She'd forgotten to switch into Isaiah's coat.

He donned his gloves and coat again and scrambled from the tent. Wearing his night vision goggles, he stomped around outside, panic engulfing him. Where was she? It had been much too long. Snow was already packing up high around the tent. A glance over at the other one told him someone had continued to dig the snow away.

"Heidi, where are you?" he called.

Oh, Lord, please help me find her!

He started toward the far side of the shelter and stumbled over something.

Oh, no...

Isaiah dropped to his knees. "Heidi!"

God in heaven, please don't let her die.

Isaiah scraped snow from her, his pulse slamming his temples. He lifted her seemingly lifeless frozen form into his arms and carried her back into the tent. He'd waited too long to check on her. What an idiot he'd been. He shouldn't have let her outside to dig, but after what he'd told her, she needed time alone to process the news, and he'd let her have her way.

He checked her pulse. Still alive. He laid her on the sleeping bag, her blue lips terrifying him. "Heidi, wake up!"

He wasn't exactly sure what had happened. She was

dressed well enough, but hypothermia could still be a risk in this weather. Maybe she had simply succumbed to exhaustion. He checked her vitals again, and searched for any obvious injury. No bump on the head. Her pulse was good and steady. Her skin didn't feel cold and more color returned to her lips. *Come on, come on, come on, Heidi. Wake up.* Other than keeping her warm there wasn't anything else he could do, except pray, and he'd never stopped doing that.

Isaiah knew he needed to dig some more, keep them from being buried alive, but he didn't want to leave Heidi. He zipped her into the sleeping bag, warm and snug. There was nothing more he could do for her.

Isaiah glanced back one more time before unzipping the tent to crawl out.

Her eyelids fluttered and she gazed at him. His heart leaped with relief.

Since finding her passed out in the snow, he'd completely forgotten about what he'd shared with her moments before. The pain in her eyes as she looked at him now brought it rolling back and into him, the force nearly knocking him over. He had to harden his heart.

He turned his attention back to exiting the tent.

"Isaiah," she whispered.

He froze, unsure that he wanted to face her. "Yeah."

"We need to leave tonight. Now. Zach is going to kill us tomorrow."

Had she forgotten about Isaiah's confession? Didn't she realize she would have died out there if he hadn't found her in time? She wasn't thinking clearly. The temperatures and the storm were more brutal than anything else they'd endured through this entire ordeal. She would die if they left this tent and hiked in the storm tonight. They both would.

"Better to bide our time and face off with Zach tomorrow. We wouldn't survive this weather." Isaiah left her to think on his words.

Heidi opened her eyes, unsure of what woke her. Tucked deep in the warm sleeping bag, she'd long ago shed her coat, but she couldn't remember where she was.

Then it all rushed back.

Only the wind wasn't howling. The storm had blown through.

The zipper again. Someone was coming inside the tent. The terror of Zach's unwanted attention rushed back at her, too. She pushed out of the sleeping bag and got into the most defensive position she could, given the small space.

Isaiah crawled inside. "Good, you're awake. We're packing up. Have to make it onto the ice field today, to Zach's coordinates. Just a little longer, Heidi."

She shrugged into her coat and grabbed her boots, her head spinning as memories of last night—everything Isaiah had told her—flooded back.

"Are you okay?"

She flicked her gaze at him, then back to her boots. "Sure. I must have slept like a rock. What did I miss?"

This time, she let her gaze linger. Something in his reaction held a question.

"No, really. Did I miss something?"

"No." He grinned.

Heidi shook off the effect it had on her. She needed time to think through all he'd told her. She'd wanted an answer. Wanted to know why he'd thrown away their friendship. Well, now she knew, and she fully understood why he'd distanced himself instead of telling her the truth. She would have done the same thing. Maybe.

She rolled up her bag. "Give me a sec."

"Heidi." He cleared his throat.

She didn't want to look at him, but realization dawned and she risked a glance up, seeing the haggard expression he'd tried to hide with his grin. "I must have slept through the whole night. Isaiah, I'm so sorry. You must be exhausted."

He nodded, a slight tuck of his chin. "A few more hours and this will be over. Knowing that will keep me going. But I'm more worried about you."

"Don't be."

"Heidi, don't you remember? You went out to dig and you never came back. I found you passed out, half-buried in the snow. Do you remember anything?"

Heidi finished with the sleeping bag and let her mind drift back to those last few moments of digging. She'd been praying, crying out to God, then finally given her burdens to Him. But she'd stopped moving, and maybe all the sweat she'd worked up from digging had dropped her body temperature even lower. It was all hazy now, but she'd been tired. So very tired.

"What's going on in there?" Zach banged on the tent. "Let's get moving."

Heidi shared a look with Isaiah and in his eyes she

saw he hoped as much as she did that they would live to finish this conversation.

They crawled out and packed the bags.

"We can leave all this," Zach said. "Get a move on. I can't afford to miss my plane this time. There's a short window before another storm. Talked to my contact last night. Curse this blasted region of the world."

Isaiah glanced up at the sky and Heidi followed his gaze. Did an odd mixture of expectation and dread roil in his gut, too? She could feel this ordeal winding down to its gritty ending. Searchers were out there, combing the mountains. David and Adam wouldn't stop searching until they found their siblings, but even they couldn't search in a storm.

And even if they looked over the ice field, they were talking fifteen hundred square miles. But surely they would be able to narrow that down to a few hundred, as if that would make a difference.

"Heidi and I'll have the basics packed up in a few. We can't afford to leave this in case things go wrong. It's a matter of survival."

Zach railed at them and Jason stepped into the fray. "They're right. Just in case he doesn't show up, we could die without the tents and supplies."

Thank goodness Jason was able to reason with his disagreeable brother. After they packed the gear, they roped themselves up and spaced apart, just like yesterday, in order to be safe as they crossed snow bridges.

They hiked through a maze of visible crevasses, and sometimes had to backtrack, but in spring, despite the storms that insisted on blasting through, a lot of the snow had melted on parts of the glacier. And yet dangers remained hidden beneath the snow. She had to pay attention, stay alert, but her energy had been drained long ago. Like Isaiah, she told herself she could make it to the end, which would come up on them much too fast.

In the distance, she could see where the glacier spilled from the ice field, which was really just a huge valley of interconnected glaciers, and the higher mountain peaks broke through. She saw the summit of Devil's Paw and Michael's Sword, gleaming snow-free in the distance, much closer now than she'd seen from miles away several nights ago. The nunataks, or rocky parts of the peaks, faced off as if in an eternal battle.

Heidi felt as though she were in an eternal battle herself.

God, I don't know what's ahead of us, but I ask for Your help and guidance over the next few hours. And I ask for Your help again, in knowing what to think about Isaiah's story. Help him to forgive himself, and help me to let it go. I'm not sure any of it even matters, considering we might both be dead in the next few hours.

A scripture drifted across her heart.

"...Because he has anointed me to proclaim good news to the poor. He has sent me to proclaim freedom for the prisoners and recovery of sight for the blind, to set the oppressed free..."

Lord, if ever captives needed setting free, that would be me and Isaiah.

Her thoughts went immediately to Cade and Rhea, though the two of them had never been far from her mind and heart.

Zach tugged on the rope, jerking Heidi forward and out of her thoughts. She'd been hiking too slowly for him.

In the distance, the sound of a small prop plane drew all gazes up. Heidi's pulse ramped up. Was it searchers?

Or Zach's personal rescuer?

Heidi got her answer. The plane circled lower and around them. She spotted Zach giving a thumbs-up. "Okay, people, let's get this train moving."

Again he tugged on the rope and Isaiah picked up the pace ahead of them, as well.

Her heart tripped over itself with dread. Zach only needed them to assist him over the dangerous parts of the glacier and then once on the ice field, when he had his plane waiting, he would shoot them both.

How could it end any other way?

Heidi was nearly breathless when they finally spotted the ski-plane landing in the distance. The guy obviously knew what he was doing. She was curious to know who the pilot was, but then again, that was just one more reason she and Isaiah had to die today, as far as Zach was concerned.

In front of her, Zach stopped, turned and made his way back to Heidi.

Oh, no. Here it comes. He's going to kill me now. Oh, God, what do I do? Help me!

When Isaiah's rope grew taut, he turned around.

Zach grabbed Heidi and pulled her close. Isaiah kept hiking toward them, rage burning behind his eyes. Heidi tried to free herself from Zach but he only tightened his grip.

And Isaiah kept hiking. He was almost on them.

Zach took a few steps back.

"This is where we part ways," he said. "And I'm taking Heidi with me."

"What?" Heidi's pulse jumped. She tried to tear away from him.

He pulled her closer and reached for the gun in his pocket.

NINETEEN

Isaiah lunged at Zach.

No more waiting until the right moment. This was do-or-die.

Zach tugged his weapon out, fired off a shot and missed.

Isaiah was on him, fighting for control of the firearm. He'd warned Zach to spare his ammunition in order to save Cade and Rhea's lives, but now Isaiah and Heidi had to face the bullets. He knocked the weapon away and it slid across the ice. Heidi ran for it but she was tied to Zach and the ropes were tangled.

Jason had a gun, too, but couldn't shoot at Isaiah with Zach on him. Isaiah didn't think Jason was a killer anyway. He pulled Isaiah away from Zach, and while he struggled to reach his weapon buried inside the coat beneath the layers of the rope and harness, Isaiah and Zach ran for the gun on the ice.

Isaiah pulled Zach back with the rope. He couldn't let him reach it first. Zach turned his attention back to Isaiah and plowed into him. They went down hard against the snow-packed ice. Pain coursed through Isaiah's face and head, magnified by the deep freeze beneath him. Jason appeared in his vision.

He couldn't fight two of them off. But he couldn't let Zach take Heidi with him, either. He'd die fighting.

She tried to pull Jason away from him, but Jason threw her back. It was a tangled mess since they were all tied together. Why hadn't Zach just taken his money and gone to the plane? Heidi's scream ripped through the air, and maybe even the ice under him. He could swear he felt it vibrate beneath him, accompanied by a deep rumble.

Oh, no!

Zach slammed his fist into Isaiah's face and the blood poured from his nose. Zach's face was bruised and bloodied, too. At least Isaiah had given as good as he'd gotten. To Jason, too. But then he noticed Heidi's swollen lip. Isaiah tried to shove Zach away.

And then it was over.

Zach stood up, staggered a little and backed away. The iced shuddered and shifted. Was the glacier moving? Zach, Jason and Heidi struggled to remain standing. Isaiah saw now what a losing battle this had been from the beginning. Two guys against one.

Then the ground beneath Isaiah caved in.

The snow and ice gave way, revealing a hidden crevasse. That was the whole reason for the ropes. They weren't in the correct formation and they would all go down if Zach didn't react.

"Use your axes!" Heidi yelled.

Isaiah couldn't get to his ice ax and, though he grappled with his gloves against the edge, he couldn't gain traction and finally fell back, free-falling, pulling them all down with him.

Screams erupted from above as the ropes slid across the ice.

A yawning, dark abyss rose up toward the bluer ice of the crevasse as if to close its jaws around him, filling him with terror. But the rope grew taught, jerking Isaiah. Someone had been quick thinking enough to stop the spiral into the crevasse.

Above him, Zach clung to the edge. He'd managed to get his ice ax in time, and crawled out. Or maybe Heidi had been able to toss it to him. Regardless, he would make it out.

Isaiah worked to free himself from the pack on his back that would weigh him down. In his worst nightmares, he had never imagined he would be the one in the crevasse, waiting to be rescued by this group. They could pull him out. But he didn't plan to wait on them.

Either way, getting out would take Isaiah time he didn't have. He dangled in the crevasse by a rope connected to two men who wanted him dead. He dropped the one remaining pack off his back, decreasing his personal weight so he could climb out, but it dangled from the rope, attached by a carabiner. The other pack he'd been carrying, but had dropped in his scuffle with Zach and Jason, had already fallen into the chasm.

He eyed the blue ice beneath him. Beautiful. God's splendor could be seen even here in the unlikeliest of places. He took it all in, wishing he could have been exposed to this amazing sight under much different circumstances. Terror grappled with a strange peace inside him. This could be it for him. This could be his death. The way his life ended. Not a bullet like he'd expected. But by a fall into these icy depths.

A few verses from Psalm 139 floated out of his heart and into his thoughts. *"Where can I go from your Spirit? Where can I flee from your presence? If I go up to the heavens, you are there; if I make my bed in the depths, you are there."*

If Isaiah fell, God would be there.

The rope budged, pulling him toward the edge. What? He couldn't believe it. They were actually going to save him? Had to be Heidi with her persuasive power over Zach. *God, please don't let her sacrifice herself for me.*

He made it to a ledge of hanging ice. Heidi carefully inched toward him and handed him an ice ax. "Use this, while we pull you out."

Isaiah took the tool and speared the ice with it.

Didn't she realize that Zach wasn't going to let him live? And Isaiah had used up his last chance to save them. Maybe this was the way it was supposed to end, and justice was being served. Isaiah was getting what he'd had coming to him all along for the part he'd played in Leslie's death.

"You have to survive this, Heidi. Do whatever it takes. Do you hear me?"

Heidi's tears dropped onto the snow. "No, you're not going to die. I won't let you. I can't lose you, too!"

Isaiah couldn't stand to hear her sobs, and he would keep fighting, keep trying, just for her. But he couldn't see a way out of this. Still, he latched onto the ice with the ax to haul himself up, knowing that in the end, it wouldn't matter. He should say what he had to say before it was too late.

"I'm sorry that I couldn't get us out of this. I love you. I think I always have."

There. He'd told her before it was too late. Well, sort of. Isaiah had probably waited too long to tell Heidi, and all the reasons for holding back seemed ridiculous now. He was within seconds of his life ending.

"Let's go, sweetheart."

Heidi tried to untie the rope attaching her to the madman as he dragged her away from the edge. He and Jason had prevented Isaiah from tumbling farther into the crevasse to begin with, since they were all tied together.

Why was the guy waiting to kill him?

Heidi watched in horror as Zach edged toward Isaiah with the gun.

She wouldn't let Zach kill Isaiah. She'd sooner die with him, for him.

Zach had a thing for her? Well, she would do as Isaiah suggested. Survive no matter what it took. Save Isaiah, no matter what it took.

"Zach, please, no. Don't shoot him. I'll go with you. I *want* to go with you. I won't cause you any trouble." Heidi softened her voice, going for an alluring tone.

That got his attention, his gaze drifting over to her. At the look in his eyes, nausea swirled in her stomach.

She wasn't sure what she was doing, making a deal with evil. "But you can't shoot Isaiah."

A lump swelled in her throat. She didn't want to go with Zach willingly, but she didn't know what else to do.

"You have a deal, sweetheart." Zach tugged out a knife, the blade flashing when the sun peeked through the clouds.

"What…what are you doing?" She couldn't believe he would twist her words around like some sick joke, but she should have known better.

What a fool Heidi had been. Zach didn't have to shoot Isaiah. *Oh, Isaiah, please use that ice ax I gave you. Hold on a little longer.*

Zach pressed the blade against the climbing ropes.

Isaiah's eyes flicked to Heidi. He held her gaze—his own conveying the love he'd held back from her all this time. Heidi wanted—no, needed—more time with him. This couldn't be happening.

"See? I'm a man of my word. I'm not going to shoot him."

She screamed, "No!"

Zach cut the rope.

Isaiah held on with the ax, but Zach shoved him into the crevasse.

Isaiah flailed back into the blue ice until it turned black and she could no longer see him. Dumbfounded, she looked on, shock squeezing the life from her body. When Zach pulled her away, she fought and kicked.

"What did you do that for, Zach?" Jason asked. "Why didn't you just shoot him?"

"No one could survive that fall. He's as good as dead,

idiot. If he survives, which I doubt, he can't get out. They'll never find him in there. Besides, that was more elegant than shooting him."

Panic and tears engulfed Heidi. Her knees buckled beneath her. Jason and Zach held her up, dragging her toward the plane in the distance. She didn't want their help.

The Bible said that vengeance was the Lord's, but her grief and sorrow would kill her. Better to let the anger, her need for revenge carry her forward. She would get even with Zach, if it was the last thing she did. He would pay for killing Isaiah. Leaving Cade behind with Rhea. For kidnapping her, and worse—for the lives of the two men she loved the most in the world.

Her brother Cade, with whom she'd always been the closest. And Isaiah.

Isaiah...

She already knew she could never overpower these men or get the upper hand as long as they held the weapons. Isaiah had already tried twice and failed. And yet he was still a hero to her. She wouldn't let Isaiah's or Cade's sacrifices be in vain.

The wind picked up again, and a few flecks of snow hit her cheeks. In the distance, she heard the prop plane starting up. Zach and Jason picked up their pace.

"Unless you want me to leave you behind, too, you need to walk on your own." He released Heidi.

She wanted to rail at him, but that wouldn't work with her plan.

"Okay, let's go." Heidi took off, leaving the two men behind. She was in better shape than either of them and had only lost her strength momentarily due to the gravity of her loss.

Heidi knew better than the two men that their window of opportunity to get rescued was quickly closing. Finally, they made it to the plane and dropped the gear they'd carried with them. The pilot climbed out and shook hands with Zach and Jason.

"You got the money?"

Zach nodded, pointing to the green vinyl bag he'd never let out of his sight.

The guy grinned. "Get it loaded."

"You heard him." Zach eyed Heidi. She was his slave now. "Load the packs."

"All of it? Some of it belongs to the SAR team." As if that mattered anymore.

Zach obviously wanted to rid himself of every shred of evidence of his involvement with the missing SAR team and would dump the packs as far from here as possible. Heidi wasn't sure the small plane could carry all their heavy packs *and* the passengers.

Fine with her.

She hefted the bags and carried them over to the open door under the wing. That's when she spotted the money bag and knew what to do.

There was only one way to truly hurt Zach.

Heidi removed the green bag and hid it under the other bags. She piled the rest of them into the plane, while kicking snow and ice over the green pack.

"Are you almost done? We have to go." Jason climbed into the front seat, as did the pilot.

Zach squeezed her shoulder and slipped by her. He

offered his hand. "Come on, sweetheart. Get in and close the door. We're going to beat the storm this time." He grinned as if he thought he could charm her.

Heidi lifted the last bag and stuffed it inside. She climbed in next to Zach. This was the moment she had to play things just right. All would be lost or won on this move.

Moisture surged from her palms. Her pulse raced. Would Zach notice her increased breathing? Panic threatened to take over as she gasped for breath.

No, not now. She had to make this work.

Still, maybe he would think her reaction normal, considering that she'd climbed into an airplane with a murderer and his friends.

Heidi pushed down her anxiety, gained control over her breathing and smiled back. In the seat, she inched forward slowly, drawing Zach's full attention. Letting him believe she would kiss him.

Why would he for one second fall for that? Guys could be so stupid. When she was mere inches from Zach's lips, she fought to control her gag reflex. Heidi slid her hand into his coat pocket where he'd left his weapon loosely hanging for easy access, just like she'd watched him do a hundred times on their journey. She also knew he always had a round chambered. Without that, her plan wouldn't work. Though she tugged on his jacket a little, he never noticed, too focused on her lips and proximity.

Heidi pointed the gun at Zach's temple before he realized what was going on.

"Okay, this is what's going to happen now. I'm getting off this plane and you men are flying away into the sunset without me."

Zach acted as though he might move to take the gun from her, but Heidi chose this moment to show her true strength. She pressed the muzzle hard and fast against his temple until he cowered.

"Yeah, sure, lady, whatever you want," the pilot said.

"We don't need her, Zach," Jason agreed. "But it's your head."

He snickered at his joke and would probably pay for that later.

"We have the money, man, just let her go."

Zach scowled, the look in his eyes foreboding. He wasn't done with her yet. Wasn't ready to let her go. In his gaze, she could read well enough that he'd had plans for her. Heidi slid away from him, but was unable to tear her eyes from the evil look in his. She used his tunnel vision to her advantage as she lifted the last pack she'd loaded and tossed it to the ground. "I'm taking this pack for myself. I need to survive the storm."

Zach didn't want anyone to live to tell their story. But he was out of options now.

She dropped the pack on top of the already buried mound. Closing the airplane door, she backed away, continuing to point the weapon at Zach's head through the window of the ski-plane. Likely his pilot had another weapon inside, but maybe not. She wasn't sure what had happened to the other weapons Jason and Zach carried, but no one moved to shoot her. Regardless, they didn't have time to waste on Heidi as the wind picked up. If the pilot waited even a minute longer, they wouldn't leave the ice field.

They couldn't afford to battle it out with her.

Nor could she afford for them to stay.

The plane moved forward and away. As she memorized the registration number along the fuselage, she kicked more snow over the green bag, but it was also hidden under the pack she'd kept for herself. If Zach thought to look for his money in the next few moments, she was in big trouble.

But he didn't.

The plane droned off into the distance until she no longer heard it. She released a breath and tried to slow her heart, but she had lost so much. How did she wrap her heart and mind around it?

And she was all alone. She had only thought she was alone in the dark place she'd lingered over the past months. That was nothing compared to this. Heidi had never imagined herself alone in the middle of the barren, snow-covered ice field.

Her thoughts jumbled together as her predicament overwhelmed her. But Heidi sucked her breaths in slowly and focused on living. She had to survive this to tell Cade's story in case he couldn't. She had to survive to tell Isaiah's story.

Her heart cried over her loss, but she opened up the pack.

Oh, no...this bag didn't hold a tent. She'd miscalculated.

Looking up at the sky she watched the clouds quickly

gathering. An unwelcome sight. If she wasn't rescued soon, she would die from exposure.

Oh, God, I've been an idiot!

All she could think about was getting back at Zach by taking the money away from him. Taking the one thing he loved away. And now here she was, stuck on the ice field with no way to live. She couldn't decide if this was better than being on that plane with Zach.

She doubted burning the money would buy her much time. She'd have to build an ice cave, but for that, she'd need an ax—the one she'd given to Isaiah.

Isaiah.

Carrying the pack with climbing gear and the bag of money, Heidi hiked toward the approaching storm clouds, snow mixed with some rain chilling her to the core.

God, if you have any plans for me to be rescued or to survive this, it had better be soon.

Finally, Heidi found the crevasse where Isaiah had met his demise. A small flame of hope ignited in her heart. Maybe he was still alive in there. She could climb down to him and haul him back up.

"Isaiah!" she called. Her voice bounced off the brilliant blue walls. Cerulean walls that lied to her, claiming their purity and innocence. But with several more calls out to Isaiah and no echoing reply, her hopes died until she knew the truth. This crevasse was a killer.

TWENTY

Isaiah woke up to dim lighting in the distance.

He blinked, taking in his surroundings, trying to remember where he was.

He must have fallen in his attempt to climb from the crevasse. When Zach had shoved him the rest of the way in, Isaiah thought he would plummet to his death, but he'd landed against a channel where water poured, like an ice luge, and simply slid the rest of the way deeper into the crevasse. That had saved his life.

Only problem was, the fall had broken his leg.

Despite the last words Isaiah had given Heidi, he wasn't about to stay here and give up. So he found a way to crawl and dealt with his injury. Pulling the ropes and gear he needed to attempt to scale the ice-walled crevasse, Isaiah began to work his way up when the ice gave and he plummeted.

The pain in his leg gut-wrenching and angry, Isaiah used focused breathing to push away the darkness edging his vision like death closing in. He had more fight left in him than he thought possible, but maybe that had something to do with the light at the bottom of the crevasse.

It was odd, really, to look down and expect darkness but to see light instead.

That gave him hope.

There was another way out. But he'd have to go deeper. There had to be a metaphor there somewhere, but he didn't have enough brainpower or energy to think of it.

Ignoring his leg, Isaiah rigged his gear, grateful for the pack that had fallen ahead of him and well out of Zach's reach. Without the climbing gear in the pack, he had no chance.

Even with it he feared he had no chance. Why did he care if he survived, when he'd failed Heidi and left her in Zach's hands? He'd wanted to be a hero to redeem his past, but it was so much more than that. His past didn't matter. He didn't matter.

What mattered was Heidi.

He almost chuckled to himself. Who did he think he was to elevate himself to the role of Heidi's hero? She could take care of herself, and he'd bet right at this moment the woman had taken control of the situation. He let that image urge him on because any other visions about what could be happening to her would crush him where he was.

He assembled his gear to rappel deeper into the crevasse, toward the light. Adam and David had explored ice caves and crevasses and all manner of glacier features, and though the wonders had always intrigued Isaiah, he'd never made the time to explore with them, always busy with his own endeavors. Maybe it was more that he felt like an outsider to the Warren family. He wanted to be one of them, but given his lie to them about who he really was, that hope was as dead as he would be if he didn't climb out of the abyss.

But if given another chance, he'd go with them. He'd take Heidi to explore, too. Do everything, and take every opportunity. A near-death experience went a long way to making a person want to slow down and take the time to see God's creation.

Finally near the bottom of the crevasse, Isaiah lowered himself the rest of the way, keeping his gear on, and took a few breaths to calm his heart, steady his focus away from his injured leg. He looked up at the wall of ice he'd just descended and wondered how in the world he'd done it with a damaged body.

God, I know You hold me in the palm of Your hand. I never doubted that. But right now, I'm struggling... Isaiah choked up. Couldn't finish his prayer, even though it was silent.

Lord, please. I pray for Heidi and for Cade and even Rhea. Protect them and save them, and if I'm blessed enough to make it out of here, then maybe I can right some wrongs.

He let his gaze follow the light again and, looking up, saw the way out. He'd have to climb. Squeezing his eyes shut, Isaiah pictured Heidi's smiling face back before all the drama. Back before he'd hurt her. If he ever had the chance to be with her, he would never hurt her again. But he reminded himself that he'd revealed everything. He doubted she would have him now.

Isaiah drew in a long, measured breath, gutted it up and half crawled, half climbed out of the crevasse. As he neared the source of the light—the small entrance to a hole in the ice—he figured he had just enough energy to make it through.

And after that?

Only God knew.

In the tunnel, he felt the cold air whipping around him already, accompanied by snow. That meant the storm would bear down on the ice field soon if it wasn't already. Isaiah would be lost forever, buried alive, if he stayed tucked away in the crevasse, but crawling out into the storm to die from exposure didn't seem like much of a choice, either.

Peering below him, his heart sank. He'd burned all his energy and couldn't make it all the way back down if he wanted to. He was almost out of the chasm. His only choice was to keep going and hope for the best.

Pulling his broken body out of the entrance to the ice cave, Isaiah fell flat against the snow, gasping for breath. In the distance, he heard helicopter rotors, growing stronger.

Louder.

Isaiah sat up the best he could and waved his arms. A coast guard helicopter hovered above him. Nothing had ever looked so good.

That is, until the rescuers hoisted him into the helicopter, and he saw Heidi—smiling and crying at the same time.

Careful of his leg, Heidi wrapped her arms around him and hugged him close and tight. It felt incredible.

He hesitated for a millisecond, then hugged her back, drawing in the scent of her hair. They held each other long and hard. He didn't want to let go.

Then his eyes drifted to that ominous green bag.

Heidi had never been more grateful for anything in her life than the moment she'd spotted Isaiah in the snow waving. She wasn't ready for him to loosen his arms around her, but she knew he had to be in pain.

Then he gripped her shoulders, a fierce look in his eyes. Not at all the look she wanted or expected. Isaiah had gazed at her with regret and with such longing right before he'd fallen into the crevasse. She wanted to see that in his eyes again. He'd told her that he loved her. Had he forgotten? Was it all a lie?

"How did you survive?" she asked, a sob in her words. "I thought you were dead, but I had to look for you. I had to hope."

He ran his thumb down her cheek. "I'm glad you did, Heidi. Thank you. I thought I was gone, too. I would have been if you hadn't come when you did. Hadn't shown them where to look."

Heidi closed her eyes, savoring the comfort and reassurance in his touch.

"I found a way out of the crevasse and followed it."

Her eyes blinked open. "With a broken leg? You have serious survival instincts."

His grin wiped away the earlier scowl. "I thought about you, Heidi. I had to get back to you. Why don't you tell me what happened? How did you escape?"

Heidi shifted in the seat. "It's a long story. I'll tell

you everything later. I promise." She didn't want to ruin this moment by sharing her tactics. Nor did she want to think about that look that had skewered her when she held the gun on Zach. She couldn't shake it. Couldn't shake the feeling that he would be back. Changing the subject was a good idea.

"They found Cade," she said. "He's going to be all right. Rhea, too. They transported her to a hospital and she's in the ICU, I think." Heidi leaned closer so she wouldn't have to yell over the steady whir of the helicopter. "I hear she's telling them everything, after the way Zach treated her."

"How do you know all this?"

"Cade, I talked to Cade. David told us that you ending your radio call with 'over and out' clued him in and the search for us was on. But with the storms and being shorthanded on teams, it took them a while to find us. So good job."

"I'm glad to hear that, Heidi."

"When they found Cade, he told them where to look for us. Where Zach had us guide him."

"Did they also capture Zach and Jason? The pilot?"

She shrugged. "I don't think so. I haven't heard." He was back to that again.

"Did you tell Cade everything?"

Pursing her lips, she shrank back. "What are you talking about?"

Isaiah's gaze slid to the green bag on the floor then back to her, the scowl returning. "I think you know. Why is the money bag in this helicopter, Heidi? What have you done?"

Heidi blew out a breath. "Can't you be happy that we are all alive? Who cares about what's in that bag? You can't think that I took it for myself."

His grin softened the intense displeasure in his eyes, but only to a point. "Funny thing. While I was crawling out of the crevasse, I pictured you escaping all by yourself. You're strong and brave and shrewd. I figured you'd get the men out of the way. Remove me, the hero wannabe, and you'd take Zach down all by yourself. Looks like I wasn't far off. So what *did* happen?"

She hadn't wanted to tell this story more than once, and she knew she'd have to tell it to the authorities. "I wanted to get back at Zach for taking everyone away from me. He made me pack the bags on the plane and I stowed this one in the snow beneath the plane. When he wasn't looking, I took the gun from his pocket before he ever knew what happened. Told the pilot to let me out and take off or I would kill Zach. He and Jason agreed they didn't need me."

Admiration brimmed in his gaze, but only for a moment. Isaiah shook his head, and then an expression of anguish crossed his face. The medic tried to administer a painkiller, but Isaiah refused.

"Let me see if I understand. The pilot took off without the money. None of them knew you'd taken it."

"That's right."

"But they know now."

Heidi couldn't stand Isaiah's recrimination and averted her gaze. Watched out the window and held on, praying this thing didn't crash with the winds whipping at it. Isaiah grabbed her hand, the gesture forcing her to look at him.

"Why did you do it?"

"I already told you!" Why did he have to grill her like this? "To hurt him. Besides, I couldn't overpower Zach or Jason and hold them until the authorities arrived, but at least I could rescue the money." Right. That had nothing at all to do with why she'd taken it, and by the look in his eyes, Isaiah knew it.

"You've put yourself in grave danger."

"No kidding. That was two million dollars."

His eyebrows shot up. "Two million dollars?"

"Yes. But there won't be any reason for him to come for me because I'll be turning the money over to the FBI. They're meeting us when we land. I've already given them the plane's registration number, too, so they can track these guys down quickly."

"You think Zach will know that you turned the money over to the government? If he finds out, do you think he'll care? He will want revenge."

The helicopter jerked and rolled. Heidi held fast, while Isaiah cried out in pain.

She eyed the medic. "Do something for him."

He nodded and administered a painkiller.

Heidi looked out the window again, trying to gain control over her roiling insides due to the turbulent flight. She hated seeing Isaiah in so much pain, most of it physical, but by his reaction she knew she'd caused him additional pain through her actions.

Oh, Lord, what have I done?

She'd brought the threat home with her. Not only was *she* in danger now, but her whole family.

Heidi let her gaze drift back to Isaiah. His eyes were closed, agony still etched on his face. He was a brave, courageous man, just like she'd always thought he was. But he'd run away from his problems, lied about who he really was. Heidi understood him better now.

The irony. Heidi might have to do the exact same thing in order to keep her family safe. She might have to look over her shoulder for the rest of her life, watching out for the day Zach would come for her.

TWENTY-ONE

Like two bodyguards, Cade and David escorted her from the FBI's satellite office in Juneau. She and Cade had both shared their stories about the ordeal more times than she could count, as if they were the criminals. Heidi had been questioned more than either of the men because she'd taken the money right out from under Zach's watchful gaze.

Heat swam up her neck as she reiterated how she'd drawn his attention away from his money. In the end, the FBI was grateful the money had been returned and appreciative of all the information the SAR team shared about Zach and his partners-in-crime. The hunt for them was on.

She climbed into Cade's truck after the boat ride from Juneau, sitting between him and David. Their longtime friend and bush pilot, Billy, usually flew them in his float plane, but he was in the Alaska bush today, so they'd taken the boat, which took much too long, in her opinion. Regardless, the ordeal was finally over and she had thought it would never end. In truth, she'd never been sure they would survive, and it seemed a little surreal to be sitting next to Cade. The rest of the world continued on—life as usual—and hadn't come to a screeching halt just because the three of them had been abducted.

But something was missing for Heidi. Or rather, someone. Isaiah had been taken to the hospital to be treated for his injuries and had been questioned there.

"Have you heard anything more about Isaiah? Is he going to be all right?" Heidi didn't dare look at Cade. She understood now why Cade had cautioned her to avoid Isaiah, but he was being a little hard on the guy.

"He's fine."

She was still working through her feelings on Isaiah's past, but that didn't mean she didn't care for him fiercely. And that was putting it mildly. She had wanted to go directly to the hospital and see him, but Cade and David insisted on getting back home. Grandma Katy and Leah were waiting.

"Did they release him?"

"Not yet." David shifted in the seat next to her. "But don't worry about him. He can take care of himself. Adam is there with him. They'll return to Mountain Cove together."

"We need to get home," Cade said.

Heidi didn't argue with Cade on that one. She knew that Leah had to be anxious to tell him about her news if she had some. Heidi hated that she knew there was a possibility that Leah was pregnant and hadn't said a word to him, but it was Leah's place to share, not Heidi's. Cade drove his truck into the driveway of the home they shared with Grandma Katy and everyone climbed out. Cade ushered Heidi to the door as if she was a child. This was getting old.

Once inside, Heidi breathed in the aroma of Italian food mingling with that of a few baked goods. Grandma Katy appeared from the kitchen and hugged Heidi and Cade. Leah, too, but she remained in Cade's arms.

Tears streaming from her face, Grandma Katy didn't seem to want to let go of Heidi, but she relinquished her hold anyway. Gripping Heidi's shoulders, she looked her up and down. Then pressed her palms against Heidi's cheeks. "I'm so thankful God saved you, Heidi."

Then she did the same to Cade, after Leah stepped out of his arms. Heidi never doubted that her grandmother cherished and loved them. And she regretted taking the money now. She never wanted to bring harm to this house. They'd already known that kind of fear with Leah's stalker.

Grandma Katy swiped at her tears, a broad smile on her face. "You must be hungry for a hot meal. The food will be ready in half an hour. Gives you time to clean up."

She went back to the kitchen.

Heidi decided she and David should leave Cade and Leah alone. Give them some space. She was surprised they didn't head back to their apartment.

"I think I'll run upstairs and take a quick shower." If Heidi could lie in her own bed and rest a little, that would make her day.

The next thing she knew, she woke up. She'd gotten her wish. She'd lain on her bed for a moment. She thought she'd only briefly closed her eyes, but looking at the clock, she'd slept three hours.

Climbing from the bed, she quickly showered.

She'd missed Grandma Katy's meal. Heidi shook off the grogginess and slipped down the stairs. Just as she reached the bottom step, someone knocked on the front door. She made her way to the foyer where Cade had already opened it.

Leaning on crutches, Isaiah stood in the door frame, filling it out with his sturdy form. Heidi had the urge to rush to him, much as Leah had done with Cade before, but with her disapproving brother looking on, she held back.

Isaiah's dark gaze slid from Cade to Heidi and he stepped inside. Cade offered him a seat in the living room but Isaiah declined. He moved to stand directly in front of Heidi. His proximity tugged at her, and she thought she could sense he wanted to hold her, but Cade's brooding stare hovered just over Isaiah's shoulder. She wanted to tell Cade to go away and give her and Isaiah privacy, just like she'd done for Cade and Leah.

She focused back on Isaiah and searched his eyes, remembering that awful moment right before Zach shoved him into the crevasse. She recalled the words he'd said.

I'm sorry that I couldn't get us out of this, Heidi. I love you. I think I always have.

Had he meant those words? Or had he said them because he thought he would die? Crazy thoughts. Heidi wanted the words to be true, but she still held on to other words he'd said about changing his name. About someone he loved being murdered.

Who are you really, Isaiah?

An invisible, unscalable wall stood between them. As the technical climber on the team, she knew everything about climbing. If only this were the kind of wall she knew how to climb.

"Why don't I see agents sitting in their car outside?" he asked. "Bodyguards next to the door. Law enforcement of some type watching the house, Cade? David?"

He asked the questions, but his eyes remained on Heidi. They were two people meant to be together but circumstances and life anchored them far apart.

"The FBI and their profiler didn't see Zach as likely to come to Mountain Cove. Heidi doesn't have the money anyway."

"Zach doesn't know that, does he?" Isaiah's expression revealed his exhaustion and he finally moved to the living room and carefully positioned himself in a chair. His leg in a cast, he rested it to the side.

Heidi followed him. She wanted to reach out to him and comfort him, but it wasn't her place, and with his foul mood, she doubted he would receive it. Doubted Cade would allow it. He tried to watch over her like an overprotective father. Even Dad, when he was alive, hadn't treated her like this. Even their oldest brother, David, didn't act this way. To be fair, she was closest to Cade, for some reason. And he appeared to want to protect her from Isaiah, and Isaiah wanted to protect her from an actual bad guy.

She huffed.

The men in her life.

Isaiah squeezed the bridge of his nose. "You have

to know your sister is in danger. What are we going to do to protect her?"

"I'm right here in the room, boys. No need to talk about me like I'm not here. I can take care of myself, so you don't need to watch out for me."

With her statement both men, who'd been staring each other down, turned to her. David entered the living room munching on a chocolate chip cookie. He looked at her, too.

Someone rang the doorbell and walked right in without waiting. Adam hurried into the living room. "I let Isaiah out close so he wouldn't have to walk so far, then parked at the curb."

Great, now Adam could stare at her, too.

"You guys sure had us worried." He hugged Cade and then Heidi. He squeezed Isaiah's shoulder. "Not to downplay the severity of your injuries, but good thing a broken leg was all you got out of this nightmare. You could have all been killed."

"Does no one but me understand this isn't over yet?" Isaiah knocked his crutches over. "Heidi took Zach's money. He's coming here for Heidi. Whether or not she has the money, she's in danger."

David put his hands on his hips. "I understand."

"Why'd you take the money, Heidi?" Cade asked.

"To right a wrong, okay?"

He blew out a breath. Funny that her brothers' ire didn't bother her nearly as much as Isaiah's.

But she was frustrated with him, too. She wanted to ask him what it felt like to be a person of interest in a murder investigation. What had it felt like to love someone who was committed to another? How could she love a man like that after everything she'd been through? Correction, she already knew she loved him with every fiber of her being, but how could she *be* with him?

"You brought the danger to everyone, not just yourself," Leah said. She knew that better than anyone because she'd done that same thing to Cade's family. She'd led a killer right to this house. And if Leah was pregnant she had even more reason to be concerned.

"Fine. I'll pack my junk and leave."

Heidi whirled and stomped away.

Cade started after her.

"No, Cade. Let me." Isaiah attempted to stand. Not so easy with his leg.

Adam handed Isaiah the crutches he'd knocked over. He really wanted to punch a hole in a wall. He climbed to his feet, surprised to see Cade hadn't followed after Heidi. David either.

When Isaiah had a good grip on the crutches, he started toward the stairs. Oh. Stairs. He frowned.

"I'm going after her," Cade said. "Someone needs to talk some sense into her."

"Cade," Leah said. "Let Isaiah do this."

"I agree," David said.

Thanks for the support. Isaiah didn't want to complicate things with Cade, so said nothing at all. He eyed the stairs. He could do this. He left one of the crutches behind and used the rail on his right side for support.

"Isaiah." Cade stepped into view. "I appreciate what you did for my sister. I know you did the best you could, and you probably saved her in ways we'll never know. And if you can actually make it up those stairs, I bet she'll be willing to listen to whatever you have to say."

Cade's nod of assurance was all the confidence Isaiah needed. It was a form of permission. At least that's how Isaiah saw it. Cade finally trusting him again. He maneuvered his way up the stairs and was near exhaustion by the time he got there. He'd have to work his strength back up. Adam appeared behind him on the stairs and handed him the crutch he'd tossed.

Isaiah moved down the hallway, looking for Heidi's room. Sure enough, she was packing her bags. When she looked up and saw Isaiah standing there with his crutches, her eyes widened.

"What are you doing?"

"What does it look like? I came up here to talk to you."

Heidi shut her suitcase. "About what? I've made up my mind. There's no talking me out of this. I made a mistake and I'm not going to sit around and wait for Zach to show up."

"My sentiments exactly." Isaiah moved all the way into the room. "I hadn't planned to sit around and do nothing, so I came up with a plan."

Heidi's wary expression wasn't what he expected. He almost changed his mind. He'd told her that he loved her. But obviously, she didn't return his feelings. That was okay. He'd never thought he deserved her love. But he would do this for her. Protect her, the only way he knew how. He would protect the woman he loved this time if it was the last thing he did.

"Come back with me to Montana. My family has a ranch. You can stay there." And he wanted to see his family to tell them again how sorry he was for all the pain he'd caused. Just like Heidi, he wanted to right a wrong. "You can stay there until the authorities catch him, if you want. And maybe I can even convince you that I'm a good guy, after all." Oops, he hadn't meant to say that out loud.

She stared up at him from where she sat on the bed, next to her luggage. "I don't know, Isaiah. I'm so confused. I need time to think things through."

Isaiah leaned against the doorjamb. "About us?"

"About us. I mean if you're taking me to Montana in hopes—"

"No, I'm not." The pain her words caused grew in his throat, and he could barely speak. "I'm doing this to protect you."

Suddenly Heidi stood from the bed and she moved closer to him. She pressed her hand against his chest. His heart. And he knew she had to feel his heart pounding at her touch.

"I...don't believe you."

"It doesn't matter if you don't return my feelings. I'll protect you." She was right. Deep inside, if he didn't lie to himself, a small part of him hoped that he could love her and she would return his love. That nothing that had happened would stand in their way this time.

"Who said I don't have feelings for you? It's more about trust. I don't even know who you are."

"All the more reason to come to Montana with me

and find out. I understand why you need someone you can trust, and maybe I can be that person for you."

Thinking of the one kiss they'd shared in the most awkward of places, he lifted his hand, pressing it against her cheek. Heidi closed her eyes, and Isaiah kissed her again. Oh, yeah, somehow he had to convince her he was one of the good guys. But what he feared most was that the price would be too high and he would fail again.

TWENTY-TWO

Heidi strolled with Isaiah toward Mountain Cove's small float-plane dock, where they would board the aircraft that would take them to Juneau. No airports or security checks here. They'd face that in Juneau. From there they would fly to Seattle and then on to Montana. Seeing the plane in the distance made her palms sweat. She was really going to do this.

Heidi had said her goodbyes to Grandma Katy, David and Adam. Cade and Leah had driven Heidi and Isaiah to the dock. But now the whole idea seemed surreal.

She gasped and paused, and Cade, walking behind her, nearly ran into her. He caught her elbow and turned her to face him. In the corner of her vision, she saw Isaiah stop and lower his bags to the ground. But he didn't approach them.

"What's wrong?" Cade asked.

"I'm worried about everyone's safety. Are you sure this is the right thing to do?" She'd never lived anywhere else except during her college years. This had been her home forever.

"You're in good hands with Isaiah. Put some distance between you and Zach, and wait it out on Isaiah's family's ranch. You're okay with that, aren't you?"

Heidi was relieved that Cade had gotten over his trust issues with Isaiah. "I'm not worried about Isaiah. This will be the perfect chance for me to get to know him better." And she wanted that, didn't she? She'd almost lost him once before and now she was getting a second chance to see what might happen between them. But going to Montana was about much more than that. It was about running away and hiding from some killer who might never show up.

Isaiah stood next to Cade now. "It's your choice, Heidi. I just thought if you went away you would be out of danger."

"I know. I think this is for the best." *As long as Zach doesn't track me down there.*

She'd been such a bad judge of character too many times, and she'd made a poor judgment call when she'd taken the bag of money.

Cade and Leah walked with them the rest of the way until Heidi finally turned and hugged her brother. "I'm so excited that I'm going to be an aunt soon. I'm thrilled for you and Leah, Cade."

Oh, God, please keep them safe. She was doing this for them as much as anyone. She couldn't stand to worry about Leah and the baby and the chance Zach would show up to harm them. Next, Heidi hugged her sister-in-law.

Leah squeezed her hard. "This is all going to work out. You'll see. And remember, the FBI will catch Zach, and all because of the details you guys shared with them."

Heidi nodded and waved goodbye to them. Sucking in a deep breath, she and Isaiah walked the length of the dock to the float plane sitting in the water.

The pilot came around to assist with their luggage. Heidi didn't recognize him. Usually Billy flew them to Juneau. Maybe he'd been busy this time.

When he stood upright and faced them, the air whooshed from Heidi's lungs.

"Zach," she whispered.

He pointed a gun at her. "I came back for my money."

"I don't have it. I turned it over to the FBI."

"Unfortunately, I believe you. If I can't have my money, then I want you. But I can't trust you, can I?"

In a flash, Isaiah threw himself in front of her, gunfire splitting her eardrums.

"No!" The scream tore from her lungs.

On the dock, she held a bleeding Isaiah. Around her, men wrestled Zach to the ground. Heidi didn't care about any of that. Isaiah blinked up at her, his eyes out of focus.

Oh, God, please, don't let Isaiah die. Tears streamed down her face.

She'd had a second chance with him and she'd thrown it away because she'd been too afraid to trust. "Oh, Isaiah, I'm so sorry. I've been such a fool to hold back my love from you. I know who you are and your past doesn't matter. That's how God looks at us, so who am I to hold that over your head?"

His eyes closed.

Heidi held him tighter. "Stay with me. Stay in the land of the living, please. I…love you. I think I always have."

Though his eyes remained shut, he grinned at that. Her heart skipped.

"Why did it have to take me almost losing you again to be willing to love? I'm ready now, to risk my heart and my life again. So you have to be all right."

Isaiah opened his eyes and looked at her, all pretense stripped away. She saw nothing but love. "The price was worth it."

"What are you talking about?"

"I knew it would cost me something to convince you I'm one of the good guys."

"I've always known you were a good guy. You didn't have to take a bullet for me."

"Oh, but I did."

Then it was over. Isaiah closed his eyes.

Isaiah woke up to bright white surroundings and the smell of a sterile environment.

A heaviness he couldn't shake clung to his thoughts and he blinked a few times to remember where he was. He was in a hospital. That much was obvious.

Someone moved from the chair on his right and was at his side, squeezing his hand.

Heidi.

She smiled at him, ran her hand down his face. Man, that felt good. Maybe he should stay right here in this hospital bed, though he wouldn't want to keep aching all over like he did at the moment.

Cade stepped into the room, followed by David and Adam. Leah lingered against the back wall with Heidi's grandmother.

"You're a real trouper, you know that?" Cade said. "You took a bullet for Heidi. You saved her. I knew I could trust you to keep her safe."

Isaiah scraped a hand down his face. "What about Zach?"

"They got him," Heidi said. "Jason wasn't too far away so they snagged him, too. Not sure about the pilot, but Zach was just crazy enough to come back. I don't know what would have happened if you hadn't been there."

Cade moved in closer. "Just want you to know how glad we are that you made it. You're one of us. You're like a brother to me."

"And me." Adam nodded.

"And me." David crossed his arms.

"I'm not going to say you're like a brother to me, I'm sorry." Heidi laughed.

Isaiah's heart was full. How could they know that's all he ever wanted? To feel as if he was one of them. "You guys are too good to me. I always wanted to be part of a family of heroes." Part of the Warren family. That more than made up for the mistakes of his past.

"And you were the hero this time." Leah winked at him from across the room.

"But I want to know why you're not going to tell me I'm like a brother." Isaiah's grin nearly hurt his face.

"Um, could you guys give us a moment?" Heidi eyed her siblings.

They chuckled and filed from the room.

"This is why." Heidi leaned in and kissed Isaiah thoroughly, holding nothing of her feelings back this time. And he pulled her closer, wanting to give her his whole heart.

He tried to ignore the pain in his side and leg, but Heidi must have sensed his discomfort and eased away. "Well, if I can't think of you as a sister, what about if I think of you as my wife?"

Her eyes widened.

Isaiah feared he'd messed up. This wasn't exactly romantic. "I'm not trying to take advantage of the fact that I took a bullet for you, I'm just simply looking at the facts. I've loved you for how long now? Three years going on four? And if you feel the same way, what are we waiting for?"

She flashed him the most beautiful smile he'd ever seen, and he was glad to be the one to put it there. He hoped to put many more of those on her face.

"How could I possibly refuse the man that I love? A man I know I can trust with my heart and with my life? How could I not take a chance on you? There is nothing that would make me happier in this world than to be your wife."

* * * * *

SPECIAL EXCERPT FROM

LOVE INSPIRED SUSPENSE
INSPIRATIONAL ROMANCE

*A K-9 officer and a forensics specialist must work
together to solve a murder and stay alive.*

Read on for a sneak preview of
Scene of the Crime *by Sharon Dunn,*
the next book in the True Blue K-9 Unit: Brooklyn *series*
available September 2020 from Love Inspired Suspense.

Brooklyn K-9 Unit Officer Jackson Davison caught
movement out of the corner of his eye: a face in the
trees fading out of view. His heart beat a little faster.
Was someone watching him? The hairs on the back
of Jackson's neck stood at attention as a light breeze
brushed his face. Even as he studied the foliage, he felt
the weight of a gaze on him. The sound of Smokey's
barking brought his mission back into focus.

When he caught up with his partner, the dog was
sitting. The signal that he'd found something. "Good
boy." Jackson tossed out the toy he carried on his belt for
Smokey to play with, his reward for doing his job. The
dog whipped the toy back and forth in his mouth.

"Drop," Jackson said. He picked up the toy and patted
Smokey on the head. "Sit. Stay."

The body, partially covered by branches, was clothed
in neutral colors and would not be easy to spot unless you
were looking for it.

He keyed his radio. "Officer Davison here. I've got a body in Prospect Park. Male Caucasian under the age of forty, about two hundred yards in, just southwest of the Brooklyn Botanic Garden."

Dispatch responded, "Ten-four. Help is on the way."

He studied the trees just in time to catch the face again, barely visible, like a fading mist. He was being watched. "Did you see something?" Jackson shouted. "Did you call this in?"

The person turned and ran, disappearing into the thick brush.

Jackson took off in the direction the runner had gone. As his feet pounded the hard earth, another thought occurred to him. Was this the person who had shot the man in the chest? Sometimes criminals hung around to witness the police response to their handiwork.

His attention was drawn to a garbage can just as an object hit the back of his head with intense force. Pain radiated from the base of his skull. He crumpled to the ground and his world went black.

Don't miss
Scene of the Crime *by Sharon Dunn,*
available wherever Love Inspired Suspense books
and ebooks are sold.

LoveInspired.com